The Dirty Deeds.

Zoee Smith

Thank you's

For Lee and My Four babies LukeFrankieKalvin&Brooklyn without you I am nothing <3

For Jodie, My Sister, My world, Chin up babes... you Finally made it ☺

To Rhian Smith: Top Proof Reader! Best friend....Family I Love you ☺

Jade&Angharad Best friends Always!

My Two crazy brothers....Love you more than Strongbow Citrus Edge :P <3

To Claire and Kevin..... Thank you for EVERTHING <3

To Uncle DaveyBaby and Auntie Sharon.... for loving me at my worst aswell as my best <3

Last but by no means least this book is dedicated to Terrie Taylor.... My Top Stalker! Whose story completely touched and melted my heart.... you've been a true inspiration... you managed to hold it all together with your beautiful family whilst battling cervical cancer, raising beautiful babies, being the next Waynetta Slob, finding the biggest custard cream in Britain! And being most importantly my number one Dom fan all at the same time! The minute you told me The Abandoned helped you through radiotherapy and some of the toughest moments of your battle.... you became a part of my world.....and I can never thank you enough for that honour! You're finally in remission! You can breathe Finally! You've become a true friend, a top stalker and a true icon for me whilst writing the book!

118 118 got your number....

Love you girl ☺ <3

To everyone who made this book possible.... I Love you <3

Author Notes

Well here we are guys the second part of the Craig Carter Series.... I hope I haven't left you pining for Craig, Jenna and Dom for too long! The Abandoned truly was the start of something amazing and I'm hoping we'll have the same success with The Dirty Deeds... As much as I love my characters I know eventually I'll have to part with them... the thought kills me! These people have become such a huge part of my life and I'll never tire of writing about them. Especially Craig, he's become my secret book boyfriend (Don't tell Lee) But I also have a life and three crazy boys to look after in the throes of the Belmonte!! As always I wish you all complete health happiness and love. Keep Tweeting&Facebooking My Tweethearts&BookBitches I'll try and get back to you all ☺ <3

My Twitter- @ZoeeSmithAuthor

Facebook- Zoee Smith ☺ (it's a personal page guys so expect pics of my kiddies haha!)

Love You Too Big!

Zoee x

Book One

The Aftermath

"And I Need You Now....

There's Too Many Miles On My Bones

I Can't Carry The Weight Of The World

No Not On My Own" <3

Flight-LifeHouse

Chapter One

Jenna Shearan sat at the foot of the hospital bed praying for nothing short of a miracle, her eyes never leaving the face of the man she loved not even momentarily. The tears rolled down her cheek as she searched his stunning features for even a flicker of movement. But he was so still, so peacefully still, lost in his thoughtless slumber. Jenna could sit and stare at his beautiful face for the rest of her life, and she would, she would wait for him. Even if it meant she never moved from his bedside again, she would wait for him. Her eyes flickered towards the ceiling in a shallow attempt to stem the tears. Her mind wandered momentarily to Craig, the poor bastard was still feeling so guilty over everything that had happened. He was paying for Dom to be kept in a highly recommended private surgery with the best medical attention money could buy. Despite currently being wheelchair bound himself. The crash had ripped apart their lives and Jenna wouldn't ever be able to feel free again until Dom opened his eyes. For five months now he had just lay there, not a single precious movement, not even a tiny attempt to show the world that he was still very much with them. It had been touch and go with him ever since he had arrived on the intensive care unit. They had worked on him for weeks, helping him off the ventilator, helping him assist his own breathing but still there was nothing. Despite Jenna being there to talk his ear off every waking moment of the day, there was still no reaction. As she sat on the foot of the bed, gazing lovingly at him, her beautiful green eyes cloudy with overcoming emotion she felt so lost, so abandoned.

Her hand instinctively reached for her slightly swollen stomach, she had found out a few days previously she was carrying a little boy. Her scan photograph sat proudly on Dom's bedside table. The tiny features highlighted perfectly, his perfect little hand waving at them unintentionally. Craig had the same photograph on his desk in his office. It had been a bittersweet moment taking Craig to the scan with her, she had felt ashamed, it was the not knowing that ate her up the most. Her little boy would be born an instant illegitimate. It was no start to life for a child really was it? She thought of Kiki then, her beautiful three year old little girl who had been immune to all of the hurt that Jenna had caused over her paternity.

Despite everything though Craig had embraced fatherhood completely; he and Kiki had created themselves an incredible bond and the little girl had grown to love her father more than anything else in the world. He had given her the world and more and she was growing to be such a smart beautiful happy little girl. Jenna rarely saw her these days, with her being in school now and Jenna always being in the hospital with Dom. She knew that Kiki was looked after impeccably well though by her Nanny Leah. The two were inseparable and Jenna knew that Leah was good for her daughter; she had the patience to play with Kiki for hours on end and keep up with her diva demands. These days Jenna's heart just wasn't in it. Of course guilt had overridden her at first for not feeling more committed to her daughter, she had no desire to deal with her tantrums or her pouting because her daddy wasn't home, but in effect Jenna had learnt to live with it.

Kiki's youth meant Jenna could make amends in the future, despite the fact her daughter was incredibly intelligent, and she was still innocent enough to accept Jenna's lacklustre excuses. She hadn't neglected her entirely, but she had definitely abandoned her role as the girl's mother. She had never meant for this to happen but she had been so wrapped up in the aftermath of the crash that all priorities had been blown out of the water. Jenna glanced up at Dom, his soft wrinkled eyes looked so serene in the bright hospital light and he was like an angel. So peaceful, so beautiful, Jenna wrenched back the tears, swiping them away with the back of her sleeve as she slid closer up the bed so that she was practically laying next to him. Her neat little bump fitting snugly between them as her slim body lay directly against his. Jenna ran her slim fingers through the overgrown black curls that invaded his head. She took in every inch of his pale skin, his slightly wonky nose, his strong cheekbones in perfect sync with his jaw line. His rippled muscles visible beneath his thin hospital blankets, to Jenna he was simple perfection. Dom was uncomplicated; he was nothing short of the ideal man. Jenna ran her fingers across his naked chest, feeling every possible sensation at the mere touch of his skin. He heart wretched sadly at the feeling of his skin against hers. Despite being caught in this horrific love triangle she had found herself entwined within, she felt herself drawn to Dom's vulnerability. He was something that was truly worth the sacrifices. Jenna had of course been forced to make a few and even now in the aftermath of it all she felt as though she was still doing the right thing. She huddled herself closer to his naked chest, breathing in every single note of his individual scent, the soft, musky scent of Dom mixed with the sickly sweet scent of his fresh sweat, he was a heady cocktail and Jenna could get easily drunk instantaneously from his power. He was everything to her, despite the war her heart raged in protest, Dom was without a doubt the one thing in life that she had got one hundred percent right.

She curled up beside him, her mascara running against the white pillow as she allowed herself to release the hurt that was wrapped up inside her. The absolute fear she felt for Dom's safety making her cling to him even more as she sobbed uncontrollably against his bare skin. She prayed he would be okay. She would kill to see his smile just one more time in her mind's eye. The short lived memories that they had shared were precious to Jenna now. She knew things had never been easy between them, but now as she sought solace in their loving memories she found that justice had been served. She plugged up her phone to her headphones; the blissful sound of Daughtry filled her enclosed space. The sultry music easing her nerves as she held him close to her, the wires and machines that loitered around them gave her no comfort at all but they were keeping him with her. She couldn't ask for more than that. She swiped aimlessly at her eyes as the nurse entered and went about her checks as though Jenna wasn't even there, barely offering the girl a look of sympathy as she pottered around Dom, checking his stats and vitals, noting any changes on her massive clipboard of notes. Jenna took her earpiece out and nodded politely towards the nurse in a gesture of respect hugging her baggy grey cardigan around her as she sat up on the bed.

"Any news?" she quizzed, her voice so full of promise, her eyes widening in hope.

"No Miss Shearan same as earlier" She replied gruffly before turning on her heel and making her exit swiftly, her high heeled boots clattered on the cold lino as she went. Jenna returned to her post, lying beside Dom, her fingers mauling his naked chest as she took in his beautiful face. His stubble slightly over grown, his hair hung floppy on his forehead in a thick black curtain but he was still beautiful. Jenna leant up and kissed his brow softly, his skin silky to the touch, his neat forehead devoid of any wrinkles. He looked simply angelic. Jenna Glanced around the scarcely furnished room, the sterile white walls almost blinded her with their fluorescent brightness. The various lights from the machines that surrounded them blinking rapidly and beeping constantly like something from a DJ set. Jenna lay back with an overbearing sigh, pushing her hair away from her face as her head hit the soft cotton pillows. The reality of her situation was still so raw in her mind's eye, Dom was hanging on by a thread, Craig was still under the impression he would never walk again and to top it all she was pregnant by one of them. The thought of it was disturbing, the not knowing who the little boy inside her belonged to. Jenna smiled as she ran her hand over her barely there baby bump, her fingers stroked against her dimpled skin as she attempted to get a reaction from the tiny life that lay growing inside her. She didn't have a clue whose baby he was but she knew without a doubt that she already loved him unconditionally. He was her little miracle baby and despite being born into this mess, Jenna knew he would have love in abundance; he would never be neglected by her. She knew Craig was cut up by it all, he had barely seen her since the accident. She had blamed him initially, really blamed him, conjuring up a vicious story of revenge that was completely untruthful. Craig had been impeccable since the crash, he had called her every day, paid for Dom to be kept in the top medical suite of the private clinic, visited a few times bringing her flowers every time. Her priorities lay with Dom; he needed her now more than ever. She curled back into Dom and Preyed silently that he would come through for her and her unborn baby.

Chapter Two

Craig lay staring at the ceiling, propped up against the thick plump pillows his whole body numb from the pain relief. His big blue eyes gazing unintentionally at the blank space before him, his hand resting against his lean taught stomach, the thick purple gauges that invaded his slim body highlighted against his paled skin. His fingers tracing against them softly, Craig lay unaware of his actions, lost deep in thought. He felt an all consuming emptiness that he wasn't at all comfortable with, he felt broken somewhat. His legs were mangled, both wrapped heavily in swaddling. For the first time in Craig's life he was scared, scared he would never recover. Scared he wouldn't be able to be a proper dad to Kiki and if the future played out the way he wanted it to, his son. He loved Jenna and he would soon show her just how much he was willing to give to be with her. The accident had put everything into perspective for him. He had found strength in the darkness and he had pushed and pushed to come out fighting. Even in the face of possible paralysis he laughed, even if it was a doubtful laugh. He had had to put his American club launch on hold while he recovered which of course had devastated him. He had sunk into an uncanny depression as he battled with his conflicting emotions. He was left with too much time alone, too much thinking time and it was slowly driving him insane. His thoughts strayed to Jenna, he had put her through so fucking much, and even now he knew he had broken her over the crash. Dom was fighting for his life, not that Craig cared too much for him, but he could see what the stress was doing to his precious Jenna. She was looking ill, despite the pregnancy giving her a few extra pounds she was still tiny. Craig's heart yearned for her, he knew she still blamed him for the crash, still thought it had been intentional. She denied it of course but Craig could see it in her eyes. He grabbed his phone off the bedside cabinet the front screen image of himself Jenna and Kiki stared at him all bright smiles and loving eyes. Craig smiled sadly and opened his messages; mainly work related emails and a few texts of Leah filling him in on what Kiki was up to. Craig shuffled as best he could up the bed, careful not to move his legs too much. His teeth clenched as he had to drag his leg slightly to the left, his breath hitched as he struggled to maintain the shooting pain that escalated through his damaged limbs. His whole body ached from sheer exhaustion and Craig wondered briefly if this was indeed what life had to offer him. Would his legs ever recover? He doubted it somehow. The nurses and doctor's weren't saying much, even when he had begged them to tell him more they had remained tight lipped, but he was hopeful that no news was indeed good news. He opened his messenger and typed a quick message back to Leah, trying his hardest to sound interested in Kiki's teddy bears tea party, but there was much going on to think about his daughters childish innocence.

He lay back against the pillows, his arm propped against his tired brow. Craig was finding it hard to adjust to the thought of Jenna sat beside Dom's bedside smothering him with affection while he was laying here alone drowning in his own self pity, thinking about her broke him. He still loved her unconditionally despite her recent frostiness towards him he hoped against hope there was a chance for them in the future. He lifted his phone up off the sheets and flicked through the numerous pictures he had of them both. His smile lingered sadly on his lips; he had never known love like what he had for Jenna. She completed him. He took in the image of the two of them that currently stared back at him, she was kissing his cheek playfully and he was smiling like a love struck teenager at the camera. They looked so carefree, so happy and Craig swallowed down the lump that had formed in his throat. Despite being a hard faced bastard, love had completely destroyed him; the emotion he felt towards the situation was nothing short of catastrophic. If he wasn't so stubborn and headstrong he knew he would have probably exploded by now. He thought of all the lovely moments they had shared since reuniting, the stolen glances, the soft chaste kisses, the all consuming fits of laughter. They had been perfect throughout all of the imperfect happenings in their complicated world, but he had loved her regardless. He was tied to Jenna, tied by their past, tied by their incredible friendship. It was where Craig had the slight advantage, he knew her weaknesses. Her biggest weakness of course, had always been him. He lay lost in deep, transcending thought; he had no idea on how to make this right. But he had vowed to himself that he would. He stared at the phone screen glowing in his hand; he flicked through to his address book and clicked on her number. In hesitance he held his finger over the call button, relentlessly trying his hardest to muster up the courage to press it.

"Hey" he smiled as his call was answered;

"Hey Hun, you feeling ok" Jenna's voice was like liquid gold to his tired ears. Despite her tone being slightly strained, she sounded as tired as he felt. The thought was comforting in his isolation.

"I'm good babe, thanks, was just wondering whether you fancied coming to visit me, I'm sick of talking to the fucking walls if I'm honest and I could do with the company and I'm not too far from Dom's ward" he smiled as he spoke, his voice full of weak camaraderie which he didn't really feel. Craig was in the rehabilitation suite of the hospital which was situated in a separate building away from the main building.

"Craig... Look I don't really want to leave..." her voice went off on a tangent slightly and she dropped a silent cough at the end to dispel the conversation.

"Please Jen, you can't avoid me forever"

"I'm scared Craig, I'm scared that if I see you, I'll forgive you" Her voice was sad, filled with a depressive sedation. Craig suppressed the urge to cry as he held his head in his hands.

"Please Jen I'm so tired of felling alone" he pleaded, his tone slightly petulant, his finger ran across his bottom lip as he spoke. If he was brutally honest he had felt alone ever since he had been admitted to the rehabilitation ward. They had a strict no children policy so he hadn't even been able to see his daughter. He had seen Ronnie a few times but other than that he was basically kept on lockdown. Despite having the Identity of Jamie Williams now, he still couldn't risk being seen by anyone who would recognise him as Craig Carter. He heard her sigh on the other end of the line and his heart literally wrenched in his chest.

"I'm not promising anything, but I'll wait for the nurse to come and do her rounds then I'll see what I can do" She replied quietly before ending the call, not even allowing him time to reply. Craig took a sip of water from the glass beside him and slumped back against the pillows, his head literally sped into overdrive and he was forced to wonder how long he could keep this up before he finally fucking snapped. He tossed his phone back onto the unit beside his bed and resumed his position, staring at the ceiling.

Chapter Three

Johnny Fenton sat in the grubby prison cell, on his bunk with his little plastic bag of belongings plonked on the floor between his legs. The cold sweat that clung to his muscular body making him giddy with anticipation, as his scruffy grey prison scrubs stuck to his back. The day had finally come when he could call himself a free man. Apart from having to spend the next three years on license he was going home, back to the real world after serving almost four years for the manslaughter of Craig Carter. He had come to the Pen a boy and now he was leaving a muscular, fit athletic young man. A man with a vicious business reputation despite being locked up, his name was still hot on the streets, Craig had seen to that. He personally couldn't wait to see his business partner and so aptly named partner in crime. Between them they had pulled off the greatest faked death of the twenty first century and now both were raking in the big coin like it was they're God given right. Johnny was now a twenty four year old fitness buff who had changed virtually overnight within his prison environment. He had instantly hardened, instantly learnt not to take any shit whether it be from the lags or the screws and undoubtedly Craig had played his hand in the ease of Johnny's time in jail. Unlike all the other bastards locked up in here he was going out to a fresh start, a brand spanking new show home, a stunning new fully furnished club that was going to make him a mint and he was coming out above all to absolve the past. He wanted to put his teenage years and the fucking Belmonte estate behind him. The place held nothing but bad memories for Johnny and despite him and Craig still having some unfinished business to contend with Kenny Kreegan, he knew this time he would never go back.

Of course he had regretted some of his decisions; he knew he had a LOT of making up to do with Cath, when he caught up with the cunt of course. When he had been sent to jail she had all but abandoned him, throwing out any excuse not to come and visit him before completely walking out of his life for good. Unluckily for Cath, Craig had conveniently had her followed by a private detective who had gathered a nice little portfolio on Cath and her new cushy little life. After spending a few stints in rehab for her eating disorder she had given birth to a gorgeous little girl called Melissa. Melissa had been born eight weeks premature, weighing a tiny three pounds one ounce and they had later learnt that she had been born Down's syndrome. Johnny didn't know whether it had been from Cath's bulimia throughout her pregnancy that had made their daughter ill but he had loved the little girl never the less and wanted nothing more than to be there to protect her. From what he had seen in the detective's photographs she was the prettiest little girl in the world, a real dead ringer for him as a toddler. He had learnt so much about her from the private detective it was almost as though he already knew her in person. Her favourite colour was orange; she adored dancing, ice cream and the kids film Frozen. Despite suffering with a speech delay she could communicate well by pointing and using sign language.

What Johnny had also discovered that not so innocent Cath had found a love for red wine and pain killers whilst sharing her life with many various sexual partners whilst their daughter was holed up in bed or with one of Cath's so called 'friends'. Once a whore, always a whore had been Johnny's opinion on that little fleck of information. What did he honestly expect after having a child with an ex prostitute. He would be paying het a visit soon though, and little Melissa would be gone. Craig had already set him up with a wicked family brief who would take his case on if any problems occurred. Of course he expected a fight from Cath, but he knew if he laid it on thick enough about all the professional help he could afford to get their daughter and coughed up a few quid. She'd be like putty in his expert hands. Johnny sighed at the thought, things were meant to have played out so differently to this, Cath was meant to have waited for him, they were meant to have made a fresh start together in their new manor house in the country. They had meant to fraternise with the lords and ladies of the criminal underworld with their lavish dinner parties, drinking expensive scotch and rubbing shoulders with the real villains. Making a name for each other and throwing themselves into their business, their future. Instead they were worlds apart and Johnny was forced to now live out that life alone, carving his own identity in the underworld.

As the hatch on his cell door opened and the screws on the outside the door informed him it was time, Johnny beamed aimlessly in their direction. Picking up his polythene bag and swinging it over his shoulder he aimed for the door, patiently waiting for the screws to lead him out. He was pleased to see some of the lags out on the wing shouting their goodbyes and clapping and jeering as he was led away, this was it. He was finally going home.

Chapter Four

It was late, almost midnight when Jenna decided to make her way across the hospital to the rehabilitation unit. Her nerves were shot as she shuffled in the darkness across the almost empty car park, clinging to her baggy cardigan as she went. The air was damp, moist with rain and slightly stuffy with the humidity. She sucked a deep breath, trying her hardest to still her erratic heartbeat. Her nervousness almost making her hyperventilate with fear. Fear of what she wasn't exactly sure but she felt it all the same. Her slippers scraped against the gravel as she trudged across through the hospital gardens, the rehabilitation unit was lit up like a beacon in the near distance. The building itself was homely looking, redbrick with all brilliant white fascias and doors. The neat little vegetable patches to the right that were cornered off by little picket fences seemed so rugged and she could almost picture them coming straight from a Beatrix Potter novel. It didn't look nor feel like a hospital suite and Jenna was pleased for the change in scenery. It was a far cry from the sterile, white wash tension that lingered in the intensive care unit and for that she was grateful. She waited for the automatic doors to allow her access and she signed herself in at the main reception. She waited patiently at the main desk before one of the nurses became available to take her over to Craig's room.

She hadn't been waiting long when a buxom red headed nurse with tired eyes and a happy smile gladly led the way over to where Craig was staying. The chatter between them was kept bare minimal as they tried not to wake the other patients all that could be heard was slightly muffled noises of snores of the patients around them and the slapping of the nurses plimsolls on the heavy lino. She pulled open a few more doors and finally her eyes rested on the door opposite them;

"He's in there, you can go straight through" she smiled as she spoke, before turning away and sauntering off with her clipboard tucked firmly underneath her arm. Jenna straightened herself up and ran her fingers through her dishevelled hair and she regretted her decision not to do something with herself beforehand. She took another deep breath as she made her way to the door, she paused as her hand skimmed the handle gently she pushed her hand downwards her breath still caught in her throat. She pushed the door open gently and was greeted with the most solemn eyes she had ever seen in her life, red rimmed and frosty blue. Her hand instinctively reached for her mouth as she rushed across to try and contain his heavy racking sobs. She held his defeated body tightly to her chest as she soothed him silently, stroking his hair softly as though he were a child.

"Shhhh, what's all this?" her voice silky as she kissed his rugged temple, his body sagged into hers, his weight lay solely on hers, crushing her slightly with his strength. He said nothing, he just continued to let out all of his pent up emotions and Jenna could do nothing more than cuddle him close to her and let him wear himself out. She of course wondered what had caused this dramatic reaction and part of her had already guessed that it was something to do with her, but she hadn't come here under false pretences. Craig was still in the dog house as far as she was concerned and he still had a LOT of explaining to do over what had happened between Dom and himself. But now was neither the right place nor the right time to be quizzing him over his intentions. She glanced down at him and met his glum gaze, he looked completely and utterly spent and Jenna held him closer again;

"Hey, what's all this" she cooed softly, taking his chin gently between her fingers and stroking his damp skin as she spoke.

"I thought you weren't coming" he whispered between his sobs, he had stopped crying but the aftermath of his attack was still lingering on his well structured body. Jenna inhaled deeply, looking almost pained as their eyes met again;

"I want going to" she admitted tiredly, settling him back against the pillows and climbing into the bed beside him, she was careful to avoid her eyes meeting his mangled legs. She had been warned by the nurse that he was very self conscious about the state of his out of action limbs and was told to tread carefully when broaching the subject with him. She snuggled into him, pulling his arm around her as she hurled the blankets up over them both, completely covering his legs so that she wouldn't feel the need to stare at them. Craig's hand slid across her stomach and he pulled her in close enough to kiss her gently on the forehead. The feeling of his lips on her skin made Jenna break out in a wave of Goosebumps. She tried her hardest to stifle the blush that spread across her cheeks, failing miserably in her attempts. She huddled close to him her fingers lingering on his scars feeling their prominence on his tanned luminous skin, the angry purple strikes where the knife had collided with his taught flesh still so fresh on his skin. Jenna had to bite her bottom lip to stop it quivering suddenly; the pain of everything that had happened was still so raw. The accident, the stabbing, the realisation that Craig had faked his own death still ate away at her like cancer. He had hurt her in ways he would never even begin to understand and yet she found herself still so torn between the two of them. Craig was her lifelong friend, the man she had loved and chased all of her life and he had never given himself to her. Until of course he had seen her with Dom and then suddenly he was offering the world and more. It didn't seem fair somehow; Jenna knew that he had been sleeping with other women during his time away. Had he expected to just sit around wallowing in her own self pity for the rest of her life pining for someone who was nothing more than a ghost? Jenna knew instinctively that he would have done just that. She sighed awkwardly she loved Craig, she really did, but she had become accustomed to the fact that he was only trying now because she had eyes for another man.

"What you thinking?" Craig muttered as though speaking to no one in particular his interest waned slightly when Jenna explained to him exactly what she thought.

"That's bullshit and you fucking know it!" he replied gruffly, taking his arm from around her and finding interest in an invisible fleck on the blankets. He sighed petulantly, if she had no trust in him then there was no point in even fucking trying and she may as well flounce back to pretty boy right now.

"How long is it going to take to get it drummed into your thick fucking head Jenna Bastarding Shearan that despite your slightly pointless reservations that I Love you, I always have and I am sick of trying to reassure you of something that I cannot make any clearer than I already have. You and Kiki and even this little man are my fucking world girl how long is it going to take eh? It's your trust I want Jen, I had your love a long time ago darling but this aint worth shit if you don't trust me" his voice was clipped now, filled with sarcasm and envious distaste. He was the expert at making people feel guilty and in that moment Jenna Shearan had never felt so small in her life. She knew he was speaking the truth but she also knew that her feelings for Dom were real; she had fallen for him even through all of the drama with Craig. He hadn't been put off with her unhealthy obsession with her ex. They had fallen head over heels for one another and Jenna knew that she could never let it rest without knowing if they could have something special. She had been thrown into a state of manic confusion and she didn't know what the fuck she was going to do. Her head was saying one thing and her heart was saying something completely different and despite her reservations she knew exactly where her loyalties lie.

"I can't come here anymore Craig until I've made up my mind. It isn't fair on the two of you if I keep flitting between you both like some dirty fucking slag, I refuse to be objectified by the two of you and unfortunately Dom can't speak for himself. I need space Craig, I hope you understand" She straightened herself out as she sloped off the bed composing herself as she turned to walk away from him again, the tears stinging in her eyes as she realised just how much the pain was hurting her. Heartache was a cruel thing and Jenna Shearan was experiencing it in true glorious Technicolor. She swiped her eyes angrily, she felt so weak in his presence and even now after all this time he was her strongest, guiltiest pleasure.

As she turned and walked out of the door Craig's thin lips turned into a slightly crooked grin. When Jenna saw just exactly what he had planned for Dom when he woke up from his coma she would never ever want to see his pretty little mug again. The thought pleased Craig a tenfold and he rubbed his hands together in sheer amusement. Picking up his phone he wondered momentarily if it was too late to make his call across the pond to America, he was just dying to let his associate in on the latest developments he held the receiver to his ear as he was put through to the international switchboard, the smile never leaving his sultry lips.....

Chapter Five

Johnny had been out a week and already he had made so much progress with his plans to track down his absconding girlfriend and their offspring. As well as helping Craig with a little business overseas Johnny's main focus was solely on gaining his beloved daughter and telling Cath exactly where she could fucking shove it. He couldn't believe how she could have just upped and left like she had but it proved one thing to Johnny. That she could never ever have loved him in the first place. He had felt slightly used at first and wondered whether Cath had sought him out just to get away from her life in Kenny's knocking shop on the Belmonte. She had worked there as the brothels Madame and had been in charge of all of Kenny's girls, Johnny had plucked her straight out of there after only a small number of meetings and had fallen for the girls bewitching charms. She had been older, wiser and amazing in the bedroom department and Johnny had been smitten. But now when he had thought after all of this time he realised that he hadn't really known her at all and had been played like a puppet in the short of it all. Cath had seen his kindness for weakness and completely evaded his trust and now after all of the time he had been given to think in prison he had come out a much more mature, much more accepting man and now he understood the truth of the situation in crystal clarity. She had wanted him for nothing more than a child and a place to go when the life got too much for her. He had been a means of escapism and Johnny the poor sod had fallen for it hook line and sinker.

He ran his hand over his closely shaved head and mused over a few of the idea's planned for the up and coming weeks at the Mamma Rouge, the place was a fucking gold mine and Johnny was pleased to say that he was fucking coining it in at the club. They were open from a Thursday through Sunday and offered the elite in fetish and all things kinky fuckery. The girls were all amazing and each preformed to the absolute best of their abilities, even with their strict no touching policy the punters flocked to see the girls in all their finery. Bondage had never interested Johnny one bit, with the exception of tying the odd girl up when he had been younger but other than that it didn't appeal to him at all. Craig on the other hand had a somewhat healthy interest in the art of bondage and submission and spent hours scouring the internet for new ideas and seeking out new props and equipment that they could use in the club.

Craig had a fascination or as he preferred to call it a "speciality" with the idea of kidnap and emotional torture which was exactly why he had played a blinder in the kidnapping of his daughter, he had used his child as a pawn, a bargaining tool to literally crush Jenna mentally and physically so that she was left nothing but a weak and tortured shell which in turn had ravished Craig's sexual appetite a tenfold. He had followed the girl for months and had kept a million photos and dossiers in the safe of her movements since his death. Johnny had always just gone along with it in the name of business and with him being banged up there wasn't a lot he could have done anyway. He had stumbled across all of Craig's findings by sheer accident. After trying to file away some of the paperwork for the club he had unlocked the wrong safe and out popped the bundles of notes and photographs that amounted to Craig's apparent stalking of his ex. Johnny had sat and read through them all out of coincidence, he missed the Belmonte and what was going on there. His sister was still living a dog's life with her prick husband and Johnny had swore on his babies life that as soon as the dust was clearer and the police and probation weren't watching him like hawks he would get him revenge on the useless cunt.

Johnny rolled himself a cigarette and continued to delve into his work, his laptop was on fire with emails from potential investors and clientele who all wanted a slice of the pervy pie. Johnny had to crack a smile over the despicable wants and needs of some of his and Craig's punters. Some liked the gagging and the blindfolding which was pretty much standard issue in a place like this but others were more darker, more dirtier and into the likes of sadism, masochism and the acts of roleplay involving brutal violence, fire play and rape. Johnny had no time for that shit, give him plain old vanilla any day where he could just stick it in, have his way and leave. But in despite of it all, sex made money, and kinky sex made millions. Johnny smiled at his little metaphor and finished his cigarette in peace, he could already see from the five figure number that leapt on the screen from a potential client that today was indeed going to be a terrific day.

Chapter Six

It had been almost five months since Dom had been in his coma and the nurses and doctors were still in limbo as to how the outcome with him would pan out. His ventilators were still keeping him alive and the previous two attempts of taking him off them had been a complete nightmare. They were again going to try and take him off the ventilator and see whether he would breathe on his own. Jenna had never felt so anxious in all of her life and had called on Craig for support; he was healing well and had regained almost eighty percent of his movement back in his legs. He still had to use the wheelchair but he hoped it wouldn't be long before he was back on his feet and back in his business. He knew that Johnny was doing a sterling job in the club and he knew the boy could be trusted implicitly, but Craig was a man with a firm belief in the mantra if a jobs worth doing well, you may as well do it yourself. Jenna clung to Craig's hand desperately as the nurses pottered around Dom, unhooking him from the various tubes and wires that had been thus far keeping him alive. They both held their breath as the nurse turned off the last of the machines, Jenna felt so light headed in that moment that she could swear she would pass out with the anticipation of it all. Craig nudged her shoulder gently and she stared in disbelief as his chest rose and fell ever so slowly, her hand reached for her mouth and the tears cascaded down her cheeks as she took in the sight before her. He was breathing, finally he was breathing unaided, and Jenna's elation was paramount as her sobs turned to cackling laughter. She grabbed Craig and held him tightly to her chest words completely failing her. She had waited so long for this and now the moment was here she relished in it entirely. Craig held her out at arm's length;

"It's time now Jen, you need to make your choice" he whispered the solemn tone of his voice wasn't lost at all on Jenna and she sighed heavily in response. Only Craig could put the dampeners on this moment and she resented him for it slightly.

"Look Jen, if he's going to be ok, I need to know what's going to happen between us. Unfortunately for you Kiki will have to stay with me, I'm not having her go back to that rancid estate. I'm sorry but that won't ever happen." He smiled sarcastically as he finished speaking and set his eyes back onto Dom, who still lay sound asleep before them. Craig couldn't help but feel nothing but ruthless hatred for the man in the bed. Even out cold and on the brink of death he was flawless. Jealousy was a horrible thing and Craig Carter was riddled with it, it ate away at him viciously. He glared at Dom and promised himself there and then that he had his card numbered. No one was taking Jenna from him, not even pretty boy Grey. He pulled up the nurse and asked to be taken back to his room; he suddenly wasn't feeling too well at all.

"Wait" Jenna jumped up from her seat and ran over to the wheelchair bound Craig; she ran her fingers across his stubbled cheek and gently kissed his slightly sweaty temple.

"He needs me Craig, at least let him come around first eh?" she smiled sadly, she couldn't begin to believe she was reasoning with him. But she knew in her heart that she was holding off because she just wasn't ready to choose between them both just yet. Craig just nodded briefly before being carted away again and Jenna didn't know why, but it felt like he was saying one final goodbye. She folded her arms over her chest and huffed sulkily as she returned to her bedside vigil of the man she knew in her heart she truly loved.

Chapter Seven

It was a week later before Dom had come to from his coma and things had not gone well to say the least, it turned out that he had no recollection of the accident, no recollection of anything that had happened before that either. Jenna was heartbroken, he had literally no idea who she was and had spent the last week trying to spark any little memory between them to try and get him to remember. But he had just stared at her for hours afterwards trying to picture her face but having no luck. It was as though his whole world was a blank canvas and Dom had sunk deeper and deeper into his relentless depression. He really was trying for the sake of the poor girl beside him who was claiming all of these ludicrous things about the two of them being together and that they had planned a future together, but Dom could never picture meeting her. He knew his name was Dominic, knew he lived in Preston and as he had already told the girl before him, he already had a wife, Ami.

Jenna had never felt so low in her entire life, the memory loss had thrown her into a fit of despair and she was trying her fucking hardest to maintain her sanity for the sake of her baby. She had bought photographs of her and Dom together and he had simply accused her of doctoring the images. He had all but told her that he wasn't interested, that he already had a wife and a child. Both of which had thrown Jenna because he had mentioned neither before and she wondered briefly if they were a figment of his lacking imagination. Jenna sat on the edge of the bed trying her hardest to try and talk him around but now he had resorted to completely ignore her.

"Often go around trying to get on other women's husbands do you, there's names for girls like you love" he scoffed sarcastically in his posh boy voice that he suddenly possessed. And Jenna's head shot back in sheer bewilderment, she suddenly felt like she had been punched in the mouth by Mike Bloody Tyson! Surely he couldn't keep up like this.

"I'll have you fucking know Dominic" she spat back vehemently "I'm no fucking slut! You were the fucking cunt who came running after me" her finger jabbed her chest as she spoke "How dare you speak to me like I'm nothing! I've sat here every fucking day since that poxy crash praying for you to be ok, praying for you to wake up.... Now I'm beginning to wish that you'd never opened your fucking eyes" she held her fucked up head in her hands as she finished her tirade. She was exhausted, hormonal and over emotional and the combination was absolutely lethal. Dom tossed his head back, laughing loudly his whole body racking with the bellowing laughter as he replied

"Well fuck me, feisty one you are aren't you, and who said you were a slut? I didn't did I?" his giggling was infectious and free spirited but Jenna couldn't even raise a grin to her mouth. She just stared at him, hard faced and completely disgusted by this man who sat in front of her. This wasn't her Dom; the one she had fought all this time to bring back from the depths, this man was a monster. A vicious, nasty monster who had no feelings and no emotions what so ever. Jenna leapt up from the bed and slapped him hard across the cheek, her fingers stinging against his skin as her hand connected with his face. Her expression wild with manic fury as she just glared at him, her breathing rapid and heavy as their eyes finally locked on to one another. The tension between them was electric and Jenna had to swallow hard to try and moisten her paper dry mouth; the imprints of her fingers on his cheek were predominant and vivid on his pasty skin. Jenna instantly felt guilty but couldn't open her mouth to apologise, she sat frozen, their eyes locked on one another. Steely grey and emerald green, neither breaking their strong gaze. Neither had the heart to speak. He was so confused and he wished that even if it was for just a second that something would click with her. She looked so defeated and sad and Dom felt awful for not remembering her.

Suddenly Jenna bent over doubled as a jolt of pain ripped through her stomach she screamed out, clutching the bedrail as another painful shot seared through her hot and heavy in its perilous assault. She clutched her heavy bump as she tried her hardest to control her erratic pains. She lunged forward accidentally as another pain swept over her so that her head was on Dom's lap and he couldn't help but run his hands through her hair and whisper that everything was going to be ok. It wasn't until he looked at the bedspread did he see the blood, so, so much blood that was splattered on the sheets. Jenna clung to him, howling mercilessly as the nurses and doctors flooded the small room;

"What happened?" one of the nurses eyed Dom speculatively as she quizzed him, pulling Jenna away from him and placing her gently into a vacant wheelchair before she was rushed away by the doctors. Dom sat frozen to the spot, staring at the gory pool of blood that had soaked his bed sheets. The shock had set in and his whole body was rigid with fear, he couldn't speak, couldn't even move. He hoped though that the poor girl would be alright.

Chapter Eight

Craig's face was knotted with worry as the tiny rat like baby was pulled away from Jenna's stomach. Craig was mesmerised momentarily before the grave fear set in at the reality of their situation. The little boy weighed a tiny two pounds two ounces and was rushed to the premature baby unit immediately. Neither parent had even got a glimpse of him as he was whisked away and that had hurt Craig immensely. Craig held onto Jenna's fragile hand as though his life depended on it as she cried uncontrollably on the operating table. Her whole face drained of colour as she sobbed whole heartedly as the sadness and the realisation that they were probably going to lose him set in. Her long awaited baby boy had arrived a full three months premature and Jenna knew she had to brace herself for the worst. Craig kissed her knuckles as his head rested on her hand.

"I'm so sorry babe" he whispered, kissing her brow softly trying to console her. He would fucking kill Dom for this, he had heard all about their little spat and Craig was fucking livid. If the baby turned out to be his son and anything happened to him. Dom was as good as dead.

"Don't let him die Craig, Don't leave him" she mumbled deliriously burying her face into his, her brow filmy with a feverous cold sweat. Craig held her tightly promising that he would go and be with him soon. His heart was heavy in his chest as he held her close, wishing all of her pain away. He hoped against hope that their poor baby would eventually find the strength to pull through. Even in his uncertainty over the child's paternity Craig felt a strong connection to the child and he would hate to see any harm come to him. As he was wheeled away he knew that he had to go and confront Dom before he returned to his son's bedside vigil.

The doctor's finished stitching Jenna up before she was taken back over to the ward, the thought of sitting over the mother and baby unit depressed her greatly. All those mothers sitting blissfully with their bonnie little bundles while she was sat there nursing her empty useless body and wondering bleakly whether her poor baby would survive. Craig had been texting her like crazy from the neonatal intensive care unit. Every time their little boy made a movement he would text, he had been amazing and Jenna was pleased that he hadn't held the boys paternity against her, for the time being at least. Her mind wandered to Dom and she thought she should at least text him to let him know the baby had arrived safely. She dismissed the thought immediately and decided against it, he wouldn't remember her being pregnant anyway, she thought bitterly. She had imagined things playing out so differently than they actually had. She had pictured Dom by her side, telling her how well she was doing, telling her he loved her as she delivered her bouncing baby boy into the world into a room filled with love. Instead she had been forced to deliver three months early, to a baby weighing barely a bag of sugar, with Craig stuck in his wheelchair praying for the life of her son. It was a tragic situation and Jenna had become so forlorn and sad with the whole sorry episode. She held her head against the pillow and sobbed until she fell into a deep, troubled sleep.

Craig wheeled into the ward where Dom was and almost had to stop himself from vomiting in his lap. His little man was putting up such a fight and Craig's heart swelled with pride at the mere thought of him. Dom lay in the bed before him, his hand over his head dosing lightly Craig clapped his hands loudly and he shot up disorientated.

"What the fuck!" he protested, rubbing his eyes sleepily. "Oh it's you, what you want?" he quizzed slouching lazily against the pillows.

"We have a son" Craig smiled half heartedly, wheeling over to the bedside and showing Dom a photo of the baby on his phone. Dom stared at him blankly, not quite registering what Craig was gabbling on about.

"You mean, you have a son" Dom corrected him, pointing at him sarcastically as he spoke his eyes darting around the room trying to focus on anything but Craig. Dom didn't know the man personally, but wheat he did know was that he was imitated by him immensely.

"No, we have a son and you better start getting your memories back you muggy cunt and be there to support that girl or I'll personally see to it that you breathe your last fucking breath in that bed right there." Craig spat angrily, mocking Dom's actions by pointing back at him. His finger flitted from Dom to the bedspread to emphasise his point further.

"Do you think I'm not trying?" he leant forward so that he was closer to Craig's face, "You think this isn't torture for me? Having to hear her tell me all of this stuff and not remember any of it! Having to try and torture myself to try and remember something" his voice was a plea now, he held his hands out in a gesture of mercy. Craig's fingers scanned his bottom lip in thought. He liked this control he had over Dom it was quite exciting to know that the man feared him, even if it was only a small quantity of fear, it was still fear nonetheless. Looking into the eyes of the man he despised most in life Craig felt nothing but aching discomfort.

"Tell me Dom, do you remember anything about the crash at all?" he quizzed; the playful smile on his lips was subtle and well hidden. As he sank back into the back of chair he arched his fingers in front of him trying to make himself look slightly intimidating. Dom shook his head in reply and Craig was angered, he couldn't read whether the man was being truthful or not. It made Craig quite resentful because he was usually so good at reading people from their gestures and mannerisms, this cunt was a complete no face.

"I meant what I said, you better start getting that memory of yours back and start being there for that girl, or you will die here Dom. I'd give my life to see Jen happy and unfortunately she seems to think she has harboured some sort of feelings toward you. So shape the fuck up and sort your head out, literally" his words were clipped and brief before he turned and left to return back to his post with his son. If one of them had to be there, then it would have to be him. That Loony cunt was still on cloud nine somewhere and Jenna had to take her time and recover both physically and mentally. He just wanted to get back to the baby and keep his eye on him. He already had a name in mind for his little off spring and he knew Jenna would agree....He just had to wait until she wasn't so caught up in all of the bullshit and drama to broach her on the subject.

<u>Chapter Nine</u>

Craig sat beside the incubator, his eyes glazed over with salty tears as he watched his beautiful son's chest rise and fall rapidly. The tubes and wires that ran in and out of his tiny body, feeding him, helping him, keeping him alive. Craig had never felt so helpless in all of his life, but he prayed that he would get to see the boy grow up. He had an insatiable bond with the little mite already and could never tire of just watching over him, praying for him to have a safe recovery. He swallowed hard; the poor bastard didn't look like a baby at all, more of a skinned rabbit or something along those lines. Not like Kiki had, she had been a bouncer, a perfect healthy sized baby girl who had been the owner of the strongest set of lungs Craig had ever witnessed. But this poor sod didn't have a chance really did he? His paper thin skin too fragile to touch and his features seemed slightly squashed, too small and bony. Craig's heart wretched every time he looked at the boy yet in the same breath, he couldn't stop himself from staring. Craig knew already that he loved the boy unconditionally and if he didn't make it, if this were to be it, he knew that he would always, always save a very special place in his heart just for the precious little angel whether he had fathered him or not. He was his, he was his son. Craig had never felt a bond like it, not even with Kiki. This little mite was special, he was needy, he was so precious and Craig knew, he would be the making of him. He placed his fingers against the glass of the incubator and made a promise to the little mite there and then that he would always be a good daddy to him, he would always be there for him, always provide for him and above all he would love him completely. The tears rolled down his cheeks as he spoke, clearing his throat loudly in the silence he continued his little speech before leaning over and planting a soft kiss on the glass. The day's events had changed Craig; he had never ever known love like he had for that baby boy and it made Craig wonder momentarily whether he already knew the boy was his. In his heart of hearts he didn't want to face the thought of the alternative, but he knew that as soon as the baby was strong enough they would have to clarify the truth.

Jenna Shearan lay in the eerie silence of the mother and baby ward, her heart ached in her chest as she thought of her beautiful little boy over in the special care baby unit. Despite being in a room of her own, all night she had been hearing the cries and whimpers of the newborns around her, and all night she had craved for that to be her. Her long awaited son, who she already loved unconditionally despite not yet having the opportunity to see his face, was alone. She hugged her pillow close to her cheek as the tears streamed from her eyes; she had never felt such a low in all of her lifetime and she hoped she would never have to feel this way again. Her vulnerability was eating away at her as her thoughts drifted to whether her little boy would make it, in her mind's eye she was already planning his funeral. There was no way they could save him and they were just clutching straws for the time being. Setting herself up for a fall was something Jenna was not comfortable with in the slightest and she hoped that it wouldn't come to the point where they were forced to say goodbye to her beautiful son. She had already lost the love of her life once, there was no way she could cope with the loss of another. She bit her bottom lip trying to stifle the sobs that threatened to enrapture her skinny body. She couldn't help but blame herself for her son's imminent arrival, had she ate enough? Probably not, had she taken on too much stress after the crash? Definitely. The questions that kept spinning around her head made her dizzy with confusion. But in the end she believed that the blame lay solely upon her shoulders and for that Jenna Shearan would be eternally guilty.

Chapter Ten

"Archie?" Jenna smiled as she took in the idea, Craig had been so enthusiastic to name the baby and now as they both stared at the little boy in the incubator, nothing had felt more right to Jenna.

"We were gunna call Keeks Archie if she was a boy, weren't we" her smile deepened at the memory as her hand lay splayed against the glass, it had been Craig's choice from day one and they had argued black and blue about it at first. But now all these years later, Jenna felt herself warming to the idea.

"And before you ask" Craig raised his hand to stop her from speaking "I want his middle name to be Drake and I suppose seems as we don't know who his dad is he'll have to go double barrels and be Carter-Grey" the babies last name bothered Craig, he had nagged his case that he wanted it to be Grey-Carter, but it had sounded awful. So he had eventually been forced swallowed his pride.

"Why Drake?" Jenna quizzed, her attention taken solely from the baby to Craig.

"Well his dad is either Dom or Craig so it's kind of a merger of the two" he winked.

"It's perfect she replied before fixing her eyes back onto the baby. He was perfect in every single sense of the word and Jenna had fallen in love the second she had clapped eyes on him. He had no hair whatsoever, his body was skinny and almost cartoon like in appearance and his features were slightly off because of how early he had been, but to Jenna he was flawless and Little Archie had taken hold of her heart. She couldn't wait for the day to come when she could finally hold him, change him and take care of him like any ordinary mother would with her child. But for now she was just happy to be able to spend time with him, looking over him keeping him safe. Craig's hand gently brushed her slender shoulders and she turned her head into his soft touch, he had been her rock throughout all of this and she honestly didn't know how she would ever have survived without him. She had given up hope with Dom, He was still in complete denial over the whole affair and Jenna had decided that she couldn't wait around for him to find his love for her again. He seemed so hung up on his ex wife to even take a second glance at her now so she had flung herself into her mutual relationship with Craig, and for the time being they were happy. The bounced off one another in perfect sync and Jenna was happy to be helping him on the road to recovery. He could walk no for short distances with the aid of a walking stick, but it was significant progress in such a short space of time. He had put all of his energy into being there for her and the baby that he had put his own rehabilitation on hold. He was dedicated to make the change for Jenna and their son even if his life depended on it.

Chapter Eleven

Ami Grey-Heller flounced through the plush suite of the Hollywood hotel she found herself staying at, subtly tossing her striking red hair over her slender shoulders as she reached the lobby, every inch the stunning socialite that she was. She opened the mulberry bag that skimmed her slender hips and took out her pocket mirror; pouting seductively she assessed her makeup and hair before striding out into the hot Florida sun. Her barely there body lovingly entwined in a Chanel sundress that hugged her delicious curves beautifully. Her gorgeous sun kissed bare legs shone in the heat with a thin film of sticky perspiration Her Gucci heels that literally screamed "I cost a bomb!" Hugging her tiny feet tightly she down the hotel steps attempting to avoid the gazes of the general public with her oversized Ray Ban sunglasses as she met her driver with a subtle rise of her over-glossed upper lip. She slid into the limousine and the outside world was shut out once more. She checked her makeup for the second time with an almost obsessive need as though the twenty seconds she had spent out in the fresh air had melted away half of her face. She patted over her heavy fringe slightly, smoothing it over her forehead so that it was a dead straight line. She glanced at her gold Rolex that hung from her tiny wrists; it was another three hours before her husband would be back and she was already drowning in the monotony of Hollywood. The Boutiques here were awful, nothing like London or Paris and she was slightly disheartened that Max had bought her here on his business trip. "It'll be fun" he said, and she had seen him for all of what? An hour or maybe it had been two? He hadn't even offered to take her out for dinner! The mindless bastard Ami scrolled through the numbers in her phone, wondering who would want to hear her pitiful drawls about how awful their trip into Hollywood had been and how the flea markets in Oregon had more to offer than the swanky modern stores here had to offer. Safe to say Prissy Ami Grey-Heller was absolutely livid that she had even offered to accompany Max on this trip. She threw her phone none too gently back into her handbag and gazed out of the tinted windows of the limousine.

Her life since she had married Max had altered dramatically, she had pot loads of money, chauffer driven cars, holidays whenever the fancy took her and a life that was the envy of all her so called friends. Cocktails on ice at every venue she entered, VIP lounges and private jets made up her life now. It was a far cry from the grotty council flat in London that she had learnt that her ex husband now occupied. She wondered briefly what had become of Dom. Obviously not a lot, but if his loony friend kept calling her trying to entice her into paying the Muppet a fly in visit he could think again. She found it hilarious that her ex husband had been cruelly robbed of his memory in a fatal car accident that had almost taken his life, in fact she relished in it. What she found even more amusing was the fact that Dom had only remembered her. He remembered her as his wife, all dyed purple hair, skinny jeans and rock concerts. She cringed to think of it, she had come so far from the shitty life she had led. She no longer had to work to survive; her job was to fucking party! Max had made sure that she never went without again. Alright she had a few sacrifices along the way, but putting Sam into a private all boys' school suited them both just fine. He came home four times a year for two weeks but was thriving within his environment and was one of the smartest boys in his year group. His peers were the pretty little rich boys of celebrities and monarchy and Ami couldn't have been prouder if she tried. She glanced down briefly at her phone in her bag that had been ringing unnoticed and disconnected the call, the international number meant one thing and one thing only and Ami wasn't ready to pay a visit to her past anytime soon. She tapped her driver on the shoulder and indicated for him to drive her to a nearby bar, she needed a stiff drink and she needed one now. Her mind was overworked with the thoughts of Dom, she truly had left him in the back of her mind when she had left all of them years ago and now she was being forced to rake it all back over. It wasn't a notion that sat well at all with Ami. Dom was her past, her dirty little secret and she didn't want to delve into old ground, especially now that her and Max were so happy. Of course they had the odd row or the odd bicker but she was convinced that she loved him. She stared out of the black tinted windows, her eyes not leaving the sidewalk as they droned through the crowded streets, hundreds of people buzzing around doing their shopping or standing around gossiping, some just dashing through the busy streets, but the hum of the city was a heady drug and stuck sat in her confined space pondering over her current situation Ami Grey-Heller realised that she was feeling very lonely indeed.

Chapter Twelve

Six Months Later

Craig sat beside Dom in the stuffy solicitor's office, the heat was stifling and he had to unbutton his thin cotton shirt to try and ease of the sweat that was pouring out of him in buckets. Jenna was running late and the two men were overly tense with nerves. The DNA results were in and due to be revealed and both were vicious with anxiety as they sat patiently in waiting. Craig's knee was bouncing ten to the dozen as he sat without movement in the uncomfortable plastic chair, and Dom kept crunching his knuckles in sheer annoyance at simply having to wait. Both had been dreading this day for months and now it was here they were both thrown into a fit of hysteria. Craig's eyes scanned the horrid space with its hideous canvas paintings and heavy oak furniture and he felt the bile rising in his throat at the sickly scent of dead sweat and whiskey that emitted from the fat, slightly balding brief who sat opposite them. The only sounds coming from the glugging water machine at the far end of the office and the erratic, hot breaths of the men situated around the room. Dom sighed heavily as he slumped further into his seat, wrapping his knuckles against his knees as he leant over on his fists that were propped against his knees. He barely registered the company around him as he let out a loud over exaggerated yawn. His hands skimming the legs of his cotton sweatpants as he relaxed further back into the chair.

"Could have dressed for the occasion" Craig muttered under his breath, of course he was sat bold as brass in his light grey Gucci suit and perfectly buffed and polished shoes. His hair cropped closely to his head, the feverish nervous grin ever present on his playful lips. He surely was nothing short of beautiful and Craig knew he was the envy of the both men who occupied the room with him. Dom looked inferior to him now, dressed in his Man Up! Track pants and hoodie, the sweat from his morning run still fresh on his clothes, the film of sweat that lingered on his slightly creased brow beading as it ran in lines down Dom's aged face.

"Fuck off Carter you Simple prick" he smirked, shaking his head as he swept away the stifling sweat with the back of his sleeve attempting to brush off Craig's words. He knew the idiot was trying to get the better of him but he wouldn't allow it today. He had been waiting for this day for the last six months and he hoped for the life of him that the kid wasn't his. In all his life he had never imagined that his life would have panned out like this. He had devoted his life to finding Ami and spending the rest of his life with her and Sam and this was a very unwelcomed spanner in the fucking works if he had ever seen one. He was fed up of waiting now and if he was honest he couldn't wait for this to be over. His memory was still extremely sketchy and he was still trying to place the girls face in his version of events. He drummed his fingers against the mahogany side table that separated himself and Craig, rolling his eyes sarcastically as he let out yet another forced yawn. The heat in the small office space was stifling and Dom could feel himself getting agitated. He almost leapt off his chair in applause when Jenna finally sauntered into the office, deliciously tanned and almost Goddess in her beauty, Dom smirked when Craig actually dived from his chair and offered it to her immediately. Before subtly taking his place behind her like a lap dog, his ample hand placed gently on her shoulder.

The fat brief, Mr James Parsons, who sat opposite them, was looking more and more uncomfortable by the second as he made his introductions and excused Jenna's lateness politely. He sympathised with her promptly because he too had children and knew all too well the sheer hard work that came with raising them. As he eyed the papers impassively on his desk unaware of the glowering eyes of the two men before him that bore into him he allowed himself a moment of solitude. Taking a sip from a plastic cup of water on his desk he cleared his throat before he began to speak. The tension in the room was raging and he couldn't wait for this to be over so that he could have a lie down before his lunch break.

"Mr Carter, Mr Grey" He nodded respectfully in both of their direction "And the Lovely miss Shearan, You all understand why you've been called here today yes?" he quizzed, his voice monotonous and flat as he spoke. Both men nodded simultaneously. Craig eyed Dom with malevolence, his face screwed into a look of pure disgust as the smarmy bastard played with a toying smile on his lips. It took Craig all his might not to thump the cunt straight in the mouth. He retained his composure though as Mr Parson's gestured his hands to continue speaking.

"Now as you both know you were both required to give a swab as was the child in question at the request of Miss Shearan. I've called you both here today because the results of those swab tests are in and Miss Shearan would like to discuss a legal plan moving forward for all involved. Mr Carter as you are aware it recently came to light that you are the biological father of Miss Shearan's daughter. So do you believe in the best interest of all parties that it would be best if you fathered this child also? I am aware that you are currently parenting the child alongside Miss Shearan with no outside interference from Mr Grey is that correct?" Mr Parsons sat back in his chair as he gestured for Craig to speak; Craig nodded subtly, no words leaving his mouth as he shot Dom a knowing glance, guarded and as cool as ice.

"Your assumptions would be correct" Craig replied snidely, his eyes still locked on Dom and the tension in the room was raised an octave. Jenna Held her gaze square in front of her, not moving an inch as she took in the vicious atmosphere that surrounded her. Craig's fingers dug unintentionally into her shoulders and she tensed further, her whole body numb with anticipation.

"Right well before we proceed I need to tell you both that Miss Shearan has issued a formal statement expressing her apologies at having to bring you both here under such unfortunate circumstances. She understands that you are both under an insurmountable amount of pressure. She would like to show you both the deepest compassion for having brought you here. So to the DNA" he scrabbled around with his papers and found a large brown envelope with their names printed on a white label "I just want to be on the understanding that neither of you will cause a ruckus in my office regardless of the outcome and that you will go about your business in an orderly and adult fashion." Both men nodded as Mr Parsons gestured for their reply.

"Right well" he added as he took a silver letter opener out of his drawer and proceeded to carefully open the envelope and taking out a singular sheet of paper. Taking another sip of water from the cup he returned his attention to the details on the sheet before him before clearing his throat deeply, coughing slightly as his throat attempted to reject the refreshing liquid.

"In the case of Master Archie Drake Carter-Grey, the paternity of said child lays ninety nine point nine percent with One Mr Dominic Grey, there are no doubts in my mind over the paternity and all of the information is clearly pointed out in section A and B of the text." He handed the sheet of paper to Jenna, who had turned a slightly sick shade of white, her hand reached for her mouth as she saw the results of the DNA for herself, there it was as clear as crystal, Dom had fathered her son.

All she heard was the violent slamming of the office door behind her and a loud, painful guttural growl from Craig as he broke down beyond the door. It took a brave man to show weakness by crying and Craig was howling with an almost animal instinct from beyond the confined space of James Parsons' office. Jenna knew that this would cut his deeper than any knife ever could, he had built such an amazing bond with Archie, and Jenna could have almost burst into tears for him. She turned to Dom who literally looked like he had swallowed a broken glass, he was completely dumbstruck. Jenna stared at him blankly, trying to register a reaction but he was a blank canvas, lost deep in thought. Mr Parsons stood and dismissed himself quietly leaving them alone in the privacy of their own thoughts.

"Well?" Jenna quizzed sternly, she had to stop herself from up and slapping him, and in that moment he looked so docile. He turned and blinked as his face registered hers.

"Oh my fucking God, Jenna I'm so sorry" his hand covered his mouth in stunned exasperation. He sighed loudly, his head lay in his hands as the hazy pieces finally began to slot together they created a complete vivid picture. Their stunning affair, the baby, Craig's faked death everything came flooding back.

"It's come back hasn't it" Jenna whispered sadly as she realised the source of Dom's silent unease. She didn't quite believe it though. Dom could only nod his head dumbly. The overwhelming guilt he felt was simply crushing. He felt nothing short of idiotic as he leant across and tried to grab her hand. She snatched it away vehemently, her face full of venom as she glowered at him relentlessly.

"Don't you fucking touch me, Very convenient that you've got your memory back now you know he's yours" she spat sadistically, her pupils dilated to the point of being almost non-existent. She rose from her chair, turning from him she attempted to flee, with no success as he grabbed her wrist before she got to the door; she flung herself around so that when they're faces met they were almost nose to nose. The sexual tension between them boiling, bubbling effortlessly to the surface and she could see the menacing lust burning in Dom's wild eyes. Their breaths rapid and forced as they just simply stared at each other for a long, drawn out moment neither backing down from the other. Both of them ablaze with anger, but passionate nevertheless. Jenna's eyes flitted momentarily from Dom to the door and she could feel herself falling so hard for him all over again. His floppy, unruly hair, his distinctive well polished cheekbones that were cut like glass, the deep grey domineering eyes that felt as though he was staring into her soul. He was effortlessly perfect and Jenna knew that if she didn't compose herself immediately then she would end up fucking him right there on Mr Parsons desk. She shifted back,

"I... have ... to ...go, I'll call you" she stammered before making her escape from the small office space. She walked out into the main foyer and scanned around for Craig, but he was nowhere to be seen. Suddenly the realisation of it all hit her and she found herself running for the exit, throwing up outside the dingy solicitors block wasn't her finest moment by far but Jenna Shearan had never ever felt so abandoned in all her life. She had nowhere to run and she had nowhere to hide. Dom was Archie's father, and hers and Craig's idyllic image of the two of them raising their child together had been shattered. Both her children were to grow up illegitimate from men who either couldn't remember what day it was or were too busy faking their own death to stick around. The shame bore into Jenna and she sighed deeply, breathing in the London air, hailing down a cab she decided it was time to go back home.

Chapter Thirteen

Jenna sat alone in her pokey council flat nursing the biggest glass of wine she could manage, it had been almost a week since the news of her son's paternity had ripped her world apart and she couldn't help but feel defeated. Dom had hounded her with texts non-stop for the past six days and Craig had all but ignored her. Claire had been knocking almost every evening since she had returned home but she couldn't even contemplate facing her. So much had happened since their last meeting and Jenna lived in fear of her finding out about Craig. She was still completely in the dark about her son's secret life and Jenna was in no position to burst her idyllic bubble. As far as Claire was aware her son was dead and buried, she had no idea of the secret life that Craig had become accustom to. It didn't seem fair somehow and Jenna knew that she was betraying the woman who had helped her through so much. Jenna gulped her wine greedily, the crisp taste taking her to a new high as she slumped back into the plump sofa cushions. The baby hadn't long dropped off and as she stared at his little face, lost deep in slumber her heart sank. He truly was a beautiful little baby, despite being six months old, he was still so small, so perfect and Jenna was completely spellbound by him. Archie had changed her life completely, he had given her purpose again, she knew Kiki would never be coming home Craig had settled that with her. Of course she couldn't even take him to court; he was supposed to be fucking dead for heaven's sake. She took in her boys beautiful features, his dark curls were his most predominant feature, glossy and wild on his little head. He had tiny, perfectly shaped dark green eyes, little pointy ears and the milkiest white soft skin Jenna had ever seen. He truly was a stunning child, with an impeccable temperament, always smiling and happy he was a marvel to be around and Jenna loved him without reservation. He had bought out a completely different side to her that she had never been able to have with Kiki, She had been Jenna and everyone else's child, Archie was hers and hers alone. Despite her hurting towards the two men whom she loved more than life itself, her life was back to its slow paced, reserved self. She held her head high when she went out and no longer lived in fear of what people thought of her. People were so blinded by their false sense of the truth that Jenna had embraced their ideologies and laughed at they're idiocy. People still showed her sympathy when she was out, it was written subtly in a look, a passing smile, the odd "how are you", they all thought she was still caught up in the grief of Craig's death and had rebelliously gone and purposely got herself up the duff by some randomer to ease her pain. Inside she laughed, they had no clue.

Jenna sat in the silence and envisaged herself with her perfect children, the two of them who lit up her life like a beacon, yet both came from different worlds. Kiki would grow up to be every inch the stunning socialite her father intended to be, growing up in money meant that you were instantly classy and Kiki Carter was nothing but the sassy little minx that her father wanted. Dressed in Cartier and Dior at three years old, packed with the mouth and flamboyancy of a teenager. Kiki was something very special indeed. Whereas Archie, would grow up in this madness, The Belmonte estate, a father who couldn't remember one day to the next, a mother who had grieved over a man who had faked his own death, then embarked on an illicit affair with him the second he reappears with his airs and graces. She had never felt so foolish in her life; she knew that Archie would need to be sheltered from it all; he needed protecting from the truth. Craig had already taken Kiki away, she would be damned if anyone came after Archie. Dom had kept his distance thus far and she knew it wouldn't be long before his head caught up with his heart and he would be round here demanding access and all sorts. It didn't settle well with Jenna at all. She loved both her kids impeccably but Archie was a lot more vulnerable than Kiki and she would do anything in her power to make sure her little boy was cosseted away from it all. She knew given the chance Dom would be an amazing dad but after the hurt of Kiki being plucked from her clutches she knew that she would never ever give Dom full access to their son because of her recent revulsion towards Craig. Her hatred had manifested itself so deeply that now even when she texted about Kiki his one word replies would make her seethe in loathing for the man who had fathered her child. Craig had become nothing but a prize winning prick and Jenna had harboured nothing but a challenging odium toward him.

She Huddled herself into the cool leather her phone burning a hole in her hand as she stared at it thoughtfully. She knew that she would have to face Dom at some point, the thought of him having a say over the parenting of her son seemed almost impossible. She had been a single mother for so long that it had never occurred to her that she would ever have to co-parent one of her children. She had never realised how much her life would change where the two men in her life was concerned. She loved them both, but loathed the way they had turned their backs on her completely. They had both done nothing more than abandon her, leaving her simply heartbroken in their tragic whirlwind. As she flicked through the pictures on her phone aimlessly she cried, bitter, angry tears that almost took her breath away in their intensity. She hovered her fingers nervously over her phone keypad, she knew she had to make right for the sake of her son. Quickly she dialled Dom's number and waited, the sound of the monotonous dial tone ringing unpleasantly in her ears, as she heard Dom's saddened voice whisper an awkward hello, she suddenly lost her confidence and hung up the phone. Staring at it blankly now as though it was some sort of foreign object, she swallowed nervously she knew that he would come round, start banging on the door but this time she knew that she would let him come. This needed to end, Tonight.

Chapter Fourteen

Kenny Kreegan sat tied to a hard backed chair, his eyes blinded from sight by a petrol stained rag, he had been in the van for a while now, he couldn't be exactly sure of how long and he hadn't known exactly whom it was that had bundled him out of his office with a barrel of a gun pushed firmly against his head. His breathing was laboured slightly and every single one of his senses tingled with anticipation. He wasn't exactly uncomfortable but it wasn't everyday you got tied to a chair and bundled into a van in broad daylight. He had already made a solemn promise to himself that whoever had been the administrator of this despicable deed would pay and pay greatly for their betrayal. The sweat was pouring across his furrowed brow, his eyes flitting from his bound hands to the door of the van, there was not a sound to be heard and the silence was making Kenny nervous. It was the not knowing that was making him jumpy and slightly out of focus, he was disorientated off his own fear, and that thought suppressed him. He had never felt so vulnerable in all his years, but as he sat there in the back of that van, his off colour teeth chattering with sheer trepidation did he realise, that for the first time in his life, Kenny Kreegan genuinely felt pure unadulterated fear cursing through his veins. He lay his head as best he could against the back of the chair and allowed his sobering thoughts to all but consume him, he knew he wasn't leaving this van alive, But he'd be fucking damned if he didn't go down without a fight.

He sat in the silence for long moments that felt like hours, his mouth was sandpaper dry and his whole body was completely deadened by the force of having to sit in the same position. His arms felt as though they had been literally plucked from the sockets, his eyes were rolling heavily from the exhaustion. He didn't know how long he had been there now but he had a feeling the night was drawing in. He hunched back into the chair, the whirring of the vans engine as it smoothly glided across the road making him sleepy and Kenny could feel himself losing focus. He refrained from breathing from his nose too much because the cunt who had tied him up had doused the rag around his eyes in fucking petrol and he was already buzzing off the smell. He was groggy, disorientated and the gram of whizz that he had been forced to bomb beforehand was making him paranoid, Kenny usually abstained from drugs and the juxtaposition between the euphoric high and his extreme exhaustion were too much for his body to take, he was an old man. As he felt the van pull into a silent almost instant stop, Kenny breathed a deep, mournful sigh, he knew that he would soon make his maker; the only thing that was flitting through his mind was his poor, demented wife Rosa. He wished he had done so much more for her, when she had been taken ill with dementia; he had been the quickest cunt pushing her out the front door. His business had been his life and he hadn't wanted Rosa to be in the way, so off to the funny farm she had been carted and Kenny had gone on to live his life as the Pimping, dirty cunt that he had always been. Rosa had barely crossed his mind, after their stint at Christmas the year previously she had rejected every single one of his attempts to reconcile with her. But now as he was at his most vulnerable Rosa was the only person who crossed his empty perverse mind.

There was an awkward silence before the van doors slid open, Kenny was suddenly alert, his whole body tense just in case one of these cunts decided to try and get a lucky shot in. Every single one of Kenny's sense's had become sensitized to his environment, the tiny beads of sweat that he could feel forming around his lips bugged him slightly as he snaked his tongue across his mouth to try and eradicate them. He tried his hardest to see through the disgusting petrol scented rag that covered his eyes, he of course was unsuccessful. He felt the heavy arms on his shoulders as they lifted him up and obviously carted him from the van. Kenny instantly felt the blistering cold as he was hauled out into the frosty evening air. He shuddered silently as the damp air lapped at his lanky body. He shouted as many obscenities as he could muster as he was carried none too gently from the chilly outdoors to the confinement of what appeared to be a warehouse space. Kenny did nothing but sit, on high alert, his whole body contorted as he heard the bold footsteps before him. Each agonising step that drew closer drew him in, he tried his utmost to try and place who could possibly want him so badly. Revenge was an intoxicating potion and Kenny knew that whoever was the other side of his blindfold would ultimately see him die. Kenny could smell the deep musk of the man's aftershave, as he lingered over Kenny. Kenny could smell the man's fresh mint hazed breath close to his face, he guessed that he wasn't even a few inches away. Staring Kenny down in the darkness; The bitter scent of musk and dazzling clean sweat hung heavily in Kenny's nose as he inhaled. The man's scent whoever he was, was simply intoxicating.

"You orite Kenny?" The voice that followed was drawn out and painfully sympathetic and Kenny couldn't help but tense his body even further as the man spoke. The voice obliviously fake and filled with malice and Kenny couldn't help but feel suddenly on pins.

"The fuck are you?" Kenny spat into the darkness before him, his lips like parchment as the words left his mouth but he would never show weakness. His eyes were still trying their hardest to see past the filthy rag that covered his eyes. He felt nothing but exhaustion coupled with a surreal numbness, the two opposing emotions conflicting as the fear took over. Every single hair on his body was prickled to attention, every sound was magnified a tenfold as he patiently tried to calm his overworked nerves. Kenny sucked in a baited breath, his mouth over sticky and dry from fear. He was sweating profusely without knowledge, his whole face drenched in a sickly film that literally poured from his pores.

"Oh I'm your worst fucking nightmare Kenny boy" The accent dropped slightly and Kenny winced as the realisation hit him that he knew exactly whom the mystery voice belonged to. His tongue ran relentlessly across his bottom lip attempting to moisten his dry lips. He didn't expect the blow that instantly collided with his jaw, he felt the bone crack relentlessly before the infectious giggling of Craig fucking Carter filled the space, bouncing off every single

"Thought you'd killed me off Kenny boy" Craig's voice was overly jovial and deliciously malicious in tone. Kenny was literally spewing inside, he had never been so bitter in his life; he genuinely felt like someone had chopped his nuts off and fed them to him whilst he was still shooting spunk. Craig Carter had done him over, the very boy he had been so quick to boast about killing was stood before him now a man and even though Kenny couldn't see him through the petrol stained rag that shielded his eyes he could feel the boys dawning, overbearing presence nonetheless. Craig stifled his chortle, trying his hardest not to piss himself with excitement. He had waited for this day for three fucking years and he had been delighted with how easy it had been. He and Johnny had literally kicked the door down to the shitty brothel that Kenny ran and taken him out none too kindly whilst he was pumping away, shagging some dirty looking black bird over his desk. For a disgusting old cunt Kenny had balls Craig would give him that he had kicked up a fuss all the way down the veranda and Craig had been surprised that firstly no one on the Belmonte had even twitched a curtain as Kenny was dragged away and two that his Armani suit was still flawlessly crease free. Despite his slight limp Craig had the full function back in his legs, the only time they played up was when it was cold but he muddled through it. He was fearless, since losing Jenna and Archie Craig had become stone faced, devoid of any emotion he had nothing left to lose so killing Kenny, even if it meant a life stretch meant nothing. The love of his life had literally been ripped away from him; he couldn't ever accept that Archie wasn't his son. He had cried, more than cried he had literally broken down and he knew that he would never ever be the same again. Despite still loving both Jenna and the baby he couldn't find a way to forgive her. Even though he had known all along that Archie may not have been his.

Craig stepped forward slipping the rag from Kenny's eyes and grinning as he stuffed it into his pocket. He glared viciously down at his victim like a bird to its prey, his eyes dancing wildly in their sockets as he took in the face of whom he loathed so much. Kenny blinked hastily as his eyes adjusted to the light, the sweat pouring from him in torrents as his eyes finally met those of the boy he had long forgotten about. Craig had matured well; barely recognisable he was now a tall, broad, muscular beautiful man. His jaw strong, his dress sense impeccable, but the eyes are what drew Kenny in the most. The sad neglected eyes that were deep set blue polished glassy and simply dead to look at. It was as though the life had been literally sucked from the poor boy. Kenny smiled; his disgusting green teeth on full display as he took in the monster before him. It was a nervous smile, one filled with sheer uncertainty, he knew Craig was going to rip the soul out of him, torture him relentlessly; but for now he would play the game, despite his body rejecting the idea. He stared into the eyes of Craig Carter and literally shivered to the core, but he swallowed his fear and continued to smile through the blood and the aching of his broken jaw.

"So Mr fucking Kreegan, this is how fear smells" Craig laughed as he sniffed the air in mock amusement, gripping the lapels of Kenny's battered suit jacket as he inhaled purposely. Kenny knew that Craig was revelling bitterly in his torment. Bathing in his imminent suffering, Kenny could feel himself crumbling before the eyes of Craig Carter. It was a thought that crippled him. Kenny slumped back further into the hard back chair and just eyed Craig sarcastically, he knew that he was fucked so he would just sit back and let the punishment come.

"Well Well Well Mr Carter you've played a blinder I'll give you that"

"But you, you vindictive little cunt" Kenny spat as his eyes met Johnny Fenton's who was stood loyally beside Craig with a crazy grin on his face, malicious and relentless as he instantly delivered a fatal blow to the other side of Kenny's face. The man crumpled beneath his fists as he strained against his restraints.

"Now now Kenny, there's no way to speak to your superiors" Craig giggled slightly as he mocked Kenny, a delicious smile playing on his thin lips as he took Kenny's chin between his expert fingers, squeezing slightly as he held the vulnerable man's pain filled glare. Craig's guard didn't drop for a second; his serene hard stare bore into Kenny, simply menacing and filled with anticipation of the illicit torture that was about to commence. The man before him held no resemblance to the boy Craig had once been, this man was an assassin, a cruel, cold, calculating killer and Kenny knew that he was about to lose his rather unimportant life. On the estate he was a man to be feared, respected, but now he felt completely inferior to the two moguls before him. Dressed sharply in designed suits and shoes, Johnny clearly still a baby at only nineteen, with a solid diamond glistening from his ear, his hair slicked over with shaved sides in the latest style, the scent of masculinity and musky aftershave was overpowering and Kenny was literally drowning in the two boys testosterone. Craig's hand slipped from his chin to his neck and Kenny felt the grip tighten hastily against his windpipe, Craig's thumb pushed against his Adams apple and Kenny almost felt it rise into his mouth. The sheer fear that the man was creating in Kenny was surprising him. Usually he would have fought back, but something told him that if he even tried it with Craig, his life would be over in an instant. Kenny didn't know if it was a good thing or not. This man held a very big grudge against Kenny Kreegan and Kenny knew that now it was time to dance with the enemy and finally meet his maker.

Johnny turned on his heel and expertly strutted over to a large storage unit, his shoes clattering on the concrete flooring as he went. He slipped his hand into his pocket and retrieved a small key from his trousers, as he slid it into the padlock the storage unit opened effortlessly. Johnny took out a large leather bound case and placed it on the floor, taking out a small docking station from the drawer of the unit he plugged up his IPod, he knew Craig needed music to work and obviously to block out the blood curdling screams that were to follow. He picked up the leather case and resumed his position beside Craig, loosening his tie slightly and sucking in a harsh breath. The silence was mesmerising and all three men simply stared at one another, completely spellbound by the situation at hand. Johnny was the first to move, guarded as he unzipped the thickly bound leather case, opening it to reveal the most beautiful marble handled samurai sword, the blade polished and sharpened ridiculously so it would slice through Kenny like a knife through butter. A smile thick with contentment played heavily on Craig's lips. He bent down and allowed his fingers to slide gently across the blade, each stroke beautifully and expertly mastered. Craig sucked his teeth inwardly as he picked the sword proficiently out of the heavily bound case. His thin fingers wrapping around the marble handle, the blade glistening magically in the dim light. Kenny swallowed the lump of vomit that had gathered in his throat. The raw burning sensation running all the way back down into the pit of his empty stomach. Johnny went over to the docking station, fiddling nervously with a few buttons before the melodic sound of UB40's Kingston Town filled the tense overbearing air. Kenny's head instantly snapped back and he chuckled in complete hysteria.

"Fucking sentimental cunt aren't we Mr Carter" he smirked through his hideous green teeth, Craig almost wretched distastefully as he stepped closer, edging ever so closer to Kenny with the blade. He could smell the bastards fear permeating off him in waves as he ran it gently down the man's cheek. Splitting the flesh instantly and allowing a crimson stain to burst across the man's sallow skin. Craig smiled in malevolence as Kenny recoiled in pain, withdrawing back as a bolt of smarting pain shot through his body. Unable to move from the confines of the chair he was bound to, Kenny could do nothing but just take his punishment.

"You plotted to kill me. You stood by my mother and faked sympathy, while you knew the nod had come directly from you." Craig whispered bitterly, his breath so incredibly close to Kenny's scarred, meaty cheek. "And now you cunt you're going to find out exactly what it feels like to be hacked at with a fucking knife." Craig's bitter words stung Kenny, the fear of God striking him down. The fear that rose inside him was crippling. He didn't dare speak for fear of something stupid spilling from his mouth. He could feel the blood from his cheek dripping down the front of his suit jacket, the scruffy over worn material soaking in every little droplet and Kenny could feel the damp patch forming on his chest. He was lost his own complete fear, drowning in his own self despair. Kenny was anxious his whole body on high alert for what was the most fearsome moment he had ever had to endure in his whole life. Craig and Johnny looked overbearingly intimidating as they hovered over him. Both so rugged, so intense as their gaze lingered over Kenny. Craig was the first to speak, the samurai sword in his hand chilling Kenny to the bone as he stepped closer towards him.

"Got anything to say for yourself you stupid cunt?" Craig whispered; his voice was low, hushed in tone. So flat and agonisingly sarcastic. Kenny almost died right where he sat. He barely felt the blade slicing through his fingers, but he heard the bitter thud of them on the concrete floor. The barely there whimper that emitted from his was almost inaudible in the silence. Kenny could only watch in sheer bewilderment as he watched the blood burst in vicious streams from the stumps of tissue that had been his knuckles. Kenny had forgotten that he was under the scrutiny of Craig Carter. The boy whom he had called dead, the boy whom he had thought he had murdered. Kenny had learnt a valuable lesson, to never trust anyone. As Craig passed the blade to Johnny, Kenny swallowed hard, he wasn't used to feeling so weak, it didn't sit well with him. Not one bit.

Chapter Fifteen

Jenna sat staring into space, embroiled with emotion as Dom laid himself out on the carpet before her. Their son gurgling happily as Dom carelessly played with him. Archie was such a contented, happy child and Dom bought out the best in him. Jenna couldn't help but be consumed with hatred towards the relationship between her son and her neighbour. She missed Craig, Missed him more than she cared to admit but the pain was still there nevertheless. She had hoped and prayed that Craig had been the father of her son and the devastation of the truth had been too much for them both. If only she hadn't slept with Dom, if only she hadn't acted like a dirty slut, then she would be fine and she and Craig would be raising their second child together as a family. Jenna took another large gulp from her glass of wine and stared around the room in disinterest. Her sad eyes taking in the pictures of her and Craig as teenagers, his smiling, carefree face had been so handsome. Jenna felt broken, emotionally and physically. The tension in the air was tragic and Jenna knew that Dom felt awkward, his facial expression was fake and full of false smiles for the son he had no time for. He would play the game, Jenna knew that much for sure, but she knew it was all a bitter never ending carousel of emotions. Dom was playing the glorified daddy well and he knew that he had finally marked one up on the invisible scoreboard between Craig and himself. The thought pleased him immensely and Jenna could feel the sarcasm coming off him in waves. She was tempted to just stab him there and then on the carpet. Get it over and done with so she could ride off into the sunset with her dream man and their make believe family. Of course pissing in the wind was more feasible and she would have to settle with awkward silence and mediation visits for the next eighteen years. She had never done this with Craig, not once had she ever felt like he had wanted to take the reins from her. Of course Craig had never known Kiki was his daughter so in reality Jenna had no comparison. Her eyes fluttered aimlessly around the room once more, the entrapment almost killing her off completely, she couldn't even attempt to speak. Words failed her almost. It took all of her strength not to look Dom square in the eyes for she knew that if she did, there was the slightest, miniscule chance that she would live to indeed regret it.

Craig paced the warehouse flooring with the speed of Mo Farrah on amphetamine, the cunt wasn't meant to have snuffed it yet, but in typical Cunt fashion Kenny Kreegan had suffered a heart attack. A fucking major one at that. Craig was livid; justice hadn't been fucking served yet! His shoes clattered as they strode back and forth. The sweat beads glistened on his forehead imminent even in the dim glow of the lights overhead. His angry flitting eyes bouncing around as he bought the blade of the sword down over the dead man's head, severing it completely. The spray of blood and flesh mixed with the eerie whimper that stemmed from Johnny Fenton urged Craig on all the more. His cackling laughs reverberated as he revelled in his own sadism. He was indeed tempted to whip his old boy out and have a wank over the proceedings. But he stilled himself, staring wildly at his work, his perfect tanned skin spattered with crimson flecks. The evil smile that fondled his lips so sarcastic and serene as he bought the blade down once more in an agonised swoop towards the lump that lay before him. This time the blade softly dipped into the fleshy lump that had once been Kenny Kreegan's nether regions.

Craig's eyes glittered wildly as he picked up the dismembered head of the man whom he hated perpetually. Now the remnants of Kenny's face a mixture of fleshy tissue and splintered bone. His dead eyes fixated, pulled wide in horror, the expression gruesome. Craig's stare was wide and filled with wondrous lust, He had killed him. He had finally killed Kenny Kreegan. The thought made him almost unload into his boxers. He picked up the protruding lump from Kenny's awful cotton trousers, the slippery flesh hot and wet in his hands. Johnny stood back, recoiling in horror, almost gagging into his shirt sleeve as Craig stuffed Johnny's flaccid dismembered penis straight into The mouth of the dismembered head he held loosely in his hand. Craig's laugh intoxicating as he ogled his handy work. He held his work of art outright at arm's length, taking in every single squalid feature, His tantalising gaze awestruck as he pulled Kenny's dead Cheek toward his lips. He kissed the awful spectacle in lip smacking fashion before he declared;

"RIP Kenny Boy You Cock Sucking Cunt" Before he smashed the dead, dissected head back onto the concrete and walking away. His shoes clattered noisily with every single step he took, his eyes rolled toward the ceiling as he realised he had blood on his flawless suit jacket. Craig spun around to find Johnny glued to the spot, his face wide with shock as he pointed aimlessly toward Kenny's cock chomping head.

"Leave it John; I've got Donny Anderson's boys cleaning this shit up" he smirked as he casually strutted off, leaving Johnny Fenton rendered speechless and completely terrified of what was yet to come. He glanced back at the face of his former boss, cut up, dismembered and completely torn after being forced to eat his own penis. Johnny turned on his heel and sauntered away, his heart not quite feeling his confident strut.

Chapter Sixteen

Johnny emptied the contents of his stomach out onto the side of the road; he was still in shock, his body not accepting of the surpassing feelings that were racing around his body. He was shaking violently, his whole body numb with acceptance that he had played his part in such a gruesome murder. Craig stood behind him laughing like a hyena, viciously mocking Johnny when he was at his lowest. He could have smashed the brazen cunt right in the face but Johnny knew which side his bread was buttered. Business was business and Kenny Kreegan had finally paid back his debt a tenfold. He was furious with Craig; he should have left Kenny alone after the poor old cunt croaked it from the heart attack. He had been instantly killed; there had been no logic in cutting him up. It's not like the cunt would have felt it. Johnny wiped his mouth with the back of his sleeve, ashamed of feeling so weak when he had for so long played the hard man; he made his way back to the van in silence. Ignoring Craig's trailing voice as he called after him. He was fucking livid, the cunt had mugged him right off and Johnny wasn't about to take it with a pinch of salt. He jumped into the van, turning the key in the ignition he sped away, leaving Craig standing in the middle of the road hurtling abuse at him.

Johnny tried his hardest to keep his composure as he raced through the country lanes, his body was shaking violently and his nerves had been shot to pieces. He hated his own nervousness as he trawled the craggy paths with vigorous pace the ground beneath him uneven and uncertain all at the same time. Johnny swallowed hard, trying to suppress the horrid emotions that boiled inside him. He was furious, Craig had pulled a real fucking blinder and he didn't understand why the fuck he had carried on standing there glued to the spot. Gawping as Craig had dismembered Kenny bit by bit. Johnny felt nothing but guilt coursing through his veins, the thought unsettled him. He gazed in the rear view mirror and took in the night before him. Craig was a world away, yet Johnny could feel him, heavy and ever apparent in his mind. Johnny pulled into a lay-by and punched the steering wheel hard, he didn't understand his turmoil over the whole Kenny situation but he had a family, he would hate to think if it was one of his own how he would react.

Johnny exhaled a loud, deep breath as he composed himself. He knew Craig was his meal ticket out of the take and he knew without him he would be straight back to the life of petty crime and wannabe gangsters. He gave himself a moment of thinking time, his head was a mess but he knew where his loyalties had laid themselves. He spun the van around full circle and sped back in the direction he had just travelled, he just hoped that Craig wouldn't be too mad at him for scarpering. Johnny swept the hair from his eyes as he rampaged through the lanes, his eyes focused, glassy and full of imminent pressure. He scanned the darkness before him; the only light came from the amber glow of the street lights overhead. Johnny closed his eyes momentarily; he had thought his life would be worth so much more than it was currently. He thought that prison would have given him the edge, a name to stand for. But he was still buried beneath the horrid curtain that was Craig Carter. He flew up the straight road; staring ahead he could see Craig wandering along the path ahead. He was completely livid and Johnny could feel his anger surging toward him in waves. He pulled alongside Craig Suddenly, Johnny's face void of any emotion as he wound down the window beside him. Craig's eyes were piercing blue with anger, literally seething as he slid into the passenger seat it took Craig every ounce of strength he had not to smack Johnny clean in the mouth. He smirked, turning towards the boy, Johnny's face was uncertain and Craig knew the boy was scared.

"Finished your fucking tantrums have you?" Craig whispered calmly, the tension between them electric as he stared ahead into the darkness, he road was clear, no traffic, no noise just blissful silence. Johnny started the engine and shunted the van away, not looking at Craig for the entire drive home. His heart sank as he realised, he would be forever known as Craig Carters Bitch.

The headlights up ahead signalled home and Johnny couldn't have been more pleased. He needed to get away from Craig at least for the night. He tipped his head back slightly, feeling the adrenaline of the night rush over him, they had finally killed Kenny. They had finally taken him out. Craig laughed jovially, Johnny's head snapped in his direction, his face etched with sudden confusion and Craig could have actually pissed himself with Johnny's sudden discomfort.

"Fuck John, He's gone, we never ever have to look over our shoulders again, the worlds ours for the taking. Don't be a prick over this!" Craig beamed, his twinkling blue eyes polished and clean shone like a beacon and Johnny had to force a weakened smile in return. Craig certainly was unhinged, slightly crazy if he was honest. But he had been true to his word, loyal to the core and Johnny had to applaud him if only for that singular fact alone. He was a true friend, despite being an arrogant, over the top hostile prick and half the time Johnny could happily murder him. But Johnny appreciated Craig's loyalty and it was better for Craig to be your friend, rather than Craig be your enemy.

Jenna finally breathed an outward sigh of relief when Dom stood to leave. The smile on her face was almost childlike and etched with delight. She couldn't stand the sight of him as he kissed the sleeping bundle that lay so contented in his arms before placing him down to sleep in the crib. Dom smiled awkwardly at her and Jenna felt his discomfort reverberating off him in waves. But she would not crumble, not tonight anyway. So with a face as sour as gone off milk she sneered at Dom and eagerly led him to the front door. There were no words, no friendly exchanges, just an awkward shrug, his worthless promises of money and gifts for his child and then he was gone back across the way to his flat. He looked back at her, smiled sadly and stepped inside. Jenna slammed the door none to gently behind him, turned and returned to her vigil, the bottle of wine staring her so blankly in the face, so tempting and so luring. As she poured another tantalising glass of the cold pinot grigio she sloped back onto the sofa and sat sipping her drink in the silence. She felt so numb, so alone. It wasn't a feeling that she could relate to, she had never felt afraid of herself before. She slugged back the remainder of the glass and instantly refilled it, taking it to her lips again her phone beeped loudly beside her. She flinched, taking the mobile in her hands she saw Dom's number automatically rolled her eyes. Opening the text she smirked at the simple "Thank you x" that he had text. She tossed the phone back down beside her and she continued to ponder over the nights events. She thought of Craig, She couldn't stop thinking of Craig. It hurt her more than she would ever admit, but he was always there, constantly. Jenna ran her hands through her hair, resting her eyes on her collection of photos, the smiles, the hurt, the love they had sacrificed all for the price of money. Craig was off living the life of luxury with their daughter and she was left, in the gutter with her cheap bottle of wine and a bastard child created from the man opposite. The thought made Jenna sick to the pit of her stomach. She had dreamt all of her life that she and Craig would be together forever, raising their children in a chic little house in the country away from the Belmonte and its clutches.

Jenna slumped against the cold leather, tucking her knees toward her and sighed as a single tear rolled down her cheek; she was exhausted emotionally and everything seemed to be mounting on top of her with each day that passed. Drink helped, a lot. It blotted out the awkward niggling of her heart and its demands. As much as she hated what Craig had done to her, she was drawn to him, like a moth to the flame, he was addictive. Craig was supernatural with his ability to possess her, completely and utterly and Jenna was left literally speechless at the mere thought of Craig. He was her perfect drug. Her one and only fix and as much as she loved him, she hated him equally. Dom had been her chance to move on, get away from Craig and he had waltzed back in as easily as he had left and taken over once more. Taking her by chance and it had been completely off guard. She closed her eyes and sucked in a fatal breath, she needed to get away from all of this and she needed to do it now. Not just for her own sanity but her children's too.

Chapter Seventeen

Dom lay in bed, wide awake; he was completely naked apart from his boxer shorts, the stifling night air drenching his body in a sticky film. The sheets lay in a crumpled lump at the foot of the bed. He had come to the analogy It was too hot to sleep, too hot to think. Agitation had taken over and he was caught inbetween the harsh reality and his ideologies of what he had dreamed his life to be. He had already been through the motions and he had reached the point where anger was starting to override all other feelings he was capable of. He hitched a breath as he suppressed the overwhelming urge to cry. His confusion taking over, the last year had been so hard on him, he had fallen in love with Jen, head over heels and he didn't quite know if those feeling would ever go away. Their son had been a miracle; he had been destined for the angels from his very first breath. But Archie was here, he was theirs and Dom was adamant that they would raise him together. Craig could only offer her money. Money was nothing over real love. A love that was unique and completely intense in its power. Dom shook his head in sheer perplexity. The whole situation was nothing but fucked up and he had no idea how to control his feelings. He had ended up in second place to a man who was supposed to be dead and Dom had questioned himself inside and out on what Craig Carter had that he obviously didn't. He had found very little to support the Craig Carter defence. He ran his fingers through his thick overgrown hair, the sweat beads that had formed on his forehead trickled down against the pillows. He had thought nothing could hurt him after the realisation of losing his memories. Losing every important speck of information he had ever known about himself. But losing Jenna which had hurt like nothing ever could. Nothing came close. He was exhausted, but his mind just wouldn't switch off, he exhaled a slow shallow breath, the rhythm of his breathing was laboured, harsh and echoed in the silence. Dom felt nothing but isolation as he lay in the solace of his own company. Bitter with anger, high of hate, it was a combination he himself couldn't even begin to handle. As he sank further into his euphoric state Dom began to wonder, was he going crazy or was he just plain tired. He closed his eyes, hoping to fuck he would picture something other than Jenna's face in his dreams. She was simply the key to everything Dom had ever wanted and Dom suddenly felt at a loss. She had taken him away from his past, she had made him better, after losing Ami he had gone off the rails, but Jenna had healed him. She had made him face the world again, made him realise that he could be ok. Now she was so close yet so far away, he had clocked the way she had been with him during his visit with Archie. Frosty had been his first perception and Dom had not been used to it one bit. He had been used to Jenna being her open usual self; Dom had been thrown by her uncanny evilness. And he vowed he would get his revenge, whether Jenna Shearan loved him or not, revenge would be his, undoubtedly. He slumped back into the sheets, feeling a little less apprehensive, and a lot more positive than he had been.

Chapter Eighteen

ONE Month Later

Donny Anderson sat at the bar in the Dewinton Inn, his attention focused on the slurring young lady on the other side of the bar. Her eyes were glassy, glazed with wine. She looked familiar to Donny but he couldn't for the life of him quite place her face. His heart went out to the poor sod if he was honest. The girl was a complete drunken mess; she was young, mid twenties at most. Her long black hair was tied on top of her head in a scraggy looking bun, her thickly lined eyes black and streaked down her hollow cheeks. Donny continued to observe patiently from his post, the girl was literally begging the bartender for another glass of white despite barely being able to stand. Donny tipped his head to one side, his curiosity was niggling at him. His vacant lingering stare was icy and cold, conniving and devious and filled with intrigue. He was still trying to place the beautiful girls face, but his mind just wouldn't focus clearly. The bartender was starting to get irate now, Ted wasn't a man with the highest volume of patience at the best of times and Donny could see he was moments away from giving the girl a fucking pasting. Donny stood just as Ted grabbed hold of the girls bony wrists, his fingers instantly leaving angry prints on her pale milky skin. The girl flinched, her lip curled into a devilish snarl before she started hurling every insult under the sun at poor Ted. Donny stormed over and pushed Ted out of the way before he did some serious damage to the girl. Donny grabbed the girl and pulled her kicking and screaming to the door, hurling her out into the street he pushed her into a siding between two shops. His angry eyes flaring as his stare caught the glazed eyes of the girl.

"What's your name?" Donny questioned sternly, his breathing slowing from his earlier temper, the girls lip began to tremble, tears threatening to spill from her hooded eyes, the glistening of her waterline made her piercing emerald green eyes literally shine in her sockets. For a moment Donny was speechless, she was completely stunning. Even with thick black makeup streaked down her cheeks. She gulped hard, the wine making her head fuzzy and Donny could swear she was either going to faint or vomit with nerves.

"Jenna, Jenna Shearan" She whispered breathlessly, trying to get her composure together, clearing her throat and standing up straight. The cold brick of the wall pressed against her spine, making her whole body shiver violently. She hadn't realised how cold it was when she had put on the lime green cocktail dress this morning. She could feel the skirt riding up her thighs, leaving Goosebumps prickling on her matchstick legs. She smiled shyly at Donny, her lips puckering slightly, deliciously plump and despite his whole body fighting the urge, he could feel the bulge in his trousers beginning to swell.

"Donny Anderson" he offered his hand in a gentlemanly manner as he introduced himself, his smile broad and friendly as he urged his body closer to the girl. He could feel the anxiousness radiating off her in waves and Donny could feel her vulnerability. Donny was confident in all aspects and he knew that he was a good looking bastard. At twenty nine he was the ultimate charmer, full lips, dark, deep brown eyes and delicious tanned skin. Despite his beautiful fiancée Sandra he still had an eye for the pretty girls. Dressed to kill in a perfectly fitting grey suit and crisp white shirt he was an Adonis, a complete God and all the girls loved to bat their eyelashes and smile their big toothy smiles at him. Donny smirked when Jenna offered her hand meekly in return, her gaze dropping from his, he took her by surprise when his fingers gently cupped her chin and he led her eyes back to his. Jenna couldn't even begin to look at him, her cheeks flushed with sudden humiliation.

"I recognise your face, but I can't for the life of me think where I've seen you before" Donny continued, his voice thick and heavy almost velvety in tone, he leant in closer, his skin almost touching Jenna's and she couldn't help but close her eyes as she bathed in the euphoria of too much wine and the musky overwhelming scent of Donny Anderson. She leant in closer and kissed his lips, the ring in his pierced lip brushed against her and she instantly shivered with anticipation. Naturally Donny stepped back; he wasn't into fucking barely awake women. He smiled at her kindly so she wouldn't feel too bad.

"Look babe, I'm not into fucking women in alleys, and in all honesty your pissed out of your head" he held her out at arm's length so he could look at her closely. He ran a finger down her cheek and finally the tears came, Jenna crumpled in a heap into the stranger's arms, he held her close. His strong hand traced the small of her back as she sniffled into his chest. Donny Led the girl away to his black Mercedes, sliding her into the passenger seat, he hadn't a clue what he was going to do with her now, but what he did know was that she wasn't going home. Donny's weakness had always been a pretty girl and Jenna Shearan had him completely captivated. He just wondered where the fuck he had seen her before and why did he have a strong feeling that she was nothing but trouble.

Chapter Nineteen

Jenna awoke with a stale mouth and a pounding head. She had little to no vivid recollections of the previous nights antics and as she stared wide eyed around the unfamiliar surroundings her heart leapt into her mouth. She had no clue of where she was and who she was with. Attempting to rack her brain she pulled the covers to her chin, scanning around the room once more trying her hardest to recall even the most minuscule speck of information. She drew a complete blank and rested herself back against the plush, plumped pillows. Her breath was sticky and reeking of wine, she felt absolutely disgusting in her dishevelled state. Her skin felt dry and sallow from too much alcohol and her whole body ached from exhaustion. She spotted the gold Rolex on the bedside table out of the corner of her eye and swallowed hard, she hoped against hope she hadn't run into Craig. She would hate for him to see her in such a state. She closed her eyes and rested her arm over her face. Her anxiety was eating away at her and the thought of not knowing who she was here with was an illicit torture. She had literally nothing to go upon other than she guessed this was a hotel room, the decor was modern, very monochrome and sterile. It obviously wasn't someone's house, it didn't appear characteristic enough to be someone's actual living quarters. It was very upscale and grand and Jenna was taken back momentarily to Craig's room in the country manor where he now resided. Jenna sighed outwardly; she missed her daughter more than anything. Every single time she tried to contact Craig to talk about Kiki he was either busy with work or out. She knew he was neither and was just being difficult in his anger over Archie's paternity, but it had been a few months now, surely he wasn't still resentful?

Jenna's thoughts were broken immediately by a fresh and drop dead gorgeous man emerging from the en suite. His body dripping wet from the shower a crisp white towel hanging skimpily from his slim waist. He smiled shyly at Jenna before sitting at the foot of the bed before her.

"Sleep well?" he asked, his voice like velvet, silky and smooth. Jenna lifted her arm away from her eyes so she was staring him square in the face, his deep brown eyes met hers and she had to hold down the urge to orgasm where she sat, he was that good looking.

"I've felt better" she smirked, yawning loudly, stretching out her arms above her head;

"You ready to divulge where I know you from then Miss Shearan?" he continued, his fingertips grazing his freshly shaved chin, his index resting subtly on his lower lip, slightly left of his piercing. He looked completely intrigued, Jenna was instantly taken aback when she realised who the Adonis before her actually was. She sat bolt upright;

"Did he fucking put you up to this?" she shrieked, ripping the covers up as she leapt off the bed. Her whole face screwed up into an angry grimace as she strutted up to Donny and slapped him hard across the cheek. The sound echoing, ringing out into the tense atmosphere and she watched his eyes flair relentlessly in her direction. His angry stare was burning into her crippling her momentarily where she stood. Donny got up from the bed grasping Jenna by her wrists; he shoved her hard against the wall, her head none too gently bouncing off the plasterboard that separated the rooms. Donny sucked in a harsh breath as he held her there, his heart thudding in his chest as he tried with all his might to contain his sudden urge to punch her square into her beautiful face.

"I know exactly who you fucking are!" Jenna spat angrily, her eyes firmly pinned to Donny's, the emerald shimmer of them was simply intoxicating and Donny found himself laboured with the sudden urge to shag the brazen bitch's brains out right where they stood. He tightened his grip around her wrists as he pinned her hands either side of her head, she squirmed beneath him but she was no match against his strong muscular frame. After what seemed like an age she eventually sagged against him, deflated from her own childish tantrum. She was exhausted with her unwanted hangover and the sheer wanting of the man before her. The electricity between them both was simply tantric as Donny cupped her chin in his hand; his finger's lingering on her soft plump lips. He leant in, his breath kissing her earlobe as he etched toward her neck. The sultry, sensuous pull of the female form before him was too much for Donny to handle; he dropped his guard momentarily and skimmed Jenna's naked thighs with his free hand. He was simply left mesmerised by the girl who stood so vulnerably in front of him, as feisty as she was, he knew that she was his now for the taking, and take her he would. Donny slipped closer toward her, almost breathless with anticipation as he planted a deep passionate kiss on her lips. She responded instantly, her tongue searching his mouth with reckless intent, Donny dropped her arms and she trailed his athletic body with her fingers, tracing every single inch of his skin as he continued his assault on her body with his merciless expert hands. He was every inch the perfect gentleman as he slowly slid his hand across her back, holding her Donny was something different, he was controlling, yet ever so lenient and as he took her there on the hotel floor his movements quick and wanting. Jenna felt nothing but endless, uncontrollable lust. In that moment she could have been Donny Anderson's woman, his wife, but she was nothing. Nothing but a whore who had lay down with Craig's close associate. She shuddered deeply as he poured himself deep inside her, her breath hitching as she took in every single drop of his wanting for her. He face scrunched into a tight, effortless ball as she found her release, calling out his name and falling against his naked chest, her body sagging against unfamiliar skin, taking her higher, making her feel wanted. Jenna kissed his chest, the tiny barely there spirals of hair that curled on his young chest tickling her lips as she continued with her merciless assault on his body. He was a stunning artefact there was no denying that, Donny had a body to die for; despite his alternative style he was completely and utterly sensual. Jenna had fallen head over heels for him and it wasn't a feeling she was used to. Despite her reservations she couldn't resist the pull of Donny Anderson and his devious allure. Jenna Lay back against the chilled rugged carpet and stilled, her orgasm finally coming to a close as she drank in the beauty that was Donny Anderson, she felt whole and the feeling was more welcomed now than it had ever been.

Chapter Twenty

Jenna pulled herself closer to Donny, her skin melting against his, he was soft, sensuous, and his scent was simply divine. Jenna could feel his breath on her neck, fresh with toothpaste and mouthwash. He held his arm around her waist as they lay there for what seemed an age, she could feel the smile on his lips radiating every single time he planted his soft chaste kisses on her shoulders. Smouldering beneath his gentle touch Jenna was literally flying on her euphoric high. She had slept with only two men in her young life until today, all different completely in their personalities. But each of them had one thing in common and that was her. Their wanting of her was compelling and almost childlike in their obsession. As she lay in the arms of her former lover's close associate she smiled sarcastically to herself, Craig who? She thought slyly as she turned back into Donny and kissed him hard as she braced herself for round two with the notorious Donny Anderson and his Adonis body.

Craig was pacing the floor, his head was up his arse and he was completely at a loss as to where the fuck the mother of his child had gone. He had been trying his hardest to reach Jenna for the last three days with no avail and in the deepest part of his anatomy, his stomach clenched in worry. He knew she had gone off the rails. Dom had informed him all about him now looking after Archie full time and Jenna being constantly out on the piss. He was livid and now the cunt had done a disappearing act. He was due to fly out to America in two days and he really didn't fancy cancelling his flight to catch the drunken cunt. He was fed up, angry at knowing that she wasn't safe. She was a beautiful young woman even in drink and she was vulnerable, at the hands of strangers she could be hurt by anyone who caught her eye with a bottle of wine. Craig knew it was his doing; it was him who had started this vicious cycle rolling. He knew she was pining over him and he did miss her, he genuinely did but it was the large obstacle of her son paternity that had rifled Craig. That had hurt him like no knife ever could. He walked into his office; he sat down by his desk and flicked through some loose papers that had been littered on his desk. He opened his laptop and gazed at the screen, not quite concentrating on what he was doing. The words before him formed nothing; he rubbed his tired eyes and ran and hand over his short prickly hair. He needed to work, it kept his mind off Jenna, it was the same torment each and every day despite his constant attempts to just say fuck it and forget about her he couldn't. They had shared so many precious memories, so many amazing times and Craig couldn't help it if he loved her, undoubtedly. He held his head in his hands and for the first time in a long time he cried, his eyes completely bursting as tears flowed a river down his cheeks. He was emotionally exhausted and despite his tough exterior he was struggling. He had a business meeting with one of Donny Anderson's crony's this afternoon, seems as Donny had mysteriously cancelled first thing and he wasn't in the fucking mood. Kristian Collins was a nice enough guy and was Donny's right hand man and most trusted confidant. But Craig Carter was a great believer in speaking to the organ grinder and not the pissing monkey. Donny cancelling on him had more or less added fuel to the fire and Craig was left absolutely fuming. He slammed the lid of his laptop down, swiping his eyes angrily and trying his hardest to compose himself. He was tempted to ask Donny to do a bit of sniffing around for him, put the feelers out so to speak. But he had never ever mixed his private life with his business associates. Besides he rationed Donny had only seen Jenna once with him at his annual Christmas Gala the year previously. Craig smiled at the memory; Jenna had looked simply stunning in a floor length red gown with a white faux fur stole. Her hair and makeup had been styled to look like a nineteen forties film star, her hair and been curled into a perfect elegant bob pale faced and red lipped she had looked simply classical. A raven haired Marilyn Monroe and Craig had been so proud to hold her on his arm. She was a breathtaking sight and Craig's heart lurched bitterly in his chest at the mere thought of her. Where the fuck was she? He picked up the phone and called Donny's number, fuck it he thought, even if Donny could find out where she had been last spotted it would help him a tenfold. He swallowed hard as the monotonous ringing of Donny's mobile left him waiting in suspense. He hated the thought of his work colleagues knowing about his home turmoil's, but if anything had happened to Jenna, he would die a thousand deaths over it. She was his, that was just the way it was and he wouldn't rest until she was home safe. As he waited for Donny to answer he typed out a text to Dom on his mobile to keep him informed if anything fresh came to light. As Donny answered the phone with a jovial Hello, Craig puffed out a longing sigh and started his story from the very beginning. All the while blind to the fact that as he was on the phone pouring his heart out to Donny about his baby's mothers vanishing act, she was sucking Donny Anderson off without a care in the bloody world.

Chapter Twenty One

Jenna sipped at the ice cold champagne in her hand, savouring every thumping beat of the music in the background, her and Donny sat high up in the plush VIP suite of the Green Rabbit nightclub, an alternative club for up and coming bands to perform live. Donny owned the little diamond and he had a soft spot for the club. The disco lights bounced around the packed out venue highlighting Donny's beautiful high cheekbones as he downed yet another neat vodka, no ice. He was grinning broadly as Jenna danced seductively before him, wearing a stunning lime cocktail dress and strappy black stilettos she looked breathtaking. Donny bit hard down on his bottom lip, he literally wanted to rip her clothes off and fuck her where she stood, but he would keep his composure for now. He had plans for Jenna and the bitch wasn't going anywhere till he had sucked her dry, she thought rejection from Craig Carter was bad? then she hadn't seen anything like Donny Anderson. He broke hearts, took names and flung you to the kerb as good as he fucked you in his bed. He was a baby faced thug and he knew there were swarms of girls who would do anything for a slice of the Donny Anderson pie. He passed her the rolled up twenty and watched as she expertly devoured the fat line of coke from the glass tabletop. He stared in wonder as her face contorted slightly as she drew back the last of the gritty substance from her nose. Her eyes were bulging, sparkling with drugs and drink. The coke was barely cut and Donny knew the poor bitch would be flying her tits off, which is exactly how he needed her for his little plan. As he sat back and enjoyed her tantalising floor show he grinned like a child with a new box of crayons, he couldn't wait to get her to work, and work she fucking would. This little beauty was going to make Donny big bucks and finally he could kiss goodbye to the tacky brasses he had working the streets and the shitty backstreet bars destined for the scrapheap. Oh yes Jenna Shearan was going to be quite the little earner. Jenna came and straddled his lap, her perky arse sweeping against his growing erection as she continued to gyrate on his lap. Donny raised his glass as toasting his silent success and marking one up on the Donny Anderson chalkboard, Jenna Shearan would definitely be the most desirable notch on his slightly shattered bedpost.

Kristian Collins stood at the far end of the bar, his eyes lay Set Square on his boss and his whore. Donny had put him in charge of getting Jenna out to work and Kristian couldn't wait to get started. She was a looker, he'd give Donny that, but like every other girl they had on their payroll Jenna was a simple down and out. She was nothing but a girl from the gutter who wanted affection. In Kristian's position of power the girl would do great things for his and Donny's little empire. He would start her off dancing in one of their seedy little strip clubs, by then she would be so out of her box on drugs that she wouldn't even recognise day and night. Then with hope, she would work the streets for him, take control of their other patches and make the girls work hard, they would be envious of a pretty face of that Kristian Collins was sure. There was nothing more rewarding than placing a cat amongst the pigeons when it came to the brasses. The girls were feisty, bitchy and overworked and from going on what Donny had said Jenna was basically a virgin, tighter than a pinhole, that would change with time but Kristian would make his money's worth from her. He saw Donny dealing out another line of coke and almost spluttered with the heat of his brandy, the girl would bloody pass out if he carried on and Kristian didn't need THAT tonight. She was meeting one of their close clients tonight and although he had asked for his victim to be practically comatose so that he could live out his little rape fetish on the girl, Donny was taking the piss. Kristian had been promised a two's up with his client and he was beginning to get impatient. The thought of that tight little cunt on his cock was enough to get his tongue wagging. He ordered another neat brandy from the bar and propped himself on one of the stools, his target never leaving his sight as he watched from afar. The night would soon get very interesting indeed.

****

Jenna could barely put one foot in front of the other as she was bundled into the back of the new, black polished Mercedes. She was completely out of her head and she couldn't quite piece together what had happened after she and Donny had left the club, they had travelled separately she could remember that much, she had travelled with his mate. He had given her a few pills and then her head had drawn a complete blank. Now as he led her away from the run down flat that stank of piss and stale cigarette smoke was a distant, slightly hazy memory. She tried desperately to piece together what had happened. She was slumped against the back seat of the car, her dress riding up her thighs, her makeup smudged across her face. She was a mess, a beautiful disaster. The feeling of the cocaine buzz mixed with the heavy head from the alcohol was enough to almost send her spiralling over the edge. She clasped her fingers around the door handle of the car and tried to compose herself. She could smell it, the stale stench of sex and sweat that emitted from her tiny body and she felt nothing but shame. She could see him, Kristian and his weird looking Goth friend as they both took it in turns to rape her. She had remained silent throughout her ordeal, separated slightly from reality and fantasy, high off the narcotics and low on her own bitter self esteem it was a potent and heady cocktail that Jenna Shearan knew would be the start of her own self destruction. She stared bleakly into the eyes of Kristian Collins as he slid into the car beside her and recoiled as he slapped her hard across the cheek,

"How fucking dare you act like you enjoyed shagging him more than me you slut" he hissed under his drunken breath, his voice laced with hideous jealousy. The striking red mark appeared across her face almost instantaneously. Jenna closed her eyes tightly and wished upon a million stars that Craig was here to save her; she would do anything in the world to be home in his arms once more. Upon opening them she focused her attention to the outside world, the basic things like cars parked along the busy roads, the girls stood freezing on the kerbs, giving head for money. Jenna knew that she soon would be joining them and in her drug fuelled stupor she lay affectionately against Kristian's chest, the exhaustion taking over, she finally succumb to a light troubled sleep. He waited briefly so that she was out cold before he lay her across the cold leather seat. His fingers grazed across her chunky thighs, he stared in wonder at the dried blood that smeared her legs, lifting the skirt of her dress he smiled devilishly, she had been discarded of her panties and there she was spread-eagled for him in all her glory, the bite marks that had been left on her were slightly horrific and he wished for a half second that he hadn't got so carried away. Donny was going to be pissed off but Kristian had enjoyed himself so he would take his lecture like a man and smile at the irony of it. He gazed at her there now and a playful smile trickled across his mouth as a very bold idea crossed his mind. He spat on his two fingers and began to slowly run them up and down her apex of her thighs, she was already soaking wet from their earlier assaults, Kristian's grin widened further. He unzipped his trousers, tugging out his semi hard penis he started to fondle it gently with his hands, when he was erect enough, he hauled Jenna up from the seat. She was a dead weight from being half asleep and Kristian could feel himself getting aroused further. He sat her upon his lap, so that her legs straddling either side of his. Slowly but roughly he forced himself inside her, feeling her thin body sag against his, he thrust into her again. This time her eyes snapped open and she sat nose to nose with the man who had so brutally raped her. She swallowed hard as their eyes finally met. She said nothing, she knew better than to kick up a fuss, Kristian respected that. He continued his frenzied assault as Jenna tried her utmost to contain her dignity and stifle her painful screams. The agony that was surging through her body was pure torture. She had never felt pain like it in her life. She placed her head on Kristian's shoulder and closed her eyes and tried to focus on anything other than where she was right now. If she could at least manage to disengage herself then she would learn to survive. It was over quickly, but for Jenna it felt like forever and as he slipped away from her she felt nothing but sad, overwhelming relief.

The last thing Jenna remembered was being carried back to another seedy hotel room, not as plush as the one she stayed in the previous night but it was comfortable all the same. She froze as Kristian leant over and kissed her lightly on the cheek, she tried her best to pretend to be asleep. He came close to her ear and whispered guiltily "I'm sorry" before climbing into the bed beside her. As he draped his heavily tattooed arms around Jenna she allowed the silent cascade of tears to flow. Her heart sank, she knew now what real pain was, physically and emotionally she had been tested to the brink of insanity and she had barely scraped through.

"You OK" she heard Kristian's faint whisper in the darkness, she couldn't move in fear of vomiting violently at the mere thought of him. So she subtly nodded her reply, sniffling through her tears, Kristian held her closer to him, nuzzling her hair gently with his nose. He said nothing and Jenna suddenly felt a pang of sympathy for him. She knew she shouldn't she should want to maul him where he lay but she was literally too exhausted to care. She turned against him and accepted his embrace; she didn't know what else to do. How was she supposed to feel? Her whole body felt as though it wasn't her own, she felt numb, inhuman unable to feel or think anything other than the night's events. She heard Kristian's soft snores and was tempted to attempt a runner, She was tempted to fucking stab him but she just lay there pinned to the spot. She took the time to every now and again steal a glance of his handsome face. He was so young, younger than she was; she guessed he was around about twenty one. Overgrown, very alternative styled glossy black hair, almost quite gothic looking Jenna thought. Two black rings pierced either side of his bottom lip and he had a loose black hoop through his nose. His skin was pale, what she could see of it through his heavy mass of tattoos. Jenna's tears came again as the thought of her babies came into her head. Her beautiful children, who she would give anything in the world to hold and to treasure at that moment,. She had been lousy with the kids in the last few months and now, she was feeling nothing but guilt and sadness. They'd be better off without her, she concluded. She had fallen for Donny Anderson and his charming ways and now she was being shunted around his friends like a dirty fucking whore. She suppressed the urge to release the vomit that protruded up into her throat. She thought of Craig, her beautiful loving Craig, the thought of him alone made her want to go and hang herself, he would never want her now, not after this. No one would want her now after this; she was damaged goods as her old mum used to say. Jenna rested back against the pillows and finally after what seemed an age drifted off into a deep, troubled sleep. A sleep filled with weird looking men, seedy council flats and bruises and Craig, her Craig coming to her rescue and taking her away from it all. But her dreams were nothing more than her trying to cope with what had happened to her and how her life would never ever be the same again.....

Chapter Twenty Two

The sun soaked in through the gap in the curtains and Jenna woke to the sound of singing from the bathroom. For a minute everything was calm, everything was normal until the realisation of the previous night hit her. She looked down her body and winced, she was black with bruises and thick welts that littered her usually pale milky skin. She stared around the barely furnished room and saw a clean jogging suit hanging on the back of the door which she assumed was for her. She sat up glaring at the en suite door, she wondered whether she could make a run for it, she daren't chance it he would find her and he would kill her. Donny was a face, a man of power and a man of substance and he would take Jenna out without a seconds thought. She lay in a hazy lull, the hangover and agonising come down taking its effect and dragging her into a state of sheer exhaustion. She flicked her hair over her skinny shoulder and ran her fingers through it with minimal effort, it was cobby, greasy and dry and Jenna felt humiliated that she had been left in such a state. She could smell the unwanted stench of sweaty body's and unwanted semen lingering on her skin and she momentarily blushed with sweet agony. She didn't know where the future was taking her and she was scared to find out. Kristian had momentarily briefed her about Donny's little slut empire and Jenna was positive she had never been bred to be part of something so despicable. Prostitution was such an ugly word, such a degrading and almost unworthy word. She had been sexually active with Craig solely with Craig for so many years that she had never even dreamt of sleeping with someone else. Until she had met Dom, he had turned her world upside down. Now here she was in some seedy, unstable hotel room, her life in tatters and her head in bits facing life as nothing more than a mere street urchin. She was heartbroken and none the less furious with herself for allowing to be drawn into the trap. Donny had snared her whilst she had been at her most vulnerable and now Jenna had to live with that sacrifice. As Kristian emerged from the en suite, his skinny body pearled with glistening beads of water, his face clean shaven and his hair perfectly straight and styled. Jenna smiled shyly at him; he returned the gesture before checking his phone. Tossing it aside when he realised he had no missed calls he turned and began to squeeze himself into the black skinny jeans that hung loosely from the chair beside the bed devoid of any underwear, Jenna sussed he had thrown his to destroy any evidence of their unwanted tryst the night before.

"Showers free if you want one mind" he announced quietly as he pulled his plain black tee shirt over his head, his accent thick with his friendly sounding American drawl and Jenna was instantly snapped from her thoughts.

"Yeah... okay" she nodded trying her hardest to stand without having her legs touching. She was in absolute agony, the bite marks and bruises were nothing compared to how she felt emotionally. She was scarred, emotionally, so deep that it cut her to the quick. That someone would want to hurt her in such a devastating, brutal way was something simply fictional. Like something she would read in a second hand book that Claire had lent her. Jenna shuddered as she held tightly onto the bedside cabinet, her knees buckling beneath her as she stood and she found herself crashing down onto the filthy carpet. Simply breathing was proving difficult for her as she just lay there in a heap. She heard the voice of Kristian above her but she couldn't register a word he said. She just saw the panic etched on his face, the dark longing for her to be alright just so he didn't have to deal with her. Jenna tried her hardest to keep her focus on him but as her body clenched and she began fitting on the floor before him, Kristian leapt up onto the bed and watched in wild bewilderment as she writhed around on the carpet like a fish out of water. Her eyes were rolling madly in their sockets as she set about frothing from her mouth, thick weightless foam that spilled like a river from her curvaceous lips. Kristian stilled upon the bed, unaware, unsure what to do to help her. His eyes were scanning the room bitterly looking for an answer as he simply observed. She was wailing now, a weird high pitched gurgling noise that emitted from her gut and Kristian Collins was literally shitting himself over the girl's prominent fitting. He stood, cursing himself as he pulled the wooden door of the hotel room open as he lit himself a cigarette. He glanced back, the puddle of piss that now dampened the floor now annoyed him, Jenna's fit had finally started to subside and now she was laying spark out cold on the floor dripping in her own urine, dribbling profusely from her mouth and making slight spasms with her legs and arms. Kristian sighed sadly, the poor girl was completely fucked up already and Kristian knew that he was going to have a wild time with the girl before him, whether she remembered it or not.

He threw the stub of his cigarette and ushered himself back into the room. Closing the door softly behind him he edged back to the bed. His eyes glassy with pending apprehension, he sucked in a harsh breath and sighed on its release. He went over to Jenna's limp body that lay in a heap on the carpet; He picked her up slowly and tentatively placed her on the bed. H e removed her clothes gently peeled the sodden layer away from her purple bruised skin. He pulled the crisp top sheet from the duvet and draped it across her. He leant in and gently kissed her icy cheek, he had never felt so guilty in all his life. Jenna was nothing more than a victim of circumstance and Kristian felt nothing but shame over his actions the previous night. His fingers flexed against her sallow cheeks. Donny had sent him to do a job, but he was in a strange way, starting to develop a liking for the girl. He had tried his hardest to keep himself under control, but he was literally crawling with disgust over his actions. It wasn't the first time he had sexually assaulted a woman, infact he had a terrible habit of doing it, but Jenna was different. He had been jealous of the other bloke touching her. He had been overwhelmed by her strength, during the whole ordeal she had barely whimpered, remained completely silent and allowed them to carry on their merciless assaults. She was simply exquisite. Kristian lay beside her on the bed, his mind completely absorbed by the beautiful girl beside him, even now after fitting on the mortifying hotel carpet she was undoubtedly stunning. Her face was milky pale, her nose slightly curved at the end, the endless mop of raven black hair that adorned her head. She was a treasure and Kristian Collins felt genuine lust for the first time in his life. The endless butterflies that fluttered in his stomach each and every time his eyes set themselves on her face he knew; Jenna Shearan was something very spectacular indeed. He lay his head against the fluffy pillows and drifted off to sleep..... Unaware that Donny was lurking in his blacked out pickup in the car park.

Chapter Twenty Three

Kristian awoke to find that most of the day had passed and that the evening was drawing swiftly in, he pulled his phone from his pocket and checked the clock, it was almost seven in the night. He checked his missed calls and his texts, Donny had been plaguing him with messages all afternoon. Kristian sank back, unsure of his next move; he at least wanted the night off. He couldn't allow Jenna to work in the state she was in. She still hadn't woken from her fit and Kristian was starting to worry, she was snoring softly beside him but he daren't attempt to wake her. She looked so peaceful, so angelic in her slumber and he almost choked as the tears welled up in his eyes. He hated the thought of what he had inflicted on her. She hadn't deserved it, she hadn't asked for it, he felt so ashamed. He crumbled at the mere thought of his actions, he held her hand tightly in his own and tried to rationalise his decisions. He knew if he went against Donny's wishes there would be ructions. But still the allure of the beautiful young woman before him was enough to make him question his loyalty to Donny. He didn't want her on the payroll; he didn't want her fucking random men for money she would never see a penny of. He certainly didn't want her shagging Donny fucking Anderson; he just wanted to know Jenna. She was Funny, bubbly simply beautiful Jenna who had blown him away with her crazy laugh and her all consuming personality. He didn't want her to be in fear of him. Despite what had happened between them, he wanted her to get to know him, just Kristian Collin's. No prostitution or drugs involved, he just wanted her to get on the same page as him. He knew of course that she would obviously detest him but his head wasn't ready to establish the thought. He halted as he lingered close to her face, her eyelids fluttering slightly in her sleep, he was captivated, absorbed by this beautiful girl and her alluring persona. She was something superhuman, something completely captivating and Kristian was slowly becoming obsessed by her. He didn't know how to handle Jenna Shearan and her pretty little mind. He rolled himself another cigarette and relaxed back into the pillows, fuck Donny he thought, the cunt could wait.

When Jenna awoke there was no sound other than the thudding of her heart, it was dark, the sun completely faded. She gazed around, her mind hazy, faded somewhat. She didn't recall much, but as she turned over and her face finally met Kristian Collins sober for the first time. He smiled shyly at her, his eyes were kind, unlike they had been the previous night she thought sadly. He could have been any normal boy in that moment as he lay there beside her, his hair floppy on his head his smile was simple and extremely handsome.

"Hey" he whispered silently the awkward tone in his voice didn't go unnoticed. Jenna sat there so conflicted; she didn't know how she should feel toward the boy before her. He seemed more gentle now, his face devoid of the angry grimace it had held, he looked almost handsome. His youth was evident and Jenna for some unknown reason found herself feeling guilty for the boy's situation.

"You feel better now? You had a fit or something" his voice trailed off as their eyes met again, he swallowed the lump that developed in his throat almost immediately, he couldn't cry. His lip trembled slightly as her green eyes caught his momentarily; the fear in them was imminent and striking. The bittersweet tension between them was sublime and as he slowly etched in closer to her she didn't feel afraid anymore. He just held her to him, her head resting against his thundering heart. Jenna felt an overwhelming sense of peace wash over her. She knew she could never mentally allow feelings for this man, but she felt serene in his company. He had taken her as his own in the most brutal way, yet she felt as though he had been simply following orders. She nodded her reply and the continued to just sit there drowning in silence. Both worrying how the fuck was Jenna going to survive, and as Kristian Collin's held her just a little bit tighter, Jenna knew that he doubted she would.

Book Two

The Change

"In the glare of a neon sign, she laid her body down.
The damned walked in beside her and he laid his money down.
He said don't try to scream now but I want this one to hurt,
And tonight my pretty one I'm gonna get my money's worth

He said they never listened, she said they'd never understand
that I don't do this for pleasure, I just do it cause I can....."

3 Doors Down- Father's Son

Chapter Twenty Four

One Year Later

The cold bitter air licked the girl's naked ankles as she clattered down the pavement. The stiletto's that hugged her tiny feet bit into her paper thin skin as she took each staggering step. She wrapped her loose cotton cardigan around her tightly trying to numb the pull of the bitter December wind. She pulled her bleach blonde hair away from her face as she attempted to half run half crawl down the narrow side streets. Her whole body was aching from days of misuse and an overwhelming come down that was lingering on her fragile frame. She was already half an hour late to meet with her boss and she knew she was going to receive another beating for her trouble. She sucked in a harsh hollow breath and almost collapsed to the pavement from sheer exhaustion. She stopped suddenly as she saw a large blacked out car slowly pull around the corner, her heart beat a tattoo in her chest as it pulled alongside her, she closed her eyes tightly, wishing she would just die on the spot, get it over and done with anything than have to give her body up again for a poxy twenty quid that she never saw a penny of.

"Well Well Well Miss Shearan I've been looking all over for you" Donny's voice came in a calm reverie from the inside of the car. Jenna's eyes plunged open and she saw instantaneously that he was waving the little white bag that she craved so longingly in his hand. She swallowed down her excitement and despondently made her way to the passenger door. She pulled it open and slid in nervously beside him, taking in his arched eyebrows and his angry snarling lips she knew that she was in for it already. He was playing her like his favourite puppet and she knew the game too well. His fingers were on her thighs then and she was suddenly propelled back into her seat with an almighty punch to the jaw. Her bone shattering completely under the pressure and Jenna felt the bottom half of her face sag in shock, she tried her hardest to stem the screams that emitted from her. She held her mouth, the blood spilling from her mouth and she knew she'd lost a tooth somewhere in the back, the splintered remains dug into her gums as she tried to move her jaw back into place. The searing pain was hot and heady and Jenna could feel the tears already streaming sadly down her face. The crimson stains were already dying the ends of her dirty blonde hair and Jenna shuddered at how horrific and barbaric Donny was toward her. She had done nothing but work endlessly and tirelessly for him, allowing men to take her body, being forced into sex with Donny and his friends as though it was second nature and in turn he fed her drugs and drink to blot out her morality. He had crushed her, emotionally and physically and she knew that there was more still to come. She was bruised, her body a complete opposite of how it had once been, she was scarily thin; her whole face had become sucked in and withdrawn. The blonde hair and tacky extensions made her look cheap and dishevelled which in effect was exactly what she was. A cheapened slut.

Suddenly Donny pounced, ripping at her over worn clothes, his hands in her hair tugging briskly from the roots. His mouth was on her neck, biting and clawing away at her flesh; his fingernails dug none too gently into her thighs. The paper thin dress she wore came away from her instantaneously revealing her bruised naked body and Donny smiled coyly when he saw that she had misplaced her underwear. He grasped her chin between his fingers, the weight of the pressure crushing her already broken jaw allowing more crimson spray to leak from the corner of her lips. Rabid ecstasy the only emotion etched on his face as he unzipped his trousers with the precision and ease of a well skilled ringleader. He held his throbbing member in his hands momentarily as he glared like a wild animal into her eyes before plunging himself into her. Jenna screamed out as he filled her forcefully, he tugged at her hair harder, biting her lip in bitter agony. Jenna felt nothing but an eerie numbness, the normality of the situation blinding her; she had been here so many times now. With men she hadn't known five minutes and then there was Donny Anderson, Lord of the manner who was the one who abused her the most in ways that were almost inhuman. She shut herself down as best she could and tried to dream away the pain, she thought of Kiki and she thought of Archie and she thought of Craig. Because in her mind's eye, in these dark, chilling times he was the only thing that kept her sane, the only thought that kept the spark from dying completely. She had to stay hopeful, for without hope she would perish and truly enslave herself to her captor. Donny was tough, but Craig was tougher and it was just a case of when he would finally put two and two together and take Donny out without a seconds thought. She remained still, not flinching once, she gathered up all of her strength to remain as clam and serene as she could. Her jaw was throbbing, the pain excruciating as he climaxed around her, his body sagging against hers, the embarrassment of her blood in his hair the only thing she felt as he pulled himself swiftly out of her. She closed her eyes tightly and allowed the humiliation to take its course. The tell tale sound of his zipper being done up and the sound of his lighter as he sparked up a cigarette the only sign that he had finished. She smelt the smoke, it lingered between them momentarily before he turned and stubbed the cigarette out on her arm, the skin blistering puckering beneath the amber glow. Jenna yelped like a wounded dog, her eyes shot open and she jolted to face him.

"Fucking awake are we?" he spat, his face contorted, twisted, her blood smeared all over his angry scowl. He looked demented, fierce and almost psychotic, like something from a bad horror movie. Jenna nodded as best she could, she could feel her jaw sliding, the splintered bones shattered underneath her sallow skin. She could feel his sticky, unwelcomed wetness between her legs and she could have easily vomited where she sat. He repulsed her, her whole stomach churned as she stared through him vacantly, she had no understanding of why he had done this to her, why he had victimised her and turned her into his plaything. His little skinny ragdoll who had developed the bone structure of a fucking greyhound, she was as dainty as a young child. She hadn't tasted a solid meal in weeks, she lived on cocaine and wine, the narcotics alone enough to kill her but anything was better than facing reality. Reality wasn't Jenna Shearan's friend, it wasn't a place she felt comfortable and if she didn't accept it, then it wasn't happening. Donny relaxed back into his seat, an angry, sly smirk played on his lips as he took another deep drawl on his cigarette, his lips pouting seductively as he eased a thin layer of smoke from his lips.

"Why do you do this" Jenna whispered blankly choking on her tears as the floodgates opened, the mixture of tears, blood and heavy mascara running down her sad face. Her face void of any expression, she didn't have anything left to give. She ran her hands through her lank greasy blonde hair and she fell back into the cold leather seats, the bones that jutted out from her tiny naked body highlighted by the dim interior lights.

"Because I can" he replied coyly a thin smile playing on his curvaceous full lips. The burning sensation in Jenna's jaw was agony, complete and utter agony. But as Johnny took the rolled up twenty from his jacket pocket and dealt out two fat lines of cocaine on the dashboard, the pain subsided and all was fine once more.... for now at least.

Chapter Twenty Five

Craig paced the floor, his bare feet slapping on the wood. His eyes blazed bright blue with worry, lack of sleep evident in the thick black suitcases under his eyes. He took a deep slug from his can of Stella and perched himself on the edge of the bed, the alarm clock beside the bed flashed 3:40am, Craig sighed heavily, running his fingers across the top of his short hair, his shoulders slumped forward. This had become his nightly routine; the reoccurring dream that played itself on repeat in his head was catastrophic. He could hear her screams. Feel her pain, her fear of the unknown. Jenna had been on the missing list for well over a year and he was still no closer to solving the mystery of what had happened to her. He was afraid, worried sick with apprehension. He could sense she was still alive, he could feel it in everything he did but he knew that she was in great danger. Jenna was his sixth sense, it was like telepathy that they shared and he knew he had to find her, because time was running out for the two of them. Craig sat there in the silence and for the first time in his life he prayed for Jenna's safe return. He knew that he may have looked a prick but still there he was on his knees, eyes closed praying to the heavens that he would be able to save her. Craig Carter knew that his life now depended on it.

Donny pulled the car into the car park that lead to a high rise block of flats and drank in his surroundings with a look of disgust on his face. He checked the slip of paper in his hands and was dismayed to find that he was indeed in the correct place. He nudged a sleeping Jenna hard in the ribs; she woke with a start, the dull ache in her jaw still ever apparent. She shuffled against the hot leather seat, the stifling warmth making her translucent skin stick fast. She peeled herself away and glanced in the sun visor mirror and attempted to tidy herself up as best as she could.

"We're here, sort your fucking self out you dirty little fucking slut" he spat with revulsion, the skin of his nose skimming Jenna's cheek, his breath staining her as his face lingered close to hers. She shuddered deeply, her heart thundering in her chest; Donny genuinely put the fear of God into her. He was nothing short of psychotic and he was having no problem tearing Jenna down bit by bit. He had taken her life, he had taken her pride and he had taken her freedom. She had been left with nothing, no emotion, no self worth just sex. She resembled a machine, designed to fuck, designed to work and earn money that she would never see. The strangers who became her abusers used her in ways that could only be described as torturous. The sex was bitter, painful and agonising both mentally and physically. She had been degraded in ways that she would never ever speak of to another living soul. Now she lived for the stolen moments of affection that she shared with Kristian, he had become her closest confidant. And as much as she hated him for what he did to her, leading her to the slaughterhouse, taking her to her sweet demise under Johnny's controlling word. He listened afterwards, he was compassionate towards her and above all he cared. He didn't treat her like a piece of meat that was ready to be fed to the bloodhounds; he showed her genuine affection, it wasn't much but she respected him. Jenna swiped away the dried blood from her mouth; the stinging sensation that followed made her breathless in its intensity. She stood shakily from the car, the cold night air biting her bare legs, her heels clipping the concrete as she walked she was exhausted and would give all the money in the world for a pair of fluffy pyjamas a bath and her bed at that moment. Donny gripped her arm tightly and led her to the entrance of the flats, the place stank of piss and degradation and Jenna instantly swallowed down the vomit as it rose to her battered mouth. He punched the entry buzzer to flat eleven and the door clicked open a few seconds later, Donny dragged her inside. The lobby of the flats was filthy, crawling with rubbish, fag butts and daily debris. Jenna even spotted a few stray condoms among the waste. She had never felt so dirty in her whole life, Donny traipsed her up the metal steps, Jenna placed one foot in front of the other forcing herself to carry on going despite her head screaming for her to run. Her eyes fearfully pulling back the tears that threatened to spill down her face. By far this was the worst place Donny had taken her; the whole place was baron, unused, dead in atmosphere completely abandoned by any form of human life.

Donny arrived at the battered door of flat eleven and cursed under his breath, he could smell the sickly heady scent of heroin. The skag head beyond the door had called him a few days previously looking for a girl they could take turns with. He knew Jenna would freak out at first but she would comply once he had put the hard word into her. He tapped the decaying wood lightly, the scuffling and hushed voices that came from beyond the dead chipped door signalling that they hadn't been awaiting his arrival. Donny's eyebrows rose in anger as he was left waiting, he gave the door a loud punch his hand instantly returning to his trouser pockets, agitation evident on his handsome face. When the door locks finally clicked and a scruffy doped up woman with not a single tooth in her scrawny head came to the door, opening it a fraction the scent of grimy bodies and drugs flooded the enclosed space between Jenna and Donny. It took Jenna every ounce of strength she had to not faint with anxiety on the spot. She could feel her knees beginning to buckle through the strain; she flashed Donny a look that was reminiscent of a deer in the headlights. Donny smiled his most beautiful smile, full mega watt pearly whites that made the girl at the door instantly gush in her unwashed knickers. She gave Donny a peek of her crumbled teeth and Jenna almost fell flat on her face, she clung desperately to Donny for support, His hand skimmed her naked back, his fingertips tracing her spine, Jenna knew the game, he was trying to comfort her make her feel like he cared for her.

"Danielle in?" he nodded to gums on the doorstep, his voice rich and velvety, thick with jovial spark. The girl nodded her head vaguely, barely able to keep her glazed eyes open, her pupils pinned and dead at the same time. The track marks on her dirty arms a dismal reminder of the life that was beyond the champagne and the riches. These people were the barrel scrapers, the filth and Jenna was suddenly hit with the realisation of it all. She had become them, her drug of choice was more expensive of course but it was all the same. Junkies were junkies in the life, regardless of what you chose to sniff, inject or smoke you were all united. Jenna almost choked as the filthy girl scurried from the door to call her boss. Her eyes were virtually standing from their sockets. Donny pulled her close, his mouth at her ear;

"Danielle is lovely, she's not like her" he whispered, his sympathetic tone wasn't convincing to Jenna, not one bit and she knew whoever Danielle was, she probably just as bad, if not worse as the girl who had just flitted from them. Whoring out druggies, Jenna shook her head, she wanted to fall to her knees and beg Donny to take her home, back to Kristian, back to the arms where she had felt safest. Despite the rape, despite the torture she suffered at his hands, he was her safe house, her only friend in this sordid ordeal. But pride made her a woman again and as she stood there head held high from the floor as she locked eyes instantaneously with the infamous Danielle Carey. She was beautiful there was no denying that, her body overly curved, highlighted delectably by her low cut blouse and sheer black pencil skirt. She looked insatiable, sexy and suddenly Jenna felt undermined, downgraded somewhat by this powerful stranger.

"For fuck sakes Don!" she screeched in her high pitched welsh accent "We thought you were the cocking police" she cackled as she extended the door out and waved for them to enter her humble abode. Jenna warily followed Donny inside, her eyes meeting the filthy antique wallpaper that had curled dramatically with age. The heavy yellow hue from cigarettes lingered the revolting stains seemingly hanging onto every inch of the ceilings walls and filthy debris ridden carpet. Jenna sucked in her last gulp of stale air before the door was closed behind them; Danielle pushed her way past Jenna and Donny and resumed her post as the head of the line. Her finely manicured hand perched on her hip as she sauntered towards the back of the hallway, her rainbow coloured leopard print stilettos clopping as she walked, her ample buttocks swaying in the dim light.

"You'll be working out of this room, it's nothing to look at but it serves its purpose" She said matter of factly as they were faced with another heavily dented wooden door. Jenna glanced sadly upwards, whatever lay behind that door would seal her fate indefinitely. Donny no longer trusted her working the streets that much was for certain. She had become a liability and now she would pay for her sins, Donny edged her towards Danielle, Jenna's nervousness making him reluctant; he was ready to thump her one in the face already. As Danielle opened the door, Jenna recoiled in horror, the sheer fear branded on her face as her eyes took in the sight before her. There in the centre of the room was a grubby, dated and overused mattress stained with fuck knows what. Jenna heaved deeply at the musky, filthy scent of sex that lingered there in the blank space before them. She felt the heavy blow to her ribs but she couldn't register a reaction. She looked up into Donny's eyes and saw nothing but rage there. He shoved her into the dark, unfurnished room. The only window in the corner covered with a My Little Pony bedcover, Jenna focused on that alone. Drinking in the irony of it all. It was Kiki's favourite, she remembered that much. Craig had bought her all of the dolls the previous Christmas and she had been bowled over by her daddy and his amazing presents. Jenna tried her hardest to focus on the happy memory as Donny slammed the door angrily behind him. He gripped her, shaking her shoulders violently before jolting her onto the heavily soiled mattress. He tugged at her dress, slapping her hard in the face with each movement his agile body made. Within seconds he was inside her, his force making her want to yelp like some sort of rabid animal. He was hard, longing and above all he was angry. She didn't scream, she barely moved as she took what she had become accustomed to. Her eyes all the while pinned to the images on the bedcover shielding the window, absorbed in the memory of her daughter as she took her punishment without a fight, As Donny spilled himself inside her, she cried. Real, fat painful tears that streamed down her face in torrents. How had she become this far gone she wondered aimlessly. She wondered sadly what she had ever done to deserve such torment. Donny spat a thick globule of spittle in her face as he stood, zipping his trousers up and walking away leaving her to mercy of Danielle and her mob of animals. The smile on his face broad and dignified almost cocky with pride. As he pulled the door open he shook hands respectably with Jenna's first customer of the night. The scruffy, grubby looking boy owned a devilish smile and a pair of eyes that glowed viciously through drugs and desire for her body. As her entered the room licking his lips, his hands already caressing the bulge in his trousers, Jenna opened her mouth to scream but not a word came out and as the boy strolled towards her, she bit down hard on her bottom lip and swallowed the last of her pride. It was to be a long night, one Jenna Shearan would never forget as she finally became a member of The Club.

Chapter Twenty Six

Jenna found herself falling, desperate to cling onto any type of hope. Her hands flailing in the darkness as she desperately tried to grasp onto the invisible edge. As she shot up, her eyes rolling around in their sockets as she tried to establish her surroundings. She exhaled deeply, the place was absolutely stinking. She eyed around the room suspiciously, used condoms littered the defiled carpet that was completely stiff from body fluids and various other muck. Jenna recoiled in horror as she noticed the pool of blood that had stained the already ancient looking mattress. Her mottled blue legs were smeared with the stuff, the sheer embarrassment of it all was too much and she began to whimper sadly. Her tears dropping onto the dirty sheet, desperately she buried her head into her hands and tugged at her dry, dirty looking bleached hair. She was physically and mentally exhausted, the drugs, drink and sex had finally caught up with her and she had never ever felt so lonely in all of her young life. She frantically craved her children and to the greatest of extents she needed Craig, his face was slowly becoming a distant memory and Jenna felt awful for that singular fact alone. She had loved him with a desire that was beyond words; he had been and still remained to be her whole world. He was the only thing keeping her sane. In her torment she curled into a tight ball and hoped and prayed to the heavens that she would just die. She heard the lock clicking on the door and was relieved when she saw Kristian lingering in the doorway. His overgrown fringe sweeping over his left eye, Jenna smiled weakly as their eyes met briefly. She pulled her glance away from his, her cheeks burning, flushed scarlet with embarrassment. She crossed her legs beneath the sheets remembering the blood that was smeared down her legs. She felt like a wounded child beneath his icy gaze, he turned away momentarily, composing himself. He strode into the room, slamming the door none too gently behind him Jenna bounced out of her skin, her movements resembling that of a cat on a hot tin roof. She looked so damaged, so fragile, like a wilted flower and it took all of Kristian's might not to sweep her up into his arms and take her away from this horrific torture. He slid beside her on the stinking dirty mattress and cupped her chin delicately between his fingers, she flinched beneath his touch and Kristian hushed her sweetly in an almost childlike manner as he saw the tears forming in her dead eyes. She had become so damaged and Kristian wondered how long she would last in this hell hole she had been taken too. He had worked with Danielle on numerous occasions, he had even fucked her on numerous occasions, but the scene before him was too much. Jenna wasn't cut out for the streets; she wasn't cut out for working in such squalor. She had no need to be here, she wasn't on junkie, and she didn't need the money. She was here out of nothing more than revenge. Revenge for Donny wanting to take Craig's place in the world;

"Hey look at me" he whispered, a tinge of desperation in his voice. His fingers lapped away a stray tear that spilled down her cheek. He gulped back his own emotions in sheer fear of showing her how hurt he was seeing her so desolate. He slid closer to her pulling her head close to his chest. He sucked in his breath as she winded him slightly. Her overwhelming sense of fear and sadness evident as her body sagged hard against his and she began to cry into his crisp white shirt. He held his own, forcing himself with all his might not to succumb to this girl and allow her to see how sorry he was for her. She didn't need his sympathy, it would only make her worse and he needed to keep reminding himself of that fact before he got in too deep.

"What am I Going to Do Kris?" she bawled as he bowled her into his lap, the sheet that had been concealing her legs tearing away from her and he recoiled in horror as he saw the blood seeping down her legs. He held her close, not knowing what else to do other than comfort her. He had no control over anything in that one moment other than her protection and he knew that if he didn't act on instinct now then within the week Jenna would be found swinging from the rafters, her neck contorted by the grubby sheet that now enveloped her broken body. He kissed her forehead, the respect and love in his movement left Jenna simply astonished but he had nothing more to offer. He knew he was battling with himself in his agony but he honestly was caught between the ropes. He looked up to see Danielle stood in the doorway, a vicious scowl written on her heavily scarlet painted pout. Her arms folded sulkily across her ample bust, her breasts almost bursting from the confines of her floral patterned silk shirt. Her heavily shadowed eyes remained smoky and sultry as she blinked in bewilderment at the endearing scene before her. The whore and her pimp in all their refined glory, Danielle swallowed her bitterness down angrily.

"She's got a customer coming on soon Kris you'll have to leave" She spat vehemently, her eyes glaring, scanning the body of the filthy girl. She wondered momentarily what on earth he saw in Jenna fucking Shearan, the filthy little whore didn't know what day it was. Kristian placed Jenna Gently back on the sheets and stood, his stance showing Danielle that he meant nothing but business, he stepped forward at almost lightening speed and grasped at Danielle's cheeks.
"You tell your fucking punter to fuck off Cunty. She stays with me today!" His eyes completely rigid with suppressed anger as he stared Danielle down viciously, his mind pondering how the fuck he had ever allowed himself to get close to this vile woman and her evil traits.

"She needs to go to a hospital, she's bleeding and her jaw's busted you can't possibly be allowing her to be dealt out in this state" he questioned harmlessly, Danielle shrugged her reply carelessly. She had no time for the likes of Jenna Shearan. The Pretty little whore had not a stitch on her. She went home at night to her husband and their two daughters with not a care in the world for the girls who she doled out like lollipops to and tom Dick and Harry who rocked up to flat eleven.

"Donny told me she was fine, I haven't seen her since late last night. And in all fairness to you Mr Collins you'd best remember what side your bread is buttered good boy. Because the minute Donny gets wind of this, you're fucked!" she whispered maliciously her mouth curling into a deep set frown with every word that leaked from her mouth. She was furious there was no denying that, the jealousy seeping through her pores. She was borderline frothing at the mouth her anger was that apparent.

"She needs the hospital Dan. The Poor fuckers Jaw is broken! She aint gunna be making you no fucking readies if she can't suck cock now is she!" He spat back, the intensity in his voice made Danielle think twice before she replied.

"Off you fuck then, but I want it back in two hours and ready for fucking work!" Her voice an almost high pitched cackle as She turned on her high patent black heels and sauntered off, her ass swinging sexily as she went.

Kristian stood, holding his hand out to Jenna he pulled her to her feet, awkwardly he hugged her close. His nose searching through her hair the over familiar scent of strange bodies lingered there and he almost found himself pulling away from her.

"I'll get you out of this I promise" He whispered his voice apologetic and sincere and Jenna almost found herself bursting into tears again at his kindness. He was so tender and sweet with her, it was as though he saw her as nothing more than an innocent child. She was his to care for and Jenna didn't find it fair on him at all. She released him coldly, remembering herself not to get too close to this man. He was still a danger to her no matter what he had promised. He had hurt her once before and he was perfectly capable of doing it again.

"Don't you ever speak about me like that again" Jenna snapped at him, "I may act like a fucking slut but do you think I do it fucking willingly eh? If it wasn't for you and that psychotic cunt you work for I'd be at fucking home with MY kids, where I'm supposed to be" she poked him hard in the chest, her face sagging slightly from the pain in her jaw, her mouth resembling that of a stroke victim. Kristian cocked his head back as though she had punched him straight in the mouth, his face stricken with sadness as he shrugged and headed for the door.

"I'll be outside" he called over his shoulder before he vanished out of sight, Jenna could feel herself losing control, slowly but surely everything that she was, was being ripped away from her. She held back her impending sobs and dressed herself as best she could; at least if she was being treated at the hospital she wasn't stuck in the hovel. She smiled sadly at the irony and walked away from her prison, her heart heavy and saddened in her chest.

****

The nurse gave Jenna the once over again with her piggy beady little eyes and sighed outwardly again before glaring wildly, her eyes glistening with venom at Kristian. She hocked the spittle from the back of her throat and eyed her notes once more. The story that the pair had strung up was nothing but utter bullshit and Patty O'Donoghue could smell it a mile off. She pressed her hand against her buxom hip and scowled once more at Jenna, the girl was a mess. She had been busted up the poor thing and Patty could sniff out a domestic abuse case like a Bloodhound could smell a premium twenty ounce steak. Her eyebrow raised itself automatically every now and again conspicuously as the two "Lovebirds" before her continued to lie blatantly to her face. If the girl in front of her had been attacked by a random girl as she claimed, the boyfriend didn't seem too keen on the police being informed. Yes Patty O'Donoghue could smell a rat and she would get to the bottom of it even if she had to miss her morning coffee and her ritual gossip in the staffroom.

"Why don't you go and get yourself a coffee from the vender Mr Collins, I'm sure you'll feel better after a nice cuppa, and I'm sure Jenna would love one too" She nattered briefly in her hideously thick Scottish accent as she bustled past Kristian. Her humungous buttocks almost sent him flying across the room as she squeezed herself between him and the bed. She began buffing Jenna's pillows and tentatively asking the girl if she was okay. Kristian stood firm, rooted to the spot, his face turned into an unimpressed grin as his eyes fluttered in sheer bewilderment of the woman who stood so openly in front of him. He picked at an imaginary fibre on his grey suit jacket before giving the bulldog faced old cunt a subtle smile and leaving the room swiftly. Not thinking twice about giving Jenna a stern hard stare before he left. The fine scent of money and expensive aftershave lingered in the room long after he had vacated. Jenna propped herself up on the bed, her whole body racking with a sweet agony that ruptured in every single muscle that she owned. She was exhausted beyond defeat; she was shut off, separated from the world she remembered so well. Yet here in the peaceful, sterile clarity of the hospital bed was her chance to come clean and escape. Her heart was leaping in her chest telling her to take the plunge, confess all of her sins to this tubby old tart hovering over her. Her head though was wise and as hard as she fought it she couldn't hold off listening to its warning. To keep her fat mouth shut, to stay with Kristian, he had promised to save her, Right? Or had it all been a merciless dream, an Idea that she had conjured up in her silly little head? She was so out of it these days that she herself couldn't separate fantasy and reality anymore. She felt numb, completely and utterly numb.

"So when did this happen Miss Shearan?" The nurse prompted, waking her momentarily from her dazed state.

"Last night" Jenna replied, the swelling in her face was becoming ridiculous, her whole mouth was throbbing. And if this hog in front of her didn't stop asking her questions she was going to launch her into next week.

"We'll have to wire your mouth bag into place; it's not too bad a fracture, more of a hairline crack so you were lucky. But you'll need rest and plenty of painkillers to dull the ache. The pain should subside in roughly six to eight weeks and we'll need to see you inbetween just to check it's healing up nicely. I'll go and get the doctor." She smiled sympathetically as she pulled a stack of leaflets from a pile on her desk she handed them solemnly to Jenna.

"You know, if you need to talk to someone there are people who can help you Hen" she held her reserve as she left the room, leaving Jenna speechless as she saw the words Domestic violence splattered all over the papers in her hands. Jenna shook her head nonchalantly, how wrong was the dog faced old hag. If only she knew the truth, that poor Jenna had been forced fed cocaine for breakfast lunch tea and dinner for the past year and then she had been made to degrade herself by shagging random men for money! And the poor, innocent minded old hag thought Kristian Collins was her bloody abusive boyfriend! Jenna could throttle the old goat for her blatant ignorance to the situation; Kristian was by no stretch of the imagination her boyfriend. He was nothing more than her glorified fucking pimp! The man who sold her to these retched urchins for money she didn't get a sniff of. Jenna sighed sadly at the poor woman's naivety. She glanced back down at the leaflets in her hands, the sad, black eyes of the battered wives staring back at her, their desolate dead eyes praying for her to escape. She closed her eyes tight and momentarily, if only for a millisecond, Craig's face flashed into her mind, his beautiful smile radiating, filling her with hope. She clenched the paper sheets with her fingers and prayed with all of her might that he would come for her soon and take her away from this awful prison. As she opened her eyes to the angry, snarling face of Donny Anderson staring down on her she swallowed down her overwhelming urge to scream, Kristian Collins had just confirmed her suspicions.... She could trust No one.

Chapter Twenty Seven

Dom sat out in the car park watching the baby playing with his toy cars on the concrete. The air was damp, muggy with the sweet feel of the evening and as Dom relaxed and took a swig of his beer, the gentle evening breeze blew gently on his face and for the first time in months he felt carefree. He felt serene; he had worked his way forward. Being a full time father had been hard on him. He had suffered with terrible post natal depression after Archie was born and now after a long, hard, almost desperate year of fighting and clawing his way back from the depths he was finally feeling okay. Jenna leaving had thrown him into a pit of despair and he had taken out his pending frustrations on his baby, for that fact alone he would be forever guilty. But he had learnt to bond, to place all his negative energy aside and turn it into something positive. And above all he had learnt to love his son, unconditionally. He had learnt that his son could be his survivor and he owed his life to the little mite who sat before him playing so innocently. Archie was perfect in every way, the perfect mixture of his mother and his father, dark jet black hair, little button nose and the most electrifying emerald eyes Dom had ever laid eyes on. He was Jenna's son there was no doubt about that, he was courageous, daring and he had the bubbliest little personality Dom had ever seen. It gave Dom comfort that Archie was like his mother; it meant that Dom hadn't lost her entirely. He missed Jenna, more than words could comprehend but he had learnt that he had to move on for the sake of his son and his sanity. He slugged another deep drink from his bottle of lager and called Archie to him. He held him close, taking in his beautiful toddler smell, the smell of his blood, his DNA, the smell he loved the most.

"You wanna go in buddy" he whispered into Archie's soft, silky hair, kissing his temples tenderly as the little boy nodded his approval. Dom scooped little Archie up into his arms, leading him back to the flats he looked across to Jenna's flat. The council had boarded the doors with metal grates despite Jenna's possessions still being inside. Dom swallowed hard, fighting back the butterflies that invaded his stomach in that passing moment. The sweet euphoric hope that one day she would return. He despised not knowing where she was, who she was with, if she was safe, but he had learnt that his life couldn't revolve around the constant heartache and he had resumed his everyday life with a sense of normality. Even if it was only for his sons sake. He made his way indoors, back to the comfort and solace of home. The familiarity of it all seemed perfect. He had created this little bubble of life for him and Archie here and he would be damned if he would ever allow someone to ruin that happiness. He had built himself a family from the ashes of Jenna's betrayal and as much as he hated what Jenna had done to him, he loved her just as equally because she had given him their son. It was a confusing state, Dom relinquished the thought, but he knew he had to keep himself together, keep moving forward for the sake of Archie. If Jenna was never found, then Dom would face the consequences of explaining to his son what had happened when they crossed that inevitable bridge. But for now, they were happy. And as long as they were coping, moving forward and enjoying their lives then there was nothing that could stop them. As Dom shut away the rest of the world he smiled, a sad melancholy smile but a smile none the less. The past was a forgotten shadow and soon it would mean nothing, the thought calmed him as much as it excited him.

Craig sat at the empty bar, hair slicked back, gelled to perfection, snappy black suit, crisp white shirt and eyes as blue as the Tahitian waters. He sipped slowly at his neat crisp vodka that sat on the bar before him. His eyes mulling over paperwork in front of him, his heart wasn't truly in it. He had been chasing a false sighting of Jenna all night, he felt defeated, hurt and hungry for answers. His mind was working overtime, the palpitations in his chest making him dizzy as he took a deep exhale. He could feel the imminent panic attack coming and he hoped that it would hurry up and pass. His temples were pounding, his bowels constricting, the horrible thundering in his chest was all too familiar now. He tried his utmost to breathe through the urge to vomit. His cheeks flushed scarlet, temperature soaring as the panic set in. His hands shook, trembling with apprehension. His whole body numb from the agony, the not knowing. He stood the effort too much and he found himself instantly on his hands and knees. His eyes were darting around the room, searching, looking for something to ease the surge of his pulse. Every single sense was heightened, his whole body tingling wildly. It felt as euphoric as a cocaine high but the fear that followed suppressed it immediately. Craig hurled, trying to force himself to vomit, anything, desperate to try and stop the horror that evaded his body. The anxiety was becoming too much, each and every panic attack more intense and deeper than the last. It was torture, pure agony and Craig didn't know how much longer they would last. He hoped against hope they6 would stop soon, because he was starting to become fearful, scared out of his wits by their intensity. Fear didn't sit well with Craig Carter, especially because it was fear of himself, of his own body. He closed his eyes, trying his hardest to fight away the scenarios in his head. He could see Jenna, naked, scared alone, she was crying profusely, screaming his name, screaming for him to help her. Craig shuddered, shooting up and punching the concrete wall before him with brute force, feeling his knuckles cracking deliciously under the strain, he retracted his hand, pummelling his fist into the wall, his head blowing its final fuse. The tears flowed down his face as he called out into the darkness, a deep guttural growl that sounded almost inhuman. The sadness and despair he felt was nothing but a tragedy. He leant against the fire exit door of the club, his back sliding down the polished wood, exhaustion taking over, his heartbeat regulating itself, slowing its electrifying pace as he came down from his hysteria. His tears tumbling down his cheeks, his head lay in his hands as he sobbed uncontrollably into his shirt sleeve. The sweat that ran down his back in torrents making his shirt cling almost magnetically to his broad frame, his eyes bloodshot and burning. He couldn't bare the sight of himself. He had become so low, so desolate and he clung to the hope mercilessly that Jenna would be found soon, he knew that if she wasn't, then he would be better off dead.

Chapter Twenty Eight

Jenna stood on the pavement of the old Shacklewell lane, her knees mottled blue from the cold, nothing but a skimpy glitter red dress concealing her modesty. She wore no underwear, her long bleached hair slung effortlessly over her shoulder, her face caked in cheap foundation and pound shop eye shadow that made her eyes look cakey. The heels she was wearing bit into her tired feet as she paced the kerb waiting for the evening's trade. She stood alone, Donny had found this little spot a few weeks ago and he had now split her between working at Danielle's flat in the mornings and evenings and working the streets in the night. She was flying her tits off, the buzz of the cocaine mixed with the amphetamines Donny kept feeding her keeping her on edge, alert, paranoid. She knew Donny had the place on lockdown; he had been following her ever since he had picked her up from the hospital a few days ago. The cold air lingered, biting, pinching her tired skin as she stood out in the cold. She had no coat, not even a wrap to fight away the damp air. She felt exposed, humiliated broken in ways no words would ever begin to describe. Donny had her captured, the suffering of him written all over her tired body in bite marks, scrams and love bites. The bruises would heal but nothing would take her away from what she had seen, what she had felt. Donny sold her to mere sadists these days; the men were big, harmful and filled with loathing towards her. She had been battered, her body crushed under the pressure of their demands. She knew she was expected to fuck at least ten men a night, sometimes more or less depending on how Donny felt. If he was in a good mood then he would leave her rest after one or two of the heavier customers. They were so needy, so wanting on the verge of being sadistic, masochistic and downright sick. Jenna recoiled at the thought, her head wasn't allowed to mull over things, she had learnt to block everything out, her emotions had become so disconnected and now she saw herself as nothing more than a mere machine. Built to satisfy, take payment and leave. Her face lit up a little when she saw the bright amber headlights turn off the road, the thought of warmth for five minutes at least pleased her a little. The car pulled alongside her, the blacked out windows slowly wound down. Jenna stepped back a moment when she saw Donny in the Driving seat. His hair preened to perfection, the ring in his lip glimmering as he puffed on a cigarette.

"You don't get in the cars, there's people watching this kerb from all areas, you'll be going to work in that abandoned shop building behind you. The one with the smashed out windows. There's a mattress and some Johnnies inside. It's a bit of a tip but you've done worse. Understood?" he nodded his head gently towards her as if dealing with an errant child. Jenna bit down hard on her lip, forcing the tears to stay in her eyes, she nodded vacantly in his direction barely registering anything else he said as her eye caught sight of the abandoned shop building behind her. Even in the darkness of the street lamps the place looked desolate. The big bright Neon pansies and the slogan "Beryl's Blooms" long faded and missing a few letters from long standing. She inhaled deeply, taking in the decaying brick and the missing glass, a broken Venetian blind hanging in the non-existent window, the slats twisted, deformed and haunting in its abandonment. Jenna swallowed down the bile that tried tactically to crawl into her throat, the hard lump of overwhelming fear not moving no matter how hard she tried.

"Good, now go and make me some fucking money or I'll leave you here all fucking night!" he spat as he wheel spun away leaving her stranded, alone in the night waiting to be flung to the vicious mercy of the dogs. She stood, frozen to the spot waiting for the inevitable to happen. The roads were completely desolate, not one car had driven by for over an hour and Jenna was starting to get anxious. She knew Donny expected payment, non payment meant a beating; a beating meant she was out of action for a few days, being out of work meant that Donny would have time to shunt her somewhere even more fucking disgusting than this doss house to sell her wares. Jenna fought down the urge to run, remembering Donny's words pummelling her brain "there are people watching". The thought exercised her brain, her paranoid edge deepened significantly with the drugs. Her eyes darted across the empty road. There was nothing. As far as her eyes could see she was alone. She stopped dead in her tracks when she heard the eerie melancholy music of Vaults, in the distance, for a moment she was catapulted back in time, her heart stopping dead in her chest as the memory of her and Craig flooded her head. In that moment she was taken back there, back to the manor house, dancing in her jogger bottoms in the crisp morning sunshine. The song had been blaring from Craig's car, the both of them smiling, happy and deeply, oh so deeply in love. Jenna's face contorted wildly as she was bought back to reality with a thundering smack as Donny's car screeched with a halt onto the kerb beside her. His eyes blazing, completely buzzing with cocaine, Jenna could spot the chemical complexion a mile off, Donny was an obvious Drug taker after a dab of Charlie, his pupils would dilate like pissholes in the snow, his lips would curl into strange grimaces, he changed after he got a gram into him.

"Someone told me you like this song Princess" he cooed softly, immediately his face softened. Jenna was caught off guard slightly the droning music seeping into her eardrums stilling her. She nodded, each movement in slow motion, she forced her body to play the game, forced herself to slide beside him in the car. She huddled to the passenger door, her eyes not leaving Donny for a second. She smiled a delicate, sombre smile, which he returned subtly, flicking his cigarette ash out onto the concrete below. His perfectly straight teeth polished white to perfection.

"I've just had a meeting with your little mate" he smiled smugly; his emphasis on the word mate didn't go unnoticed. Donny turned off the ignition and turned to face Jenna, his lips contorting playfully, he reached out and caressed her sallow cheek, stroking at the degrading cheap makeup that she had caked on. His eyelashes fluttering innocently as he took in the face of the beautiful girl he had destroyed. He felt sorry for her more than anything, she had made him a mint and he had taken her so many times as his own he knew her body like the back of his hand. He would be sad to see her go, but go she would if she didn't perform her best tonight. He tucked a loose strand of bleached, bedraggled hair behind her ear and leant in for a quick kiss on her dry, chapped lips. Her breath hitched beneath his touch and Donny smiled at her want for him.

"Was he OK?" she whispered, cutting the tension between them with the force of a samurai sword, her eyes glistening, wet with unshed tears. Donny placed his fingers across his bottom lip, scanning Jenna's face, devoid of any emotion he turned and pulled something from the glove box, sneakily he tucked it away into the door compartment and turned back to Jenna, his eyes molten, ablaze with the look of lust. He moved closer, his skin inches away from hers, his breath so fragrant, so close to her ear.

"He misses you" Donny whispered "but then again, who wouldn't?" he quizzed as his mouth pressed gently against Jenna's. There was no fight, the mind games had become too much and as usual Jenna found herself submitting to him once more. His sweet addictive kiss, almost as powerful as the cocaine he was shunting up her nose. She shuddered beneath his fingers as he rode his hands along her tiny thighs, his kiss deepening, his tongue rolling in her mouth, searching every orifice deeply between each breathy lap of his tongue. Jenna moaned gently against his lips, despite everything he was still as desirable as the first day she had met him. The mind games warped her, sucked her in, pulled her to him and kept her there. She pulled him closer, gripping onto his plain black T shirt for the life of her, her nails digging into his soft flesh, making him groan deliciously in unison. He pulled away momentarily, staring into her dead jewelled eyes, serenading how beautiful the girl had once been in place of the girl before him now. Suddenly everything was business again and in his moment of weakness Donny lapsed. Her bewildered gaze, setting her off again as she pulled back in her seat, looking at Donny for the answers she relinquished so desperately. He was a head fuck, a complete and utter ride on the sick cycle carousel. She stared at him blankly through heavy mascara and black kohl liner. Her emerald green eyes still glistening, the only thing that was still Jenna about her face. Those eyes could never be replaced.

"I have you scheduled for a little work tonight" he grinned with an almost school boy veneer, rubbing his hands together as he spoke. The words like liquid venom stinging Jenna as soon as they had left his beautiful plump lips. She almost choked on his audacity, her eyes widened substantially as the words left his mouth. She had been stood on the kerb for the last 3 hours with nothing. She had shagged every Tom Dick and Harry who had graced Danielle's that morning without effort and here the brash bastard was demanding more. More that she didn't have, more that she couldn't force herself to give, but she knew she would. Like a lamb to the slaughter she would give. She looked back at Donny, nothing but contempt written on her face. He glanced away; he couldn't bring himself to revel in her sadness. He knew the night would be the breaking of the girl. As he pulled the syringe from the driver's panel, he gulped hard. Holding it out at arm's length he saw the fear, the sheer panic shoot across Jenna's face as he grabbed her arm. She couldn't fight, no matter how hard her body urged her to, her eyes remained pinned to the needle in Donny's hand, and she knew instantaneously it was Heroin. The prostitutes poison. She saw Sammy in her mind's eye, poor battered and broken Sammy. If only for a second she felt Sammy's pain. As the needle pricked her skin for the first time, puncturing her vein, she felt nothing. She watched in sheer horror as Donny pressed down on the plunger, her body devoid of any possible action. She thought about screaming, fighting, trying to stop Donny, but her body was frozen. As though every single moment was tragically stolen by time, her gaze at last met Donny, his face so serene, so calm as he pulled the needle away from her broken flesh, the smile on his face almost satanic. He resembled a child at Christmas with the most wanted toy as he watched her succumb, plunging to the depths as the sweet, overbearing rush hit her. She had never felt a high like it in her life, the feeling of overpowering sickness mixed with sheer oblivion had never felt so good. As she felt the impending heroin pull, the tasty rush before the dizziness and the sickness. It was the best feeling in the world, but the strangest at the same time and as she found her sleep she succumb, her body taking over. Donny grinned as she slumped against the leather interior. He hoped she was ready because she was going to reach her limit tonight. He started the ignition and sped away, the dead looking female in his passenger seat a constant reminder that he was in control, and control he would always maintain. Donny smiled his devilish, slightly uncanny smile as he hit the motorway. Tonight was a night that Jenna Shearan showed her worth and Donny Anderson was ready for the downfall, whether he wanted it or not.

Chapter Twenty Nine

The room was musky, thick with the heavy scent of cigarette smoke. The lighting dim and almost barely visible as Donny swept across the room surrounded by the lingering smog. He stood proud, glancing across at the moguls that scattered the barely furnished flat. He sat in the corner, painting his face with black. The Camera was set up in the corner, a man concealing his face with a fox mask nodded subtly in his direction. The man's dark grey eyes resumed position locked on the distorted body of the unconscious, naked girl who lay completely out of it on the bare mattress that lay on the floor. The other faces around the room, Concealed with random masquerade masks and facepaint. It was quite the mad hatter's tea party. Donny placed his face palette down and lit himself a cigarette, his palms sweating profusely. His darkest fantasies were coming true before his eyes and already he could feel the swelling in his trousers as his erection bulged uncontrollably. His lips curled into a slight snarl as he saw the room filling with more men, their faces covered, and their clothes the compulsory black tuxedo. Donny stubbed out the butt of his cigarette, billowing out the last stream of grey smog before he returned to his makeup palette. He began painting stitches in heavy black liner across his lips, his eyes already panda rimmed with thick black paint. The idea was to conceal their identities so when the videos went viral no one could point them out. The masquerade masks added to the erotica, the intensity, the drama. Donny raised his eyes as another man sauntered in, his face covered with a huge Raven faced mask, the beak studded with beautiful black crystals. The eyes ruffled with dark, thick black feathers, he recognised him easily as the boss. Carrick Reynolds was into the sex game, he ran many successful brothels around the world. With a stake in the red light district in Amsterdam and a multimillion dollar Sex cellar in America from where he filmed many of his fetish videos. This however was a much darker affair. The masquerade group sex event that he had conjured up this time offered all types of sex to the man who paid the most. There was just one girl; the meat that they all lusted over. Each man took it in turns to rape the prize. No matter how brutally, nor how out of it the female was they never stopped. Each trying their hardest to outdo the other whilst being streamed live to several secret fetish websites all run by Reynolds himself. Sometimes the events could go on for over twenty four hours before they had all had their fill. High on drugs and excitement the men had paid in excess of over one hundred thousand pounds apiece just to get a slice of the pie.

Donny's gaze darted suspiciously around his dank surroundings, he felt small here, almost inferior to the men around him as his eyes continued taking in the grubbiness. The sheer filth of the hovel that these millionaires that surrounded him had chosen for their dirty little party was not lost on Donny. They saw this girl as nothing but a piece of meat, a dirty filthy little whore that was theirs for the taking. It was in every corner of the room from the peeling wallpaper that crept down the walls, the ends decayed brown with smoke. The threadbare carpet that had clearly been laid by someone who was registered blind was snagged and ripped; As though someone had gone at it with a fucking machete. The stench that came off it was musty, almost ancient. The whole room had the look of despair drawn all over it. Donny glared across the empty space, his whole face resenting the position he was left in. He hated the filthy surroundings. It wasn't normal to him. He was accustomed to his plush clubs, the overtly upmarket hotels that offered him at least a bed sheet and a blanket! Hell even Danielle's little whorehouse seemed like a palace compared to this. His lip curved into a disgusted scowl, taking mental note to wipe his feet on leaving this fine establishment. He lit himself another cigarette off the butt of the previous, his nerves would not calm. The fear of being caught, the fear if being recognised excited him equally as much as it scared the shit out of him. His torso was heavily tattooed, there was always the possibility that someone would notice his markings. His eyes caught sight of Jenna once more and his heart punched a heavy beat in his chest. She looked dead, that was the only way he could describe her. Her long legs twisted, distorted into an unfamiliar angle, her flat chest rising and falling at a shallow barely there pace. Her dark roots coming through the dirty bleach blonde dye in her hair that she had been forced into having. Her skin pastel blue in shade, it was as though she was no longer human. The blood stained dress she wore hung loosely from her exposing her, leaving her vulnerable to these monsters around her. The tattoos on her tiny wrists were the only thing that stood out to Donny most of all, the names of her babies that shone like a beacon. He gulped hard, battling the guilt. Donny could feel himself losing control of his emotions; he had never ever felt so torn in all his life. It truly was the feeling of fight or flight. He felt himself stand, his body on autopilot as he grappled with himself to just sit down and let the show go on, he couldn't. He leapt across the room in amongst the feathered faces and the flurry of jet black suits, the colours all merging into one as though time had frozen. Disorientated and euphoric he darted forward, struggling to place one foot in front of the other and hauled the dainty body from the grubby mattress. She was feather light, like picking up a doll or a small child and Donny had to suppress the urge to cry hysterically right there where he stood. Without a word nor a whisper he left, not sparing a thought for the shouts and the screams that erupted on his departure.

As he hit the cold night air Donny sucked in fresh breaths, trying his hardest to still the drumming of his heart as he made his way back to his car. He couldn't quite pace himself and almost ended up in the gutter as a result. He held on to Jenna's body tightly, clinging on for her to pull through. He didn't need a murder charge on his records. He wasn't about to let her get gang banged by a bunch of fox faced cunts either! He had been all for it at first, the whole affair had seemed classy and had been portrayed as this massive orgy. That had appealed to him, but it had become nothing more than a bunch of dirty old men playing dress up. Donny wanted no part in it. He placed Jenna into the back of the motor, unaware of his next move he just slid into the driver's seat, punching the steering wheel at his stupidity. He bit down hard on his bottom lip taking in a deep breath he exhaled, the magic of it all smashing around him in glorious particles. The proverbial salt being rubbed deeply into the flesh wound that was this crazy scenario. Donny sat back, his lip quivering profusely as the salty fat tears began to roll down his cheeks. As cunning and as hard faced as he appeared, Jenna Shearan had captured a spot of his cold heart and he had melted. He felt pity for her, nothing more than that. He had made her do things that he wouldn't ever dream of doing to any other woman, he had taken her to the brink and back again with catastrophic force and this was outcome. He had a fully grown woman with the body of a child laid smacked out of her face on his back seat. He leant over and looked at her, she was crumpled, her face was free of any pore or imperfection, and she was still beautiful even if she was drugged up to the nines. She looked at peace now, her whole face calmed with sleep, she looked rested. He knew beneath those closed lids was a woman whose soul had long abandoned her. All hope had been lost, but as she lay now, she looked like Jenna. The girl who had so famously stole his heart despite him being a married man. He had fallen for her hook line and sinker as had every man who crossed her wicked path. But Donny had pushed her to her limits and here she was his little wounded flower all battered and bruised from the neck down but still she remained the same. Her face always seemed so polished, even when she was off her nut on coke she seemed so flawless. Donny loved how beautiful she was, he could manipulate her in ways that the other whores would never dream of allowing. She was innocent; the game was nothing to Jenna, She was a concrete angel. She felt nothing; her whole body had completely shut down. She knew nothing of the life that Donny had pulled her into and he would be damned if she escaped his clutches just yet, as he took the motorway back to Danielle's he found a weird, twisted little smile had merged on his face, who needed to share when he could have the main prize all to himself. Donny turned up the radio, the sound of an unfamiliar DJ filling his ears. The music melodic and serene as he sped along the rain splattered road at seventy, his windscreen wipers swishing back and forth at rapid speed, his eyes fixed on the tarmac as he pondered what his next move was. He had no idea what he was going to do or say, but he would be keeping a closer eye on Jenna after this. He could feel her slipping away from him, he could feel her precious bubbly personality slipping from her with each and every pump of her aching heart. Donny knew one more incident like this and she would be gone. He wouldn't give her the smack again, he didn't want her becoming reliant on the stuff. Coke seemed to fetch her back a bit. He found himself reasoning with the idea. If he kept her on the sniff then her addiction was mental. It could be easily reversed. Smack was a different kettle of fish altogether. He didn't want her to become some desperate smack rat who would sell her Grannies fanny for just a line of the black magic. She meant more to him than that, the fact scared Donny. He had a wife he shouldn't have these feelings for any other woman than her, but Jenna Shearan had surprised him. He had been in the whoring game since the age of nineteen, the baby faced villain, and every girl had swooned without question to his feet. He had made million off his girls but he would give it all up tomorrow if he thought for an instant that Jenna would actually want him. Ever since she had arrived at his winter ball with Craig Carter hung on her arm, her smile like poison, lips flushed with deep scarlet paint he had wanted her, needed her to fulfil him completely. She had become his obsession and as long as he was forcing himself inside her, forcing her to sleep with whatever Tom Dick and Harry he could line up for her, Then she was his. Hook line and bastard sinker she belonged to him, whether she wanted it or not. And as long as Donny had that control then he was happy. As he cut away from the motorway back to the familiar pull of the side streets he loved the most he smiled humbly. She had survived another night.... Barely.

Chapter Thirty

Jenna slipped away from the bed, her naked body encased in nothing more than a cotton sheet as she tip toed quietly along the tiles to the bathroom, her feet padding the surface gently scared to wake him from his slumber. She entered the plush bathroom, turning on the shower she stood in front of the full length mirror shamefully. Her bones highlighted by the bright neon lights that were pinpointed around the ceiling. She felt dirty, unwashed, whipped in the potent scent of sex and alcohol. She stood under the heavy spray of warmed water and welcomed the feeling of cleanliness it instantly gave her. Shaking her heavy head beneath the jets of water she gathered her thoughts. Trying to piece together the nights events with no avail. Tragically her memory had all but abandoned her, but she felt good. That was a bonus, she didn't feel so negative about herself. Donny had stopped feeding her cocaine and where the first few days had made her feel like she may as well be dead, the comedown had been horrific. She had bit each and every one of her finely polished nails to the quick, soaking in the feeling of being even headed. She now felt like facing the day was becoming easier. She didn't like to dwell on the negatives and the last seven days had proven that if she could beat begging Donny for "one more line!" and pleading with him to "help her" then she could overcome anything. He had taken her back to Danielle's initially, Jenna didn't remember much, the whole memory was distorted but what she did remember was the fight, Danielle had battered her. Her whole body had ached so severely from heroin and meaty fists that she had almost succumb to death. Kristian, her little guardian angel had arrived to take her away, she remembered him screaming at Danielle. The memory was short; nothing else came back to her head. But she remembered the bruises, the thick welts that still adorned her face. She remembered Danielle, her face distorted, screwed up like a hyena as she flew toward Jenna. For what reason Jenna was still unsure but the woman had literally pounded seven bells of shit out of her that night. The black eyes were only now fading but in all honesty Jenna felt like she had deserved it somehow. She knew Danielle was hooked on Kristian, Jenna sleeping with him had obviously come as a shock to her and the poor woman had caught a case of the green eyed monster. But ever the optimist Jenna had moved on, her recovery overnight had been effortless and within the twenty four hours that had followed she had taken pride of place in Donny's bed at his stunning Mansion just out of town. She knew it wasn't the home he shared with his wife but it was the next best thing. Jenna loved it here, even thought she had to pretend to be the housemaid whenever Donny's wife decided to pop by. But she was fine with it; she would do whatever he asked not to be back out on the streets again. The house itself was worth millions, a full red brick affair with a trellis to one side. Fully serviced Gardens surrounded by acres and acres of Greenery. It was simplistic, rustic and stunning all at once. In their time together they had become quite the Bonnie and Clyde, he took her to swanky bars and clubs, drinking till the early hours and tumbling beneath the sheets till early morning. It was rewarding as much as it was poker faced. Jenna relished in his company, he had become all consuming. He couldn't apologise enough for his previous actions, he had smothered her in luxurious expensive gifts that accumulated bills of well in excess of £100,000 just to say sorry for all he had done. Although Jenna couldn't help but feel the victory would be short lived she was enjoying the freedom and the thrills while they lasted. She sat out on the decking, the glorious sun bathing her tiny body in a delicious glow as she soaked in the afternoon sun. The sound of Taylor Swift hummed from the radio indoors, she had a cool crisp glass of white wine in one hand, a Mills and Boon novel in the other. A pair of black Ray Bans concealing her eyes from the glare, it was heaven. She felt content, for the first time in months the smog was finally beginning to clear. She sensed she may as well play the game as long as she was in Donny's good books then she wasn't in danger.

A while later Donny stepped out from the patio doors, his overgrown hair glistening wet from the shower. He strode over to her with just a towel covering his lower half, his muscular tanned chest beaded with droplets water. He lit a cigarette and swiftly lay on the sun lounger beside her, bending his knees up towards his chest; the towel rode up his thighs deliciously, tempting, teasing Jenna into submission. She slid her sunglasses down the bridge of her nose, her lips curving into a seductive pout as she leered at his perfect physical form. She tilted the wine glass to her full lips, taking a long sip, the taste of the wine bitter-sweet on her palate. Her eyes not leaving her master for a second, she watching inquisitively as he popped the seal on his can of lager, the movement reminded her momentarily of Craig and his beloved Stella. She swallowed the thought instantaneously, pushed Craig Carter straight to the back of her mind. She smiled alluringly at Donny, her face strikingly beautiful, her piercing green eyes framed bewitchingly by the heavy jet black false lashes she wore that fanned out over the dark kohl eyeliner that traced her eyelids. She fluttered her eyes at him, biting down hard on her bottom as she took in the rise and fall of his handsome chest. The sun bouncing off his perfectly jewelled skin, the water from his shower mixing sweetly with his fresh perspiration. He truly was a marvel to look at. He took another deep drink from his can, taking in the breathtaking views before them. The miles of luscious greenery that belonged solely to him. There was no talk between them, they just lavished in one another's solace, both compelled and star struck at the beauty of this place. She wondered every moment of the day though what it had been that had made Donny change his tune so drastically. She was convinced he was playing a game of sorts, trying to fuck her head up further; she was scared of him, scared of his overactive mind. He could have her trussed up and back selling herself for cocaine at a click of his fingers and that was what stopped Jenna from developing any kind of emotional bond with the man beside her. Sex was sex, that was a given and it was a necessity if she were to survive. She stood, wobbling slightly in her heels as the wine shot straight to her head, she allowed her fingers to skim her flat stomach as she stretched out languidly, her body bending to the seductive rhythm of the song that came echoing from the conservatory. The soft bouncy melody of some DJ singing about firing a gun filled her senses and she came alive, her whole body responding as she flung her hair over her shoulders, The bleached blonde locks now dyed a stunning plum tone, the purple hues picked up significantly in the sunlight. Jenna knew Donny had noticed her despite his face still being shielded by the newspaper that he was engrossed in. she started swaying her hips to the music, her arms above her head as she got lost in the tune, she felt free, if only for a moment. These were the times she treasured, when she could just become herself again. Her head bounced as she continued to sway in time to the music, the scent of wine playing beautifully on her tongue, the fuzzy feeling of alcohol taking its effect, cradling her like a babe in a new cotton blanket. She was at one with herself, the feeling was amazing. Despite her longing to be home, with the people who she knew so well, in her pokey little flat on the Belmonte, she had to admit that these were the days where she felt she could cope, she could move on with her fast paced life. She had been dealt nothing but the joker card for so long she felt as though she should take this welcomed break and enjoy the happy moments that were few and far between. She laid herself next to Donny on his sun lounger, feeling the warmth of his skin melt against hers, he truly was exquisite. He placed his paper beside him on the over varnished decking, he placed his arm around her, his arm resting slightly against her jutting hipbone. His fingers stroking her pale skin, bowing over her bones, he winced, guiltily drawing back. She rose her hips to his touch once more, Her skin still bruised from the numerous assaults she had suffered and Donny found himself scared to touch her, he swallowed hard, his thin pianist fingers skimming against a deep purple welt that plastered her thigh. He imagined her in his mind's eye being tied and gagged by the monster who had abused her like this; his heart strained knowing he had placed her there. He had never felt guilt like this in his life. He had over sixty girls working for him, under his spell like moths to the flame but none had ever taken a hold of him like Jenna Shearan had. She was simply fascinating. All of his other girls ran the streets because they had an addiction of sorts to feed. But Jenna, she had done it all on the fact alone that he scared her. To Donny that was a potent cocktail and he was drunk off of the girl's heady allure. She was a beautiful, crazy creature was Jenna. Set on fulfilling his every single desire and Donny respected her no end as much as he never showed it. He kissed her cheek briefly, his breath contorting briefly as he touched her petal soft skin. She turned into him, her soft lips puckering into his, his tongue exploring her mouth deeply as he returned her agonisingly strong kiss. His hand travelling the apex of her thighs without him barely recognising she truly was a delight to behold. He cupped her ample breast with his skilled fingers, the feeling of her delicious pink nipples hardening beneath her bikini top enticing him to explore her further. He felt her chest tense as he ran his hand along her washboard stomach, her dazzling white skin puckering into magnificent goose bumps beneath his touch. His expert fingers lingering on her skin as he snatched his hand away, his kiss deepening as his hands found her hair; he pulled gently forcing her to moan gently against his lips. He pulled her body against him so she was almost straddling his hips, he felt her sweet arousal as she brushed against his swelling erection. Her body wanting him, he could feel it, he was almost swimming in her wetness as she cocked her leg across him, his penis digging politely into the apex of her thighs, his wanting of her never more apparent than it was in that moment. She dug her fingers into his cheeks as she pulled him into her, her kiss deepening, imploring his mouth with desperation. Her long dark hair tumbling down her thin back as she tilted her head in ecstasy, Donny set about smothering her neck with soft kisses as he researched her body. His fingers imploring her, the soft subtle pull of her ivory skin dimpling as his agile fingers imprinted her skin. She sucked in an anxious breath as the towel that concealed Donny's bulging erection fell to the floor and he became completely exposed to her. The smile on her full lips was undeniable as she hovered over him, her supple skin inches from his as his eyes found hers. He looked bewildered, like a deer in the proverbial headlights. She dipped her hips expertly and Donny sank into her, his bulging erection filling her, she was wet to the touch, so wanting of him and he hummed in sweet anticipation as she began her merciless assault. Bouncing so expertly on his cock as his hands traced her jutting spine, his eyes locked so dumbfounded on hers as she rose and fell onto him, her pert ass springing deliciously in rhythm to the music that still played behind them. Donny was left to drown in his hazy stupor as he relaxed into the comfort of the sun lounger, watching intently as the beautiful vixen before him relished in her duties. She moaned deeply, an overwhelming sexy sound that echoed, reverberating around the stillness that surrounded them. Her moan was incredibly alluring and Donny was captivated. He continued to survey her body greedily, his eyes taking on more than they could handle as his hands felt every inch of her skin puckering beneath his touch. She truly was a beautiful sight as she rode him like a fine jockey. She tipped her head back, her long slender neck bowed straight, her mouth slack, the flirtatious red she wore on her lips slightly smudged from their kiss. Donny could feel her tightening around him and he knew it wouldn't be long before she came hard on him. He pushed his hips up to greet hers as they found the perfect rhythm she clenched his knees for support, her nails biting his flesh as she moaned loudly into the stifling hot air. Donny drove into her a few thrusts more before they both exploded into orgasm, Jenna shuddered on top of him as he poured himself into her, her lips shaped into the perfect "o" as she spiralled back to normality, panting deliciously as she fell on top of his naked chest. Donny pulled his arm around her naked back and caressed her tight pale skin. Their breathing regulated finally, his chest resting as she listened contentedly to the thundering of his erratic heartbeat. She smiled, swiping away the smudged lipstick from her mouth as Donny planted a swift kiss onto her temple. He tilted her chin so that they're eyes met, glazed with lust and affection each of them glancing for long moments, not a word said between them. Jenna's lip started to quiver and Donny swiped at a tear that spilled from her eye.

"I'm so sorry Jen. I'm so fucking sorry" he repeated it over and over like a mantra as he huddled her close to him. He meant it, for now. He had become attached despite trying his hardest to keep her at arm's length. Despite trying his hardest put her to work the streets, her resilience had stunned him. It had attracted him to her even more. She was a rarity a complete Jewel and momentarily Donny was completely bewitched by her. She had been to the depths, through the roughest, dirtiest ordeal and here she was like a phoenix from the ashes a beautiful, remarkable young woman. Donny was saddened and ashamed by his actions but of course business was business and Jenna Shearan had at a time been a means to an end. But his feelings for her had changed, blossomed somewhat and now he was besotted, head over heels in lust of the girl he had used, abused and branded with the name prostitute for the rest of her life. But He cared; he wanted her to know that despite everything, he had never stopped caring for her. He puckered his lips and kissed her faintly on the mouth, she smiled warmly in response. Her teeth chattering slightly as the breeze hit her bare skin, another prickle of Goosebumps flurried across her back. Donny sat up, shifting her slightly on his dead thighs before asking her whether they should head indoors. Jenna nodded as she uncurled herself away from Donny and his warm arms. She stood confidently, her lithe polished body turning on heel and sauntering away from him, her pert naked ass bouncing delightfully with each over powering stride she took. Yes she was a beautiful, intriguing creature was Jenna Shearan and Donny was going to crack her, whatever the cost.

Chapter Thirty One

Sandra Anderson awoke with a start. She wondered briefly if she had been dreaming. She glanced at the bedside clock. Two thirty in the bastard morning? She hesitated as she heard shuffling downstairs; she turned over to find the empty space beside her. She assumed immediately that it had been Donny who was making the ruckus downstairs. She would fucking murder Donny when he finally graced her with his presence. This had been happening a lot lately. Donny would go out dressed to kill, the scent of his icy, Jean Paul Gaultier cologne lingering in her home like a bad habit. She shot up, hair rollers flailing in her bleached blonde hair as she fumbled about in the darkness trying to find her phone. She tumbled out of bed, keeping her ears on high alert as she followed the dim glow from her mobile. She stalked across the room, her heart beating a tattoo in her chest as she tugged on her plush silk dressing robe. She tried her hardest not to make a single sound as she fleeted across the room. Her back stilled against the white panel door the solid gold cast door knob digging forcefully into her back. Her ears pricked against the wood as she tried her hardest to try and dissect what was going on down the stairs. She heard giggling, at least she thought she did as she pinned herself closer to the door. She tried her hardest to decipher whether Donny was alone or in company, failing obliviously. She heard muttering, a woman's laughter, high pitched and filled with alcohol before the silence. Strange; she thought. Sandra held her ear close to the wood, her attempts pointless as she heard the back door shut once more and the screech of the tyres of Donny's car as he sped away, leaving her, undecided, hanging virtually abandoned by her own husband and his slut. She had sensed it for a while, the late nights, and the scent of sex lingering on his clothes, the faint floral perfume of a girl on his tuxedo jacket. She had fought the urge to stab him over his infidelity on numerous occasions but now, he had bought the fucking cunt into her home.

To say she was livid was an understatement. She stalked towards her bedside cupboard; taking out the scissors from her drawer she sauntered over to Donny's walk in wardrobe, the cunt would feel her hurt this time. As she plunged into his Gucci suits, her mouth wide screaming bitterly as she sliced away at the expensive fabric. She was something completely catastrophic. Her voice cutting through the silence as she resembled something of a banshees standards. She would find the despicable bitch who had done this to her, and when she did she would rip the fuckers head off and feed it to the slut raw. She was inconsolable, beyond words as she slumped against the pile of mottled greys and blacks, the fabric soft against her skin, her patience wearing bald as she stifled her screams with the flats of her palms. She was seething, frenzied almost rabid as she trashed the bedroom she shared so frequently with her new husband. He had cut her so deep her blood ran cold. The bad blood sizzling, boiling in her veins as she fought viciously against her own emotions. She stormed down the stairs, the dressing gown she wore fanning out over the opulent black carpet as she traced each step. Her carpet slippers clunking against each step as she thundered downstairs, she ran her fingers through her pigmented blonde mane as she cursed, swore angrily at the nothing before her. The darkness absorbing her, the only light coming from the shallow, dimly lit outdoor lighting. The whole house was plunged into the murkiness of the receding light. Something that Sandra had never noticed before. It made her home feel alien. It wasn't a thought Sandra relished to say the least. She felt inferior, almost unknown. Donny had been her life for so long, he had kept her sane, kept her in the fine and ignorant lifestyle she had become accustom. This diversion, this piece of skirt he had been chasing offered him nothing. Nothing she couldn't give anyway. She was incensed, her body shaking from the indignation that burned deep in her veins. This was torture, illicit, sweet persecution and Sandra could feel every last drop as it rained down over her. She was beyond control, a caged feral animal as she charged across the gravel driveway to Donny's beloved Jaguar; she leaped onto the bonnet like something possessed driving her foot into the glass windshield. Screaming with carnivorous rage as the glass erupted into a million tiny shards beneath her strong pounding foot. Her senses on high alert as she saw the blood splatter from her wounded leg, she leapt down from the car, collapsing into a heap on the gravel as she cried a million tears for the love of her life who had scorned her so blatantly. He was her husband, the love of her life and now he was gone. She could never ever forgive him for bringing one of his sluts back to their home. She looked down at her leg momentarily, instantly wishing she hadn't, the mass of splintered bone and messy flesh that painted her driveway was enough to make her pass out there on the spot. As she bled dry onto the concrete, the life draining from her Sandra had one final thought in her head.

Revenge.

Chapter Thirty Two

Craig Carter was miffed somewhat as he sat out in the garden with Kiki. They had been playing tea parties for well over an hour and he was beginning to get bored. He took a long glug from his beer as he sang "I'm a little Teapot" in the flattest voice he could muster to vindicate his boredom. He stopped midflow and stared sadly into the solemn eyes of his baby daughter and felt the same pang of guilt he always felt when he paid attention to her. She was the double of her mother; age had made her a pintsize Jenna.

"Don't you want to play anymore daddy?" she whispered sweetly, her gorgeous singsong voice like balm to Craig's ears. She truly was an angel and he was blessed with her despite his ignorance towards her of late. He found it hard to bond with Kiki without grieving Jenna, he found it hard to look at the love of his life just as she had been when they first met one another. Kiki was Jenna down to the glossy hair and her sassy attitude and Craig loved her as much as he envied her. He hated how torn he had become but his daughter scared him beyond words. He had never loved another like he loved Kiki, apart from Jenna and he knew as much as he would go to the end of the earth for this little Madame, she was too much like Jenna for him to be able to move on.

"It's not that babe, Daddy's just thinking about mummy that's all" he replied honestly, he didn't know what else to say or how else to explain how he felt. Kiki looked up at him, her face ashen, saddened again by the mention of her mother. As little as she was Kiki had been graced with old shoulders and it was in one way a blessing in another it was a curse. She felt the pain of losing her mother as though she was a teenager, not a babe and Craig felt stricken as he took the little girl into his arms and huddled her close. The smell of his baby girl flooded his nostrils as she cuddled into him. To her Craig was her hero, her Daddy who would always protect her. But she missed her mummy terribly and Craig swallowed down the overwhelming emotion that filled him as Kiki laid her tiny head on his chest.

"Don't worry Daddy, I won't leave you like mummy did" she whispered in her tiny little singsong voice, her chubby little arm snaking preciously around Craig's burly neck. It was that tiny little observation, from his tiny little girl that was his undoing and he cried so hard he thought he would never stop. He held her so tightly, so lovingly as he repeated "I know baby, I Know" against her baby soft, mass of hair. The tears rolled down his cheeks as he revelled in the innocence of his baby. The daughter he shared with the woman he loved singularly more than anything else on the planet. Jenna had been his one true love, his one and only solace and despite him having no knowledge of her whereabouts he had a feeling, a hunch so to speak that she was close. As his crying subsided, he swiped the back of his shirt sleeves across his cheeks as he heard his Nanny Leah calling them in for supper from the patio doors. Craig nodded in reply and stood, stumbling slightly as he held Kiki still in his arms. The dusk was setting in and the sky sang with colour. The pinks and burnt oranges blending to make a spectacular show, Craig sucked in a harsh and baited breath as he wondered what the future was to hold for him and his little family. He knew that he was missing the most important piece and that feeling wasn't going to be complete until her return. As he looked up into the dusky sky he prayed to God for a miracle, he prayed to God to show him a sign. Little did he know that it wouldn't be long before he got his prayers answered.

Chapter Thirty Three

Jenna stood in the full length mirror. The sound of Darren Styles flittering in the background her hands skimming her slim thighs delicately as she rubbed in the dark mousse fake tan, prying her eyes away from her bruised body she swallowed hard. Her game face on as her glance fell back to Donny who was fast asleep in the glamorous four poster bed, the sheets dipped across his lean muscles, his deeply rippled abdomen on show. She wanted to slice open his throat there and then as his pulse bopped around in his neck. His strong muscular jaw relaxed with sleep, he looked almost human as he dreamt wildly. His lip quivering slightly, Jenna sighed; he was perfect in every way. Despite the fact that he was a hardened criminal mastermind, his allure was simply pulling. She found herself falling for him almost instantly. She flicked her long tumbling curls over her shoulder as she worked on her other leg, attempting to hide the bruises that Donny's previous customers had left littering her ivory skin. She shuddered at the thought. So Many strange men had lingered on her, her skin poisoned by their touch, the smell of their arousal still so heavy on her. She felt bitter, used and in a way, she felt deserving of it. She had been a terrible mother to her children; she had been nothing but a disappointment. She had lost her daughter and in turn she had lost her beautiful baby boy. She has missed so much in their development, Archie's first word, his first smile, his first steps. She swallowed hard once more, she couldn't think of them, not now. She would break if she did. They were all that kept her sane. The thought of them filled her with such joy that she could burst at the seams. She swiped away at the tears that filled her heavy lined eyes. The kohl running slightly, then the thought of Craig invaded her, his kiss still so fragrant on her lips, his touch still so fresh on her skin. She exhaled, blocking out the handsome face that absorbed her thoughts. Craig was forbidden territory, Donny had made the point exceptionally clear to her multiple times. She closed her eyes tightly relishing in her over fond memories of the man she loved so much. Craig was still her world, despite the catastrophic twist of fate she had been dealt, Craig was her reason for breathing. He held her world so high even without his presence in the physical form he had kept Jenna in a normal state of mind. Each lonely night she had spent with some random had been defused by the memory of Craig Carter. Each time she had been forced to collide sexually with a man, he had been her solace, the thought of him taking her through. As long as she closed her eyes and thought of him hard enough, he was there. His delicious smile revving her to go on, to continue, she knew in her heart of hearts her would disapprove. He would hate her for what she had done; He would see it as a moment of weakness. She had seen how he had reacted when he had found out the paternity of her son. Craig had been devastated, He had seen Archie being born, and he had cradled him, sang to him and loved him as his own. It had been the fact that Archie was Dom's child that had torn their prefect world down and now Jenna found herself living on what ifs. She had been going through the motions for months. She wondered whether Craig still thought about her as often as she did him. Her thoughts so vivid, so trusting, she smiled again but it was sadder, melancholy as she wondered how long the hurt would last. He was everything. He was nothing but her life. Craig had been her entirety for years and now she was faced with the idea that Craig would finally be his own person, she shuddered. Craig had never been on his own. Jenna lay back against the covers, her head all over the place as she contemplated a life without her beloved Mr Carter. She closed her eyes and saw nothing but his piercing blue eyes, cornflower blue, so enticing alluring her out of her mind. His soft baby smooth skin, the delicious dimples in his cheeks that made him look every inch the charmer. He was such a striking man to look at, almost flawless. His skin perfect, stubble free, contoured perfectly with his high cheekbones and strong jaw line he was just a completely bewitching creature. Jenna laid her arm across her face, contemplating every single scenario that was running through her head. She was upset to say the least. Craig was everything to her. She loved him with such affliction, such necessity. He was her better half, without question. She smiled as his face flooded her thoughts, his perfect smile glistening at her, she suppressed the urge to grasp out into the nothing before her and plunge him from her dreams. She stood once more, her glorious naked body glowing in the morning sun, beautiful beyond words she hummed along to the song that played faintly in the background. She sauntered around the vast bedroom floor, swaying her head to the bouncy rhythm; music was her sanctuary she could truly lose herself within her favourite records. Although Donny had banned Ke$ha because he thought it reminded Jenna too much of Craig. She spun around in tune to the music and came practically nose to nose with Donny. She was stopped immediately in her tracks, her breath catching in her throat as she surveyed the tiredness and the disdain in his face, the face she loathed so much, yet was attracted to none the less. Her lips parted slightly as she smiled at him, embarrassment in her hollow eyes highlighted so perfectly.

"Morning" she whispered subtly, batting her eyelids as she felt her cheeks flush scarlet. Donny smirked, his eyes wide with amusement as his fingers stroked her cheek she felt her skin puckering beneath his touch, his fingers stretching into her long thick mane of hair, each tendril slipping through his fingers, he pulled her close and kissed her temples. He looked so fresh from bed, his hair slightly resembling a crazed lunatic, his eyes heavy from sleep but he was a marvel. She pouted her lips seductively as he planted a chaste kiss on them, she swayed beneath his touch. He was mesmerising, despite everything that he had made her do, she admired him somewhat he was a man with power, by his own admission he was a man who over indulged in desire. The art of making women bow down to him was his forte. Jenna gulped hard as he kissed her once more. Taking her breath away as his sickly sweet morning breath drifted across her lips. His hand traipsed across her naked flesh, his fingers searching her skin, her milky completion melting beneath his touch as he fondled her objectively.

"You, look, so beautiful," he whispered breathlessly, his mouth at her ear lobe as he spoke. He was captivated her naked body on show like an art exhibition just for him. She sucked in a baited breath as his lips traced her swan like neck, every inch of her skin tingling with his touch. He pulled her around to his sensuous embrace, his fingers tracing the small dips in her naked back. She moaned softly against his lips, making a wicked smile burst suddenly across his mouth as the sultry sound of Skylar Grey filled the space between them. Her beautifully haunting voice mesmerising them, lost deep in their lust as they stared at one another, drowning in each other's hard wild glare.

"I can take you to so many places, Show you so many things" Donny whispered, his hand still riding up her naked back, the thin sheen of sweat on her skin allowing his fingers to glide across her effortlessly.

"I'll give you anything you wish" he smirked as her teeth skimmed her bottom lip, she was anxious, he could feel it. She nodded, thinking his words over, her eyes hazy, fluttering beneath dark inquisitive lashes. Her eyebrow arched as she stepped closer, catching Donny's lips with a swift kiss before she met his earlobe.

"If you meant that statement Donny, you would release me" She pleaded. Her voice breaking slightly, higher pitched than normal. She caressed his cheek lightly, her eyes full of wanting hope. Maybe now he would finally understand that as much as she enjoyed sleeping with him, enjoyed his company, she didn't want him. Not as a boyfriend anyway. He was silent, not a word nor an audible breath escaping his mouth. He was thinking over her proposition and Jenna could see the hurt sneaking across his face. He was wounded by her admission she could see that much.

"Don, Look" she whispered, her hand skimming his cheek once more. He snapped back, his lips opening briefly in disdain. Displeasure leaking from every single pore as he looked at her as though she had grown two heads.

"Don't Jen" He whispered vehemently, spinning on his heel as he sauntered toward his office, leaving her standing there in all of her naked splendour. Her breath literally plummeted from her chest as she sat down on the edge of the bed. Her heart thumping in her chest, cardiac arrest imminent as she flustered, and her eyes locked on the door still ajar. Donny's scent contaminated every single inch of the room, suffocating her yet intoxicating her at the very same time. He would be perfect if he wasn't so self absorbed in the world of forced prostitution and drugs. She huddled close to the comforter, swallowing back the tears, Skylar Grey still singing sweetly as Jenna tried her hardest to contain her strained emotions. She heard Donny screaming from the office and she shot from the bed, tugging on his T-shirt from the crumpled heap on the floor she left to find him. She stumbled from the room; she caught the glimpse of him as he stood in the hallway. Vulnerable needing eyes peeking from between his eyes.

"Don!" she cried, running toward him, scooping him into her embrace. Soothing him, her fingers deep in his hair as she tried to spur an answer from him. Her eyes seeking his, as she met his gaze.

"She's dead, she's fucking dead!" he sobbed between baited breaths. Jenna clutched him tighter to her breast. Clinging to his sagging shoulders as he cried out his pain. She ushered him towards the bedroom, setting him seated on the bed, she knelt before him. Her palms flat on his thighs as she tried her hardest to consolidate her with her words. He inhaled deeply, finally spiralling downwards from his euphoric high; he held his hands solid on Jenna's shoulders, looking around the room as though everything was alien to him. Like a child Jenna held him close to her breast, hushing away his anxiety until he was paled, staring blankly into the vast space before him. His expression sullen, almost unrecognisable as he just stared into the nothingness, he was sad. There was no denying that. But beyond the sadness Jenna could make out another emotion, relief almost. She didn't want to say it aloud in case she was wrong but she guessed that the loss was nothing more than a convenience to Donny. She laid a kiss on his brow out of respect and left him to grieve. Not fully engaging with her efforts as she caught one last glimpse of his cold calculating stare. She wanted out now; there was nothing more to say. She paced the dense carpet floor, clutching to the banister as she made her way down the spiralling staircase, everything suddenly a foreign object as her face finally fell against the dark oak of the front door. Her head electrifyingly close to exploding. She couldn't think straight, her head pounding viciously to the beat of its own drum, she was scared, scared of how things were going to go. She knew that Donny's wife was out of the picture he would be even more brutal toward her. She could sense the imminent change already but as she paced the lawn, her naked feet between the grass she couldn't force herself to leave him. Morally it didn't feel right. She turned on her heel, each and every sense in her body telling her to turn around and run as fast as she could into the distance, but her heart, the vicious cruel beast that it was plagued her to stay. She looked back at the gates, demoralised, afraid, uncertain and alone. She was confused as to how far this could go if she stayed, Donny had already taken her to the brink and she had survived. She knew going back to him was for the best and so she made her way back inside, her cheeks a little pinker, her heart a little heavier. But she couldn't leave him now, could she? She felt the grass sinking inbetween her toes one last time. She sucked in the fresh air as she catapulted herself back into a life of uncertainty, her hesitant breath shallow as she pulled open the heavy wooden door. The opulent smell of money and expense was not lost on her as she entered the grand hallway. The familiarity of the place lost and she felt almost strange in her surroundings. She clambered back up the stairs, each step heavier than the last, she felt almost giddy as she reached the top stair, the net finally closing in on her as she pulled open the bedroom door.

Donny sat on the edge of the bed his head in his hands, stifled sobs escaping his mouth in pools of breathlessness, his whole body shaking clearly before Jenna's eyes, the sound of some slow Rihanna track humming in the background. Jenna crept toward him, her pale legs quivering beneath her; she knew she was doing right by being here, she stood before him, kneeling at his feet as a good girl would, stroking his tear stained cheek with her ice cold fingers. His head turned into her touch, comforting her as she realised he wasn't angry.

"You didn't run? He whispered softly against her palms, his red rimmed eyes locked on hers as a sad smile crept across his mouth. He was stunning when he was vulnerable, a complete God. Jenna ran her fingers across his lip, slightly grazing his piercing, his lips trembling as she touched his over enhanced cupids bow, he was beautiful in his timidity and Jenna was blown away by him. He was such an enigma, in one sense he was dangerous, sworn to be avoided, in the next he was placid and loving, she was drunk on his questionability. He truly was a marvel as he sat before her now, breathless and tearful; his eyes rimmed red from tears. He was handsome, his features soft, still carrying the cunning shine in his eyes but he was still flawless. He was nothing but serene. Jenna gazed intently into his aching eyes, full of devotion for the dangerous soul at her mercy. She was breathless as his thumb skimmed her cheek.

"I'm not your enemy Jen, I never meant for any of this" He whispered, his voice solemn, his palms open in front of her signalling his contempt. His face was dead almost with guilt. She choked slightly as his words hit her ear drums with brute force. Her lip creased into a sad smile. The electricity between them completely disarming, so wrong but it felt so perfect all at the same time. Donny was a charmer, a complete enigma and Jenna was in awe of him. She sat upon her knees and pulled him close, the feel of muscular frame on hers was a comfort. Her cheeks flushed as she felt him pull her tighter, his need for her was soothing and Jenna welcomed it completely. She had to stay with him now, if only for a few days for the sake of his sanity. She promised herself that tomorrow she would be gone. Resigned to that fact she returned Donny's embrace, the vixen like glare in her eye not quite matching the sadness that hung like a dead weight in her heavy heart. Her doe eyes wide, the ducts full to swelling as she once more put Craig's face back to her memory.

Chapter Thirty Four

Jenna sat in the bathroom, her robe tugged tightly around her as she wished the child she was so imminently carrying to come away from her, a miscarriage had never been on her list of things to achieve but she felt nothing but serenity washing over as she realised that whatever happened the child would NOT be born, would not know how treacherous life could be. It had no father, no prospects and now it had a mother who wished it dead. As she felt the inevitable cramping and the jolts of pain that followed, she could do nothing but beam with glory. She chalked up another score on The Donny Anderson chalkboard and gave herself a moment's light relief. She was amazed, sick with apprehension of the vile secret she had just lost ever being brought to life. It was a relief for her body to be finally freed of it, no matter what the child would never have been loved. She had not one maternal bone left in her body. Seeing them made her weak, sad even and she couldn't be sad. Her body devoid now of any emotion wouldn't allow it. She swallowed hard, giving her the good grace to say goodbye as she felt the animal within her slip away. Not a moment's pity was shed, not a single ounce of love lost. Jenna stood and quickly flushed away the evidence, taking her small pocket mirror from the shelf she lined herself up a small pick me up before snorting up the white powder from the surface in one without a second thought. She was emotionless, thoughtless and in the wrong frame of mind for any of this shit. She stumbled away from the toilet bowl, feeling a moments triumph as she head out of the bathroom, her mind clear as the day, she flounced back to the bedroom trying her hardest to forget the cramping that continued to knot her stomach, it was gone, Finally there was no baby.

She headed to the shower, her face sticky with sweat from the pressure of pushing out the lifeless blob that now lay vacant in a drain somewhere, Jenna snorted at the thought, the coke making her feel ten feet tall, disorientated somewhat. Donny was being difficult; He was still in shock mode, what with his wife deciding to bleed to death all over their precision cut lawn because she had guessed he was shagging someone else. Jenna had to hold back her hysteria, the woman he was shagging being her of course. She thought of poor old bleached blonde bleeding away on the driveway; it was highly amusing to Jenna in her opulent state of despondency, doped up on the coke Donny had been force feeding her for the duration of his heartache. Jenna was sick and tired of him. He had become overnight a petulant child. He did nothing but cry; over and over again he repeated his memoirs like a mantra. All in all she had heard his wedding day speech at least fifteen times, the night they had met a dozen and if she was physically honest talk of Sandra was turning her sick. He didn't seem interested in occupying her and Jenna instantly was thrown off guard. He had played to her fiddle so far but now, it seemed as though he was trying to force her to leave. The constant talk of his ex and their hedonic love life was something Jenna could not sit physically through anymore. She sauntered past the Ensuite and down into the kitchen,

Donny sat at his laptop tapping away at random keys, emails from what Jenna could make of them. She sat at the breakfast bar, stifling a sob as another vicious stab of pain injected into her stomach, she gasped strenuously as she took a seat. Her face contorted into disarray. She plunged helplessly between pain and acceptance as Donny lunged at her. His fingers sinking into her supple skin as he kissed her hard on the mouth. Her breath literally billowed out of her lungs as he pulled away from her. Jenna coughed, stunned at his affections, confused as he leapt back toward the cooker. His nervousness killed her stone dead. She speculated from her seat, puzzled at his opulent gesture of affection. She continued to stare at him, bypassing his tremendous athletic frame, seeing nothing but deep into his soul. Longing for him to get back to his normal self, she prayed silently as he played around with whatever it was he had on the stove. His actions contrite with nervousness she knew him, really? He was a riddle of a man and Jenna, despite how much she tried couldn't crack him. He smiled a full over enthusiastic smile at her before setting two plates on the counter top. His eyes dancing with the same old tune as they always did when he was flying from the coke. A potent mixture of grief and lust ever apparent in his over enthusiastic eyes as he toyed with whatever it was he had bubbling away on the stove. Jenna fidgeted on the stool, her agitation uncontainable as Donny flashed her, his brightest grin as he plated up their meal. The thought of eating bought Jenna to a standstill, the bile rising high in her throat as she swallowed down the urge to vomit. She shuffled away her nausea, looking vacantly into space. Donny plated up and pushed two steaming plates of Eggs Benedict and fresh asparagus onto the counter top. Jenna took the plate graciously as Donny sat opposite her. He shovelled the first few forkfuls of his breakfast into his mouth before setting his cutlery down either side of his plate. He wiped his mouth casually with the back of his hand; silence bestowed upon them once more.

"Jen I've been thinking....A Lot." He started. His fingers slowly teased his slightly overgrown mass of black hair. His face contrite with sadness, his cheeks hollow and sunken inward, lack of sleep and torment making him look dirty. She squinted, her eyebrows raised as she urged him to continue, glad of the distraction from her unwanted meal.

"I'm letting you go" He whispered the pain written all over his expression like a tattoo. Jenna recoiled in shock as the words hit her like a blow to the jaw. Her eyes wide with unexpected surprise as she tried to get her head around Donny's words. Her neck snapped back as her eyes locked viciously on his, stalking green and glorious in all her wide eyed splendour. It wasn't until the plate of food that leapt from her hands crashed above Donny's head did he finally come to and react. Plunging from his seat he caught a vivid glance of eggs and whatever else sliding down his white washed walls in a burst of vibrant colours. He clasped her chin firmly between his fingers.

"If its work you want Jen I can always find you a place in with the girls you know that" his voice lingered with confusion, he hadn't gauged her reaction properly in his opulent haze he probably should have. As she stepped back, observing at arm's length as though seeing him for the first time. Donny saw nothing but the red mist descending in her eyes as she swung her tiny fists at his face. She screamed some random, unrecognisable words as she tumbled towards him like a feral animal. The high pitched wails were heady and long howls of distinction. Almost inhuman as she catapulted her tiny frame into him, her fists colliding with his skin, the blows weren't painful as such, more irritating, but the cry that emitted from her was what scared Donny the most. As she went to catch him once more on the jaw he swung his hand up to catch her arm. Regretting it instantaneously as his fist collided with her perfect mouth. Spraying a delicious crimson spray across his white marble flooring in its wake as Jenna snapped back away from him. Her reaction was that of a child as she cowered down away from him, stumbling backward. The blood stained her teeth making her cackle like a nervous hyena as she swiped at her mouth to stop the overflow. She looked cannibalistic, psychotic even and Donny was slightly taken aback by her strange presence.

"You cheeky cunt Donny Anderson, You complete and utter cunt!" She screamed straight in his direction, her head shaking rhythmically as she spat her vehemence in a red ocean at his feet. The blood pooling on the floor could easily be mistaken for a murder scene. Jenna stumbled forward her glazed eyes not leaving Donny for a second.

"Do you honestly think I like working for you eh? You took my life, my fucking home, my kids. Making me sell my body, being plied with whatever drugs you see fit to take the edge of? Being shipped about and touched up by men old enough to be my fucking father! Who the fuck do you think I am Don?" her voice reaching an overwhelming crescendo as her nose came tip to tip with his. The feeling of her skin so close to his now unnerved Donny. He had never seen this side of her before, this side of her had floored him.

"Jen look" he stepped forward, retrieving her wrists in his vice like grip as he looked her up and down with fearful eyes. "Do you think I wanted this? Do you think I wanted you like this? Well you're fucking mistaken darling! I kept you at arm's length for a fucking reason; I thought if you were away from me, working the streets, you would disgust me in the end." His hand was at the arch of her back now as he pulled her close. "I thought it would all make me stop" he whispered into her hair as he inhaled deeply.

"Stop what?" Jenna spat sarcastically, trying her hardest to squirm from his grip. His whole demeanour had changed, his breathing had become shallow, his eyes were brighter and Jenna felt torn between the devil and the deep blue sea as he choked on his words.

"Stop me from falling in love with you!" he whispered, his teeth sinking into his bottom lip as he finally looked honest for the first time since she had met him. It was as though she was meeting him for the first time all over again, he had become innocent in seconds, his face devoid of any emotion other than guilt.

"But after the last few days Jen, after everything with Sandra. I don't want any questions; I don't want any suspicious glances from anyone because I was shagging one of my brasses. Fingers will point and my name will be dirt and I'm not in the game for that." He replied heartlessly. The juxtaposition between his previous statement and this completely mind blowing. Jenna stepped back, nodding silently to herself. She sucked in a much needed breath, her green eyes full of unshed tears and within seconds she was on the floor howling like a wounded animal, her whole body shaking violently as she just let the last year go, The endless nights of fear, the exhaustion of being used for sex, the love that she had lost and the love she had gained. She cried for what felt like an eternity, Donny held her close to his chest, like a babe as she shed every bitter emotion from her, she was finally free. Donny smiled, he knew this was all he could ever give her, true he loved her, true he wanted nothing more than for her to stay. But morally, it wouldn't ever feel right. Jenna had turned his world upside down, showed him emotions he had never and would never feel again. She was a treasure, a special completely flawless woman and he would never have the good grace of hurting her again. He rocked her gently in his arms, praying to god that he was finally forgiven. He kissed her hair gently, bathing in her delicious scent, her beautiful delicious scent. Letting her go would be the hardest thing he had ever done. But he knew in his heart of hearts it was time. He bought her to her feet, holding her close to his beating heart as he took in all of her for what he knew would be the very last time. He was angry, he was upset at himself but he knew it was for the best. Jenna was not his possession. As much as he prayed for her to conform to his ideologies of the perfect woman. He knew she was not destined for his lifestyle. She stepped away from him then, her body rejecting his touch as she spun on her heel and left without another word. Donny heard the floorboards above him creaking as she went about filling her suitcase he imagined with her belongings, he was sad to see her leave. She had been a joy to have in his company, but as all things, this had to come to an end Donny was glad they would part on at least decent terms. She tumbled down the stairs noisily. Her over stuffed pink suitcase making a loud thumping noise behind her as she struggled to drag it down the steps. Donny smiled; he could see her face, streaked black with mascara, puffy and red from crying. He felt the strange knotting in his stomach commence as he sank in the fact that this was it, she was going home. He couldn't help but wrench at the thought in his surprise as he pondered that, her home was here with him. He sauntered toward her, all confident fake smiles and greeted her with his hand. Flamboyant Donny Anderson had been reduced to a mere mute by the simply bewitching young lady before him.

"Jenna Please" he pleaded, trying to offer an explanation which he didn't have. She lifted her hand, summoning him to say no more as she gathered herself together and strode away from him without another word. Her head held high, taking with her the small, minuscule dab of self respect and pride she could muster. And then with a flick of her long purple hair and a wink of her beautiful green eyes she was gone.

Chapter Thirty Five

Johnny Fenton sat in the shadows of the overcrowded bar, his mouth locked onto the rim of his pint of cider. He was enjoying the company of a few of the locals, the banter was consistent and the drinks were flowing. Despite it being a Tuesday night and work was ever so constant on his mind, Johnny was relaxed, and the atmosphere was jovial and almost pleasant despite being surrounded by a bunch of drunks and trouble makers. He took another long drink of his pint, savouring the taste of its cheap refreshment. He was stuck in a debate between the two of the locals about the state on the economy and how the world relied on alcohol and drugs to keep everyone sane. He didn't notice the pretty young girl storming through the pub doors, drenched through from the rain, her jade green dress; opaque, clinging to each and every dimple and curve in her silky milk white skin. She sat at the bar, ordering herself a large double vodka she knocked it back in one, then she proceeded in ordering another and downing that with equal pace. It wasn't until Johnny went to stand to get himself another drink that he was floored back into his seat with catastrophic force, the cider he had been gradually downing all afternoon coming to the forefront of his mouth as he suddenly caught sight of the stunning Jenna Shearan. He shot back into his seat, his eyes jolting back and forth across the bar as she carried on handing out notes to the barman to refill her glass. Johnny was enthralled as he eyed his prey; he pushed himself further into the background as everything around him became a blur. His fingers slipped scattily into his jacket pocket, he fumbled out his mobile. His calculating stare never leaving the delectable Miss Shearan as his fingers shook, scrolling for Craig's number his eyes flitting between the phone and the gorgeous girl who propped up the bar. Her high pitched drunken laugh sliced the air as she exchanged floaty chit chat with the handsome bartender. Her eyelashes fluttering like butterflies on her lids as she took back another shot with the savvy of a sailor. She was exquisite, she had changed somewhat since Johnny had seen her last, she was tiny, her body devoid of her delicious curves, her hair no longer the dark raven black mane it had once been. The dark crimson colour she had taken didn't suit her, it washed her complexion out and made her look slightly like a drug addict somewhat. She had become a cheap version of herself. Yet she was still unique, a complete stunner. Johnny's eyes refused to stray from Jenna, his finger hovering desperately over the call button. He stared a few seconds more, before pressing the button, his heart thumping in his chest, the blood pulsing through his veins at lightning speed as the sound of the monotonous dial tone echoed repetitively in his ears. Finally after what seemed an age he heard Craig's mumbled voice echo down the phone, he was obviously drowsy from sleep. His voice was stretched, filled with lethargy as he answered with a vague hello.

"I've found her, I'll text you details get here fucking now!" he whispered down the phone. His mouth barely opening as he continued to stalk Jenna, he mouthed each word delicately so she didn't accidentally catch sight of him. She was drunk, her eyes were rolling, her voice was slurring but he knew she wouldn't leave just yet. He hung up the phone and text Craig the address. He stressed his urgency in his text, slipping his phone back into his pocket he continued to eye out his victim she had not a care in the world as she tapped her foot along to the Chris Brown track that thumped in over the jukebox, she smiled innocently at the familiarity. Johnny took in each vulnerable movement. His every single sense heightened by the alcohol that lined his veins as he watched her every delicate movement. The way she tossed her hair over her shoulder carelessly. The way she giggled like a child at the barman's unfunny jokes. The way her hand kept nervously smoothing down the pleated skirt of her Grecian style dress. The way her teeth hesitantly skimmed her bottom lip as she ordered another drink. Her eyes were hungry with longing, for what of course Johnny was unaware. But watching her as he did now, seeing her in the plain light, he was captivated. She was nothing short of mesmerising. He slithered back into his seat and glowered at her from afar. She was nothing short of captivating. Johnny couldn't help though even in his state of euphoria at finding her but notice the bruises. Faded slightly but still a pungent deep purple, her legs and arms were covered in them, trailing right from her barely there thighs to her slim ankles. Johnny gulped hard wondering what on earth it was that had happened to her since her disappearance a little over a year ago. Johnnie downed a large gulp from the fresh pint that had been placed in front of him, his eyes transfixed on Jenna. He slunk into the background, trying his damnedest to stay hidden. He felt his skin melting against his thin cotton shirt; he loosened his tie, the sweat beading across his temples as anxiety crept in. He couldn't risk being seen; she would run if she knew. Of that he was certain. All he could do was wait, and hope and pray that Craig would hurry the fuck up!

Craig sped down the motorway, his windscreen wipers fleeting back and forth as the vicious heavy rain bounced off the glass. He was thankful for the little traffic that evaded the roads. Apart from the odd car bumbling along in the treacherous weather the roads were virtually clear allowing Craig to push the car as fast as he could down the long stretch of road. As he finally reached the exit slip his heart leapt out of his chest, the address Johnny had given was literally ten minutes away. He swallowed down the vomit that rose high in his throat, his eyes bulging painfully in their sockets as he tried his hardest to scout out the pub where his most treasured possession lay in waiting for him. He turned off into a small side lane which ran alongside the public house, as he turned off the ignition he was plunged into darkness, the headlights fizzling out leaving only the dimly lit street lamps across the street to guide him out of the alleyway. The echoing of drunken voices spilled from inside, the stench of stale beer ever apparent as Craig traced the red brick with his fingers, each step making his heart race faster and faster in his chest. She was barely meters away now and Craig was convinced he could smell her, although he knew he was imagining things the thought gave him little comfort at the prospect of his quest. He had no clue of how she would react, he had no idea how she would take to him, and he was nervous, agitated and elated all in one.

His legs like jelly beneath him as he physically had to force himself to complete each weary step. After what felt like an age he finally reached the door, his fingertips resting on the old faded brass of the door handle. His forehead rested on the decaying chipped wood as he gasped breathlessly for air, trying to still his thundering heartbeat. He yanked open the swinging doors and was greeted with a fresh waft of sweaty no hopers and alcohol, he wretched slightly, his hand shot to his mouth. The foyer was cold and damp with no lightening other than that from inside the pub that shone dimly through two tiny panel windows on each door. The place was a fucking dive. Craig composed himself one last time. He pulled open the final set of double doors, set alight from within, in a cloud of cigarette smoke and as confident a stride that he could muster. As though everything had frozen in time, he caught glances of the jaws hitting the floor as he headed straight for the girl sat at the bar. He tapped her shoulder lightly. Giving her a second to spin around and register his face. Her complexion paled, as though someone had injected ice into her cheeks. The colour literally drained out of her face. He winked at her as he tossed her surprisingly over his shoulder. Her piercing shriek was enough to pop everyone in the pub from their fuddled daze. One man rose gallantly from his seat, Johnny snapped viciously like the loyal partner that he was. He flew at the man's throat before he even managed to get into a full standing position.

"Sit down you muggy little cunt or I'll cut you up like confetti in front of every single fucker in here. You understand." Johnny tightened his grip around the man's scrawny neck. His stale breath billowed nervously against Johnny's cheek.
"Understand!" Johnny spat aggressively, his nostrils flaring, eyes wide with malice. The scruffy man nodded repeatedly as Johnny shoved him back into his seat with maximum force.

"Good" Johnny smiled jovially before turning on his heel and sauntering away confidently. He stopped at the bar signalling to Craig that he would be just a minute more. He called the bar tender over and gave him a five pound note.

"Get that cunt over there a pint will you" he laughed. Turning back to an angry looking Craig and the flailing, crying, girl that was pounding his back with her tiny fists, he ushered them out of the doors and out into the bitter wind. The rain was still pouring down in torrents and as Johnny pulled his suit jacket around himself he followed Craig around to the side of the pub. He had to hold his breath as the stench of rotting food and stale alcohol drenched his nostrils. He could feel the cider bubbling in the pit of his stomach. He fought away the urge to vomit as he tackled his way through the grime and debris underneath his patent leather shoes.

"Put me fucking down Craig or I swear to fucking god" the girl continued to moan, her face beet red from fighting, her skimpy dress flopping up her back exposing her gorgeous, slightly bruised behind in the dim light. Craig just stood still, by the trunk of the car. Johnny paused momentarily taking in the scene before him. Even in the turbulent rain and the wind Craig looked spent. His eyes hollow and emotionless, he looked pained. Johnny knew it was the shock of seeing Jenna again and how she had reacted to him. But right now there was no time for games. They had to get her home and hopefully get her back on an even keel with them. It was going to be a long night. Johnny could feel the apprehension creeping into his bones. It was a fear he would never live down and he hoped against hope that he would never see Craig look so fearsome ever ever again. It wasn't until Craig skipped the passenger seat and bundled the girl into the boot of the car did he realise that Craig's last nerve had finally gone. As he motioned silently for Johnny to get in the car, Johnny knew that Craig needed him now more than ever, not only as a business partner, but as a friend too.

Chapter Thirty Six

Jenna lay against the carpeted interior, sweating profusely through fear and anxiety and sheer effort of punching and kicking her way in the darkness. She was breathless; all her efforts thus far had been fruitless. She had pleaded and begged for well over an hour to be released, she had screamed at the top of her lungs in anger. Throwing every insult she could muster at her captors. Now she was lost in the final phase, she had given in. She was exhausted from the fight and now her whole body felt incapacitated and useless. She just stared into space, the vodka doping her, making her feel as though the whole enclosed space was spinning, whirling around and she was struggling not to vomit. The bumpiness of the car on the road bringing her back to life suddenly, she froze her ears on high alert for the slightest sound. There was music then from the front as they stopped dead in their tracks. A song Jenna recognised, about being a king or something. It was something she had heard in some of the clubs she had graced with Donny. The sound making her shiver now, the haunting bass of the beat was excruciating with familiarity. Jenna's body prickled, every single hair on her slim body stood to attention. The song making her heart pound in her chest, her anxiety overbearing and in the darkness she truly feared herself. It was desperately quiet beyond the confines of her prison. The heat from her body radiating in the small space making her sweat profusely. Torrents of sickly heat crept across her body and her head pounded so hard she thought she would pass out from hyperventilating any second. She began to bite viciously down on her fake nail extensions, the plastic giving her a source of stress relief and she felt calmed slightly, even though her nervousness could still be felt by the rest of her body she didn't like the stillness. The world around her had come to a complete standstill. She felt defeated. Her whole body was rigid, every sense heightened by the anticipation of what was to come. She felt nothing but a strange sense of delirium. She heard muffled voices and the gravel crunching underfoot. The sound coming closer, as her hearing peeked, every single sound sensitising her further. She finally knew what real fear smelt like. Completely giddy off her own strange ideas of what may happen here and now. As the hood was pulled up and the light burst in through the cracks, she squinted, her vision blurred. Her eyes straining to focus as she saw Craig and Johnny's faces staring hard at her. Steely eyes bore into her, pupils dilated fully, fuelled with anger and rage as they're gazes darted over her. She smiled nervously, their expressions concrete cast, not changing an inch, their faces stony, grey in tone. Almost dusty looking in their vehemence, Craig ushered for her to grasp his hand. She shuddered, her skin puckered with blistering bumps as her hand enveloped his. Their skin electrifying as they touched. The spark between them effortless as he took her in his arms, she shivered deeply. Burying her body deep into his rippling muscles. His skin silky soft against hers, he was a marvel. He smiled unintentionally, catching Jenna's bitter eyes as he stood unaffected by her presence. As though she was almost unborn, Craig pulled her close to his chest, his nostrils literally flaring at her scent. The sweetness of musk and dark fruits filling his nose as he inhaled deeply, Jenna was a heady potion. Her body entwined between the river and the waves. She was nothing short of perfect. She was perfect. Craig's eyes lit at the prospect of her. Dressed in nothing but her tiny see through Grecian dress she was stunning. He had found her, finally she was home. The tears flew then in torrents from his eyes, he was a man with pride but in her arms he crumbled like a child. He wilted to his knees, taking her with him as they cradled one another delicately. Johnny looked on as the dramatic scene before him unfolded; swiping away a stray tear with the palm of his hand he smiled a sad but sincere smile. They had finally found her. As he melted into the background, his eyes not leaving the broken scene before him he felt himself dissolve with pride. All of their hard work had finally paid off. Although Johnny had a sinking feeling knotted deep in his stomach that the worst was still to come.

Chapter Thirty Seven

Craig stared down at Jenna as she slept peacefully beside him in the passenger seat. Her face was calm, devoid of any marks other than the bruises that donned her eyes. In this state she was truly beautiful, her hair fanned out across her bony shoulders. Her dress riding up her elegant thighs, but still she remained a classy looking young woman. Craig had never loved her more than he did now. Of course he wanted answers, but they would come in time. He wanted to know every sordid secret this beautiful girl harboured. He needed to know, he craved information if only to finally put his mind to rest. He knew that whatever it was, he wasn't ready to hear it. She had cried so bitterly tonight, he had thought she may burst with the upset. He had done nothing but console her. There had been nothing more he could do. She had changed significantly; he had noticed that almost instantly. Not just in her everyday appearance, but her whole demeanour. She had become shy, unsure about herself, about her body and Craig had been stunned. He had tried to hold her, show her how much he had missed her and she had recoiled away from him. It was as though the thought of intimacy with him sickened her. Every single hair on Craig's body stood to attention as his fingers strayed from the gear stick to Jenna's soft skin. His thin fingers brushing against her sallow cheek, he tried his hardest not to grasp hold her where she was and hug her until her bones crushed between his weight. She looked so fragile, so frail. Like a dainty flower in the breeze, wilted slightly but still extremely empowering with its beauty. Craig smiled sadly a he headed home, his heart heavy in his chest. He didn't know how the fuck they were to move forward, time would tell if they were ever to be right again. He knew exactly where he needed to go. But as he saw the estate in the distance he felt his stomach twist maliciously. She needed to go home, Kiki didn't need the confusion and Jenna needed time alone. Craig would stay with her for tonight but as of tomorrow she would be alone, for now at least. She would need the solace of her own home. Craig bought the tears in his eyes to control as he pulled into the Belmonte. The place was like a ghost town in the early hours. The high rise flats dimly lit with the odd up all nighters; otherwise the place was completely absorbed in darkness. He saw his childhood home for the reality that it was, he swallowed down the vomit as he saw his mother's lights were still shining brightly in the darkness. His nerves prattled as he parked the car directly opposite Jenna's flat. The familiarity of the place was haunting. The Belmonte was a ground plagued for people with no hope and Craig almost shed a tear for the fact that his poor old mother still hovelled there. And as he looked up at the flat in which he was raised, the tears spilled slightly onto his cheeks. Claire was a homing bird and he knew that she was probably sat there now, in her finest sale bought pyjamas. Doing nothing but nursing a corner shop cider in one hand whilst counting her blessings on the other. Craig smiled, the thought of his mother almost making him crumble to his knees with guilt. As much as he loved his old mum, this life would never ever be for him again and he knew he needed to address the issue sooner rather than later. He eased Jenna out of the passenger seat, her flimsy body like a babe in his arms as he carried her effortlessly across the tarmac to her flat. Quickly he checked the metres making sure there was still gas and electric there he opened the front door with his key. The instant smell of degradation and abandon filled his nostrils. The place was a dive, stinking with the whiff of sheer damp, dust and inhabitation. He made his way across the living room, avoiding the furniture as though he was following a map on the back of his hand. He made his way up the stairs and lay her down in the bedding. Her ritualistic flower filled bedspread wrapped around her despite the fact her body hadn't lay amongst it in months. Craig lay a soft kiss upon her head, watching her contently as she huddled herself among the blankets in sleep. Her tiny body cradling against the warmth, Craig glanced back once more before pulling the door behind him. He tried his damn hardest not to inhale the sheer stench of neglect filling his nostrils once more. As he traced the hall toward his daughter's bedroom he sighed, his heart as heavy as a boulder in his chest. His thin fingers skimming the white wood of Kiki's bed as he entered the small space. The scent of her skin lingering on her sheets as Craig took one bewitching final breath of the sweet stale air. The place didn't seem so appealing now and he made a mental note to send his team of decorators over in the morning to help her do the place out. It hadn't changed a bit since he had last been here, but now he felt saddened by their memories here. Archie being born, his finding out the Dom had fathered the precious child he had longed to be his own. He felt as though he was still mourning the loss of his son, it still ached in his heart to know that he and the boy would never again had the bond they had shared in the first few vital weeks of his life. It had been Craig who had sat beside him morning noon and night, watching over him, watching each tender movement his limp little body had made. It had been Craig who had held him close in the dead of night to comfort him as he cried. It had been Craig who had loved him with strength so unnatural that it had frightened Craig. He would have gone to the ends of the earth for that little boy and now as he stared at a picture of Kiki and Archie that hung above Kiki's bed in a beautiful silver frame with My Little Brother engraved into the metal. His lip quivered as he ran his finger over the faces of Jenna's two beautiful children, their similarities so striking yet now Craig could see with vivid clarity their differences.

He turned away from the room; the house was completely silent apart from Jenna's light snuffles coming from the bedroom. He would leave her to sleep now and maybe pop by later in the week to see how she was getting on. He needed to distance himself from her. He needed time to think about all that had happened. He knew she wouldn't be willing to talk to him just yet and he accepted that, he had taken it on the chin that it would take a lot of time and a lot of healing. But he would find the cunt who had done this to her and when he did, he would kill. Taking the stairs now back to the ground floor he recoiled as the stench from the kitchen almost floored him once more. Pulling off his cuff links and depositing them on the mantle he rolled his shirt sleeves up. He couldn't leave the place in this state; even if he made the place at least smell a bit more attractive then he was onto a winner. He strode across the carpet, holding his nose as he went into the kitchen. The place smelt absolutely foul but Craig had guessed that there had been people here since Jenna had been here last. The newspapers and sandwich wrappers that adorned the bin were all dated from at least the last three months and she had been gone over a year. Whoever it was that had been back and forth here hadn't long fled, a month maybe two tops since the place had been last touched. The stench of decaying food and just neglect was ever apparent as he began sweeping everything from the debris covered units into a black bag. He knew the place like the back of his hands. He tore into the cupboard under the sink to drag out the bleach and the floor cleaner and a pack of cloths so he could at least tackle some of the cleaning before the morning came.

He got to work scrubbing and bagging the unwanted shit that filled the enclosed kitchen space. He swiped away at the sweat beads that spewed out across his forehead as he splashed the soapy water across the now bare counter top. He had thrown at least six black bags out in the process and finally thank fuckIng god the place was getting back to some sort of normality. He had emptied the vulgar smelling fridge of the rotten food and long stale baby bottles and doused it in neat bleach to try and shield the smell. He wondered who the fuck had been in here looking over the place because not a single thing of value had been touched. Even Jenna's jewellery box on the mantle in the living room was still intact. So it must have just been someone sent to just check in on the gaff from time to time. He was surprised though that none of the fucking Belmonte junkies had rammed raided the place for a pair of knickers to flog on. He smiled at the irony. His thoughts strayed to his mother once more as he swept the kitchen floor free of the last load of dirt and debris. He wondered why on earth she would still be awake at this hour. She had always been an early bird had Claire, always in bed by nine after the soaps had finished and she had drank her cup of Horlicks. The thought of seeing her again scared him now; he knew she would never ever handle the truth. That he had lied to her of all people about his plans would kill her. He loved her so very much and he missed her with each and every day that passed but he knew that he had paved this road for himself. He had been the one who had faked his own death, played with his own life in the hope he could make a better one for him and Johnny in the process. He had always dreamed of coming back, bigger, stronger and bolder than ever before. He had imagined him and Jenna getting married, her wearing his ring like a medal of honour as they raised beautiful babies together. But it had all been simply that. A fucking dream. The reality so vivid now as he stood in the pokey little flat where it had all began, their little love story played out before him in a series of pictures and unheard words. The love they had felt for one another was like nothing else imaginable. The love they had shared between them simply superhuman and he would give his left arms now to have that euphoria back. The bond they had shared had been unbreakable and the trust they had for one another had been implicit. Now though as reality sank slowly into his pores he realised that they had become distant strangers, cut from one another by the clutches of fate. They had been one another's everything and now they stood separated, spurred on by their stubborn ways and their need to be right. His heart thudded in his chest as he caught the beaming faces of the drunken teenagers that drenched every inch of the room. Their smiles were wide, happy and beautiful. So carefree. Craig slumped down onto the settee and held his aching head in his hands. Why had life done this to them? They had been so perfect for one another and if only he had seen it back then. Then he knew he would have done something about it instead of constantly fighting his feelings. He wished now that he had showed her the love and the affection that she had deserved instead of using her like a skilled puppeteer uses his puppets. He saw her on his strings as she had been then. So ready, so driven to give him anything he wanted from her and he had just ignored her advances. They had made love here, had fought here and laughed, smiled and loved here and now as the room spun around him in glorious Technicolor, his memories flushed to the forefront. Surrounded by the painted smiles of his younger self Craig felt inferior. As thought the smarmy cunt in the pictures was mocking him, showing him exactly what he had missed, he slumped back into the cold leather and he allowed the tears to come. There was no fight; there was no denial just pure exhaustion and sadness. Sadness for all he knew he had lost and all he knew was yet to come. This night would be the start of many more to come of feeling like he had failed. Failed to protect his family, his best friend, the mother of his child, he had let her down in ways he couldn't even begin to fathom. He composed himself then, wiping away the angry tears with the flats of his palms. His eyes puffy and dry from the tears, he looked around once more satisfied that the place was up to standard he pulled a pen from his trouser pocket and scrawled a brief note to Jenna and left it on the fridge. He pulled on his jacket and stalked out into the night.

He glanced around making sure no one was about he almost leapt out of his skin when he heard a voice resembling a foghorn come hollering from the upstairs veranda. He froze, not even turning around to look as he registered the fact that the voice undoubtedly belonged to his mother.

"She back then is she love??" she called over the veranda, her voice thick with alcohol, Craig noticed the slur in her voice almost immediately, he turned his head as if to look up he put on his best attempt at a Scottish accent as he shouted back a simple "Yeah aye She's home" back in response. He paused long enough just in case she replied, but the simple snort that emitted from her was enough to tell Craig he was dismissed. Before he quickly paced back to the car, jumped into the driver's seat and pulled none too gently out of the Belmonte. His heart literally sitting on his tongue as he realised just how much of a close shave he had just had. She hadn't noticed him that much he knew, but she was probably too pissed to notice. His body was literally shaking with intensity; he shook his head in wonder, bemused suddenly by his brazenness. He had just come second best to staring his mother in the face and he had come away laughing. He pulled out onto the empty motorway, the morning was just creeping in and Craig couldn't wait to crawl into bed for a few hours before he began his day. It had been a crazy old night that he was certain of. He marked it up on the chalkboard as one he wouldn't forget in a bloody hurry that was for sure.

Chapter Thirty Eight

Claire Horran pounded on the door of the flat with her meaty fist possibly as hard as she could muster without breaking the glass panel. She was dressed in a flannel dressing gown and huge fluffy slippers. Her usually razor straight bob was frizzy and messed up on the top of her head. Her face set into an angry grimace as she waited as patiently as she could muster given the circumstances. Eventually she saw the shadows emerging beyond the glass she sighed an over dramatic huff of relief. As Dom pulled open the door, babe in arms half asleep in his boxers Claire flew past him and sauntered into the hallway. Her arms folded over her humongous breasts as she leant against the wall. Dom stood open mouthed the shock on his face imminent as he closed the door silently behind him.

"Good Morning to you too" he yawned tiredly, hoisting the baby up higher onto his hip as he tried to provoke an answer from Claire as to why she felt the need to be banging his door like the bastard IRA at half past six in the morning! She looked completely bewildered and Dom couldn't help but smile at her urgency. He placed the baby down onto the carpeted floor and his face flushed a secret shade of crimson as he realised he was still stood in only his boxer briefs.

"She's Home Dom" She shuffled nervously in her slippers, her voice muted, barely audible as the words spilled from her abnormally quiet mouth. Dom Stilled, his eyes flitting nervously from the door, to his son who sat oblivious to his surroundings on the floor. Dom's eyes closed then, he bit down forcefully on his bottom lip, and his head shaking slowly as he fully digested the information he had been given. The blood rushed around in his veins at almost lightening speed. His body refusing to move a muscle, every single inch of his skin was smothered in delicious Goosebumps that pimpled across every inch of him. He sucked in a harsh breath, the air frosty with change as he scooped Archie up into his arms. He held the boy close to his naked chest. His nose diving into his sons sweet smells Jet black baby hair. The boy was his entire world; despite being his mother personified Archie was sweet, mild natured child who was beautiful in every single sense of the world. His personality was kind, soft and gentle and he was the most striking boy that Dom had ever lay eyes on. He was pale; almost porcelain white in complexion with over accentuated pink rosebud lips, which on any other little boy would look slightly strange but they complemented Archie's face beautifully. But it was his eyes, the piercing almost luminous green of his irises that took Dom's breath away with almost a knockout force. They were deep and mesmerising just like his mothers. Dom could sit and drown for hours into the boys wide pooling stare. He was a completely stunning child there was no denying that, everyone who met him commented on how marvelled they were at him. He was Jenna Shearan reborn there was no denial on that note. Dom loved him with a passion that burned holes in his equilibrium. The child was perfect in every single way and Dom was as proud as punch that the child was his and his alone. He couldn't have her turning up here and expecting to take charge. He wouldn't allow it. He handed the child gently to Claire, he needed to confront her. As the mother of his child she deserved to be respected but as a Mother she also had a duty to her son. She hadn't served her duty as a mother and Dom needed answers. She couldn't just waltz back in and resume her position after being absent for over twelve months. The boy needed stability, love and protection and he had that in abundance from Dom. He would be dead if he saw any harm come to his boy. He had allowed a child to slip away from him once he would never make that mistake again. He swallowed down hard as the darkness that crept into his stomach threatened to spill, he suppressed it. His memories of that fateful night were still so vivid. But he wouldn't go there now, that was dead and had been buried such a long time ago. He couldn't change what had happened. But he would be damned if he was about to let history repeat itself. He strode to the door with as much confidence as he could muster. His eyes were glazed grey and cold and Claire's heart palpitated thick and fast in her buxom chest. She cuddled the boy tight to her, his scent beautifully fresh beneath her nostrils. He nestled against her and immediately Claire felt comfort. The boy had become her solace, her grandchildren ran her ragged. So demanding were they in their needs but this child in her arms had been a blessing. She had missed Kiki so much; the beautiful little boy had filled a very narrow void. She had played him UB40 and nursed him until he slept soundly. In a way she hungered for her granddaughter in every single moment spent with the child but he was a balm to her tortured soul. Dom's lip arched as he crossed her, his face wise and courageous as he strode past Claire. Like a peacock with its feathers on show he exhumed confidence. But as Claire had learnt it was Dom's eyes that were the giveaway. He looked hurt, baffled and somewhat demented as his fingers flexed around the door handle. Claire held her breath; she didn't know just how to react as he turned back once more. He gave both her and the baby one last glance of his subdued smile before he slammed the door shut behind him. Claire finally found the power to exhale. Whatever happened now, it would be a cruel twist of fate to add to the vicious circle that Dom and Jenna were already riding. Claire knew that the girl would never be able to dedicate herself entirely to the boy. She was still chasing the hapless ghost of Craig, which being something that Dom, no matter how hard he tried. She could never in a million years contend with? She felt for the poor sod, there was no denying that. But as she lay the baby back down onto the rug she kept her eye very close to the window and was almost tempted to grab her Craig's old binoculars out! She hugged her dressing gown tighter around her and waited for the storm to ensue.

Chapter Thirty Nine

Dom snaked across the concrete hall. His face flushed, his eyes pinned back into their sockets, and he was sweating. It was an unappealing sweat that had seized his control. He fanned himself with his left hand. He was swallowing and sucking down on harsh breaths. His whole body was clammy as he came face to face with Jenna's front door. He looked around him in case of anyone watching as he rapped his knuckles against the wood. He scratched nervously on his arm, his nails tearing the flesh as the blood snaked through the graze. He flexed his muscles, trying his hardest to relax into himself. His mind was obliterated by a thousand thoughts. How would she react toward him? Would he be greeted or shunned away. He felt so haunted, sad as he stood there. As an afterthought he wished he had put some clothes on. But he was here now so there and such was his urgency he saw that there was no point trying to hide the fact that he was nervous. He let another breath his head bowing now, all effort of exhuming confidence had been taken from him. He was sweating profusely, the tiny beads bubbling across his skin, making him look even more vulnerable than he felt. He saw a shadow in the glass and for a moment he felt as though this whole set up was a dream. His eyes wide as he looked for a clue, a deep necessity screeching from the pit of his stomach as he left a film of vapour against the glass, he was so close he could almost smell her from deep within her hovel. Her scent was a visceral scent. It was potent mixture that Dom had continuously got high on. Again he knocked the glass; he saw the grey shadows pressed against the glass. It was the small movements made beyond his gaze that kept him meticulously in wait. He saw a small shadow fill the panel and he swallowed down the rock hard lump that had formed in his throat. He stood as confident as his body would allow as a small crease appeared in the door. As quick as the wind she was in his plain view. For a second he didn't recognise her. The woman before him was a shadow of his former lover. Her cheeks were sullen, sunk deep within her hollows. Her body was emaciated beyond relief, each bone in her body jutted forward without purpose. Her once jet black hair strip dyed a horrific purple colour. She was a mess, her face devoid of makeup making her look almost dead. She stood with nothing but a scruffy duvet to cover her modesty. Her hair was escaping in dirty tendrils against her cheek from the top knot on her head. He could see where her hair had been bleached blonde. The disgusting patches were evident on her scalp. It was as though she had morphed overnight. He attempted a half smile, trying his hardest not to grimace.

She almost fell against the door frame in shock. She claimed the wood in her hands as she took in the sight before her. She had been waiting upon this moment all night and now he was here she didn't quite know how to take him. He looked amazing. He was even more muscular than she had remembered. His hair was like a blanketed veil across his brow, slightly overgrown and messy but still alluring all at once. Jenna paused as she took a quick stride towards him. Her heart thundered in her chest, he was without a doubt the sexiest man she had ever witnessed. Even Donny played a casual second to Dom. She stood before him as vacant as she could muster, her open mouth tantalisingly waiting for him. Her bottom lip protruding in a delicious pout, all Dom could do was stare. His eyes were looking her up and down with lust. Jenna stepped toward him, her eyes glassy against his. Dom stood back, He didn't know what to do with his body, and it was as though he had lost all control of his functions.

"Hi" she whispered her voice so nervous, so small. She pulled the duvet tighter around her, trying her hardest to hide the shame of her body. The veil of pink that shot across her cheek said different though. Dom held his hands out and carefully cupped her delicate face as though she was made of the finest china. He scanned each of her features with such precision as though he didn't believe that this was really happening. She bit down hard on her bottom lip as she saw the sadness etched like charcoal in his grey eyes. He glanced away from her, shaking his head before he snapped her into his warm embrace without a moment's hesitance. The duvet slid away from her shoulders and he winced when he felt the true extent of her childlike body against his. She felt so different to the once curvy petite girl she had once been. Now she just felt too skinny, her body held no shape her once lush figure now girlish and unformed in his hands. It didn't feel right him holding her so close like this. She was unappealing like this. Unattractive despite him knowing that it was her, she didn't feel like she was Jenna, despite having her face, her voice, her tentativeness. This girl before him was rough, hardened somewhat. She smelt unclean, dirty and unkempt it wasn't the Jenna he had known at all. He slowly held her away from him, taking in the grubbiness of her dress, the bruises that kissed her skin, the scratch marks on her cheeks he sucked in a loud breath. Unbelievably he said nothing, words were beyond him as he just stared, like someone about to buy a dog. Doubt cursing through each and every pore as he wondered just what had caused her to end up like this.

"Say something" she urged. Pain sketched across her furrowed brow, as though his opinion would probably kill her if she were to hear it.

"Jen...I...I Just don't know." He paused after every single word, his hands in his hair again through nerves. His mind was scatty, filled with questions. But nothing seemed to surface from his mouth. His expression was one of confusion, an uncanny almost childlike need for information. Jenna moistened her dry lips with a quick flick of her tongue and noisily cleared her throat. She held her hand up to him to stop him from speaking.

"How about I go and put the kettle on eh? Have you got any milk though because I haven't gone to get anything in just yet" the embarrassment in her voice didn't go unnoticed. He gave her a small, sliver of a smile and turned to leave.

"I'll fetch the coffee and sugar and all. I don't know how long the shit you've got have been here. Can't afford to be poisoned by your mouldy coffee" he replied jokingly. His voice was full of mock dread as he pulled his hand across his mouth to feign shock. He turned and winked at her, flashing his amazing bright smile. And without a second carefree glance he was gone. And momentarily it felt as though she had never been gone. She placed the latch of the door on and went through to the kitchen; she stopped dead in her tracks when she saw the little note on the coffee table. Knowing exactly who it was from just by looking at the handwriting she had to swallow down the tears that threatened to spill. She had to stay in control, he could know nothing. She had a long hard road ahead of her, that was a given, but she would get her revenge. Of that she was a million percent sure. She had been used, abused battered and broken and now like a phoenix amongst the ashes, she would rise.

 She needed to get it all off her chest, a problem shared was a problem halved as she and Claire had always said. Well now the problem would be dissected and ripped apart just as she had been. She pulled the kettle off the unit and walked casually over to the sink to fill it. She tucked the note away in her bra, she would read it later. She glanced at the clock on the microwave, quarter past seven in the morning! He could have bloody waited she thought as she put the kettle back to boil. She tugged her topknot out of her hair and pulled it loose, her long flowing locks spilt down her slender back as she tossed her head back and took in a full blown breath of what felt like freedom. She pulled her hair back up into a ponytail before she went back through the living room and took to the stairs. She had to get these grubby clothes off and get into something that actually belonged to her. That hadn't been given to her by Donny or purchased with his hard earned pimp money. She strode into her bedroom, ripping the flimsy material away from her with a subtle swipe of her hand; she tossed it aside with the rest of the junk she didn't want. She needed a complete image overhaul. She needed to get herself back to Jenna. She fished around in the overflowing wardrobe, she tugged at her dresses, her jeans at her tops and t shirts but every single thing she tried swamped her. She heard the door go downstairs and very nearly bounced out of her skin. She breathed a huge sigh of relief as she heard Dom calling up to her that he was back after he had done a firm inspection of the downstairs.

"Be down in a sec, I'm just getting dressed" she replied, trying not to sound too disheartened as she pulled on a pair of black leggings (which of course hung away from her as though they were flares) and an old T shirt of Craig's. Although she would have probably had more luck raiding her daughters wardrobe for something fitting. She sighed as she caught sight of herself in the full mirror that hung on the wardrobe door. She lifted her t shirt and winced as though in pain at the sight of her tiny ribcage and her heavily bruised torso. She bundled the top back down and headed for the stairs, shutting the door of her bedroom behind her. As she did so she wrote a mental note to self to take the mirror down later on. She tip toed down each of the carpeted steps, her toes sinking deeply into its familiarity. She slowly poked her head around the door frame and smiled as she caught a glimpse of Dom stood in the kitchen, his back to her making coffee's on the counter top. She smiled languidly, like a teenager with a stupid crush. She stood tall; with as much confidence as she could muster she cleared her throat purposely to signal her arrival. He stopped in his tracks and turned to greet her with a half smile. He passed the steaming mug to her and took his perch on the sofa. He took a drink before placing the mug down on the table; he stared blankly before patting the seat beside him. Both were unaware of how they should act or how they should speak without it being deemed inappropriate. Gone was the witty flirtatious banter they had shared, in its place stone cold atmosphere it was as though they were strangers meeting awkwardly for the first time.

"So" he began when she had taken up her seat "Tell me what's been going on. From the very beginning. I want the full unedited version warts and all." He sat back in his seat, pulling his feet up onto the sofa crossing his legs and placing his hands into his lap; he was offering her an ear. That was a start.

"That's what you really want?" she sighed, closing her eyes to gain composure. She could not cry; she wouldn't. She was already weak enough without this dragging her down any further. She sat back too, mocking each of Dom's movements; she stared up at the ceiling as she began to speak. She couldn't look at him through fear of breaking her control. And boldly she began, as though she was the only person in the room. She spilled out her vicious angry monologue from the very beginning.........

<u>Book Three</u>

<u>Revenge.</u>

"It's No Surprise I won't be here tomorrow

I can't believe that I stayed till today

There's nothing here in this Heart left to borrow

There's nothing here in this soul left to say

Don't be surprised when we hate this tomorrow

God knows I tried to find an easier way

Yeah you and I will be a tough act to follow

But I know in time we'll find this was

No Surprise"

Daughtry- No Surprise.

Chapter Forty

Dom just sat and stared open mouthed at Jenna, not quite breathing right. He was rendered simply speechless. Completely and utterly distraught as he swiped away the nasty heartfelt tears that trickled down his cheek in torrential streams. He was furious, livid even. His fingers traced his clean shaved chin again as he continued to listen in sheer awe of the brave woman before him. He now saw Jenna in a whole new light, he was scared for her. Scared of what she had been forced to endure, it was alien to him. Prostitution was something you read about in seedy crime novels. It wasn't something that happened to young girls like Jen. He was molten angry, his temper flaring as she sat there lost in her own tainted thoughts. Dom recoiled in horror as she retold to him some of the treacherous deeds she had been made to perform at the hands of Donny Anderson and his fucking cronies. He cursed Craig deep in the pit of his stomach, had he known of all of this all along? He worked too close to Donny for him not to have some inkling! Dom was trying his damn hardest to remain calm. Despite his hands shaking like leaves in a tornado. His nerves were frayed. He thought of her being so vulnerable, so lost and it made him extremely sad, not just for her but for her poor children. Kiki and Archie had been the ones here who had truly suffered. Kiki especially, she was older, wiser than her years. She had been told her mother had left them, guilt flooded Dom. All of these months he had thought Jenna to be this heartless selfish bitch for disowning their son and now everything was collecting together in crystal clear clarity he felt nothing but sweet remorse for his actions. He had never felt so helpless in all of his life. He glanced up into her beautiful face; she was choking back the tears as she unveiled the story of how Donny had taken her to some abandoned flats and made her work from some grotty room his stomach twisted into vicious knots, he had to suppress the urge to vomit right there on the carpet. He had never heard anything like it in all of his life. He pulled his coffee cup to his lips and took a mouthful of the freezing cold liquid, his brow furrowed as he stared down into the cup distastefully.

He grabbed Jenna's hand in his own and smiled, urging her to continue when she began to trip on her words.

"Its fine, Carry on" he whispered sadly, he could see the shame tattooed on her face as she recalled her darkest moments. When she spoke of the heroin he flinched. No wonder she was so fucking thin! The cunt had been plugging her with bastard gear and making her fuck strangers for money! Dom felt his skin crawling. It was nothing short of miraculous that the girl wasn't dead, never mind signed to a bastard nut house. Dom was completely bouncing in his seat; he couldn't quite contain the sparks of anger that flecked in his bright grey eyes.

It wasn't until she mentioned a woman by the name of Danielle did his blood run cold in his veins.

"What did you say?" he spat, his hands virtually clanging in his wrists as he shook with sheer fury. He knew the name, well; just the sound of it brought back such horrific memories. He pictured his beautiful wife Ami and the curvy girl pictured at the bar. Ami chattering away to her boss beside her their colleague Danielle sumping vodka from the bottle. Her high pitched cackle vibrated off the walls. He pictured the man, the sleazy eyes bewitched by a woman who wasn't his for the taking. His hand riding up Ami's thighs as he stared longingly into her stunning eyes. Dom stood watching, captivated from his post in the lobby of the shitty pub on the high street. Not wanting to watch but of course his eyes not allowing him to even flinch. He witnesses the two girls knocking back the Prosecco while the filthy rich toad continued to maul his wife like a kitten with a new ball. Ami just sat there without a care in the world. Her eyes wicked and filled with lustrous ardour as she continued to giggle and his jokes and pet him lovingly. Her hooded eyes were smoky and black, her eyelashes fluttering seductively against the dim light as she carried on unaware of Dom's presence. His watchful eyes didn't dare to stray even if it was only for a second. He bore witness to everything, from the way the man skimmed her lips with his fingers to the way he watched her intently with his come to bed eyes. And yet she was so compelled, so stupefied as to obey his commands like the Seductress she was. When the man eventually locked lips with his wife, Dom had turned on his heel and sharply he had left. There had been no going back and from that night on He had hated Ami and that cunt Danielle for her part in it. The woman had been their friend; she had come to their house, played with Sam on the carpet whilst Dom and Ami cooked dinner for them all. It didn't seem right that now here she was goading Ami to cheat on him with a man worth a million dollars. Dom had seen it all, he had dealt with it all but this had been the straw that had broken the camel's back. He had never been the same again and from that day on he had hardened. Completely solid on the surface he had become and now as the name echoed in his mind he felt his walls quivering. Danielle had been such a faded memory in his past, like the forgotten sands she had shifted, become nothing more than a faint speck from his imagination but now, as he heard Jenna speaking of her, doing such despicable acts to the girl he loved the most he could feel his hackles rising. He imminently pushed them away, this wasn't about him, and this was about Jenna not him. He stood up from the sofa and knelt before Jenna. His hands found their place on her tilted shoulders as he stared her square on in the face.

"I know the girl you're talking about, she was a friend of my wife. I swear to god Jen I would never ever have allowed this to happen to you if only I knew" his voice went off on a tangent as he attempted to hold her. She fell forward awkwardly into his arms, her breath literally plunging from her lungs as he almost suffocated her with his embrace.

"I promise you this will never ever happen again" he whispered, his shallow breath lingering on her cheek. He planted a soft kiss onto her sweaty temple before he gradually pulled himself away. It was all becoming too much to take in, Dom felt like he was caught between the devil and the deep blue.

"You can't tell Craig" she replied sternly, her eyes like dark pools against her pale complexion.

"Jen he could help you!" He protested but he was cut off mid sentence by dead fingers grasping hold of his forearms. He flinched, his face a mixture of confusion and heady lust for the young girl before him, even now after all of this, it was still there. That weird bubbling in the pit of his stomach, that deafening crescendo of the blood flooding in his ears every single time their skin touched, it was like being on the world's biggest roller coaster, he was pumped full of the adrenaline high. His whole body rigid from the sweetness of her voice, he had missed her more than he would allow himself to admit. He couldn't let himself fall back into that trap. He had worked too hard and fought off too many to be where he was now.

"I need to go and sort Archie out babe, Claire's over there with him. Why don't you go have a nice long bath and get back to bed for a few hours eh? I'll call in with some dinner for you later if you like? Maybe we could order?" he sympathised, his voice soft and soothing like balm to her ears. No one deserved what she was going through now. It must have been torture these hellacious months, the torment and the terrifying things she had been forced to do, to strangers. It didn't bare thinking about really. She nodded slowly, a minuscule flush of pink crept across her cheeks.

"You won't tell anyone about this will you?" she begged, her voice thick with embarrassment and humiliation as she stood to see him out. He turned and held her hands in his own tightly, he smiled at her with loving eyes and shook his head before he left her without another word. Jenna sighed contentedly, finally she had unburdened herself, and she felt better than she had in months for it.

Chapter Forty One

Craig buttoned up his crisp white shirt and knotted the pale blue tie in front of the full length mirror in his bedroom. He checked the time on his watch and smiled with glorious appreciation. He had almost half an hour to spare before his date would arrive and he actually couldn't wait to take the young lady out and treat her like an absolute princess for the night. He splashed on some expensive aftershave before checking his reflection once more. He had made maximum effort for tonight. From the Snappy grey trouser suit, the pants slack around his hips, minus the jacket of course. A slick new haircut and freshly shaven skin splashed in the woody and hypnotising scent of his cologne. His shoes were polished and buffed to an almost sparkling finish and a brand new clean cut Diamond stud in his ear. He knew he was a fucking handsome bastard; there was no fucking denying it when even his reflection winked back at him in appreciation. He smoothed a hand over his head once more, just checking that there wasn't a hair out of place, he pulled his hand back and sighed as he spotted the gold "Daddy" band that adorned his ring finger. It had been a gift from Jenna after Archie had been born, despite the fact he had worn it ever since it didn't feel right to him. He was Kiki's dad no Archie's, the fact killed him even still. So much time had passed yet the grief was still so raw in his aching heart. He longed for his baby, his little boy whom he had spent those precious moments with. The baby he had cuddled, kissed, sang to and loved as his own was now just a dent in his over-active imagination. Archie had been destined to be his child, he still felt that same rush of paternal love every single time the boy crept into his mind. But he had to learn to let it go. Even the mere thought of it cut Craig to the quick but it was time. He slid the ring away from his finger, glancing at the message engraved inside his heart constricted in his chest "With Love your little soldier" Craig sighed as he dropped down onto the bed, planting the ring down on the dresser as he stared aimlessly at the ceiling. He didn't fully know how he was going to deal with Jenna just yet. It was like dealing with a forlorn needy child and if he was honest with himself, it wasn't something that he needed. Things had been going well recently business wise things were booming, his fetish clubs were raking it in overseas as were his little drug rings in and around London. Truth of the matter was he didn't need the drama. He knew Jenna had been in a mess that much had been evident by the fucking state of her. The stench of her had been enough, but Craig was her best friend and he wasn't about to turn his back. As much as right now it was tempting. He knew his body would never allow him to leave her stuck in the lurch. It was his biggest curse, being guilty to the charms of the beautiful Jenna Shearan. Although of course she had looked better. He didn't like to hinder on the thought. He stood back in front of the mirror, checking himself over once more as though lying down on the bed would have messed his whole face up. He took in his own perfectly chiselled features and smiled. He couldn't wait for his little date tonight. His excitement mirrored that of a child. No business meetings, no drama just some good food and some amazing company. He straightened himself out one last time and smiled to his reflection. He was ready.

Craig's palms were sweaty as he took to the stairs one by one, his finely polished feet making a bare minimum thud on the heavily carpeted stairs. He smiled his mega watt smile at Leah his nanny as she greeted him at the foot of the stairwell with her freshly washed skirt and shirt combination pressed to a remarkable finish, her respectable flat carpet slippers encasing her unusually small feet. Her hair tied slickly back into its usual tight bun, her no nonsense face perfectly made up in a hue of simple pink blush and a slick of mascara. She was a bewitching woman, so quiet and so contented. Craig was completely credited by her. He nodded toward her in a friendly hello and he could have sworn he saw her lips twitch into what could have been described as a discreet smile. She stepped away from the steps and laid her hand gently against Craig's chest straightening his tie with her bony fingers.

"Mr Carter, You'll do." She stated firmly through pursed lips. She was trying her hardest to dispel her elation at the thought of the boss finally trying to get his life back to a state of normality. She held him at arm's length and checked him over once more with her beady mysterious eyes before smoothing down her own skirt and scurrying away to the back of the house. Craig stood there by the old grandfather clock at the bottom of the stairs and waited as patiently as he could muster without breaking into a cold sweat, he had never feared a date so much in his life. He would have loosened his tie but he daren't touch Leah's handy work. His brow slightly sticky from sweat and his fingers rapping against the spindle banister he swallowed down his nervousness. His piercing blue eyes stuck glued to the glass of the foyer door. His palms were clingy with sticky film, his nervousness was something simply school boy. But still patiently he waited. It seemed like hours until Leah made her return, despite it only being a few minutes. Her shadow filled the luxurious patterned glass of the foyer door and Craig held his breath as he saw his simply beautiful date strutting through the door. Her body dressed in a stunning regal blue floor length gown. Her hair was piled into a curly up do on the top of her head. Craig winked cheekily in the girl's direction and she returned the compliment with a poke of her little tongue.

"Took your time" Craig giggled softly as he took the girls hand.

"No daddy I'm early" Kiki replied sarcastically as she grasped her father's hand. Her pretend handbag slipped slightly off her shoulder as she tried to strut away from him confidently in her little patent white shoes.

"You look beautiful Keeks" he smiled sincerely. She was a breathtakingly beautiful child. She was a doppelgänger version of Craig with her mother's beautiful spirit. Kiki was Sass personified; she was a delicious combination of Jenna and Craig in a tiny little bubble of good looks and simply breathtaking personality.

"I know daddy, now can we go for dinner please" she replied in her soft petulant tone, her bottom lip protruding in full pout. She truly was stunning. Craig was taken aback with the simple presence of his beautiful daughter. He linked his fingers in hers and suddenly everything was forgotten. They walked toward the entrance of the grand home that Craig habituated and within and instant they were both compelled by one another. Kiki despite her delicate years felt completely under the spotlight with her father's charms. As they walked down the grand polished stone steps of the Mansion and out to the jet black limousine that was waiting on the gravel driveway for them. Kiki squealed with delight as the door was opened for her to slip inside the luxurious interior of the car. She shuffled across the bench allowing her father to slide in beside her. Craig closed the door silently and they were away. The mocktails and bite sized snacks that littered the Diamanté encrusted table made Craig smile as he endured his daughter lapping up the luxury before her. She took the straw to her mouth and took a deep drink from her blueberry crush sorbet, her pretty little face scrunched at the sourness and Craig had to hold back his perilous laughter. Kiki was incredulous as she held a finger sandwich to her lips; she sniffed the contents wisely as any other toddler would. Wincing when she realised it was Tuna and opting for a ham and cheese one instead.

"I like these ones daddy" she smiled approvingly. Her mouth filled with half chewed ham sandwich and cheese but still she was adorable. Craig smiled quaintly as he popped an olive and feta cube into his mouth, she was a little treasure. It was times like this that he loved the most when he could just spoil her and love her like a proper father should. He was always so busy with work commitments and endless meetings he barely had time to eat let alone play princesses. He knew he was lousy, he felt it no end but he knew his daughter treasured his time. So they spent it doing extravagant things like tonight's date night. He had planned a lovely night starting with a slap up meal at a top Italian restaurant in the city, followed by ice cream at his favourite desert place and back home for a princess DVD and popcorn night in their onesies. It was nice to spend some down time away from the hustle and stress of work. Even better when he had such fantastic company, they chatted away without a care in the back of the limousine oblivious to the world around them, right now it was just the two of them and that was all that mattered.

When they finally came to a standstill a while later Craig ever the gentleman he was went around to open the door and hand in hand he escorted her into the beautiful entrance foyer to "Sergio's Finest Italian restaurant" The air con blasting in the clammy evening heat was comforting and Craig instantly relaxed as he was booked in and let to his pre reserved table. It was adorned already with a fresh ice bucket and a bottle of white wine and a sparkling water for the little lady. The cream napkins expertly folded to resemble swans on the table.

"Only the best for the Lord and his lady right Keeks?" he laughed heartily as he led her into her seat opposite him before he shuffled comfortably onto his. He pulled the menu out and handed the separate child's one to Kiki, who perused it with a tight lipped affliction. Craig browsed over his own menu in the silence, the delectable notes of a classical piece lingering softly in the background. The high brass candelabra on the table were the only form of light apart from the dim over head spotlights casting a dim, private light onto the table. It really was a remarkable place to enjoy a quiet meal with a beautiful, soft ambience. It was peaceful, atmospheric with tentative staff that catered to your every whim without question. And the food was out of this fucking world. Craig glanced over his menu to survey his daughter's movements and grinned when he saw her attempting to read the upside down menu in her tiny girlish hands.

"What you fancying Keeks?" he muttered, still browsing his own menu with minimal effort . She shrugged her little shoulders heftily in reply as she let out a loud sigh before folding her arms across her tiny chest.

"Daddy I just can't decide and that books no good." She pointed at the menu that now stared at her open on the tabletop. "I just can't read the words" she protested. Before picking the card up and attempting a second go. Craig nearly spat his wine across the room as he stared at her with mock serious eyes.

"That Kiki Marie is your problem" his eye brow arched sarcastically as he spoke, Kiki's face suddenly twisted into a look of confusion "you do realise babe there's only pictures in your menu, there aren't any words" he replied, holding back his laughter as best he could. He saw the girls eyes widen like saucers in disbelief before she picked the menu back up and stared at it, her mouth shaped into the perfect little "O" as she scanned the pictures before pointing to the Lasagne.

"That's what I want Daddy, Sanya like Mummy used to make me" She replied matter of factly before taking a sip of her sparkling water from the plastic champagne flute the restaurant had so nicely provided for her. Craig smiled as she relaxed back into her seat, her elbows on the table, her palm cradling her chin. She looked so much older than her years and Craig knew she was going to be trouble this one was. With her fiery attitude and her bewitching looks, she was going to be a little heartbreaker!

"Do you want Peas and sweet potato chips?" Craig replied, simplifying the words on the menu that boasted of Thrice cooked sweet potato wedges garnished in molten black pepper with some sort of dip and sweet sugar snap peas. He waited for the waitress who had been loitering by their table since they had walked in through the door to make her way to them before he gave his order. The girl was practically gushing at the knees, over placating him with her heavy chavvy accent. Making remarks about how Stunnin' his daughter was with her oversized blood red mouth and fluttering her horrifically over lined hooded eyes that were layered thick with about fifty coats of clumpy mascara at him. Craig was almost tempted to use the ice bucket to vomit in but he held it back as best he could. He thanked the lord when she finally decided to sway her huge hips away from the table and he could finally be free to breathe without choking on the horrific scent of Charlie Red and fag breath. Kiki sat pinned to her chair, a look of absolute mortification etched on her tiny features, her nose scrunched up in disgust as she stared wild eyed at her father.

"Daddy, That woman was crazy, I just know it" she whispered sternly before returning her gaze back to the waitress who was grinning like a Cheshire cat at them over by the cash register, she waved frantically at Kiki when she noticed the girl looking at her. Kiki raised her hand and slowly waved back before returning her attention back to Craig.

"Daddy she's looking at us still" she whispered again before Craig finally silenced her with his hand. He was raising a young lady here not a judgemental little notright.

"Aye little miss perfect just because she looks a bit mad doesn't mean she is, she could be a lovely lady for all you know" he added quaintly before placing his napkin across his lap and taking a large slug of wine from the glass. It was a delicious Moscato, fresh and fruity and right there and then Craig was tempted to polish the whole bottle. He made light conversation with Kiki whilst they waited patiently for their meal; Craig was absolutely famished after not eating since the previous morning, he could smell the delicious scents coming from the kitchen and he was sure the whole dining room could hear his stomach growling in sweet anticipation and desire to be filled. When the bread basket came he almost took the poor waitresses hand off for the garlic buttered baguette, his mouth watering as he brought it to his lips, oh good god it was better than sex, he rolled his eyes to the ceiling as he savoured the taste. He really hadn't realised how hungry he actually was. Until the steaming platter was placed before him and Craig came face to face with the biggest plate of Fresh caught seafood linguine he had ever laid eyes on. He took in the heady salt scent of the sea mixed with fresh tomatoes and mushrooms and the delicious herb and white wine sauce. The meal smelt and looked incredible and Craig's taste buds flew to life at the mere sight of it. He picked up his cutlery and dived straight in with his fork, trying to remain as casual he could without shoving the plate straight into his face and going at it like a pig in a bloody trough. The food was as usual a sheer delight and Craig almost came in his pants after the first few forkfuls were safe and secure in his gullet. He glanced up from his plate and saw Kiki delicately cutting her lasagne up with her knife and fork and popping the tiny mouthfuls into her lips. She was becoming such a little Madame, a pure bred little lady and he smiled to think of her and her nanny Leah playing tea parties with her little vintage china tea set, nattering on about afternoon high tea with the teddy bears and the unicorns. It reminded him of how his mum had been with his sister Sammy when they were small. Sammy had always been rebellious though and preferred dirt bikes and mud slides compared to tea and princesses. Craig hoped against hope his daughter would never turn out like her aunt. The thought sent shivers straight to his bones. Sammy had been completely out of control nothing like his precious little girl who he had sworn to himself he would try his hardest to keep as innocent as he could for as long as he could. She was a little sweetheart, all doe eyes and cupids bow lips she was simply divine to look at, a picturesque little girl with a super personality. She was Craig's whole world and more and he loved her more than he could ever express in a vocal form. She was everything to him. As he watched her just sat there eating her meal, drowning in the splendour he knew he had made the right choice by taking her away from the estate that fateful afternoon and despite everything that had happened since, he knew the girl was just right where she belonged. He reached his hand out across the table and stroked her plump little cheeks.

"Daddy loves you so much princess" he whispered softly as his eyes met hers, he felt his heart pound just that little bit faster as her reply resonated in his ears that she loved him too. Her mucky face smothered in tomato sauce yet still she was breathtakingly beautiful, she was Craig's little angel, his saving grace. She was to him everything a man could want, she didn't complain, she was polite and despite her youth she was expertly wise. Craig had been ludicrously blessed with the child. Craig continued to devour the rest of his meal, blissfully unaware as he shovelled forkfuls of pasta to his lips that his beautiful daughter had fallen asleep in her plate of lasagne and was now wearing a delicious coat of tomato sauce and cheese on her face. When he did eventually notice he burst out in a fit of boyish laughter to himself, and pulled his phone out of his pocket to take a photo. Kiki would be absolutely mortified when she found out! She was such a little diva when it came to her hair and her clothes and here she was face down in her dinner snoring like a little piglet smeared in mince meat and tomato Craig smiled at the irony of it as he placed his phone down on the table and just stared momentarily at his baby. The miracle that was Kiki never failed to knock him down stone dead, he could never quite get over the fact that she was his daughter, his flesh and blood. The thought never ceased to amaze him. She was a little bit of him and a little bit of Jenna all bundled into one and Craig was mesmerised by her. He pulled the napkin off his lap and went to her aid, attempting to wipe the mess away from her cheek as gently as he could so that he didn't disturb her. He cleaned her up as best he could before paying the bill, tipping almost the same amount that he had paid for his dinner before he lifted Kiki's tiny body up into his overwhelming arms and making his way to the door. He had planned such a lovely night for them both, but his little partner in crime had bailed out on him on the first hurdle. As he bundled her into the back seat of the Limo he directed his driver to take them back home. An early night and a cuddle in bed sounded even better than the night he had planned. He bent down to kiss her gently on the temple, the scent of tomato sauce still lingering on her silky soft skin.

"Daddy loves you Keeks" he whispered once more before settling himself back against the plush leather seats and allowing his body to rest finally. He checked his emails and found a few from Donny about a new business venture they had on the cards but other than that nothing too pressing. He yawned loudly, raising his hand to his mouth to try and stem the sound. He hadn't realised how tired he actually was until then. He was actually exhausted if he thought about it. He closed his eyes momentarily, blocking out the hum of the limo as it plodded through the street at a snail's pace. Craig felt lazy, dazed from the last 24 hours and all they had held for him. The future of course was a different story altogether. He still wasn't sure just how far things were going to go, but he knew that he had to dig a little deeper beneath the surface. Jenna wouldn't spill the fucking can so he would have to do a little investigating of his own. His fingertips brushed his naked knuckles where his Daddy ring was usually cemented, he swallowed down hard. There was no time for anymore guilt, he had already felt enough. He knew now that it was time to get some answers but he also knew there would be a fight to get those answers. What he also knew was that when he had the information he so desperately needed. Then there would be fucking murders.

Dom and Jenna sat on the sofa in her flat sharing a pack of lagers and a Chinese reminiscing over all of the wonderful times they had shared together. Both laughing and finally feeling carefree despite everything that had happened, Dom had decided to push all of the negative thoughts that had been plaguing him to the back of his mind. There was soft guitar music and James Bay's beautiful voice playing in the background accidentally. The song was called let it go or something, whatever it was it was making Dom feel overly relaxed. He pushed his plate onto the coffee table and huddled into the sofa, sucking on his bottle, his head bobbing delicately to the track as he felt the alcohol slowly take effect. Claire had decided to take the baby from him for the night so he could get some time alone with Jenna. He felt the need to parent her somewhat. Now she was alone she needed help to get back to a regular routine. She was completely out of sorts. Even down to the basics, it was like he was dealing with a child not the mother of his child. Now that she had finally taken a long bath and washed away the stench of moral degradation she was starting to shine like the old Jenna had. What was now a dull and dim light would soon be a bright shining flame that would light up the sky Dom was sure of it. Of course she needed some work, she needed love and she needed care but Dom was dedicated to making her heal. Forcing her to deal with herself head on, it was the only way he knew how. But he knew he could help her, he would make sure she recovered from this. He popped open another beer as they cuddled up together on the sofa as only friends knew how and settled down to a box set of The Pirates of The Caribbean. Jenna burst out laughing when she saw the credits roll in front of her and the music began to kick in

"Surely this wasn't the only box set you had?" she quizzed, taking a quick slurp from her can, nestling into his shoulder, careful not to rest too close. She couldn't bear the thought of him getting the wrong idea. She hated the thought of being cheapened by his sympathy. Her insecurities climbing the walls as he placed his arm loosely around her shoulder, she held her breath unhealthily, fear to move too much. She didn't quite understand how to deal with his affections. She wanted to go down kicking and screaming, she wanted to lunge at him for even contemplating putting his hands on her skin, but the other half of her begged for him to touch her. She pleaded with him to want her as though she was a normal person again. He was special, he was worthy of everything he had. Dom was something else entirely. There was no judgement with him, just acceptance and Jenna was eternally grateful for his presence, even if she didn't know just how to take it. It felt nice to have company; it felt nice to have familiarity. That was all she could have hoped for. Even in silence just him being there was enough.

"You don't hate me do you?" She whispered in the silence, her fingers clasping the aluminium can harder in their grip.

Dom's head snapped toward her, his steely grey gaze alight with blazing fire as he shook his head sadly. It was all the answer Jenna needed. There wasn't another word spoken as they sat in the silence. Both tired, both exhausted with the events of the day but neither wanting the company to end. His hand lay rested on her bony knee and Jenna daren't flinch in case he got the wrong idea but she was quite comforted by the fact that he was trying. She yawned unapologetically, her lithe body stretching out in a catlike pose, her tiny limbs protruding beneath the paper thin flesh. Dom fought back the urge to speak, biting down hard on his tongue. He wanted to rip Donny's smug fucking head off with his bare hands and he would. Revenge would be a dish that would be best served stone cold.

"I Best get going" he said quietly, glugging back the rest of his beer and standing. Jenna stretched once more and smiled at him through dreary over tired eyes. Her eyelids were droopy and bleary with the haze of sleep. She looked so young, and so desperate for his attention as she sat before him all doe eyed and wanting and Dom could do nothing but stare. His subtle blush slowly creeping across his cheek as he gazed down on her, his whole body rigid with anticipation he couldn't quite stipulate what was to happen. Shifting so nervously from one foot to the other as he prayed she would look away first. His stomach tied up in delicious scout worthy knots as he tried his hardest to push his feelings aside. She needed him now, this he knew but strangely the pull that stirred deep in his gut, needed her too. He couldn't fathom it she wasn't his woman to want, she was in no fit state to call herself anyone's woman, but there it was, still driving, working its way around deep in his gullet. He felt sick, incredibly sick with delectable craving. Like a shark delving its praying teeth into the unknown. The heavenly scent of Jenna and tension was a lethal cocktail and Dom was perplexed, high from her amnesia. As much as he tried to propel himself away from her amorous pull. She was nothing short of spectacular even in her state.

"You can stay if you want" she replied in probably the tiniest voice she could muster. Her eyes were bright, wild with desire. Dom froze; he didn't want to give her the wrong impression especially after all she had told her today. But he couldn't help but linger, his whole body speaking to her in some kind of broken code. The two of them were playing to a full house, both entangled in a beautiful broken masterpiece. Dom knew that they could have been so much more than they were. A shattered portrait they had become and they were pulling at the weeds if they thought that they could be recovered. But somewhere deep in the disdain there was a slim, dull light that kept shining despite their obvious friction. Dom didn't know how the fuck to respond, his eyes glassy with a cold anticipation. Half of him was tempted, overly tempted even. But he knew that Jenna was forbidden fruit. She was the broken link in their crowd and Dom was almost resenting toward her. The Belmonte was something completely alien to him. Despite the drama he had to face every single day. The place was still crazy. The hum of everyday life was serene, even with the junkies strolling about, doing their daily. Dom remained even keel. He saw the estate for what it was. A crazy, eclectic mix of real life and paradise. Both were torn between their morals and their impending chaos should they choose to collide once more. Dom Swallowed down the sudden urge to vomit with anxiety and made his excuse to leave. As much as he felt the need to stay, he knew what the outcome would be and he knew they would both regret it come the morning. As much as he knew she wanted him, she was still so fragile, so tender and Dom couldn't risk upsetting her anymore with the reality that they would never work. He knew too much.

Craig had arrived home in high spirits; he had put Kiki to bed as soon as they had arrived back home and had taken up seat in his study with a cold can of Stella. His head ticking into overdrive as his fingers brushed the keys on his work phone softly. The thought of the impending phone call he had to make making his stomach tie in knots. He thought it too soon to make contact, but not knowing if she was okay was killing him slowly. He had put all of his attention into making sure that she had got home safely that he had forgotten how much of a pull she had over him. His mind was raging a tirade war against his heart and he knew eventually he would cave and his heart would surrender. Mercy when it finally did because he had a feeling that the fireworks would be too much for him to handle. Jenna had been his first and only Love from the very beginning they had lived this dramatic love story from behind the barricades and now they were heading to war. Heads would fucking roll when Craig found out what had happened, then vengeance would be his. No matter how big the fellow mans army was Craig would build a bigger force. But for now he just had to dig around as best he could. So far everyone was acting clueless, playing dumb but he knew liars when he saw them. He opened his laptop and began sending monotonous business replies ploughing of the various design briefs he had been sent. His heart wasn't in work; he needed his bed and a few sleepers to knock him out for the night. He hated the valium he had been prescribed by the doctors but some nights, like tonight when his anxiety was through the roof he relied on them heavily. Although they lingered on him like a bitch and he knew he'd be a nightmare to work with the following morning through slurring and generally acting like a stroke victim. He closed the laptop lid and abandoned his office he kicked off his shoes at the stairwell and paced the winding staircase. He swigged the last of his beer as he padded softly on each step. His fingers knotted in his short hair as he ran his hand through it in agitation. He couldn't wait to settle down for the night and attempt to deal with his feelings in the morning. He tiptoed past Kiki's bedroom door trying not to make a single noise as he crept toward his bedroom. The minute he strode over the threshold he stripped down to his boxers and dived into the fresh linen and without popping the blue tablets from the bottle on his bedside cabinet he drifted off into a peaceful drunken sleep.

Chapter Forty Two

Donny lay awake in the darkness, the silence was overbearing and the loneliness was beginning to hurt. He spread his hand out and touched the cold empty space beside him and sighed. He glanced over at the alarm clock, 2:30am flashed sadly back at him. He wasn't used to feeling so connected to his emotions, he was a cold hearted monster of a man in everyday life but now that the night dawned in around him and he realised that he was actually alone he felt bitter. He had lost his precious wife and he had lost his beautiful lover all at once and the reality was finally sinking in. Being a man of his word he would never run back to her but he missed sharing his bed with Jenna. She had become his sanctuary from all of the gruesome entrails of his everyday life. Despite the fact he had pimped her out, he had fed her drugs like sweets and he had knocked her about a few times. He knew they had shared something special, well to him they had anyway. He mused over the thought of phoning her, asking her to come back for a cuddle but he almost slapped himself for being so fucking sappy. But he had to admit she was amazing at being the model girlfriend. The sex was unbeatable and the romantic shit, well he wasn't used to it, but he had liked it all the same. He wasn't used to taking girls on fucking dates and to dinner. Fuck his wife had been lucky to get a Chinese on their anniversary never mind dinner at a five star restaurant mid week for nothing. It hadn't boded well with him at first but he had become accustomed to giving Jenna the finer things. Since the night he had witnessed Danielle beating Jenna to within an inch of her life he had sworn from that day on he would protect her. And he had meant every single word and had been trying his best up until his stupid wife decided to stick her fat foot through the windscreen of his car and bleed to death on their driveway. She was now facing down in a river somewhere and Donny was fine with that. His wife had no family who would ask after her, her mother was dead. Donny should know he was the one that had killed her. And her fucking father if that's what he could be called was a strange fucking not right who was holed up in some bedsit in Islington with his twenty cats for company so Donny knew he had no threats there. It was the vicious little fucking stepchild that had his back up and Donny knew it wouldn't be long before he came sniffing around.

Tommy was a little wannabe gang lord who had never fully cut away from his stepmothers apron strings. Sandra's first marriage had been to some millionaire businessman called Max Heller. Who had fucked off with his secretary to America and hadn't been seen since. Tommy had been left to fend for himself since the tender age of sixteen and had stuck to his step mothers backside like a leach ever since. Donny had never liked the boy. His baby face and big powder blue eyes were disarming and made him look a hell of a lot younger than his years. Even with his slightly stubbled face the boy still looked about eighteen, Donny had never taken to him. From their first meeting Donny had shunned the boy like a mother bird does a bad egg and tossed him straight out of the nest. Sandra met with him three times a week, spoilt him, took him out or whatever she did to please him but Donny had played no part in it. Tommy was a little fucking cretin and the minute he started sniffing around was the minute Donny was going to bring out the big guns and frighten the little tosser into not saying a fucking word about his precious step mummy and where she had disappeared to. He took a deep drag and blew out a thick grey plume of smoke out through his mouth. The nicotine haze allowing him to rest even if it was only momentarily. He lay back against the plush silk pillows, comforted by their chilly embrace. He felt a bit disheartened about facing the future alone; he had enjoyed the company while it had lasted. The girl had made him feel alive again, taken away the morbid loneliness he felt every day. Even though his marriage was still in the early years Sandra had known nothing about affection, she had known only how to slug wine and spend money that was a given. But when it had come down to the having a physical, loving relationship Sandra had been as passionate as a dry ham Sandwich. She enjoyed the title of gangster's moll more than anything else if it hadn't been for the term she wouldn't have been bothered with him one iota. Oh Yes she loved the opulence and the grandeur that money gave her but she turned her little piggy nose up to the person who kept her in her Pearl earrings and high heels. Donny put the thought to the back of his mind. He didn't like placating himself it made him feel weakened. The female form was such a desperate, cruel mistress and he was indeed glutton for punishment. Donny stubbed the cigarette end into the ashtray and for a moment just took in the space around him. It felt too roomy in the bed; he was used to having Jenna sprawled out beside him, taking up half of the bed despite how small she was. He was used to the feel of her skin against his, the warmth of her hair at his nose in the early morning. He missed the way she used to roll over onto his side of the bed and snuggle close to his pillow if he got up in the night. She had become a necessity in his everyday routine and Donny was beginning to feel saddened by the fact that she was gone. He had never expected it to happen and so he had taken her for granted. He wished he hadn't but he couldn't change reality. She had abandoned ship. Left him high and dry with nothing but his mind that was in over drive, he was sure he loved Jenna. His filthy mind would never be willing to admit it but he was sure he did. It was the little things, from the way she walked, to the way she opulently bathed her skin in decadent vanilla bubble bath. The way her hair was drenched in the scent of melons from her specific hair mask. The way it still dripped off of the pillows was intoxicating. The elevating smell of her that was more apparent in his home than he was lifted him. Jenna was his conviction. He was caught in a sticky situation here and it didn't fix well with Donny. He wasn't used to feeling like he needed something so much. He sat back up; he knew the sandman would be avoiding him like the plague tonight so he pushed the covers aside and clambered out of bed, stretching in the moonlight that spilled through the thin voile panels in the windows. His body glistening with a sticky hot sweat, the bulge in his boxer shorts aching as he stretched languidly. He sighed heavily wondering what the fuck he was going to do. He didn't want to run back to her, he would be weak if he did. But part of him really wanted to, just to say goodbye properly. He had left her go in such a heated way, he just wanted to clear the air between them. She had become a vast part of his life in such a short space of time. Now was gone. Donny grabbed his notebook computer from under the bed and plugged it in beside the bed. He stared blankly at the screen as he pulled up a few of his business notes and some plot sites he had found to build himself some properties on nothing seemed of interest but there were a few nice places that he would have to take a closer look into in the future. He sat at the foot of the bed fiddling about with his business affairs for another hour before he eventually got bored and called himself a cab. This would be sorted. Tonight.

Chapter Forty Three

Dom sat perched on the edge of his sofa sucking desperately on his half a spliff that he had lain in the ashtray. Claire had taken the baby for the night and he needed something to calm his nerves. His hands were jangling uncontrollably as he took another few puffs before setting the ashtray down on the coffee table and settling back lazily onto the sofa. His mind was completely in overdrive and the paranoia was starting to creep upon him. Lingering as he thought over the day's events. His mind was hazed, caught viciously between sedation and being over alert. He could feel his temples pounding in his head, wary of what the fuck he was to do next. He was flustered, his heart skipping merry beats in his chest, fluttering at a heavy pace. He thought momentarily he would pass out. But he held consciousness wearily he stood, trying to shake off the feeling of fear that was sat numbly on his aching shoulders. He felt nothing, other than complete emptiness. His head was a mess; he hadn't felt so down in a long time. But he knew that he had to confide in someone. He could see Donny now ripped into a million pieces, the blood draining from his ugly face, distorted dead eyes that hung in their sockets like treasured heirlooms. Dom pictured Donny with his throat slit, hanging from the rafters by his own fucking tie. Dom closed his eyes as the rush of euphoria finally hit him and he began to relax into himself. The thoughts his mind were plucking up were a comfort. He held all the cards now, and close to his chest he would keep them until the time was right. Donny would pay for this, and he would pay with his treacherous, unworthy life. The cunt wasn't worth the proverbial wank yet he still had the fucking bare nerve to saunter the back streets as though they were paved in gold just for him. Well it would all end soon. All Dom had to do was get Craig on side and they would be laughing, standing victorious with dirty blood smeared gloriously on their hands.

Chapter Forty Four

Donny sat in his car, the lights dimmed to an eerie glow as the rain hammered against the windscreen. He had driven out into the middle of nowhere just for the calm. The serenity of the outdoors bringing his wayward mind to reason. He wanted so badly to go and be with Jenna, but the fear of rejection struck a chord in his ugly heart and he felt merciless in his assaults. He couldn't be with her; they were toxic together, a heady mix of fire and gasoline. He knew that more than anyone could fathom, but living without her, even now in the premature hours since her departure seemed virtually impossible. If sleeping alone had been anything to go by he could never handle it, he had just felt her presence everywhere. But not being able to touch her, hold her, kiss her goodnight was killing him deep inside. Even though he had been a fucking cunt to her, he had fallen in love like the silly bastard he was and now he was trapped between the devil and the deep blue. He was drowning with no sense of security or safety to abide him. He was for the first time in his life, missing another human being and the thought alone was sobering. She had become a part of his routine and now that it was broken he felt knocked viciously out of joint. He had shed a tear tonight for all he had made her go through, he imagined her alone in Danielle's the night he had dumped her there. She had shone bright even then and just got on with things. She had been a good worker despite her obvious hesitance at being a whore she had done the job well. But Donny had felt a change in himself. Seeing her with punters had made him angry, jealous and he had begun lashing out on his business associates for touching her up the wrong way or saying a harsh word to her and it was then he knew that he was punching well above his weight. He pulled a cigarette from his ever ready box and lit, filling the interior with an angry purple plume of smoke. He inhaled the sultry hit of the nicotine, the rush hitting him like a bolt of lightning where he sat. He coughed slightly, absorbing the heave in his chest that only a dedicated smoker feels when their stressed. The warmth of familiarity was overwhelming and welcoming all at once and Donny felt nothing but distinct pleasure as he lounged back in his seat. He ran a hand across his aching neck, a flicker of a playful smile lingered on his full lips. He had the devil in his mindset and nothing was bringing him to heel. He needed to lose some of this pent up frustration so he spun the car around with a screeching u turn and decided, he had to go to the Belmonte tonight if only to see her.

Jenna had just fallen into a troubled sleep on the sofa when she as woken by the slightest tapping noise against her kitchen window. She shot up wide eyed in the dark, stiff against the sofa back as her eyes shot across the room. Her fingers dug deeply into the leather as the tapping ensued once more, cold and eerie as each finger struck the glass. Jenna swallowed down the scream that emerged in her throat. Her body rigid with sheer panic, eyes bulging in her head as she stood, trying not to make the slightest noise as she padded barefoot to the kitchen. She saw the darkened shadow beyond the glass outlined by the sliver of moonlight outside. The heavy beating of the rain bounced off the window pane as she slithered into the kitchen on her hands and knees to avoid being seen. She held her raspy breath as she stalked across the lino floor, bringing her back against the cold glass panel of the back door so she was just millimetres away from the culprit she closed her eyes as the stem of tears rolled down her solemn cheek. Was this really what her life had become? Hiding away from the threat of the shadows, in her desperation she snatched an empty wine bottle from beside the bin and lay in wait. The fingers rapped against the glass once more and Jenna almost dove out of her skin. Jenna hitched a tainted, much needed breath trying to dispel the feeling of craziness from her warped mind.

"Who is it" she wailed, her voice strained. Her fingers clutched the bottle tighter as she waited patiently for a response. Her heart almost bouncing out of her chest, every second that ticked by making her even more nervous. She sat in wait, her whole body pricked with intense emotion until she heard the whispers coming through the cracks in the door frame.

"Craig?"She called out into the darkness. Confusion written over furrowed brow, she froze as the shallow cackles of the man behind the glass echoed around the kitchen space. The bizarre giggling brought Jenna crashing back to reality, she would know that laugh anywhere. The noise so distinct and filled with the venom of a cocaine high. She pulled herself wearily to her feet and pinned her body to the wall of glass that separated them. He couldn't hurt her as long as she stayed inside. She knew he wouldn't smash the window, it would make too much noise and people on the Belmonte were light sleepers and heavy talkers' news would spread like wildfire and she knew he wouldn't risk being seen. There was no way she was going back now, which was of course why he was here. He had realised his mistake in letting her leave and now he was here to take back what he saw as rightfully his.

"What do you want Donny" Her voice breaking with nerves, she imagined she sounded even more petulant to him.

"I had to see you. To say goodbye" he whispered after a few long moments of agonising silence, Jenna sensed the urgency in his voice. Sympathised only for a second. Her heart screaming for her to pull him inside and comfort him. Run her long fingers through his dark hair, to feel his thick full lips on hers she could feel her knees trembling beneath her at the thought. Despite what he had done Donny was an amazing lover. The perfect mix of give and take regardless of his actions he had given her the world.

"Jen please, you know I need you, you know I would never hurt you again don't you" Jenna could hear the slur in his voice, drugs had him stupefied and she knew if she allowed him in she would regret it in an instant. Donny was an expert at mind games and Jenna knew exactly what he was doing. She needed to get out of the flat immediately if she had any chance of survival. She pushed herself against the door, her slim body pressed firm against the glass.

"Aye Jen. If you don't open up I'm gunna have to chuck you over me knee" he slurred once more rattling the doorknob loudly. Jenna inhaled a long relaxing breath.

"I need some time babe, to think about things" she replied gently, trying her utmost to keep her voice calm and neutral. She couldn't risk tipping him over the edge. Donny wasn't a man to be crossed at the best of times, but when he had a line him he was lethal. She stepped back, her eyes closing momentarily as he rattled the door again.

"I just want to talk to you" the temper was starting to flair now and Jenna could feel his annoyance at her defiance reverberating in waves. Jenna backed away into the hallway, desperately trying not to make a single sound. The street lamp outside lit her passage up like a beacon so she edged herself slowly to the front door, He was still stood by the back door so she had enough time to make her escape before he noticed she had fled. She pulled the keys from the sideboard at the bottom of the stairs, fumbling with the bunch as she finally grasped the front door key. Slowly she pushed the key into the lock, her heart banging in her chest as with the slightest flick of her tiny wrist the lock clicked open. One more deep breath inward and Jenna bolted straight out of the door. Her bare feet slapping against the concrete as she sprinted across the hallway and began to bang her tiny fists on Dom's front door. She was screaming, her voice desperate and high pitched and for a second she didn't even realise the blood curdling sound was coming from her. There were hot tears spilling down her cheeks in torrents. As though time had stood deathly still, everything seemed to be in slow motion she felt a heavy hand on her shoulder. She spun around and came face to face with Donny Anderson in all his coked up glory. His eyes wide, filled with angry menace as he delivered the painful blow that connected to her jaw before Donny slung her to the ground. She heard Dom's door open, there was shouting but she couldn't make out the words in her dazed state. She felt herself being lifted up into a pair of strapping arms and she wished and prayed with all of her might in that moment that they belonged to Dom. All that could be heard was heavy breathing and the sound of car tyres screeching in the near distance. She felt herself slipping out of consciousness. Then suddenly her world turned black, her body finally giving into peaceful undisturbed sleep.

Chapter Forty Five

"Dom what the fuck!" Craig yawned sleepily as he answered his mobile. He had heard it ringing on the bedside cabinet at least five times before he had finally decided to answer. Groggily he swiped at his eyes, holding his phone lazily to his ear and hearing his nemesis mouthing off down the receiver wasn't what he wanted to hear in the small hours of the morning. He sat up shaking off the tired ache that racked his body. He pulled his pillow behind his back and leant against the headboard. His hand skimmed his head as he tried to make sense of Dom's lunatic ramblings.

"Oi you stupid cunt, fucking slow the fuck down now then!" he snapped down the mouthpiece when he had finally had enough of the idiots fucking gabbling.

"It was fucking Donny!" Dom mouthed breathlessly when he finally had gathered himself some composure.

"What was fucking Donny now princess?" Craig smiled sarcastically as he took a swig of water from the tumbler on the bedside cabinet. He wondered why the fuck Dom felt the need to hare his little bit of gossip with him though. Surely he knew by now Craig couldn't stand the fucking sight of him.

"He was the one who took Jenna you muggy cunt" Dom spat in response to Craig's childish remarks. Craig grinned at the boys' bravado; he found it quite cute that Dom had actually challenged him. Well if calling him a cunt was all Dom could manage then he was sadly mistaken if he thought for a second Craig would be offended.

"When did you work that out then genius? If you remember correctly I work with Donny, don't you think I'd realise if he had Jenna? Now if you don't mind some of us are trying to sleep!" Craig laughed now, a proper childish giggle that to anyone else would sound beautiful. Almost enough to charm the birds from the trees but to Dom resembled nails down a chalkboard.

"I fucking swear to you Craig on Archie's life, he's had her. He's been whoring her out all this time." His voice was a plea suddenly and Craig couldn't help but feel the tightening in his stomach. Could Dom be telling him the truth? It easily could have been done. Donny had clubs and women all over the country he easily could have shunted Jenna off elsewhere to work. He didn't want to believe it to be true but he knew if Dom was telling the truth then vengeance would indeed be his. Although Donny was a close business associate of his and what Craig had believed to be a friend. But this little bombshell had blown any chance of that now. He paused once more, letting it all sink in. He questioned Dom meticulously then. The second Dom informed him that Donny had been over there kicking off and Jenna had been hurt he immediately hung up the phone and raced to get dressed. He had to be with her now. Whether Dom was there or not. She needed him.

* * * * * * * * * * * * * * * * *

A while later Craig was sat in Dom's living room nursing a steaming coffee and a face like a smacked backside as he watched Dom mollycoddle Jenna as though she was a little fucking kid. He felt as though his nose had been put clean out of joint as he just sat there blankly staring into space. When he had arrived he could hear the voices all around the estate, despite it being the early hours of the morning the curtain twitchers were up and gossiping already. The fucking place was a disease. Craig held the cup to his thin scowling lips as he looked on at the tragic scene before him. Jenna was still out for the count, she had come too twice but had fallen back to sleep after a few minutes. Exhaustion was the more likely cause than the blow to her face. It was bruised, a horrific black and purple blotch on the side of her cheek. Dom had suppressed the swelling with a bag of frozen parsnips, he'd run out of peas apparently. Not that Craig had been listening. He had been too enthralled in judging Dom's awful décor of baby toys and fake posed photography of him and the baby. It cut Craig to the quick to see how much the boy had changed. Deathly pale skin and bright green eyes just like his mother. Craig felt bad for immediately thinking that Kiki was the prettier of the two children. But the mood he was in now Dom was lucky the thought hadn't escaped his mouth instead.

"Want another?" Dom asked as politely as he could muster when Craig placed his cup down on the coffee table.

Craig shook his head and stood, resuming his position by the mantelpiece. His eyes narrowing as he scanned each perfectly placed photograph on the surface. Each smiling face, each and every expertly captured smile screaming out happily at Craig. He stopped at the photo of Dom and Claire that had been taken at a meal or function of some sort. Craig swallowed down hard as he saw the beaming faces of his niece and nephew and the wide mouthed laughing face of his beautiful mother. Craig instantly felt gunned down, his heart heavy with regret as he held the picture in his hands, his fingers tracing his mothers smile. He had missed her so much and now knowing she was so close, just metres away he felt that it was time for him to go to her now. He had tried to kill the idea stone dead but it was there, still buzzing around in his head.

"Where was this taken?" Craig asked gently, his eyes still lingering to the face of his loved ones. His eyes were sad, lightly creased with crow's feet that made his face look slightly older than what he was. Dom stood beside him. Staring slightly over the strapping mans shoulder,

"It was a charity fundraiser they had for Lily's playgroup" he replied, smiling warmly at the memory before slumping down on the sofa to drink his now stone cold coffee.

"I'm sorry for the way I spoke to you earlier, just had a lot on my mind the last few days that's all. You didn't deserve it" Craig said quietly, before setting the picture back in its rightful place. And sitting on the chair opposite Dom. His Crystal blue eyes wide with sincerity, his hands placed casually between his legs, his head bowed slightly to the floor. Dom shook his head and shrugged the incident off as nothing.

"I completely understand mate" he replied lighting his trusty spliff that was placed neatly behind his ear. He threw his lighter down on the coffee table before he began pulling a few long puffs on the cigarette before setting it down in the ashtray and handing it to Craig. Craig smiled humbly at the man's generosity before taking a few tokes himself. God he had missed smoking weed, it had always calmed him, even though he only dabbled in it occasionally now, there was nothing like a spliff to calm you down in stressful situations. So he guessed tonight he could make the exception. Feeling a little lighter hearted after a few more puffs he passed back to Dom and relaxed back in the chair. The thought of seeing his mother still lingering like a bad smell in the back of his mind. He knew the time was shortly coming where he would have to finally face her. He turned to do Dom then;

"What would you do if you were in my position" he asked through reddened stoner eyes and an electric boyish grin.

"With your mother?" Dom quizzed "Mate if I were you I'd go and sort it out. She's found it tough since your sister died not having you around. She misses you so much, she doesn't shut up about you half of the time. It's like your God's gift or something" he grinned flicking the ash into the tray frequently when he spoke as though he had a nervous disposition. Craig nodded once more and stood. This needed solving and as his old grand had once told him "there's no time like the present Craig" Dom was stunned as Craig pulled the front door shut behind him. He wanted suddenly to go to Claire. Dom knew Claire would be devastated. But he was cast firm to the sofa, the whole affair had never been his business but Dom had understood Craig's need to get everything cleared up. He needed his mother now, they all did. Claire was like the glue that had held them all together in their darkest moments and now it was their turn to repay the favour. Dom lit the last of the spliff in the ashtray and sat watch over the sleeping Jenna. Her delicious rosy pink lips puckering as she snored softly, shifting her position slightly. Her mouth slack, curved slightly in slumber. She was picturesque. Dom was in complete awe of her. He smiled at the memory of the first night they had spent together, she had looked exactly the same that night, and he had stayed up into the small hours just looking at her, drowning in her beauty. She truly was a marvel. Stunning in both looks and personality. Despite her faults, and she had more than a few, she remained exquisite. Dom crept slowly from his seat and tucked a stray hair behind her ear so that she now looked completely angelic, her hair flowing in a plum veil, framing her beautiful heart shaped face perfectly. He bent down and gently kissed her soft temple, the skin warm and plump beneath his lips and Dom instantly felt the stirring begin deep in the pit of his stomach. Things were going to turn ugly very quickly from here on out, he didn't know whether they would all survive. But he knew Donny would be out for their blood after tonight and Dom didn't know now whether he would be sticking around for the fireworks.

Craig stood face to face with the PVC front door that led to his mothers flat. He had been stood staring at the window pane for at least twenty minutes contemplating what the fuck he was going to say when they finally came face to face. His palms were sweating profusely, would she even recognise him? He had changed so much from the chavvy teenage boy he had been when he had faked his own death. He was now a man, a fine one at that. He had outgrown the Belmonte and all of the fucking saps that occupied it. He hopped from one foot to the other trying to beat out of the cold and dispel the feeling of hopelessness that was bubbling inside him. He swiped the sweat from his forehead with the back of his sleeve and braced himself once more. He held his hand to the knocker and froze, he honestly didn't know if he could go through with all of the heartache that would come from Claire when she realised the truth. When she found out that he had deceived her all in the name of his own self greed. She would be devastated there was no denial on that front. She would be more than hurt and Craig wasn't sure he could put her through all that, especially since his sister had died so tragically. He felt guilty for not being there when he was needed the most. He had taken the cowardly option and stepped away instead being the man he claimed he was. He had mourned Sammy's passing alone in his office with a bottle of whiskey and his treasured ub40 album. When all along he knew he should have been here instead, lifting his mother up, healing her with his loving embrace, but instead he had his away in the shadows, allowing everyone else to pick up the pieces that he had left in his wake. He sucked in a final heavy breath before he finally brought his knuckles down onto the glass. He rapped noisily three times before stepping back out onto the veranda. He saw the light go on upstairs, his eyes darting to the window that remained in darkness, his old bedroom. He sighed heavily as he heard the sounds of shuffling feet coming closer and closer. The house was now bathed in a dim glow and Craig could see his mother's buxom shadow in the background shuffling into her dressing gown that she always left on the bottom of the stairs. She was cursing to herself and Craig couldn't help but raise the small smile that leaked onto his lips. She was a game old bird was his mam. He heard the million locks that Claire had on the front door unbolting one by one, followed by Claire's continuous swearing.

"Who the fuck do you think you are knocking here at this time don't you realise what time of the morning it is you fucker" She screeched as she yanked the door open. For a single moment when she clapped eyes on the beautiful young man on her doorstep, she had no clue who he was and was about to question him. At a second glance she was rendered entirely speechless. As though all of the wind had been knocked clean out of her. She held her hand to her mouth as the tears began to flood her eyes. Her crazy red bob sticking up all over the place as she fell back into the door. She was shaking now, physically rattling as she just repeated "No" over and over like a rhythmic mantra. Her eyes never leaving his, he felt the sting of tears developing in his own as he stepped forward and wrapped her in his arms.

"Its okay mam, I'm home" He whispered as she began to sob viciously against his shoulder, her body sagging against his with need as she clutched him tightly. Clinging to him with an almost feral need, she was spluttering unheard words between furiously heavy breaths as she tried to make sense of how this miracle had occurred. But he was here, her baby was alive. Craig knew the happiness would be short lived, he knew eventually he would have to explain his actions. But until then he would just enjoy having his mother back. She was holding him out at arm's length now, scanning every single feature of his handsome face. He had changed so much. He was barely recognisable now, his soft boyish features had all but disappeared and in their place was fine athletic bone structure and fresh well shaven skin. He was a stunning man, with the most bewitching topaz blue eyes and fresh youthful skin. He had evolved into a gentleman and in that moment Claire was bursting with pride. Despite her anger, despite the fact that she herself could kill him stone dead where he stood for all he put her through. She had never in a million years thought she would ever feel this happy ever again. Her head was swimming, full of unanswered thoughts that would for now remain unanswered as she revelled in the company of her golden child. The apple of her eye was home and all that mattered now was that she kept him safe and away from harm.

"Cup of tea wouldn't go a miss mind, I'm parched" Craig winked cheekily, his face just a little bit pink from blushing under his mothers gaze. As if he had never left Claire just nodded her head and practically skipped off into the kitchen and filled the kettle. As she set about fussing with the mugs she turned and grinned with a smile as wide as the Cheshire cat as she whispered softly through her happy tears.

"I can't believe it's you"

Craig gave a shrug of his heavy shoulders and yawned loudly as Claire set the two steaming mugs of tea down on the table and grabbing the biscuit tin from the cupboard. She sat opposite him, still grinning broadly as she dipped a rich tea into her mug. Craig looked at her in mock disgust, he had always hated people dunking things in tea, tea was to be drunk, not eaten. He took a biscuit from the tin and ate it dry. His mother tutted her disapproval.

"Still haven't changed then" she laughed through a mouthful of biscuit.

"God no" Craig shook his head "Dunking is for pigs mother" he replied in a fake posh accent.

"So I'm assuming it's you who has the baby" she quizzed. Her voice was thick with sarcasm, her eyes twinkling with knowledge.

"Yes Kiki lives with me, we have a manor house out in the country" he stated proudly, taking a quick sip of tea. "It's a lovely house, we have a few acres of land, indoor pool, gym and sauna, Kiki has a lovely princess bedroom and playroom and my staff live on site so its easy access for the Nanny and My driver. You'd love it." He smiled warmly. As he grabbed another biscuit from the tin, Claire placed her hand on top of his.

"You've done well for yourself then, were you hurt badly after the attack or?" she had to stop mid sentence to stop herself from crying once more.

"I was in recovery for three months, maybe a little longer. But yeah I'm left with scars. Johnny though he works for me full time, he runs one of my clubs actually" Craig laughed at his mother and her obvious shock to learn that Johnny had been in on the whole bloody thing. She was so confused; her head was genuinely fit to burst. She picked at her dressing gown as she mulled the whole thing over in her mind. Craig had been her whole world and he hadn't trusted her with his plans to fake his own death. No matter whatever happened she was his mother. She had believed them to be closer than that, but he had proved her wrong with his deception.

"Who else knows that your alive then?" she quizzed once more, this time through slightly gritted teeth, her voice thick with aggression. Craig knew immediately she was on the defensive and she would be able to sniff a lie like a fart in a lift. So his only option was to be as honest as he physically could be.

"Jenna, Dom, Lee, Lisa" they all know, they're the only people from around here who do. I have a new identity and that for my business affairs" he grinned coyly. He didn't know how else to reply. As much as he loved his mother. He knew that she would now pose a problem for him. He knew that now was the time she would scrutinise every single detail of his life since the attack. He couldn't deal with it tonight, it wasn't the right time. He sat back and downed the last of his tea. Looking around awkwardly at the old mismatched appliances and the run down appearance of the place Craig saw how badly his lies had affected Claire. She had always been so house proud, so enveloped in her home and the shitty little NicNaks she had accumulated over the years. Now the place just looked grubby and cluttered. There were dished piled high in the sink, the units looked unpolished and even her poor spider plant that adorned the window had seen better days. Craig knew in that very moment that he had definitely outgrown this fucking shithole estate. If he had his way he would pluck his mother right out of this pit and take her away from here. But it wasn't just Claire he would be taking and that is exactly what made Craig think twice. As much as he cared for his niece and his nephew, they were well and truly broken children, estate kids and there was no fucking way they were casting their ways off on his little jewel Kiki. He knew he looked upon his mother now with his nose in the air and he would forever feel guilty for doing so, but this place was a fucking dump. The people who occupied the place were all jumped up junkies or dole trolls and Craig couldn't help but feel his skin crawl at the mere thought of returning here ever again in his life. It would take his every single ounce of strength in his body not to wipe his feet on the way out of the flat. The whole set-up screamed bad memories to Craig and he would be glad to leave the demons here dead and buried. He would always want a relationship with his mother but he wouldn't ever be letting his daughter back on this concrete jungle even if his life depended on it.

"So why have you come back now or should I take a wild guess that you've come back for her downstairs and not to fucking explain yourself" Claire quizzed, her lip still quivering slightly as she spoke. She was angry now, seething in fact and Craig couldn't wait to fucking leave as it stood. She was starting to get on his tits, he had expected anger, he had expected her to smack him in the face with a fucking saucepan if he was honest. But the whinging and the petulant arrogance on the woman was starting to grind his gears. He was beginning to think he had made a mistake in coming here. He slid his chair across the lino and stood.

"Jenna needs me mam; she's in a lot of trouble. I don't know how big this is going to get and I can't tell you who will lose their lives in the process. But only I can help her." He whispered sadly, pulling his head into his hands.

"I have to put Kiki first and she needs her mother, more than I ever realised before. I need to end this and soon. The longer it's left the worse it will be for us all. I don't know how long I've got as it is but I need your support in this. I don't want you sat there pondering over the fact that you think I've deceived you. I did it to fucking protect you and Sammy and them kids or Kenny would have killed you fucking all without a seconds thought. So spare me the fucking sour face and the attitude wont you" He scolded before he turned and left without another word leaving Claire open mouthed and sorry she had ever opened the bastard door. She pulled her ever apparent whiskey bottle from the kitchen cupboard and poured herself a large measure straight into her coffee mug. She would think about it all again tomorrow. She lit herself a cigarette and allowed herself to cry.

Kristian Collins was away with the fairies, slumped in the corner of Danielle's flat, his eyes low and moody as he sucked another line of coke with the tatty rolled up twenty from the Thomas the Tank plate that sat on his lap. His nose burning with the chemical intoxication as he drew back the remaining particles of powder that invaded his nostrils. He was completely off his nut and he couldn't wait to give Danielle a good fucking when business calmed down a bit. His cock was fit to burst in his trousers such was his rabid erection. He shuffled uncomfortably in his skinny jeans trying to reduce the swelling. He took a long swig from his can of cheap cider that was perched on an upturned crate that acted as a coffee table. The bed sheet curtain flapping from the open window letting in a sliver of a breeze from outside. The night was slowly breaking into morning, the darkness breaking slowly into another new day. Kristian polished off the remainder of his beer and slung the empty can amongst the other rotten debris and broken bottles that had mounted in the corner. Kristian closed his eyes and took in the cocaine rush that evaded his body, the sweat was leaking profusely from his brow, and his jaw was bouncing around his face as he ground his teeth together harshly. He took in the sounds of the sex trade that echoed from the walls all around him.

The harsh banging of headboards and over exaggerated moans from the dirty slags that Danielle had working the rooms. The girls who walked around with their toffee noses stuck high in the fucking air during the day, chatting shit about every other female on the planet with voices thick with jealous negativity. When by night they were nothing more than filthy sluts with their barely there knickers round their shapely ankles. They were Dirty whores that played the dirty game. Kristian forced a slightly sloping smile to himself, his off it eyes glazed and pinned so much that his pupils were practically invisible. He coughed the hackles from his chest and spat them out onto the already stained to fuck carpet and stood up, stumbling slightly, holding his hand out to the wall as he steadied himself.

"Dan! Come here you filthy bitch and suck my fucking cock" he called out, laughing to himself like a creepy hyena, his tongue snaking in and out of his overly dry lips. As he pawed his way across the room, spluttering and coughing as he went, his heart thumping a tattoo in his chest, he felt the first shot of mind bending pain shoot up his arm and he collapsed to his knees. He roared angrily in pain as he grit his teeth clenched tightly as another electrifying jolt pumped through his system, he felt immediately helpless, his whole body was numb from shock as though there was a fucking elephant sitting on each and every muscle in his body. His vision was blurred, but the last image he saw vividly was the working girls stood open mouthed, screaming completely stark naked as they watched Kristian Collins die of a heart attack right there on the brothel floor.

Chapter Forty Six

Donny was fucking livid as his car screeched to a thundering halt on the gravel drive. He leapt out of the car and sucked in the bitterly cold morning air. His nostrils flaring with sheer demonic anger and rage. His temper heated almost to the point of boiling over. He yanked open his suit jacket and tossed it in a heap on the floor as he entered his vast beautiful home. The lights were dimmed down so everything was cast in eerie shadows. The spindles on the staircase drenched in the sickly scent of pine polish, a little more than subtle in the air as Donny took the stairs in twos. He needed a run to clear his head; there was no way he would be getting any sleep. The dawn was beginning to break, an eclectic mix of heavy pinks and Smokey purples flooded through the large bay windows. Donny stood and bathed in the glorious beauty of the morning, the sun was just coming up over the horizon casting everything in the distance into a shadow of black. It was like a beautifully painted oil canvas, vibrant colours and heady thick shadows. Donny sucked in a calming breath and for a moment he felt serene, at one with himself. It was strange how cocaine made you have these almost out of body experiences, as thought you were on the outside looking in. It truly was breathtaking although stupidly simple. Donny smiled to himself then before pulling a pair of sweats from his wardrobe. He took off his suit pants and shirt, tugging at the knot in his tie with little tolerance. He turned on the radio, Jenna's CD was still in the player, Donny swallowed down the razorblades that lurched into his neck, and he puffed a breath gruffly. This was going to be harder than he thought, letting her go was something he had never fathomed in his wildest dreams. He pulled on his sweatpants and caught his reflection in the mirror. He was a handsome fucker; there was no denial of that, with his short dark hair, his cute button nose and the sparsely dispersed stubble that coated his chin. He was the rugged kind of perfect, but he was perfect none the less. Tattooed and with a body to kill for he was in everyone's eyes the image of picturesque beauty. He was a superior mix of good looks and bad boy charm. The girls were flocking to him, but to Donny, they may as well be invisible. He had been dumbstruck by only two women in his life, his wife and Jenna. Jenna more so because she had been the forbidden one. He had used her, abused her and still she had gazed at him with her big doe eyes and her pouting thick lips. Donny was stunned by her. He stood now gazing at himself in the mirror; his hands trailing across his ripped torso were her hands had left their subtly perfumed trail. He liked the way that his joggers hung from his slim hips, just above his pubic bone. He imagined her there; her cheek nestled amongst his pubic hair as she went down on him. He could just see her now, on her knees before him. At his mercy completely. He had loved her then, but he loved her even more now. The fact that she had run away from him had proved only one thing. She was scared, scared that she was falling for him too. He pulled on his hooded jumper and pulled the hood up over his head. He slipped into his Nikes and once more glanced at his reflection in the mirror. He was a handsome fucker there was no denying that. His eyes caught the slightly blurred picture of him and Jenna that was stuck to the inside of the wardrobe door. His face was slightly distorted, but there she was with her luminous eyes and her perfect curves in all the right places, smiling broadly for the camera, her arm wrapped around Donny's waist as she sipped on a glass of champagne. The shot was perfectly natural, Jenna at her most stunning without a single doubt. Her milk white skin was flawless despite its unnatural deathly colour. She was hauntingly beautiful. Donny stroked the picture with delicate fingers before turning and heading for the door. He looked back once more, pulling his hood up further on his face and darting down the stairs. He needed to figure out his next move. Grey had marked his cards, but Jenna was a different kettle of fish altogether. He would face that little mishap tomorrow. As he pulled open the front door and took a deep drag of the fresh air. The sound of some second rate rap track filling his ears as he pounded the pavement. His trainers slapping the pavement as he went, steady paced and feeling invisible. Donny traced each and every step, slightly breathless and over tired but still buzzing from the coke. He was running at a slightly over energetic pace, more of a gentle sprint than a jog. The crisp morning breeze billowing around him, Donny felt peace, nothing but serenity as his feet pounded the pavement. There was something about being alone in the early hours that calmed Donny. Despite his head being a complete fucking scatty mess at the moment, he couldn't deny how fresh he felt after a run. Despite the sweat raining down his forehead in torrents through his over indulgence in cocaine he felt amazing. The fact that he could probably indulge in a liquid breakfast and a read of the morning paper comforted him somewhat. Although apparently vodka and lemonade wasn't a suitable breakfast but whom the hell was he to say no. The thought was tantalising. He began to slow down his pace, his muscles leg burning, his heart banging in his chest; he bent over double, sucking in the wild torrents of fresh air. His head was spinning; he sat down on the wet dew dripped grass and gathered his composure for a moment. The damp grass was soaking against his thick cotton jogging trousers. He was sweating profusely his temples pounding as he held his head between his knees. From out of nowhere he felt the sting of angry tears in his eyes and right there on the concrete pavement in the middle of the desolated park, Donny cried his eyes out like a fucking baby. He cried for his wife, he cried for the loss of his lover and he cried for the complete feeling of loneliness that had become his day to day. There was no escaping his emotions. Donny Anderson, broken bitter man with a chip on his shoulder. The tag didn't suit him at all. He was strong willed, so much more than this and he would prove it. He would bide his time, but he would make her his again. He was the perfect artist of manipulation and if it meant him serving her hearts and flowers on a gold platter, then so be fucking it. He picked himself up after what felt like an age and began running off into the distance, his head thinking overtime and his mouth wired into the most devilish smile. Fuck Jenna Shearan, she'd come crawling back in her own time.

Chapter Forty Seven

The girls were raving around the knocking shop in a flurry of skimpy knickers and swinging tits. All trying to keep their squeals and dry heaves of sickness to a minimum. The dead body that was slumped in the lounge was causing more than a bloody grievance and Danielle was at her wits end trying to shut the fucking trollops up. The noise was reaching a deafening crescendo and Danielle was beginning to panic, the neighbours ere nosey bastards as it was and she didn't need old bill doing a random welfare check to find a fucking dead druggie in her living quarters. She was fucking furious. Donny's mobile was going straight to answer phone and every single one of the girls were throwing a fit over a stiffy. Not in a good way either. She stormed through to the small kitchenette and filled the kettle with water, she needed a fucking brew and a fag to try and clear her head. She slammed the door behind her, silencing the almost cat like tone of the girls voices. She couldn't handle being a Madame on days like these. She slid her ample body down the cracked wooden door, the tears damp in her eyes. Her head in her hands as she tried her hardest to deviate away from the situation at hand. She could hear the faint whispers of the brasses from beyond the door, the gossiping had begun and Danielle knew it wouldn't be long before the news got back to Donny. The girls were little slutty grasses when they wanted to be and if it meant getting themselves licked out like a cream cake for a tenner then they would stitch Danielle up like the proverbial kipper. She got to her feet clumsily, steadying herself against the kitchen units, willing herself not to faint in the process. She ran her fingers through her thick mop of hair, straightening herself out as she popped a heaped spoonful of instant coffee and two sweeteners into a mug. She poured water in and stirred, she despised black coffee but it seemed necessary under the circumstances. She had to get Kristian's body put of here immediately, she had punters coming in first thing and didn't need them sniffing around because of a fucking dead body in her living room. She took a large gulp of the sour liquid and grimaced at the sickly flavour, she didn't know whether she was being paranoid or not but she could swear she could hear her name being whispered outside in the hallway. She shook it off almost immediately. Leave them fucking talk the dirty slappers, it gave their fucking fanny's a break anyway while their mouths were going like the clappers. Danielle picked up her mobile from the counter top, her finely manicured talons tapping away on the keys wildly as she send a quick text to Donny. If she told him first then he couldn't accuse her of keeping him in the dark. She knocked back the remainder of her coffee and pulled her loose around her face.

"RIGHT!" She bellowed at the procession of half naked girls and their open mouthed punters that had been hanging around the kitchen door like a bad smell. Their faces dirty a mix of smudged lipstick and streaked mascara, eyes slightly bulging in their drugged up stares. Paranoia etched on every single broken face that stared back at her. Their bodies twitching with anticipation as Danielle held her hand out to silence them before they had even began speaking.

"You lot get back in your rooms, get on with your fucking work! Donny's been informed and is on his way. My colleague will be removed from the premises sooner rather than later and you can all get on with your early birds. Now get fucking lost before you end up like him in there" She spat pointing angrily at the closed living room door. Just as everyone started scurrying back into their holes where they belonged, Ali, one of the newer girls piped up from the throng of unwashed bodies and limp cocks.

"Dan, d'ya think I should ring a ambulance or summin?" She quizzed, her lank mousey brown hair framing her face in a veil as she spoke. Her sallow cheekbones protruding sickly as every syllable left her lips. Danielle stared at her in sheer bewilderment. Was this bitch fucking crazy? She wondered as she took a stride closer to the girl, her eyes not leaving Ali's for a second as she rammed her hands in the girls hair until she had it bound tightly in her fists.

"Surely you're not that fucking stupid are you?" Danielle screeched, her cheeks burning scarlet in anger. The girls paper skin just skimming hers, a complete juxtaposition in comparison. Danielle slammed the girls head hard off of the wall as she suddenly began babbling her apologies. Danielle was completely out of control, she was slinging the tiny girl around like she was literally a rag doll. Her temper flaring as she began punching the girl clean in the face, blood spraying the grubby magnolia walls as the girls nose burst underneath Danielle's fist. Every single one of the working girls stood glued to the spot, completely motionless as they witnessed their boss beating lumps into one of their own. Not one of them attempting to move, not one of them willing to help. Despite how unfair they felt the attack was, in a strange sense the girls understood why. It was common knowledge that Danielle and Kristian were lovers. Despite Danielle's long suffering husband and two children at home. Poor Darren still not knowing that she was a brothel Madame, he still stupidly believed she was working nights in a factory! Despite the dirty scent of sex on her shapely body and the cheap perfume she used to mask it. He at best would have expected an affair. Not that he would ever admit it of course he loved her too much for that. They had got married in a cheap registrar office do, promising to devote themselves to one another forever. But Danielle had been a delicious Wall Flower; she had flown away from her newly wedded husband. Darren had shown her little affection, forcing her into working longer hours with people she loved. Then she had met Kristian. At first she had laughed like a school girl at his boyish charm and his pointless flirty gestures. But in the end she had fallen, head over leopard print heels in love with the young, slightly crazy Kristian Collins. He had wooed her with his crazy simplicity. He had wanted nothing more than her, nothing more than her crazy heart. Danielle had never known passion like Kristian's. Staying up until the small hours singing love songs to one another had become their norm. Looking over their little empire, the girls, the drugs and the money had Danielle tripping over herself.

Kristian had been the perfect distraction away from her normality. Her two daughters were her life, but everyday life had never been Danielle's style. Yes she did the school run; yes she made dinosaur nuggets for tea whilst her wretched husband stroked her face and whispered sweet nothings in her ear as though his words would instantaneously make her faithful. But he knew, he knew more than ever that his words made no sense. They had grown distances apart; her desires belonged to another man. The thought killed Darren; but he combed through the mill. Scraping at scraps that would never fully belong to him now. He knew she had another man. Of course he had no idea whom the man was but he lived for the knowledge that Danielle still slept in his bed, well for most nights she did anyway. Darren had learnt to love and live in an applicable silence. If she was home, then she was with him, if she wasn't, well she simply wasn't. But above all Danielle was an impeccable mother. She was there through the calm and the suffering with her girls. She took them and collected them from school each and every morning without fail. Despite her profession, she was there for every single step of her girls development. They went to dance two times a week. They divulged in swimming, art and recorder lessons. Despite everything she was there even when Darren couldn't be. She was an amazing mother. Even now as she held Ali by the scruff against the plasterboard wall. The poor girls' neck was buckled, she was disorientated through drugs but still Danielle was grasping her as though she had offended her. Her head slightly lolling to one side as Danielle raised her nose towards the girls' earlobe.

"We don't deal with the fucking police in this camp you little fucking rat!" She whispered in the girls' ear before she shovelled her onto the filthy threadbare carpet in sheer disgust. She turned her back on the girl, sucking in tiny gulps of breath. She felt slightly guilty as she saw the bruises that were already starting to form on the neck that Danielle had inflicted so viciously. In the flick of a switch she had turned into Jekyll and Hyde. The girls pulse was bumping wildly beneath her paper like skin as she fought desperately to hide her humiliation. Danielle held her hand to the girl, she felt awful, she had always prided herself on treating the girls with respect and dignity. She was normally one of them, always ready for a laugh and a joke to make light of their shitty situation.

"Look Al I'm sorry" She whimpered, feeling slightly defeated when the girl shook her head in disgust and scuttled off back to her room without another word. The procession slowly returned back to their rooms, each one with a grimace of shock and discontentment tattooed on their ghost white faces. Some still completely stark naked, their pale flesh mottled a sickly stagnant blue from the lack of central heating in the flat. Danielle maintained her rested face and sauntered back into the living room with as much pride as she could gather. The sullen heap of skinny jeans and floppy black hair shadowed in the dim light of the corner lamp was too much. She sat beside Kristian and pulled his lifeless head into her lap. Her fingers tracing his drooping still slightly warm lips, his body so limp and heavy beneath her touch. Her fingertips lingered softly on his milky complexion, the skin baby soft and tepid to the touch. The tears came then, as did the almost inhuman howling of pain as she cradled Kristian's face, his cheek nestled closely to her breast. Her tears trickling down into is damp sweat soaked hair, the scent of his manly shampoo lingering subtly in her nostrils mixing with the heady scent of his fresh sweat. She couldn't believe he was gone, the thought was unnerving. She had loved him with a passion so strong, he had been a true friend, a listening ear for when things at home had become too much. He was an excellent lover, sensitive and rough at the same time. The perfect mix of seduction and mystery. He had been a kinky little fucker, but she had enjoyed it. He had been her special little secret. The two of them had been fire and gasoline together. Trapped within their web of deceit and destruction, but now he was gone. Ripped away from her without warning. He had been her solace in her darkest of times, when throwing herself into work had simply never been enough, he was there, offering her a warm embrace and a kind word. She hadn't a clue on what she was going to do now. All she did know was that now she was alone. She had to face Donny and his attitude problem when he eventually showed up. She had to go home now every night to a husband that she no longer loved, all their hopes and dreams would remain just that, dreams. They had been planning on running off into the sunset together with the kids, a moonlight flit abroad so they would never be found and could be left to live their lives out together in peace. The dream seemed so fitting now, so perfect. In hindsight she wished she had plucked the courage to runaway sooner. But loyalty to Darren had her bound in its vicious clutches, torn was she between the rock and the hard place. Whereas now, she had lost it all, in the wreckage she could salvage nothing. She would go home as she did every other night; she would sleep in bed rigid with fear that her estranged husband would want sex with her. They no longer made love, they hadn't done for months, the desire to love him was all too much and now she felt like a machine in her own home. She simply just functioned; there was no emotion in her life anymore. Kristian had been her energy, with him she could laugh, she could cry, she could be herself without the fear of being called immature. She had lived only for their stolen moments together. And now as she held his lifeless body in her hands, her heart breaking bit by aching bit. Her whole body numb, she felt absolutely nothing.

Danielle's sordid reminiscing was broken instantaneously as a wide eyed and almost feral looking Donny Anderson stormed in, face drenched in a silvery film of sweat, his face beet red in colour as he puffed and panted wearily. He slumped down onto the ripped leather couch and draped his hand over his face. This was all he fucking needed. He spotted the lines and lines of coke and the rolled up twenties that adorned the shattered mirror face in the corner of the room. The beer cans that were tossed in a pile in the corner of the room, that was bathed heavy with the stench of stale alcohol and even staler sex. Donny placed his hand to his mouth, swallowing down the dry heaves that racked his throat. He locked eyes with Danielle, black tears running in streams from her heavily mascaraed eyes. Her makeup had run in trails across her tear stained cheeks, her nose packed thick with cocaine, her hair a rabid mess upon her head. She looked like a train wreck. Donny had never really liked her as such, he'd always thought of her as a bit too much of a "Housewife" to run a brothel. Despite that fact she was coining it in! Her little establishment was quite the place to be according to his business counterparts. Despite there not being a scrap of decent fucking furniture throughout the whole fucking place, you'd feel like you hit the fucking jackpot if you were lucky enough to get a fucking mattress. What she did have though was more drugs than the bastard Colombians and sex coming out of her earlobes. All the girls were either out of it druggies or freaky little nymphomaniacs who just loved a good fuck from the richest payer. They weren't picky either, if you had the readies, they had the pussy. But if you looked at it now, as Donny could see it in the cold light of day, you could really see just how degrading, shabby and desperate the place was. In the end these girls would have nothing, most were lucky to see their twenty fifth birthdays because they were all so young and all so drug hungry that their bodies just couldn't handle the over abuse. He had even known of one girl of Danielle's to suffer a stillbirth at the age of nineteen because she had been so over worked by one of her punters. The guy in question had pushed a sex toy too far inside her and caused her waters to haemorrhage and her amniotic sack to rupture. She had been almost twenty five weeks pregnant and the child hadn't ever stood a chance at life. The poor sod had ended up killing herself after Danielle had made her go back to work once she had returned from the hospital. It had been Donny who had cut down her body, he could still remember the flower patterned dressing gown chord that had been strung around her neck.

The chilling suicide note that had been penned by what looked like a child, detailing her need to be with her baby. Donny could still see her contorted face, her bulging wide open eyes, struck with fear yet bathed in an eerie glow of peace. As though the girl had finally found her way back home. She had been battered, bruised, unwashed but she still had dignity in her eyes. As though she knew that she would finally be free. Even know when Donny closed his eyes he saw the girl how she had been left hanging there from the shower, wrists slashed with a dirty razor blade. Blood splashed grimly across the grimy off white tiles. Donny would never forget that day as long as he lived. They had cleaned up, shipped the body out and covered their backs in less than an hour; the girl was just another statistic, another footnote on the underbelly of society. With no face, no name; the same fate was about to come to his best friend. His advocate, business partner and confidante. He had loved Kristian like a brother. But in business there was no such thing as brotherhood. The boy would soon be propping up the nearest fly over. Donny glared at Danielle through hooded eyes, there was nothing more he would like than to smack her clean in the face. He could see the sadness there, but the stench of fear lingered on her more. He could sense that she thought that he would blame her for the tragedy that had unfolded here tonight. And he did. But she wouldn't realise that just yet. He pulled his mobile from his sweatpants pocket and made a move for the door.

"Don't move, I'm going to make some calls, get this mess cleaned up" he gestured subtly, his voice flat and emotionless as he turned and left her once more in the darkness. Danielle was chewing on her fingernails wildly as she sat in wait, the grubbiness of the room scared her. The thought of the dirty needles piled high in the corner, the thought of the rancid excrement stained carpet beneath and the thought of the dead body in her hands making her almost vomit clean in her mouth. Clean this mess up he had said, how the fuck was she going to ever get this mess clean? There was a dead man in her fucking clutches with at least ten witnesses who could spill their guts at any moment. The girls were in disarray and it wouldn't be long before Donny turned from Mr Nice to Mr Murderous. He was under too much stress, Danielle knew all about his wife dying and the fact he was still pining like some lovesick puppy over that slut Jenna Shearan. Well Danielle couldn't be bothered for the hassle tonight. She just wanted to get home to a large glass of wine and a cuddle with her girls. She felt completely deflated and despite everything was actually looking forward to seeing Darren. Nice, Normal, drug free Darren who was simple to please. She closed her eyes tightly and prayed for Donny to go lightly on her.

Chapter Forty Eight

One Month Later

The evening air was bitterly cold and crisp, almost dead despite an eerie shrill in the breeze through the open bay window. Craig pulled on his thick leather gloves and buttoned his dark grey suit jacket. He nodded his approval to himself in the thick framed full mirror that adorned his bedroom wall. His eyes were rimmed black with lack of sleep, his heart pounding visibly in his chest. He grasped hold of the glass tumbler on the sideboard and took a deep swig of the fine malt whiskey in the glass. Some spilt subtly from the corner of his lips. He turned around to face Jenna who sat nervously on the edge of the bed.

"You promise me you're not doing anything stupid?" She whispered sadly, taking a sip from the glass Craig had passed her. She fucking despised whiskey, it had been her mother's poison; but the mood Craig had on now she would happily gargle on tramps piss than annoy him further. The change in air between them had happened literally overnight, it was as though he had turned cold toward her, as though just having her there was an inconvenience to him. He rolled his head around, his neck clicking rhythmically as he stretched widely. He was zoned, there was no denying it, and Jenna knew trouble was afoot. She could taste it on her tongue along with the bitter after sting of the burning alcohol. She tossed her hair over her shoulder and gazed at him longingly with deep set green eyes and millions of fluttering lashes. Craig turned away from her immediately; he didn't have the heart to tell her that he honestly had no clue on what was going to happen. He slipped on his thick black suede coat from the clothes peg on the over door hanger and sighed a heavy breath. Silently he bent down and kissed her gently on the cheek. His lips warm and soft on her flesh sending her into a flurry of goosebumps as he walked away.

"I'll see you later" he sighed as he closed the door gently behind him leaving her sat there with a look of horror smacked on her skinny face. She held her head in her hands helplessly as she lay down amongst the mountain of pillows that made up his side of the bed and hugged one close to her face. The scent of his hair at her nose was exhilarating and Jenna found herself momentarily whisked back to better days. When life wasn't so fucking hard and they're future together had seemed so bright, so beautiful. When he had been just that chavvy kid from the Belmonte, who would do anything for her. The one who would tear down walls with his bare hands just to be near her. He had been his completely. Yet now here they were worlds apart with barely a word between them. She knew that whatever he had planned tonight, she knew blood would be spilled. She shut her eyes tightly and prayed for the first time in her whole life, she prayed for Craig's safe return. She prayed for him to want her again just like he had all those years ago. Those days seemed so fucking far away now, so much had changed between them. The fight was slowly beginning to drain from her now. Too much time had passed and so much had been said. He knew everything about

Donny and Kristian and the abuse she had suffered at their hands and she had noticed the way he stared at her sometimes in the night when they were alone. He would just stare at her over his wine glass with sad sad eyes as though she were nothing but a child. As though she needed his sympathy to survive. She had been saddened to hear that Kristian had passed away, despite everything in her most darkened hours he had in his own sick way been her only friend. She would miss him somewhat, why she couldn't quite explain, but she would grieve for him alone. There was no way she was telling anyone about how close they had become, no one else would understand it. He had been the one to embrace her, despite the fact he had raped her. He had been the one to kiss her despite having her gagged and whipped with a riding crop moments before. He had been the one to tell her she was beautiful after he had allowed her to be mauled by the dirty men that had used her day in day out. He had been the little bit of positivity to come out of her shitty situation. In her own little way, Jenna would always respect him for that.

Her head though was a complete mess. She didn't even know what the fuck she wanted anymore. She could barely get out of bed in the morning let alone be trusted to make any adult decisions. She wrapped the silk duvet around herself and buried her head into the pillows drenched in the only scent that seemed human to her anymore. Craig had been so patient with her, so delicate, like she was made purely of the finest china. He hadn't rushed her to spill her guts about Donny and he hadn't pressed the issue when she had clammed up and lashed out at him. He had just done what he knew best, waited for her. She had been so grateful for him these last few weeks. Dom had kept his distance since Craig had taken her back to stay at his for a few nights. She had been too scared to even step into her own flat in case Donny had decided to send one of his cronies to finish off what he had started. She barely recognised herself anymore such was her paranoia. Even the slightest noise set off her anxiety like a bullet leaping from a gun. She would try her hardest to block out the reality of it all by sleeping her days away. But it was her nightmares that really scared the living shit out of her. The same old reoccurring dream that Donny was chasing her. The faces of the strange men who had taken her lingering in the background. They were all full of evil eyes and snarling lips. Knives in hands in a glorious ricochet of blood and bone. Jenna would wake each night screaming, drenched in sweat, clinging to Craig for all it was worth. Confused and in a daze she would mumble how scared she was until he embraced her, even if he was on his knees with tiredness he would hold her and reassure her with his gentle, loving words until she fell back to sleep. He had been her rock absolutely, despite their relationship being slightly different now. Craig felt more like her carer than her lover and he treated her with the same admiration that he treated their daughter. Like a child. He was constantly running around after her plumping her pillows and making sure she was okay. Not once had he told her though that she was beautiful, not once had he hinted any interest in her. And although she had been slightly disheartened, she understood it all the same. He wasn't expected to love her anymore. The thought killed Jenna inside and she vowed that she would get better and that she would get back to herself even if it killed her. It was the anxiety though that was proving difficult to shift. She had become so paranoid about her looks that she walked around in grubby pyjama bottoms and Craig's running hoodies. Hair scraped back high on her head. She had become accustomed to bathing in water and bleach so much that her skin had become deathly dry. The fact that she was scrubbing herself with a scouring pad hadn't helped. She was covered in disgusting red raw scabs that had blistered and thick heavy black bruises. Her skin had burnt so bad that she could no longer wear underwear or anything other than leggings. She felt completely shit about herself. Craig had secretly cried buckets when he had saw the state of her. Not that she knew of course. Now though as she lay in his bed, amongst his things, in his home she realised that she was now what she had always been, slave to Craig Carter.

Craig pulled up along the kerbside with a silvery glint in his aqua blue eyes, his skin prickled with dangerous anxiety as he swung open the car door and saw Dom stood on the kerbside. Dressed subtly in all black. Looking slightly smarter than usual Craig almost cracked a smile at him. He hopped into the passenger seat, his floppy black hair in his face. Craig was tempted to ask him did he want a fucking bobble for his overlap but he protested. The man had a face filled with simplicity, he was almost emotionless. Dom knew why, he understood it completely. Their faces mirrored slightly, both concrete in their ways, both desperate for justice.

"You ready?" he quizzed as Dom slipped on the spare gloves that adorned the dashboard. He gave nothing more than a nod as they slipped away into the intoxicating calm of the dark. Both ferociously nervous, knots in their bellies with a scout's precision. Both silent, drowning in the solace of their own thoughts. Both high with the delicious twist of fate that they were about to encounter, this was revenge. This was all they had thought about for the last four weeks, enduring precise, agonising hours of planning and now the time had come to bring Donny and his empire crashing to the ground in a flurry of flame and fury. They were ready, although tensions were high and emotions were mixed for the first time since they had crossed paths, they were both on the exact same page. This was for Jenna, this was for their children and the twelve months of agony they had suffered but above all it was for each other. For the sleepless nights they had lay awake, heads spinning wondering what the fuck had happened. For their broken sanity, for their broken hearts and their broken heads. Both were completely compelled by revenge and what it would mean for them both. It would mean freedom for Jenna, freedom for her to heal, freedom for her to spread her wings and finally be free. Until Donny was down and out of the game, she would forever live in fear. They had already been tracking Donny for the last few weeks, despite almost being caught red handed on two separate occasions the pair had pushed through and finally they're plan was in place.

The car pulled into a narrow side lane leading off onto a winding country road. Craig parked into the small gap and wound down his window. The stench of nature blasted the car with the smells of earthy leaves and twisted roots. Craig lit two cigarettes and passed one to Dom. His face was deathly straight, emotionless devoid of a single glimmer of what he was thinking. His hands were stiff, not a single jingle of fear in his rigid body. Dom knew instinctively that Craig had done this before Dom was bricking it at the thought. The thought of killing another human being was completely alien to him, even in his wildest dreams he would never have thought about murder. No matter how much he hated someone, it was never a comprehension of his. Until now of course, now that someone had harmed the mother of his child. That was his driving force, the reason why he was here now, next to the man he loathed most on the planet, to exercise revenge for the woman they both would give the whole world and more for. Dom cleared his throat and took a few dainty puffs of the cigarette, his hands shaking nervously as he tried his hardest to keep his calm facade. He had never been in trouble before and the thought of being caught by the police scared him out of his wits.

"So are you ready?" Craig murmured through the fog of apprehension and cigarette smoke, His lips twisted into the craziest grin, his eyes twinkling with excitement. Almost like a kid at Christmas at one with his delusional happiness. Dom swallowed down hard before he shook his head slowly.

"To be honest mate I feel like I'm going to shit my fucking boxers" He grinned trying his hardest to hide his uncertainty of it all despite his obvious honesty. Craig smiled, he hadn't expected anything less from Dom. He could sense the man's fear, and that's where Donny would find weakness when they finally grasped hold of him. Craig knew Donny would tear Dom down within seconds, Dom needed to thicken his skin and fucking quickly. Otherwise Donny would think this whole fucking set up was a joke. He turned in his seat so he was facing directly at Dom, his lip quivering with anger.

"Look mate, I know your probably fucking cacking yourself yeah. But this is the big time, this cunt will tear you to fucking pieces unless you find your fucking backbone." He replied smugly, tossing his cigarette butt casually out of the window before blowing a giant plume of smoke out wildly into the confines of the small cab space. Dom almost choked as the grey fog hit him directly in the face, his face contorted in displeasure. He could have happily smacked Craig clean in the face, but he refrained. Of course Craig was a fucking psycho, he'd been dragged up in a shitty two bed in the middle of the fucking jungle! The boy may as well start calling himself fucking Tarzan the amount of humanity he had in him. Dom almost chortled at his own wit, but refrained of course. He wasn't looking for a slap off the fucking dimwit ape before him. He just nodded in Craig's direction and finished his cigarette in silence. The night was going to take them into the unknown, Dom wasn't prepared no matter how much planning they had shoved into the last few weeks. Nothing could prepare you for murder. His palms were thick with sweat, his head swimming with his preconceptions of where the night would take them. He knew though with a million percent certainty that he would never ever as long as he lived put himself in this position again. It was the sad reality that they had been bought here under such circumstances. As They pulled back out onto the open road, Craig turned up the UB40 CD he had on loop, Dom almost chuckled at the stupidity of a twenty something young man being so madly in love with a reggae band twice his senior. Craig hummed along jovially beside him, his face jovial slightly, his skin was glowing with apparent smugness. There wasn't another word spoken between them as they drove along the winding country roads, the car dipping into every single fucking pothole in the road on their way until they finally pulled up into a secluded bank of over head trees and plants. Craig stepped out of the car, straightening out his attire before he addressed Dom.

"Get the stuff out of the boot, its about a ten minute walk just up that pathway. We'll walk up the hill there" he pointed as he spoke signalling his directions "You stay outside, I'll take the front door. There's no security, no one knows about this place. Donny's in there with some brass. I'll shoot her first. No witness no problem." he chuckled heartily. He stood lighting a cigarette off the butt of his previous. His body slouched against the car as he waited eagerly for Dom to shift his fucking backside out of his seat. Craig was pumped high, filled with adrenaline and blood hungry thirst that was imploding in his veins. He left no time for answers as he began to trudge ahead, the earth of the bank soft beneath his feet, almost crumbling beneath his weight as his feet sank into the ground. He cursed under his breath for wearing such expensive shoes at such a time. He glanced back only momentarily to faintly see Dom rummaging in the boot of the car, the darkness suppressing his vision slightly but Craig pummelled on regardless. His heart rate accelerating as he finally caught sight of the top of the grassy bank. He wiped the sweat from his brow with the back of his sleeve, Dom's footsteps were slapping behind him dismally, Craig grinned to himself, the man's heavy breathing was laboured and heavy. Craig stood rooted to the spot sucking in calm, cool breaths until Dom was finally beside him. They paced the final few steps together, both drenched in sweat, both racked with anticipation as they finally reached the top of the bank. In the distance stood a small country lodge placed in the middle of nowhere. It was a pretty place even now, as it was shadowed in the darkness. All redbrick and fake thatch roof, surrounded by fresh vegetable patches and shrubs. Bathed in the humble glow of tiny spotlights that were embedded into the gravel driveway. It looked like something out of a picturesque fairy tale book such was its simple beauty. Gingham curtains and fine lace nets adorned the windows and immediately they were like Hansel and Gretel being drawn toward the witches' cove. They began to stealth through the over grown grass that surrounded the little open space, keeping as low to the ground as they physically could without being spotted. Craig signalled for Dom to take the lead, checking that all of the lights were out first before they made their move. It was the element of surprise that would give Donny the disadvantage. The fact that the lodge had no upstairs would become an advantage, nowhere to hide. Craig drew his thin athletic body so that he was face first against the cold wood. The wind was picking up around them, the howling whistling through the nearby trees and shrubbery. Dom appeared and signalled him that the coast was clear before resuming his place by the back door, just in case the occupants had been tipped off and decided to do a runner through the back. Craig reached gently into his pocket, the metal of the pistol felt ice cold as Craig's fingertips brushed gently against it. He smiled sadistically as he snatched the gun from his pocket, he had never in his life been forced to use one before, but he would make Donny fucking suffer tonight if his life depended on it. The Cunt was going to be squealing for his life by the time Craig was finished with him. He stood back slightly away from the door and swung his foot back. With one short sharp kick the door was left swinging on its hinges and he was flailing through the hallway. His mouth spilling obscenities, his feet were pounding against the heavy woollen rug in the hallway but everything was running to an almost stand still pace in bitter slow motion. He saw the red headed girl first, open mouthed as Donny stood there stark naked at the foot of the bed. His hands trying their hardest to cover his sweaty modesty from where he had been shovelling himself inside the poor girl. Immediately Craig aimed the gun at the girls head, his eyes wide with malice. His lip was quivering with distaste as Donny's eyes met his, the flash if fear didn't go unnoticed, he hadn't been expecting company. Especially not the company of the almost animal Craig Carter. His face was enough to tell Donny that he wouldn't be walking out of the comfort of his little country getaway tonight.

"You know why I'm here?" Craig questioned flatly, his face once more devoid of expression. His stony blue eyes burning with carnal lust, blood drunk waiting for his prey. The gun was still pointing square at the poor girls head. She was quivering like a rat on helium on the bed, her tousled long hair resting just over her bulging fake breasts, her vagina on full display as she bunched herself up on the top of the bed, her back pinned uncomfortably against the headboard. She was crying now, big fat tears rolling down her mascara stained cheeks. Her emaciated body riddled with pin marks and bruises. Craig almost felt sorry for the poor cunt until she looked at him with her dead eyes, all he saw there was his sister, it could have very easily been Sammy sat there staring at him. Large doe eyes, glaring at him with fear, still glazed over from the previous hit. Craig took a step forward, his glare pinned on Donny, the cunt looked like a fucking mug, a weakened little mug as he stood there with his hand covering his cock, his wedding ring absent from his finger, yet the white tan line still so apparent there. His face a mix of the devastation of being caught and the fear of what was to come. Craig knew immediately that the man had been wondering when this was going to happen. As though Donny knew that he had in effect signed his own death warrant by taking advantage of Jenna. He offered no explanation, not even a glimmer of emotion. There wasn't even an ounce of fight in him. Craig was of course disappointed but none the less he was here to get the job done. But the night was still young for Donny Anderson Just yet. Craig tossed him aside like a rag doll before he gripped the young brass by the long box dyed red hair. He pulled the girl up to her feet, the poor cunt could barely stand and Craig guessed correctly that she was one of Donny's most worked girls. He pushed her toward the door and immediately began to give her a lecture of being stupid to get involved with the like of Donny. She mumbled something about needing the money to feed her kids. Craig was undone, he sent the girl out toward the kitchen to make herself a brew whilst he dealt with the big guy. He called Dom in from outside the front door where he had been lingering for the last few minutes and made him sit with the poor dab. He ordered him to make the girl a large mug of coffee to sober up whilst he sorted Donny out.

Dom took the girls hand and gently led her away from the room, she was in a daze, shock setting in on her tired muscles and she was almost flopping out of the door as Dom led her through to the kitchen. She was flying her tits off on whatever drug Donny had been plugging her with, the girl didn't even realise that she had been sat there naked until Dom had wrapped an old sheet around her skeletal frame. She was lifeless, limp from exhaustion. Dom sat her down at the filthy table, the dirty needles and spoons burnt black from the heroin that adorned the counter top making him shudder deep into his bones. He almost slung the poor girl into the chair before sitting down opposite her. This was another fucking world to him. This poor girl couldn't have been a day older than seventeen. Her skin soaked in the foul, sour stench of sex, her embarrassment evident in the blush that crept across her stone grey cheeks. Dom wrinkled his nose as discreetly as he could not to offend the poor thing.

"What's your name love?" he smiled softly as he spoke. His hands trembling in anticipation as he waited for a response. There was nothing, her face hid a faint sliver of interest as she looked straight through him with her dead eyes. The pupils dilated so small that all Dom could see was her mysterious brown iris's as she glared at him. Her mouth slack slightly at the corner and he wondered momentarily if she was indeed having a stroke. He repeated his sentence once more and patiently he waited for a response. She blinked at him as though in quaint disbelief. She shrugged her bony shoulders before spluttering something in what appeared to be Romanian. Dom couldn't believe his fucking ears! He was literally rendered speechless. Not only was the girl scraping the legal age for sex, she couldn't speak a fucking syllable of English! Dom scraped his chair back on the filthy lino and stood. He sucked in gulps of breath furiously as he paced the kitchen. There was no fucking way he was allowing this little scrap of information to bypass Craig before he blew the cunts head off. He muttered to the girl to stay put whilst he ran up the stairs.

Katriana Polkov slid from the table with the stealth of a deranged cheetah, as quietly as she could she tiptoed across the kitchen tiles to the open cutlery drawer and pulled out the biggest bread knife she could find sitting on top of the throng of silverware. Slowly she crept to the bottom of the stairwell her feet padding softly across the thin carpet runner that lay in the hallway. She could hear a commotion coming from upstairs. Raised voices and feet shuffling on the bare floorboards above her head. She tested the bottom stair for any noise, finding her footing easily among the noise that the men were making, gingerly she made claim and began to clamber silently up each step. Her heartbeat leaping in her chest from fear of being caught red handed. She flinched as the door opened a crack, spilling golden light onto the densely carpeted hallway. She clung to the spindle banister for dear life praying to God that no one was about to blow her cover. The din didn't calm and the voices could be heard now louder than ever. She pinned her back against the wall as she slid across the landing, trying her hardest not to make a single decibel of sound as she went. She peeked between the gap in the door, Donny was on his knees. His hands ties behind his back with the rope from her dressing gown. Sweat spilling down his forehead as he trash talked the two men who stood either side of him. Their faces twisted into the most salacious grins as they taunted Donny. Both hungry for justice, both crazy with malice like children as they danced around Donny's defeated body, with his slumped shoulders and his unfunny come backs to the insults that were being chucked in his direction. Katriana sucked in one final breath, the blade ice cold against her tiny thigh, the degrading sheet she held so tightly around her body filling her nostrils with the scent of her own wretched body as she stood helplessly in wait. Her fingers strong, clasped around the handle of the blade as she took another bold step toward the door. Her fingers clutching the handle. Her body shivering with ruthless assault as she tried her hardest to force her body to stop. The eerie red mist descending in front of her eyes as she gasped desperately for vital puffs of air. Her whole body locked in the vice like grip of her own anxiety. She swung back her foot and with one swift kick the door flew open. She stared open mouthed as the barrel of the gun met her sweat soaked temple. Donny glanced up at her and shook his head, the men had known all along that she was coming.

"Your little mate by here sang like a fucking birdy when we threatened to chop his cock off" Craig grinned as he pushed the barrel of the gun closer to the girls skin, he felt her shiver with fear beneath his steely gaze. The silly bitch had honesty thought she had one over him. He almost broke out into an almost girlish giggle at the fact. Here he was standing like king fucking Dick with his backstabbing business associate strung up like the proverbial Christmas turkey. OH he was going to enjoy this moment. This was what justice felt like, and by damn it felt good knowing that it had been this easy. It had been this fucking simple to get one over on Donny Anderson and his army of goons. He winked at Dom who was stood over Donny smirking like the Cheshire cat. Donny thought that this was it? He thought they were just going to kill him off. The cunt was going to suffer at their hands, he would feel fear in its most wildest form as he had inflicted on the mother of the two of their children. They would make his last hours on this earth a living fucking hell. Craig hadn't told him exactly what he had in mind, but he knew now he was ready to partake in whatever it was. Donny had shown no remorse for his actions. He had barely creased a brow in consternation as they had relayed what he had done to Jenna back to him. He wasn't fazed one fucking bit and that's what had raged Dom the most, the inhumanity of it all. The lack of sympathy, the lack of compassion for the pain he had inflicted, for the hurt he had caused. Donny showed nothing other than bravado, he had seen the whole thing as a joke. Well they would see with clarity very fucking soon who would have the last laugh. And Dom assured as long as he had breath in his body and a beat in his heart that it wouldn't be Donny fucking Anderson.

 Craig began chuckling to himself bitterly, his face the ultimate picture of disbelief as Donny begged him to spare the life of Katriana. The girl was still wielding the knife in her left hand. A puddle of stinking urine soaked her bare milk white feet as she stood shaking so wildly where she stood. Her face had turned the colour of concrete, as though the life had been scared out of her. She was mumbling to herself in Russian, praying to the gods for her safety.

"Is this what Jenna was like?" Craig snarled viciously. His lips curling in disgust as the words escaped his mouth. The thought of knowing the truth scared him; he was scared at what his reaction would be. But he had to know. He knew Jenna had held back from telling him everything so not to hurt him. But it was that hurt that would spur him on all the fucking more in his revenge. He couldn't wait to start torturing the sad bastard in front of him. And he would savour every delicious moment like a lion with a fine cut steak. His blood lust was strong, heady for the scent of sweet metallic revenge. There was nothing more to be said now, actions spoke bigger volumes than any words ever could.

Donny began cackling like a twisted hyena, his eyes bulbous in his head; he was flying high on a adrenaline and drugs. His confidence abundant;

"Oh she was fucking begging alright, begging for my fucking cock in her big fat fucking gob!" he spat back in distaste. Within seconds Katriana Polkov's blood decorated the shabby cigarette stained walls with a deep crimson spray as Craig shot her straight in the head without a moment's hesitation. The bullet penetrating the flesh instantaneously sending splintered bone and freshly butchered flesh flying into the air. Dom stood open mouthed, his face splattered with blood as the degrading body dropped limp to the carpet. Donny was deathly silent suddenly as the sight of his dead lover flooded his eyes. He almost had the gumption to look away until he felt two hands pinned to the sides of his temples.

"No fucking chance you cunt!" Dom spat as his grip tightened on the man's head. He wanted Donny to feel pain; he wanted him to hurt just as much as he had been forced to for the last twelve months. The sleepless nights, the threat of not knowing whether she had been alive or dead that had eaten away at him for months on end. No Donny would know just how much they had hurt between them.

"if it wasn't for the morals my good old mum installed into me as a kid you cunt I'd fuck her now, even with her fucking face all over yours" Craig spat vehemently, the malice in his sickening words echoing in the enclosed space. His voice quivering with his own loathing, completely abandoning each2 and every ounce of humanity he owned as he leant down over the body at his feet. He grabbed the mangled mass of broken skull by the scabby mane of hair that hung lifelessly on her head and spat straight at the empty face in disgust. Before slamming the girls face back down onto the flood. The thud of her sparse flesh hitting the carpet sent Donny into a tirade of abuse.

"You sick Cunt Carter!" he screeched, tears pricking his eyes as he strained angrily against his restraints. The broken acts of the broken man never seemed more adequate than now. Craig brought the pillowcase over Donny's eyes and tied the bottom securely with a few cable ties around the man's neck. Now the games would begin and Craig Carter was in his fucking element. He signalled Dom to go and get the car. He couldn't wait for the night to begin. He licked his over dry lips and smiled with an almost boyish voyeurism. Tonight he really would become King Dick Afterall.

Chapter Forty Nine

Donny was crawling on his knees like an unsteady baby as his face collided with the bitterly cold concrete. The Blood Spilling from his lips as yet another tooth came buckling from his gums. Another vicious blow was delivered to his knee caps, the vicious crunch that followed was almost enough to make him vomit. His head was filled with a crescendo of the unknown. His whole body was on lock down, left naked from the boy's merciless assaults. simply enduring whatever was thrown at him with humiliation. Another fateful blow to his knees sent him sprawling across the floor with a roar of anger. Never in his life had he once felt sympathy for himself. Yet now he would happily curl up in a ball and die if he could. Craig stood over him, cackling like a hapless hyena, he was in his element. Donny could tell how much the boy was enjoying executing his revenge. This was Craig's moment, Donny understood that now was the time to just step back and allow the boy his time. In a way he admired the boys gumption, he admired the boys love for the girl they had all been poisoned by. Well by fuck he was feeling the effects of taking advantage of that girl now. He had never meant for things to get so sour between them all. Craig had been his most cherished business associate, dedicated to pleasing him, dedicated to raising the Anderson firm. Yet now here they were, worlds away from the honesty and the solid friendship they had shared. Their relationship was in tatters and his life was now hanging in the balance and for what? The allure of a pretty lady. Donny could almost taste his own demise in his mouth. The sting was all too much. For once in his squalid life Donny Anderson actually felt genuine guilt. He didn't know whether it was because death was staring him plain in the face or whether he was in the middle of a premature midlife crisis.

The sound of Craig's shoes clattering behind him brought Donny back to reality, his body immediately tensed against attack. He was rigid with apprehension as he waited patiently for whatever was coming next. Craig's vice like grip grasped his shoulders pulling him to his feet. The deathly ache in his kneecaps making him wince painfully as he tried his hardest to keep up with Craig's fast pace. He was thrown none too gently into a hard backed chair; his feet were secured to the solid wooden legs. Not that he could feel anything past his thighs of course. Finally he came face to face with his rival. The boy had become a man almost overnight and the transformation was immaculate. Craig was everything that Donny had taught him to be. Success would follow him wherever he went, he was a marvel. Donny was proud that despite everything that had happened that he had seen Craig flourish. But now he would meet his maker at the hands of the boy he had fed so humbly. Craig had practically devoured the hand that had been feeding him so long and Now Donny would pay his dues for his mistake. Not that Donny saw it as a mistake, it had been an opportunity that had manifested itself so deeply in his pores and he had snatched the opportunity with both hands and had run like the wind. He had always found Jenna attractive, the night he had met her at his annual Christmas ball she had rendered him simply speechless. Almost like Jessica

Rabbit in her looks, beautiful and curvaceous with a personality that could captivate a whole room. She was absolutely stunning. Donny had vowed from that night on that he would play the waiting game with her and he had caught her completely unaware. Attack was the best form of defence as his old mum had always said. But as he had learnt the hard way, you play with fire eventually you would get burnt. Now as Craig Carter stood over him with a large knife in his hands ready to slice his face from ear to ear Donny couldn't help but feel slightly defeated by his usurped attempts of playing the charmer.

"Got anything to say before I chop you up and feed you to next doors fucking cat you muggy cunt?" Craig muttered. His jaw line was strong and tight as he spoke, the words literally chilling Donny to the bone. The desire in the boys was burning bright, like piss holes in the snow. He was panting breathlessly; his handsome face was contorted with an angry pair of lips that were twisted into the most sinister pout. The knife slashed Donny's left cheek as though it were butter. The crimson river that began splattering down his bare chest, creating a zigzag effect around the mass of bruises and cigarette burns that were embedded deep in his suntanned skin from the assaults of Craig Carter and his little bitch. Donny let out a deep guttural roar of pain as his body flinched heavily with shock. Nothing could have prepared him from the feeling of sheer helplessness that he had acquired in those desperate seconds. His pride was literally leaking out of his pores as these two apes before him stood mocking him like a pair of fucking gay boys with their handbags in a twist Donny literally felt the fire of defeat burning deep inside him and if he could have he would have rather Craig just stab him there and then on the spot and get it over and done with. All he had left now was words, and at the end of it all, words would mean absolutely nothing. His jaw was stinging, the dull ache of his partial Chelsea smile setting in. Donny felt like the joker from the batman films! The sheer humility of it was enough to almost break Donny to tears. As his right cheek gained an identical mark to his left he was undone. The venom pouring out as best he could manage, each muttered syllable completely disorientated, he was left babbling almost like an uneducated child. A mixture of sticky metallic blood and torn flesh filled the gap where his lips had been sliced so brutally. He coughed deep in his throat, the blood spilling into his mouth making him gargle and choke disgustingly. Craig like the master artiste stood back and gazed intently at his work. Dom stood slightly behind him, his face almost luminous green with the urge to upchuck the contents of his stomach. The gory sight before them like something from a modern day horror film, as though they were on the outside looking in almost. Dom wretched silently into his shirt sleeve as Donny's head slumped forward, sending blood spilling all over his naked skin landing in a neat pool at his feet. Craig smacked him across the head to make sure he was still alive. His reaction was a barely audible grunt from the bloody mess.

Craig took the blade in his hand and with cold and calculated ferocity he lunged toward Donny. His hands grasping Donny's naked penis as he brought the knife down in torrents on his shrivelled member. Donny was screaming, spluttering between each wild screech that came from the man's aching body. Donny's was rigid with fear as Craig yanked away his flaccid penis, dangling it before Donny's eyes like something possessed. His savage powder blue eyes glimmering recklessly as he pulled Donny's head back by the hair. His mouth at the man's bloody ear, his breath was deathly low against Donny's sticky skin.

"This One is for Jenna" he spat in a hushed whisper against Donny's ear before shoving the man's own penis straight into his own mouth. Donny's eyes were wide with incredulous pain and obvious displeasure. Craig lapped up each and every single moment as he rammed the fleshy article deep into Donny's throat. The playful smile on Craig's face was enough to almost send Dom vomiting on the spot. Although he kept his composure as best he could. Craig Carter wasn't a man Dom wanted to tip over the edge especially with their current state of affairs. Dom swallowed hard, the lump in his throat practically bulging as Donny's desperate eyes met his own Dom remembered his form immediately and shrugged off his moment of guilt passively as he stood his ground once more, and acting the hard man wasn't his forte. He fucking hated it in fact. He was nowhere near Craig's league and if he was honest he never fucking wanted to be! He couldn't wait to get home to his son and have a cup of pissing tea!

Seconds later in a fit of childish laughter and glorious blood spray, Craig sliced open Donny's throat right there where they stood. They both watched in amazement as the man took his final breaths in a heap of molten blood, eerie broken flesh and disgusting gut wrenching gargles from the man's throat. Dom and Craig stared one another down for long moments afterwards. Both unsure of what to say, both untrustworthy of the other yet they still nodded respectfully towards one another. Both completely exhausted from their excitement, both riding high on the fact that they had finally laid the demon to rest. Jenna was free. That in all was what they had both wanted from the beginning. Now they could walk away now knowing the biggest battle had been won while silently they both wondered to themselves who would triumph when the real battle came. The fight for Jenna's affections was officially on. And both men knew that it was going to take a hell of a lot of time and a hell of a lot of patience before she would even consider looking at either of them again.

"You ready to go home then mate?" Craig asked blankly, dropping the knife with a staggering clatter on the bare tile floor. He ignored the splash of blood that speckled his trouser leg as he turned to walk away. He couldn't wait to get home for a shower; the stench of Donny Anderson was lingering on him. The thought of a cold beer was overly tempting and if he was honest it was all he needed to calm his hyperactivity. There would be no sleep in him tonight that was for certain.

Dom nodded his reply and slowly followed him outside. The fresh air hitting him for six as he stumbled across the car park in a sickened daze, he felt completely numb. The fear and elation all at once had finally defeated him and now he was left completely exhausted. He fell into the passenger seat as soon as he opened the door and fell into a deep, restless seep. Filled with pictures of blood and severed heads, he felt washed with an unexplainable guilt and he knew Jenna would never thank them for this. It had all been too soon, the poor girl was still suffering from withdrawals; her moods were all over the place. She was still confused, still stuck in an empty daze of what to do from one hour to the next. Dom knew that this would break her. Both mentally and physically she didn't have the strength to accept that he was gone. Although she would have to eventually. It didn't seem fair for her to have to endure all of this now on top of everything else. Dom knew Craig had been having her see a therapist, Rhian or something her name was. Dom didn't care to listen to Craig half of the time. He seemed to be pushing and pushing for Jenna to recover before she was ready to decide what pyjamas she would be lounging about in from one week to the next. Never mind going to therapy sessions with one of Craig's stuck up mates who probably had a fake degree and a pair of stilettos longer than her bloody legs. The reality of course was much different. Rhian Smith had come highly recommended by Craig's work colleague Jeff. Who had fought for months on end with his wife to come through post natal depression. Rhian had put in hours and hours of work and stopped Jeff's wife from ending up in asylum because of her lunacy. She was patient, over indulgent in the lives of all of her patients and above all she was kind, with a track record of being the best in the business. Rhian had been Craig's saviour these last few weeks. She had been nothing short of a minor miracle. Jenna had adapted to Rhian like a duck to water. She had opened up to the girl; she had been nothing short of perfect when it came to business.

Jeff was one of Craig's henchmen. Of course Dom had taken an immediate dislike to him from the second they had met. He could charm the bird's right out of the fucking trees with his overly good looks and his slick allure. He was a modern day Johnny Cash with his smart black suits and his dark jet black hair that he wore spiked on his head like some wannabe pop star. Dom though thought the guy was a complete and utter cunt. The way he swanned around with Craig you could have sworn they were the fucking Kray twins. Both as thick as the each other and both thinking they were God's gift to the female form. Jeff was older though and slightly more refined than Craig. Matured thoroughly, he had lived the life a hundred times over and still he was fighting. Despite that, the man was a tosser. In Dom's eyes he was anyway.

"Who's doing the cleanup?" Dom quizzed blearily when he opened his eyes. They were driving down the motorway. Craig's face was fixed straight ahead, emotionless, and he was deep in thought, drowning deeply in his own little bubble. Dom already knew the answer, but conversation was easier than an awkward drive in silence. It was bad enough that Craig was playing some shitty CD that he had made. Dom could have almost vomited over the high pitched serenades coming from the in car stereo. Craig eyes him suspiciously out of the corner of his eye. As if the moment hadn't been weird enough in itself. They had just fucking killed someone and now here they were talking about who was going to wipe up Donny Anderson's windpipe! It was all very surreal for Dom, as much as he tried his hardest to hold his calm reserve. The whole thing was making him extremely uncomfortable.

"Jeff and his team are." He replied matter of factly "Johnny's had to go. He's found Cath and the baby." His voice was taught, gruff and silent as he continued to glare at the vast open road. His blank expression not dropping for a second. Dom began to panic slightly, his nerves not being able to cope with the reality of their situation. What if something had gone wrong? What if they had been seen? What if the police had gotten there first before the men in fucking black? Within a split second Dom was hurtling abuse at Craig, throwing his fists at his tormentor, slinging Jenna in his face. She would never ever forgive him after this. She would never ever want to know them again. In a sick sense she had loved Donny. She had fell in love with Donny's control of her, she had loved his mind games, had been sucked in by them. She had been caught in the web of deceit, burning in her own squalid sorrow. She had begged for him to love her, had striven to please his every single command. Of course she hadn't loved being a prostitute, she hadn't loved being force fed heroin. But she had been plagued by Donny and his bewitching control of her. She had been completely compelled by his demented spell. Among the lunacy and the festering sadness, she had genuinely become part of Donny and his crazy world. And now like vultures they had torn her apart limb from rancid, sex soaked limb whilst she was sat at home at her most vulnerable. They, the two men she trusted more than anything else in the world, had betrayed her more than Donny had ever managed. Between them they had created a monster that they would now have to captivate. She would be out for their blood, completely drunk on her own self loathing and her unrequited love for a man who had done nothing but use and abuse her. Dom knew that it was the bitterest of all pills to swallow, but swallow it they would have to if they had any chance of saving her. Craig slammed on the brakes of the car, sending Dom almost crashing through the glass. His face beetroot red in anger as he slapped Dom hard around the head.

"You muggy cunt! Don't you remember the last time you fucking tried it with me in a fucking car! Got a fucking death wish have we? Don't think I won't hesitate in chopping you up like that other fucker back there!" Craig screeched, his lip twisted into a sickening nasty snarl "The difference between me and you Dominic, is that I won't fucking stop when it comes to that girl. I'll murder me own muvver stone fucking dead if it meant Jenna coming away with a smile on her fucking face and don't you even think of forgetting that!" His blue eyes were blazing with contempt as he threw another badly aimed smack at Dom's head. The rage and the hurt were written all over his young face.

Dom was rendered speechless, quickly he descended from his high horse and suddenly he had become the victim. He stared at Craig for long breathtaking moments, there was no man alive he fucking hated more than Craig Carter. The sheer thought of his name sent Dom's stomach churning in agonising knots. It was as though Craig had been the standard setter for all things vulgar and dishonest. He was a complete and utter scum bag in Dom's eyes. The less he had to see the psychotic prick the better. Tonight had just proven to Dom that Craig was nothing but a heartless, fucked up villain who prided himself on the tyranny of others.

People who were weaker than him excited him, he was sick, twisted even. But as Dom's mother had always said, you couldn't educate pork!

"Yeah I get you, crystal fucking clear you dopey jumped up prick" Dom nodded sarcastically before setting himself back in his seat for the long, agonising drive home. He could have happily suffocated Craig right there where the smug cunt was sat. But if he lost his temper tonight, he would be up on a murder charge. Craig had really trod on each and every single one of his nerves now. It was time the cunt was knocked off his fucking peg! And if he thought for a fucking second that Dom was just going to let Craig and Jenna just waltz into the sunset together then he was in for a fucking shock. Dom gritted his teeth in anger and resumed his place staring at the dead open road between them. There was no fucking way was he being mugged off any fucking more, Craig Carter was living on borrowed time and sooner or later his word would come crashing down around him. And he was bringing down the whole force with him, each and every single one of Craig's associates would be in Shit Street with him. Dom smiled secretly to himself and noted another score on the invisible scoreboard as they drove away in silence.

Chapter Fifty

Jeff Harding was soaked through to his boxers with congealed blood and dirty sweat as him and his expert team of lads began the long job of cleaning down the murder scene of Donny Anderson. In all fairness he had expected more blood and gore than what he had been the recipient of. They had arrived at the warehouse an hour earlier and had been laughing all the way through the job. Donny's invisible empire would crumble overnight and now Craig Carter would take his rightful crown as king. In Hindsight Jeff was gutted that he hadn't been part of Donny's demise. He would have loved to see that sad cunt begging for his life. But Jeff had other fish to fry tonight. He had another two cleanups and a drug run to finish before he could head home. He had been dreading the thought all day, the thought of going back to a hotel with his lover seemed so much more appetising.

His long suffering wife Katie was a wreck at the best of times, popping pills for every form of anxiety possible. She was a recluse who feared the outside world more than she feared Jeff ever leaving her. She was a lost cause, doped up on the strongest medication she could get her fucking hands on. Jeff knew as soon as he walked through the door where she would be, perched on the end of the bed in her disgusting pensioners nighty, peeking through the permanently shut blinds that adored every single window of their house, flinching at every single sound coming from the outside world. Whereas his lover Saskia Kanellis on the other hand was a red blooded filthy young woman with a dangerous sexual appetite and the most amazing personality to match. She was the ultimate trophy girlfriend with her fake tits and her thigh high outfits. Jeff was smitten with her in every single sense of the word. And she was exactly the same in return. They hung off of each other's words, yet she respected his loyalties to Katie. The moments they stole together were worth every single second of deceit that they felt afterwards. It wasn't that they had intended to fall for one another. Saskia had been a Dominatrix at one of Craig Carter's bondage dens that he ran alongside his other business deals. Jeff had been introduced to Saskia as one of Craig's best working female Dominants. He had been bewitched by the girl's scarily mellow attitude and her placid nature beneath the thick eye makeup and the platinum bleached Barbie hairdo. She had been a true sweetheart ever since their first meeting and their affair had blossomed. Of course Saskia knew her boundaries where Jeff was concerned. She herself was a single parent to two babies under the age of three. So she accepted that they both had their priorities set in other places.

Although she had developed feelings for Jeff surface pretty early on in their relationship, She had always kept them concealed from him. Her calm exterior was the perfect facade for her love of the man she knew would never truly be hers. Saskia spent her nights crying into the plump pillows of the hotel rooms that they often frequented as Jeff slept soundly beside her. Some nights she felt like telling him out deep she actually was swimming in her over indulgence in him. But he was the perfect escape for her everyday life. She was seeing herself through a university degree in criminal psychology as well as looking after her two girl's full time. Both children were fathered by two different men from her days as a dominatrix. She had never been happy of the fact that her babies would never know they're fathers. But she threw herself into being a brilliant mother to them. But it was her breaks away from stress of everyday life with the man of her dreams that allowed her to capture some sort of normality. She knew Jeff worked long hours, she understood to a point the need to nurse his batshit wife who was loonier than a fucking crack head on giro day. The woman was the local laughing stock, not that Jeff knew that of course! But she was still a fucking joke. Saskia had never pleaded with Jeff to leave Katie, she knew that they didn't have a physical relationship anymore; they barely had anything other than Jeff's need to nurse the poor fucker despite her being nothing but a hopeless cause. Jeff would never mention Katie around her unless she asked him outright and she was fine with that. She only asked in all fairness out of sympathy for him. She guessed he didn't have anyone else to offload his burdens on so she may as well fill in the space. Sometimes though the thought of him mothering his wife as though she were a sick child frightened her, it was as though she could see his loyalties as plainly as painted boats on the squalid horizon. That he would Always, without a moment's hesitation be with his wife over her. That was the thought that always brought Saskia Kanellis Crashing down to earth with a mighty wallop. But tonight as she sat out on her front veranda, nursing a cold glass of wine and a joint in her pyjamas she would wait. As patiently as she could manage for him to arrive, she knew he was out of town on some job but she would give it another hour before she turned in for the night. It was still early enough for him to show up yet. She sipped her glass of white and sucked on her herb laced cigarette. The haze restoring her faith in her powers of seduction, she hoped it was only a matter of time before Jeff came running with his suitcases and his divorce papers. She was sure of it, or at least she thought she was. The reality of course was all too different.

She forced back the remainder of her glass, the cool crisp liquid quenching her overindulgent thirst. She whined as the burn travelled to her stomach. She coiled herself up in the small tub chair and hugged her cardigan tightly around her slim waist. The morning skyline was a beautiful eclectic mix of deep plums and smoky blues twinkling with a million tiny stars, it truly was a spectacle and momentarily Saskia thought she was dreaming it all. Her eyes wide in wonder as she stared out at the vast space filled with skyscrapers, office buildings and street lights ablaze, the night was her favourite time to wind down and see the world for how truly beautiful it was. There was something truly spectacular about the early hours of the morning and the peace that it brought. She closed her eyes and whimpered as a stray tear clung to her cheekbone, tonight was not her night after all and she would be going to sleep in her oversized empty bed, alone and unwanted. It was enough to send Saskia into a fit of unshed tears as she realised that without a doubt, she would always be, second best.

Jeff stormed through his front door like a hurricane; he could smell the wine before he even saw his wife and wondered how the fuck once again she had got her mitts on alcohol when the dopey bitch never left the fucking house. He was almost murderous with rage, he had spent the whole night working his arse off on jobs and now he was coming home to this. She had been texting him well into the early hours with her nonsense and now Jeff literally felt like his head was about to blow a fucking top. He strolled into the familiar darkness, the blinds and curtains drawn so tightly that not a crack of light dared creep through the drapes. The scent of long decayed cigarette butts and cheap wine filled his nostrils, churning his guts in the process. Katie was hard to judge in her mental state. She suffered from chronic bipolar, that coupled with her post natal depression was a lethal combination to say the least. She was literally a walking junkie. The amount of tablets that she downed on a daily was no man's business other than Jeff's of course who had been tied to the woman so viciously. Since losing their children to her mother, Katie had changed. She despised anyone and everything. And despite her best efforts to put on a brave face she rejected every single effort to even see the child that she had given birth to. Jeff saw their daughter three times a week at his mother in laws home. The baby was a placid enough child. A little terror of course, but that was to be expected with a two year old but Jeff loved her regardless. He hated Katie's mother though, she was like Katie just a million years older, slightly fucking prehistoric and warped in the head, and Jeff of course knew that the feeling was mutual. The whole fucking family had suffocated him, had hated him on impact. Katie's mother had taken a particular disapproval as had her fat fucking father who sat on his three seater leather sofa every night downing cans of Lager and reading The Sun, banging the world to rights as he went along. In Jeff's eyes the whole fucking family were a joke. But they had custody of his child so he would entertain them to the least of his ability just to ensure his daughter had the most out of her childhood. Not that she would have such a childhood with Grandma Terror and her fat hubby! But Jeff had to participate and he had to respect his in laws if nothing else. They were doing the Job that he and his wife had fell short upon. And so he was of course forever in their debt.

But now as he stumbled upon the broken glass that scrunched beneath his feet, he prayed to god that he was thankful for his daughter not being around for the fireworks. He trudged into the living room with the feet of a burglar as he glanced around the familiar yet strange settings. The broken chandelier that hung above his head was glowing dimly, almost in a visceral dimness as he met the squalor that had once been is living room. He saw first the upturned sofas and the bleak grey furnishings that had once made his private place so beautiful. Then he saw her, his socially oppressed wife sprawled in the corner of the lounge, an empty monopoly board at her knees. Her mortifying grey scale nightdress was lingering at her ankles. Their daughters stuffed toys in a circle at her feet. Westlife was on repeat somewhere in the background. Jeff was stunned. He finally saw with deep clarity the awkwardness of his life. He had never in a million years felt so defeated. He just watched her for long agonising moments. The rage bubbling in the pit of his stomach, He almost lunged at her but refrained. He had no idea what her mental state was.

"Kate, what the fuck is this?" he whispered sternly. His voice bounced off the hollow walls. His heart was thudding in his chest; the thought of pasting her across the walls was all too tempting. She just stared through him, completely away with the fairies. Her pure milk white face splashed with flecks of blood from her slashed wrists, she hadn't done a very good job mind, Jeff thought, the cunt was still breathing. He took a step forward, his boots crunching the glass from his wedding pictures beneath his feet. She flinched suddenly almost leaping from her chair; her hands were trembling like leaves caught in a disastrous wind.

"He didn't have enough money to buy Trafalgar square" She spat viciously, nodding her head in the direction of one of their daughters teddy bears. She folded her arms across her chest, leaving blood stains on her nightdress. Her dark steel coloured eyes were glistening from drink, Jeff could smell her from here he was stood, that and the stench of stale urine from where she'd pissed herself. He had to try his utmost hardest not to go over and smack her clean in the fucking mouth.

"What do you mean he didn't have enough fucking money? You do realise that's a fucking toy don't you!?" He quizzed, sceptical of course if she was even on the same fucking planet that he was. He could feel his temper creeping inside him, almost fit to combust as his wife glared at him through her nasty eyes. Her face twisted and bitter as she stared hard at him every single emotion stirring inside her.

"How fucking dare you" she spat plummeting from her chair and flying towards Jeff, her hands flailing wildly as she tried to attack him, her feet mangled with blood as she cut her skin on the glass, not feeling a single stab of pain as she flew at her husband with an almost feral rage. A wild inferno of lank flame red hair blew behind her as her fists made contact with her husband's strong burly frame. Her release finally found as she began smacking him hard, her screams murderous as she tried her hardest to lay into him. But her petulant strength was no match for Jeff's as he flung her none too gently onto the oak wood flooring. The blood spilling from her open wounds onto the plush cream shagpile rug. He stepped back, his eyes wide with anger as he looked down upon the woman who had caused him so much anguish over the years yet so much happiness in the beginning he felt nothing but animosity. Sympathy had overridden him and now he was beginning to feel as though he was the victim in all of this not his wife and her fifty personalities. He turned and walked away from her as she began sobbing into the rug about how "crazy" the bear had gone when he realised he didn't have enough money. Jeff knew in his heart of hearts that it was time for her to be sectioned, but loyalty to Katie made him think twice. She was his wife and he had vowed to protect her in sickness and in health, so he had to abide by his promises and look after her as best as he could manage. He trudged up the stairs completely heartbroken. His head in his hands as he run a bath, he needed to get away from that fucking mess downstairs for a bit and gather himself before he really did kick off. He stared at his reflection in the mirror. He was freakishly handsome, youthful looking still despite his age and the deep red scram marks that now adorned his left cheek. He liked to take care of himself and did so with an almost military precision. He was in the gym five days a week, he ate cleanly and very rare did he drink. And it showed, he could have passed for a man half his age if he wanted to. He slipped out of his shoes and he swiftly removed his black trousers and his shirt and slipped into the hot soapy water. His skin shading slightly red with the burn almost instantly but he found it relaxing somewhat. He could hear Katie nattering away to herself downstairs, her voice thick with malice and he knew that he would have earache for the rest of the night with her. He closed his eyes momentarily and saw Saskia's face clouding his thoughts, her beautiful pearly white smile and her delectable curvaceous body that he owned completely. She was a real treasure. And despite everything Jeff was proud of her patience. The girl was a saint, she had never ever become too possessive of him, and she above all knew her place. She wasn't the type of girl who needed reassurance and Jeff liked that in a mistress. She was his ideal woman in an ideal world. When he was away from her he craved her so desperately, she was his escape route from his life of misery. She was the balm to ease his hurt. And lately he had been relying on her company heavily just to keep sane. The thought of not having her there through all of this almost drove Jeff to drown himself right there where he lay. If it hadn't been for Saskia he probably would have started playing monopoly with the loony bitch downstairs!

His phone buzzed in his jacket pocket and for a second he smiled like a naughty schoolboy thinking it could have been her. He stretched out from the bath and grabbed his mobile from the breast pocket. His brother Jason had text him asking him to go out for the day for a few beers up west. Jason was the ultimate playboy, ruggedly handsome and he had more money to blow than the royal mint. He lived in Ireland and was only over on a business trip. Jeff pondered over the thought and immediately text back that he would love to. Anything to get away from Nutty Nora and her monopoly board! He smirked at the irony, although he was a little disheartened that Saskia hadn't even bothered to text him. He thought about calling her first for a little while but immediately decided against it. He didn't want her getting the wrong ideas. He lay in the water until it was almost freezing cold over thinking, his head was in a fucking pickle and he hated it, he couldn't handle it in fact. He had work to focus on Craig would play fuck if he thought there was trouble in the camp and so Jeff plastered on his fake smile, got out of the bath and get dressed ready to face another day of lying to himself.

Chapter Fifty One

Jason Harding stood under the fierce jet of water, his perfectly sculpted body dripping with sweat from his morning workout. He couldn't wait to see his brother, it had been nearly two years since he had seen him last. Jason had lived in County Wicklow Ireland for almost ten years running his own highly successful business in fishing and trawling, he also spoke fluent Gaelic and participated in training local children in sports. He was all in all everyone's best friend. And he liked it like that. Everyone who knew him envied him, because he was genuinely such a nice guy. He threw on his jeans and a plain white t shirt taking his time to perfect his hair in the hotel mirror. By God he was a handsome bastard! His mother had told him so from day one how he should have been a girl. With his playful dimples and slightly curly overgrown brown hair, milk white skin and beautiful green eyes he was the complete opposite of his older brother. His charm offensive was better too if he did say so himself. He ran his fingers through his slight stubble his cheeks baby soft beneath his touch. He checked his phone, his brother was meeting him in just under an hour and he was already dressed and ready to go. He opened the mini bar and pulled himself out a beer while he waited. He settled down on the bed and turned on the TV, aimlessly he flicked through the channels trying his utmost to keep his attention on the blurred images that were skating before his eyes. He had been out on the town the previous night and the pretty little half caste girl called Kyra or something had been blowing his phone up all day for a second date. But Jason Harding didn't do second dates; he didn't even do first fucking dates. He fucked and then he chucked. It was plain and simple, when a girl started to get too clingy, he dropped them swiftly like a bad, over indulged habit. Jason didn't do commitment, not after he had caught his ex wife in bed with his old boss. Anything that had happened after that was nothing more than casual sex. It had broken his heart and he had vowed to never ever trust another woman with his love for as long as he lived. He had done his fair share of heartbreaking in the years since though! The women literally fell to their knees after just a smile.

But Jason hadn't let it fill his life with venom, he had cut free from dull over bearing factory work that paid fucking pennies and he had up sticks and caught the first ferry to Ireland. It had been hard saying goodbye to his family, of course being away from his brother was painful; they were like the bloody Kray's when they were together, although they were simply chalk and cheese they were the best of friends. Upon leaving London he had invested all of the money his brother had gifted to him into his trawling business and now he earned millions of pounds ever year whilst the business practically ran itself. He had learnt the hard way, tears had been shed and blood had of course been spilled and he had vowed that he would never ever have to feel so shitty ever again. Especially since his ex's new lover was now propping up a flyover somewhere in London with his cock rammed up his fucking arsehole. Courtesy of Jason's brother of course. The thought even now made Jason grin from ear to fucking ear. His brother was a fucking legend nowadays though; even when he was away on the trawlers the boys would have stories about Jeff Harding and the Carter crew. Jason had only met Craig once, but it had been before Jeff had had any involvement with him in a professional sense. It was at a gala for the criminal underworlds elite that his brother had dragged him along to that apparently a Mafia don was hosting. Of course on the night there was no sign of said Don and they'd all just got slaughtered on expensive champagne instead.

Jason very rarely drank anymore though unless he was out with friends, he had gone through a bout of acute alcoholism after he and his ex wife had broken up and had ended up rushed to hospital having his stomach pumped of booze and drugs. It hadn't been his proudest moment if he was honest. But jumping on the wagon had been the best decision he had ever made and now he only drank socially instead of on his own in front of the tele for no apparent reason. He had lived enough to know the dangers of living life in the fast lane and so now the simple things pleased him. He enjoyed sports, enjoyed being the coach for his local youth football squad. He enjoyed fine dining and champagne, he was the ultimate consumer. He loved having the financial freedom to do whatever he pleased without even having to question how much the cost of anything was. He had the freedom to do whatever he pleased without having to answer to anyone. It felt great too, to know he was young with a million possibilities. It was a breath of fresh air to him. He was buzzing with excitement to see his big brother, they spoke every single day without fail but nothing beat spending time with him in the flesh. And Jason thanked the fucking lord that Jeff wouldn't be bringing the fucking loony toon with him! It was a joke in their family that Jeff's wife was a few sandwiches short of the proverbial picnic. She very rarely ventured out of their home and every time Jason had gone to the house she had acted like a delusional little fucking prat. He had caught her talking to herself no less than three times the last time he had turned up on the doorstep unannounced and his reception had been to say the least frosty. Nutty Nora couldn't stand anyone other than her fucking self and whatever friend she could conjure up in her broken mind. He did feel sorry for her though, Jeff was like a dog with two fucking dicks when he wanted to be. He had really tried to make things work with Katie, he was her full time carer and like any red blooded male he liked to let off a bit of steam. But in Jeff's case letting off steam was fucking whores and taking his dirty dick home to bed his crazy wife. But hey, who was Jason to judge. He smirked at the irony and was glad, thankful even that it wasn't him in that position. Jason finished his beer in amicable silence, glancing at his watch he realised that an hour had almost passed. He got up from the bed and tossed his empty bottle in the waste paper basket beside the bed. He checked himself over once more in the mirror before slipping his shoes on by the door and heading out.

The mid morning London traffic was hectic, chaotic even and Jeff wasn't amused in the fucking slightest! It had taken him over an hour to make the usually twenty minute drive into town. He was though beginning to wish he had chosen a different place to meet his bloody brother! The place was on fucking lock down because of a crash on the main road and Jeff would have been quicker if he had walked the whole fucking way there. He beeped his horn loudly in disapproval, and banged hard on the steering wheel in distaste. He didn't give a flying fuck for the fuckers in the crashed car that was practically on its side, the fuckers should have been looking where they were fucking going, he thought. He pulled his phone out of his pocket and quickly typed a text to his brother explaining his lateness. He was still fucked off with Saskia for not calling him, he understood she must be upset for him not calling by but these things couldn't be helped, could they? He checked his emails just to see if she had tried to contact him through that instead, but nothing. Jeff couldn't help but feel disheartened. If she didn't call him soon he would have to react. He couldn't lose her, it would be like chopping off his right arm, literally. He hoped she wasn't too pissed off with him, nothing that some kind words and wine wouldn't cure of course. He grinned at the mere suggestion of having to grovel to Saskia, it made him almost laugh like a hyena. Oh and grovel he would have to if he was going to get straight back into her good books. He felt bad for not making the effort to explain to her what had happened the night before with Katie, but he didn't want her to think that he couldn't handle his wife either. In other words, Jeff was stuck between a rock and a very hard place.

He wasn't looking forward to when the two of them crossed paths again, but he knew it was going to have to happen eventually. She wouldn't be able to stay away for too long. He grinned at the thought; his mood instantly lightened by the thought of Saskia sitting in her onesie with a pout on her beautiful mouth amused him greatly. The thought of her needing him, wanting his just that little bit too much was the reason he was so attracted to her, it was desire. It was a crazy twist of lust and forbidden ecstasy. It felt so wrong and so right all at the same time and Jeff thrived on the danger of the unknown. The traffic started to clear and Jeff could have actually leapt up and screamed Hallelujah as the cars began swirling off in all different junctions with frantic pace, not wanting to get stuck again.

He finally escaped the mad rush, literally beaming as he pulled up outside the plush looking Greek restaurant that his brother had asked him to meet him in. The smell of fresh spices and home cooking filled Jeff's nostrils the second he opened his car door. He suddenly came over completely famished and couldn't wait to fill his boots with the delicious food he was about to be in recipient of. He walked through to the bar, he immediately spotted Jason, propping himself up on a barstool with a vodka and coke chatting up the beautiful brunette barmaid with a look of pure indulgence written on his handsome face. He popped an olive in his mouth from the bowl on the bar and began to laugh playfully with the dazed girl who seemed completely captivated by Jason and his extrovert charm. Her poor breasts were spilling from the confines of her tight black cocktail dress that she wore with plain black patent shoes. She was completely compelled by Jason, it was written all over her pretty little face and she was practically drooling over him. He like the vain little bastard he was sat there sucking it up like the local sleaze. He was a funny boy was Jason, all brooding good looks and natural charm. Jeff coughed under his breath and immediately Jason spun around on his seat. He dove from his seat and enveloped Jeff in a massive bear hug all the while mumbling on about how much he had missed him. The side splitting grin on his face was enough to light up the whole room. Jason had never in his life been so happy to see his brother's face. He regained his position on his chair and began asking a million questions all at once. Jeff held up his hand and cut him off mid sentence as he ordered himself a drink from miss big boobs behind the bar and her over toothed almost goofy looking smile. She immediately went and occupied herself pouring out the measure of neat vodka and mixers as though they were her best friends.

"So bruv how's things?" Jason quipped taking a sip from his freshly filled glass as the girl lay them down on the counter. His sexy eyes winking at her cheekily, the poor girls face turned almost bloody red with embarrassment as she left them too it. Jeff heard her moments later giggling like a naughty schoolgirl to her colleague about the whole crazy episode. Jeff took a swift glug of his drink before they made their way over to their table that was already laid and ready waiting for them. They both took their seats opposite one another, Jeff fixed his tie slightly so it was looser around his neck while Jason perused the menu whilst making flirty eyes at the still giggling barmaid. He hadn't changed a bit other than some fine lines that lingered close to his eyes but other than that he was the same old Jason he had always been. If not just slightly more big headed than the last time Jeff had seen him. But Jeff loved his baby brother more than anyone else in the world. He had been his best friend from the moment he had been born and they had carried each other all the way through to adulthood. Together they were better and that was the only way they had ever saw things. Jeff grabbed the spare menu from the table and began to scan over the mouth-watering dishes that were on offer. He had no clue what he fancied but he knew if he didn't eat soon he was going to throw a paddy fit. He hadn't had the chance to grab something at home because Nutty Nora had taken a turn for the worst and had began to smash up their kitchen with her bare hands. Jeff swore blind that if she didn't shape her ideas up he was going to bury her alive in the fucking garden with her bastard nighty and her monopoly board!

Once they'd finally ordered and settled themselves down with a drink the brothers sat reminiscing and catching up on each other's affairs. Both laughing until their sides split in two and just mellowing in one another's company. Jeff had forgotten how nice it was just to have some downtime with his little brother although it also made him realise how much he missed Jason when he wasn't around. As He lifted another forkful of the delicious moussaka before him to his lips, Jeff raised his glass of amaretto in a toast to them. Jason being the joker he was shrugged it off as nothing but his brothers' strange attempt at humour but secretly he was bursting to have his brothers' attention. Jeff had always been so reserved and so calm whereas he had always been the charmer of the two. They had both had a rough start in life, born to a drug abusing mother and a violent father, their childhood was filled with abandoned memories of fights, strangers and the crack fuelled haze that constantly lingered in their third storey one bedroom flat on a shitty council estate. Their mother had been a prostitute selling herself for a measly £10 a time just to get her fix. The boys had been lucky to see a tin of beans and piece of dry toast for their daily meal but as brothers they had come through the worst, both keeping each other sane both sheltering one another from the emotional torment. Both had been completely alien to the concept of love and genuine affection from their parents. Their old man was a fucking tosser of almost epic standard. He wasn't even sorry for the years of endless beatings and the years of emotional torture he had placed on his boys' shoulders. Jeff and Jason had lived the life a million times over yet here they were. Without a single scar or blemish to show how much they had suffered. Here they were dining like kings, pure business men through and through. Yet they had grown from the gutter.

Jeff had been the worst hit by their past, he was extremely shy. This in turn of course made everyone think he was extremely silent. Jason had learnt that confidence was everything in life and loving yourself was the most important tool in success. He had forever tried to drum into Jeff how bloody amazing he really was without seeming like his brothers stalker or anything. They had both learnt to forgive their mother over time although. It had taken every ounce of their strength to just speak to her nowadays, their father was a different story altogether. The boys had blanked him for years and now he was senile old prick banged up in a nursing home somewhere. This of course was nothing more than he deserved. The last they had heard he was talking to himself and playing with his heroin bruises. Jeff and Jason had always persevered through it. Both had kept on smiling through the tears, both leaning on one another for the towering strength of each other's support. They had the strongest bond, completely and utterly bound together by their love and determination to stick together. They had fought every single odd that had ever become a barrier between them and now they could finally say they were free. The thought was humbling and they both knew the triumph that each other felt at knowing they were untouchable. The Harding brothers were the closest living example of the Kray twins personified. They enjoyed the rest of their meal with drinks flowing freely, their banter passing and back and forth effortlessly. Until of course the subject of Jeff's wife cropped up.

It wasn't that Jeff was uncomfortable with the woman he married, but he was uncomfortable when the subject of her illness came up. It was no secret in their family about Katie; of course his family weren't aware of the full extent of her illness. They were aware of the postnatal depression, they were aware of the social anxiety and the fear of going outside. They didn't however understand how far gone Katie actually was. In all ideals she was a fucking fruit loop. A complete and utter crazed lunatic who should be on the bastard funny farm with the rest of the nut cases but Jeff couldn't bare the thought of her being under the spell of the medical profession. He had seen hundreds of news reports about how mentally challenged patients were kept in those asylums and the thought made his skin crawl. She was way too fragile, way too delicate for that. And as much as she did his fucking head in and as much as she was a burden to him at the best of times, he did love her in his own way. It was a weird way, of course that was a given, but he had married her for a reason and those darker days didn't seem so important when he thought of how amazing their relationship had been before the depression. She had been almost perfect. Katie had once been the most gorgeous jewel in a crown of thorns. She was impeccable yet reserved. She had once had the longest legs a man had ever seen, with the glossiest hair and the most beautiful shade of porcelain skin. She had been Jeff's dirty little secret, similar to how Saskia was now. Jeff's first wife had been a fucking dragon and Katie had been his fucking relief. She had been wild between the sheets and a complete lady in the streets. But as he did to everything that he touched he had ruined her with his constant cheating. The amount of times he had strolled in at two in the morning smelling of another woman and her cheap perfume was no one's business. The amount of times Katie had found the texts on his phone, answered the phone to the purring voices of his latest fumble and yet she had never whispered a word of her findings to him. She had kept it bottled up for years and finally the shit had hit the fan and her meltdown had all but consumed her. With each violent outburst came the inconsolable guilt that engulfed her, made her swear never to utter a word of her secrets to anyone. She was so scared to leave the confines of her own prison just in case she said the wrong thing to the wrong person and landed Jeff in trouble. She loved him with a hurricane force that had all but torn her apart limb by aching limb. She was emotionally exhausted, a complete stranger to herself now. She had become so far gone that now when she stared at her torn reflection in the mirror all she saw was the ghost of herself staring back at her. Her thick matted hair that hung lank at her shoulders, her sallow skin that was borderline grey in appearance filled with blemishes and hollow cheekbones that protruded deep beneath her skin. She had become so depressed that she couldn't even bear the thought of the everyday things that she used to love. The simplicity of getting dressed, putting on a slick of her favourite lipstain, going for a coffee on her own or even curling up with a good book and a glass of zinfandel. She had become literally a nothing and Jeff had to take the blame for that partly if not wholly. He had been her addiction; she had loved him so fiercely, so rabidly that she had never believed he would have a reason to be unfaithful. But Jeff of course was like a dog with two fucking dicks and would slip a sly one into any girl who so much as fluttered an eyelash at him. He was a player, a fucking good one at that! He was Slipperier than a fucking eel with his oozing charm and his delectable etiquette, almost gentlemanly if it wasn't for his constant fucking hard on and his wandering eye.

Jeff of course just thought that Katie had been depressed over their child. It had killed her when she had been told that their daughter was being taken away from them. But she had been caught trying to walk the poor newborn around in the freezing cold with just a vest on in the middle of fucking December. Katie had been disorientated and intoxicated on her daily pharmaceuticals when the police had accidentally come across her. And so they had had no other option other than to take the child from her without a single moment's consideration for Katie's welfare. They had sectioned Katie under the mental health act and she had spent four months trying her hardest to keep her sanity intact. For a while she had been doing excellent, seeking advice from a therapist had helped her in abundance, she had begun to show flecks of the old Katie, the one he had fallen head over heels in love with. Until of course the courts had ruled that Katie's mother would have primary custody of their daughter. It was then that Katie had completely lost control of every emotion that she had left and she finally submitted herself to a life of being fucked by her own warped mind.

"Jase fucking leave it out!" Jeff warned, keeping his eyes firmly transfixed on the flawless white tablecloth. His eyes bulbous and raging as his fist connected with the wood making the other diners turn to glare at them suspiciously. Momentarily the whole restaurant fell into a mind numbing silence as fellow diners stared at their otherwise quite private table. Mouths hanging open in almost comical grandeur. Jeff took one sideways glance at the gawping crowd and immediately all eyes were back on plates and the sudden hum of voices began to pick back up. He had the look of venom in his over alert eyes and immediately from one sudden glance Jeff put the fear of God into the souls of each and every single one of the diners. Every single cheek in sight slightly pink with embarrassment as people searched for a new source of entertainment other than the two handsome boys arguing at the table.

"Fuck sorry bro, I didn't realise Madame marbles was something to get your knickers in a twist over" Jason joked back, almost giggling into his wine as he spoke.

Jeff could feel his knees twitching underneath the tablecloth and for a split second he envisaged himself turning the fucking table upside down and giving his brother a fucking pasting. But his temper subsided almost as quickly as the idea had planted itself. Jason wasn't to understand the enormity of the situation with Katie. He had kept his torment away from his brother and he intended to keep it that way. The finished their meal in complete silence, the atmosphere between them was tense and almost unbearable. Jeff refused to utter another word within his brothers company. The boy would learn that as much as Jeff may despise his wife, he would never allow another living soul to breathe a bad word about her. She was his, his only sole possession and he cared about her dearly. He cared about the way she felt even if she herself didn't even know how she felt herself. He wanted Katie to be happy and as much as she was a fuck short without an ounce of compassion left in her skinny body. She was still his wife and commitment was something that Jeff had always believed in strongly. He felt like the biggest hypocrite walking of course, with the amount of affairs he had notched on his bedpost, yet here he was spouting about loyalty. It was entirely laughable really. A complete fucking joke, but he wasn't willing to admit that the laugh was on him. The fact that he felt no guilt was what ate away at Jeff the most. He felt only pity, pity for the fact that he had slipped a stunning platinum ring on the psycho cunts fingers without thinking things through and now here he was glued to her for life. That was the sad part; he was enslaved to a woman whose love he no longer desired. He would always appreciate Katie; he would always love and respect her as the mother of his child but beyond that respect was a world filled with love of the passionate kind that Jeff was so desperate to chase. Katie could just continue to play fuck with her teddies and her fucking board games as far as he was concerned, he wanted no part in her demise.

But he of course would take a part of the blame for her and her antics. As much as he hated to admit the fact that he had been the reason for his wife's decay. He would still sit there and deny any wrong doing on his part if anyone dared to question it. To everyone else he was a fucking hero. What man wanted to cater to his ill wife whilst running a successful business empire? Fucking Jeff Harding of course! Jeff the fucking snake who would fuck anything with a pair of tits if it meant he was getting his cock wet behind his deranged wife's back. But of course people only saw him as the poor man who was responsible for his poor senile wife, the one who found entertainment in children's colouring books to relieve her fucking stress. The woman was a bloody mess of epic standard! But to everyone else, to the alluring eyes of others Jeff was a fucking saint. He of course felt the pressure of playing the martyr, but the image was easier to maintain with his line of fucking slags ready with their knickers around their ankles and their dresses around their waists. Jeff Harding of course was willing to lap it up like a fucking dog. The dirty cunt that he was.

Before the boys knew it they were trawling the streets at two in the morning with a greasy kebab in their clutches and an imminent hangover in the morning. Their earlier argument had been long forgotten. Both completely out of their heads on vodka shots and house champagne sweat soaked and smelling like the local brewery. Jason was slurring some story about one of his fishing trips as he staggered up the road. The silent London streets deathly quiet as not a sound could be heard in the distance other than the bitter autumn winds that slashed their bare cheeks as they walked. Jeff almost toppled over as he dithered away beside his brother, nodding his head and muttering the occasional grunt under his breath as he attempted to get a word in edge ways. His brother could natter away with the best of them; by fuck he would put the curtain twitchers of his street to fucking shame. Even old fucking Doreen in number forty five would have been rigid stiff through boredom by now, and she loved nothing more than a good old scandal to get her through the day. Jeff took a deep gulp from the half full champagne bottle in his hand, offering it to his brother he expected him to shut up for at least twenty seconds as he took a drink. They were both freezing cold, shivering excessively as the cold wind battered they're alcohol drenched skin. Both were out of their fucking skulls. Both high on life as they trawled the dimly lit street, the overhead street lights bathing them with light amber glow.

 Jason was still bumbling on, blissfully unaware of anything until he heard the screaming tyres of a speeding car that came hurtling around the corner at lightning speed, sending his brother hurtling through the air as it collided with him until it was too late. All he heard was the screech of the tyres as the car flew away around the corner. It had been a personal attack on his brother; Jason suspected it had been intentional. Suddenly everything was playing in slow motion as Jason threw his food bag in the air and quickly scarpered over to his brother who was laying face down on the concrete. The champagne and smashed glass formed the perfect puddle beside his battered face. Jason was screaming then, howling like a wolf to the silvery moon but it didn't feel as though it was coming from himself, it was as though he was having a fucking out of body experience or something as he pulled his brother over onto his back and began to attempt to resuscitate Jeff's limp body. The seconds felt like hours as he pumped his hands against his brother's sagged chest, each pump draining the life from Jason's arms as the tears flooded his cheeks. He wouldn't look down; the thought of his poor siblings' mangled bloody legs in front of him was too much. Jason swallowed down the vomit that he found was swimming in the back of his burning throat. The acidity stinging his stomach as it hit for the second time, almost spilling from his lips ferociously as he wretched once more. His gut twisted in a million knots, his eyes locked firmly on his brothers' dead eyes. The shock still tattooed on his face, his lip contorted into a strange curvaceous line, grim and thinly set, almost invisible through the paleness of his skin. The sound of the ambulance sirens in the background notified Jeff that thank fuck someone had phoned for help. He hadn't even noticed the congregation that had encircled them. Despite the fact that Jason had been screaming at them for the last ten minutes to get fucking help he honestly didn't know what the fuck he was doing. He wasn't sure whether there was a God out there somewhere, but by fuck he was praying with every single ounce he had in his body that his brother would survive. His whole body was aching with need, need for the knowledge that his big brother was going to be ok.

When the paramedics finally arrived, Jason was immediately pulled aside by one of the young male paramedics who wrapped him in a foil blanket and sat him in the back of the ambulance as he helplessly watched on as his brother was mauled by the strangers who now had the job of saving his life. Jason was shaking like a leaf In a storm, his lip was quivering though sheer helplessness. He felt terrible, heartbroken even as though the world had stopped around him and it was just him and his broken feelings. It was almost as though Jeff was a million miles away and he couldn't reach out his hand to help the one person who had guided him through life. Seeing Jeff laying there lifeless on the concrete was soul crushing for Jason and all he could do was watch on, as though this were all but a mere soap opera and they were the actors. He wondered momentarily whether this was all but a nasty dream and that he would wake up soon and the day would be new and his brother would still be laughing and joking with him over the everyday things. But here was the reality; he didn't know whether Jeff would survive the night. And even if he did, what life was he to lead? The poor man's legs had been taken straight from underneath him. He would never ever walk again after this. That much was already a given. His career with the Carter lot would be crumbled to dust already and he would have been replaced by the morning. But as Jason looked on, the fear of god was put into him. Whatever his brother was involved in, it was obviously deadly fucking serious and he hoped to fuck that whoever had given the nod to this attack didn't have his name on their card next. Jason couldn't handle watching his life from over his shoulder and as much as he loved his brother, he wasn't about to throw himself to the wolves in the name of brotherhood. He was scared, for the first time in his life Jason Harding was actually petrified of what was to happen. As the paramedic fussed around him like some fucking lunatic he honestly felt like nutting the poor fucker straight in the face just because he was annoying him so bloody much! The idiot was now mumbling on about how he shouldn't look at Jeff because it could make emotional shock set in. It was enough to make Jason almost clip the poor sod over the fucking head for sounding so bastard stupid. Of course he was in fucking shock! His only brother had just been mowed down in front of him, his brother was lain out on the fucking cold tarmac streets of fucking London, probably gasping his last breath but here he was being told not to look! Surely this idiot was thick if he thought that Jason's eyes would stay away from the broken body of his dismantled brother who lay in the middle of the fucking road. Blue lights blasted the area in a simultaneous pattern. Over and over the sirens wailed as each stroke of light highlighted

Jeff's' petrified expression. The sound of muttering voices from the crowd that had gathered around was almost reaching an agonising crescendo in Jason's head as his brother was stretchered into the back of an ambulance. He was hooked up to at least a million wires from the umpteen beeping machines that the paramedics had laced him in. Jason stared open mouthed, trying to voice his speechless concerns to the paramedic. He needed to be with his brother there was no other words for it. He needed to be beside Jeff now. He needed to be there for his brother, whether he survived or not. Jason would have to pick up the pieces bit by broken bit. He hurtled from the ambulance at almost lightening speed. He began to slow jog beside the men who were quickly carting his brother into the back of the second ambulance. Their voices were miffed and almost annoyed at the fact that he was here. But Jason didn't give a fuck as long as his brother was ok. He quickly took the seat beside his brother in the ambulance. He clutched the man's hand, Jeff's cold fingers entwined within his own, felt almost alien. The paramedic looked at Jason with distaste as they pulled away from the wretched scene. The blue lights were blaring and the siren screeched over head as they raced through the cars that had gathered for a nose of the shenanigans. Jason clutched his brothers hand tightly as the paramedics began working on him in the back of the ambulance. His trousers were cut away so that they could assess the damage to his legs while another was administering oxygen through a mask placed carefully over Jeff's mouth. The paramedics were silent as they worked, Jason was glad though because he couldn't handle hearing how fucked up his brothers battered body was. He just hoped against hope that Jeff found the strength inside him to get through this. Then Jason would strike out and put an end to the cunt who had committed these wrong doings against the Harding Brothers.

The sound of the bedroom door creaking slowly open awoke Jenna from her light doze. She turned herself around to find Craig at the foot of the bed getting undressed as quietly as he could. She smiled subtly as she admired his fine physique. His lean muscles rippled in all of the right places, his soft skin delicately tanned and peachy. He was like a Greek God personified with his short sandy coloured hair and his mesmerising blue eyes. He really was a spectacular sight in all of his glory. Despite the angry red scars that adorned his torso, he was comfortable around her and the thought was as much of a stress as it was a relief. She didn't know where to put her eyes half of the bloody time. But as they lay transfixed on the ever alluring Craig Carter and his impeccable good looks, Jenna could feel the overbearing familiar feeling of the butterflies flapping around in her stomach. The over frenzied attack of nausea that she faced every time she caught sight of him because he crippled her with nerves. She had never intended to fall for Craig, too much water had passed under the bridge for them now, she was sure of it. But still she couldn't help but stare at him, hungry for his rabid touch on her delicate skin. As unstable as she felt emotionally she knew that Craig could give her everything she had ever desired. A life for her and their daughter, a home that they could call theirs and they could live happily together. Kiki was still young, Jenna would give the world to have both of her children back with her. Without a worry or a burden laid on their little shoulders. Despite all that had happened she had never once lost touch with the fact that she was a mother. The aching need to see her babies had all but killed her whilst she had been under Donny's spell. They had been all that had kept her going even in her darkest moments. When she felt like taking her own life just to save herself the torment. Her children had been her only reassurance that she was never alone.

She saw her own smile mirrored intently on Craig's gentle handsome face, the way his eyes instantly softened when they met hers that he felt the same way in return. He slid off his trousers and tossed them aside as he perched himself at the foot of the bed. His hand tracing an invisible crease in the covers, his body glistening with a thin veneer of perspiration as the shimmering light from the full moon seeped in through the thin voile curtains. He truly was a remarkable creature. Even in the darkness he was strikingly beautiful. His hand slid up the bedspread until it rested neatly on hers, Jenna's lip curved slightly as a smouldering smile played against her mouth. She allowed Craig's fingers to playfully entwine within her own as her knuckles brushed against his hand. The feeling of his skin against hers sending a prickling shiver to envelope Jenna as they continued just to stare at each other. She pulled herself up against the headboard, her eyes not leaving Craig's for a second as she pulled him closer, pulling his head down onto her chest as she just held him too her. Feeling his heartbeat so close to hers was a invigorating experience, one that she had missed so much. He had always been her world, her rock and she was so glad to be back home where she belonged. She began to stroke his hair, his head snuggled so deeply into her chest. His head buried do gently against her naked flesh. The touch of his warm breath against her bare breasts as he lay on her sending delicious shivers down her spine as she kissed the top of his forehead gently. Inhaling the intoxicating scent of body wash and Craig's fresh clean sweat. She closed her eyes momentarily and all of the sadness and all of the frustration and the fear she had felt for all of these months was suddenly washed away. He was everything and more to her. It felt so perfect holding him in her arms, she was so desperate for normality after the craziness of the last few months. She had been broken, she had been torn down piece by piece but she knew deep down that the worst was over and now she could finally breathe easy.

"He's gone isn't he" she whispered, resting her forehead against Craig's. Her saddened eyes direct with his. She felt his heart rate quicken against her and immediately she knew the truth. He nodded sadly, staring deep into the eyes of the girl who he had risked his everything for. Here she was, in his bed, wearing nothing but his satin sheets. Despite everything that had happened. He couldn't just fall out of love with her and he couldn't lie to her either.

"Yes he is, you're free." he whispered. His aching voice quivering slightly as he swallowed down the tears that were pricking his electric blue eyes. His face was blazing with sadness as she cupped his face in her hands. She kissed the bridge of his nose gently. She knew Donny had suffered in his final moments, no words would ever describe how much the thought tore her apart. Like a hot iron through her heart she felt the burn. The knowledge that

Donny was gone, that Kristian was gone it was mental torture. The fact that she never got to say goodbye, the fact that she had never got to see him begging for forgiveness for all of the horrible pain he had inflicted on her. The fact that even though Craig swore she was free, she honestly didn't feel it. She still had so much to prove. She still had so much to fight back against. Dom being the next biggest monster she had to face head on over their son. She wanted Archie back so desperately but she knew the impending fight was going to be brutal. Dom would wipe the fucking floor with her the second he found out that she was going to try and get the baby back.

"Everything is going to be OK Jen. I promise" he reassured, he sat up and crawled into the bed beside her. He pulled her close into his body, her tiny frame almost buried against him. He nestled his nose in her hair, sucking in the delicious scent of her skin, the smell of her shampoo invading his nostrils. He could feel the heat of her skin radiating against his, the two of them metaphorically melting into one another. He had always loved this girl with a passion so strong that it confused him each and every single day. She had him spell bound. Completely captivated with her beauty and her awe inspiring personality. Even though she was broken, she was damaged way beyond repair, but Craig would do anything in his power to see his beautiful butterfly spread her wings once again. He held her there into the small hours, just telling her how he was going to make her happy. And he meant each and every word that escaped his mouth. This time there would be no mistakes, there would be no more suffering and no more sadness. He wanted to get her back to being herself , he wanted her to learn to love again and to love herself in return.

 Craig could feel the nervousness kicking in, he felt a catastrophic amount of nausea as he leant in and kissed her. He didn't know how she would react to him being so forward with her. But the second their lips collided it was like she had never been away and Craig knew from that instant that he would never ever allow her to be gone from him again. They had so much happiness waiting in their future and there was no way that she was ever ever leaving him go through all of this heartache again. He had to let her know exactly how dedicated he was to making her happy. He wanted to see her beautiful smile every morning when he woke up and he wanted to be the last person she kissed each night before they went to sleep. He wanted to look after her, make her well again and show her what real love really was. He had been scared of her rejection for so long, scared of ruining the only thing they had got perfectly right. Their impeccable friendship. But now after all of what had happened he realised that she was worth the risk. Even if they crashed and they burnt at least he could say they had tried. . His palms were sweating profusely and his mouth was as dry as a bone. He felt vulnerable and it wasn't a feeling Craig Carter was familiar with. He had grappled with his feelings for so long now that everything was finally coming to the boil and if he didn't react now then she would be gone forever. She needed more than just a friendship, she needed more than just the craziness of a one night stand once in a blue moon. She deserved more respect and she deserved someone who would dedicate their life and soul to making her happy. And Craig was as sure as he was his own name that he was the man for the job.

 They lay entwined in each others arms and she laughed, a genuine beautiful laugh that made Craig beam with pride as she said the one thing that he had been waiting to hear since he had been a snotty nosed four year old.

Yes.... She would marry him.

Chapter Fifty Two

One Year Later

Jenna squeezed into the beautiful white flowing gown, careful not to put too much pressure on her vast growing bump. The beautiful hand stitched gown had been expertly tailored by one of Italy's most influential designers. The bodice was intricately clustered with thousands of crystals and beads that when coupled against Jenna's flawless pregnancy skin was simply breathtaking. She wore her hair long and curly, perfectly dyed in a delectable caramel brown that suited her despite her paleness. She looked absolutely fabulous, effortlessly striking and for the first time in a long time she actually felt good about herself.

 Her unexpected pregnancy had been a beautiful and effortless experience. It had been easy and stress free and she was absolutely glowing. With only a month left till the birth of baby Carter they had decided to move the wedding forward. That coupled with the fact that they had found out not three weeks before that Craig's mother was riddled with breast cancer and her days were few and far between. Craig had stepped in and arranged for the day to be moved forward and he done an exceptional job. The absolutely wonderful manor hotel where they had picked their venue was decorated in accustom to their chosen theme of white and lilac. Every surface was adorned in pretty flowers leading to the exquisite marquee where they were to exchange their vows. They had invited only a small number of their friends and family to share their intimate ceremony with and that had suited them both to the ground. It wasn't about showing off and it wasn't about making a scene it was about them showing each other how much they loved each other. Jenna stared out at the dazzling blue sky from the double bay windows, not a single cloud could be seen, if she hadn't been to the depths of hell herself she would have said that life indeed could be perfect if you really did put your heart into it. As sad as she was to say goodbye to her old life she knew that today would be the final chapter as Jenna Shearan and her new novel would start as Mrs Carter. And she couldn't bloody wait.

She had overcome a lot in the past twelve months and she was proud of all she had achieved. As a family they had unified and fought off the world. Craig had mended all of the wrongs he had done by flying out and visiting Donny's stepson, he had told him everything about what Donny had done to Jenna and of Course what Donny had done to Tommy's mother. Tommy of course had been heartbroken, blood thirsty for revenge he was never going to execute and so Craig had taken him under his wing. Had trained the boy well and now he ran one of The Carter nightclubs as a manager. He had a lot of prospects and Craig was sure Tommy would continue to flourish under his careful control. Of course then there were Craig's two best men, whom he couldn't have thanked nor could he have loved any more than he did. The Harding boys were his closest and most valued friends. He looked upon Jason and Jeff as though they were brothers.

Jeff had taken to losing his legs badly at first. He had constantly battled with post traumatic stress disorder and had attempted suicide on several occasions before Craig had told him he needed him on his feet for the wedding. As promised Craig had booked him in with one of the best prosthetic specialists money could buy and within eight months Jeff had been on his new trendy legs. Of course he was still stung over the car accident. After he had been in hospital Jason had done some digging around and it had been discovered that it had been Saskia driving the car that night. She had gone fishing around Jeff's house and had found Jeff's wife Katie alone and helpless. Katie had attacked Saskia, she wasn't as fucking lacking as she had appeared and had fucking battered Saskia for shagging her husband. Katie had been sectioned and was apparently doing well. Jeff saw her once a month now at the lovely residential home where Katie's care was based. Jeff's biggest achievement though was winning the custody battle against Katie's parents for his daughter. Jeff was an amazing father and he doted on his beautiful happy little girl with a pride that was simply exquisite to watch. Although he had been sceptical at first Jeff had taken to parenthood like a duck to water and his little family were thriving. He still worked alongside Craig, but as his right hand man. The brains behind the planning and design briefs of all of Craig's new building plans. He was happy enough and that was all Craig had ever wanted was for his friend to find his inner peace. They had all learnt a few hard life lessons in the space of a year. Jason of course had packed his job in the fishing industry and moved himself back to London where he was now married to the Beautiful Abigail who he met on Craig's stag do six months prior. After a whirlwind romance they had married in a simple, elegant ceremony in front of only three people. Jenna, Craig and Jeff. It was all the witness they had needed to show their committal to one another. They were a stunning couple and both were excited to be godparents to Jenna's baby when it arrived.

Jenna glanced up at the clock, in less than an hour she would be marrying the love of her life. It didn't feel real, it was as though this was a scene from one of her wildest dreams. She couldn't believe that finally after all of the years that had passed between them she was finally going to be brandishing herself with the Carter name. It felt almost like all of her Christmases had come all at once. He was such a special man and despite everything, he had always been the one who truly had her heart from the very beginning. There was a knock on the door then and Jenna almost jumped out of her skin. Craig couldn't see her in her dress! It was bad luck! She ushered her make up artist Carla to the door to see who it was. She beamed almost instantly when Dom walked into the room holding their little boy in his arms. Archie was dressed in a beautiful little black tailored suit and lilac shirt. His overgrown floppy hair was the image of his fathers. In fact they were almost like twins. Jenna rushed over and enveloped them both in a unified hug. The year had been tough on Dom, he had taken the heartache of losing Jenna quite badly and had spiralled off the rails for a while. He had ignored her calls and texts and her constant begging to see their son for months on end and in a last ditched attempt Jenna had sent him a text saying she wanted him to give her away at the wedding. At first he had protested against it, had called every little slut under the sun. But he had arranged to meet up with her to go over everything and they had finally gotten onto the same page. She understood that Dom would never willingly hand over their son and as much as Jenna hated to admit it, Archie was in the best place. He was settled and he was happy with Dom and for Jenna and Craig to try and uproot the little boy wouldn't have been fair on him. They had worked out a plan that stated that Archie stayed with her and Craig every weekend Friday evening through to a Sunday afternoon and she saw him as often as she could in the weekdays. Dom had become her most treasured friend and even with their history he was the only man who ever truly understood her and she loved and respected him now more than ever. He had been excellent with Craig's mother since her illness had been discovered and he would still go up and see her every single morning with a fresh cuppa and cake and a natter out on the veranda as they watched the sunrise. Dom was a complete treasure, one of the only men Jenna Shearan trusted implicitly and so it was deemed appropriate that he was the one to give her away. Despite Craig's protests at first because he thought people would find it weird. But Jenna had shrugged him off and threatened to call the whole thing off if he didn't accept her wishes.

Dom looked strikingly handsome in his black tight fitted suit, his overgrown jet black hair slicked over to one side yet still messy in true Dom style. He was exquisite and Jenna knew that one day he would make a woman extremely happy. She kissed him lightly on the cheek and took her son from his arms and held Archie tight to her chest. Trying not to get any marks on her dress and trying not to lay the child's weight onto her bump. She loved her son, there was no doubt about that, he had come at a time in life where everything had been wrong and it hadn't been his fault that she had gone so far down the wrong path. She was a dedicated mother to him even though everything was on Dom's terms. She promised each and every single day that he would never be pushed out of hers and Craig's lives. Even more so now that she was expecting another baby.

"You Look Beautiful Jen" He smiled as he spoke and expression spoke volumes. Jenna knew that he truly did mean it. He may not have been happy with the situation but he had swallowed it and he had turned up and that made the world of difference to her. She would always love Dom, that was a given. He had been there for her in her darkest moments and she wouldn't ever forget the compassion and the kindness he had shown her.

"Thank you Mr Grey! You haven't done so bad yourself" she contested, her eyes sparkling with happiness. Her skin shining with luminosity. Dom's heart sank momentarily, jealousy invading each and every single pore in his body. He had loved this girl before him with a colossal strength, it was superhuman the feelings that he had for Jenna. She was like the oxygen he breathed, the beat in his heart, he needed her. This was tearing him apart, he knew Craig couldn't make her happy, not like he could anyway. She would see it for herself soon enough. They would last mere months, Dom was certain of it. But for now all he could do was smile and be happy for her and plaster on his stupidest happy face. Although desperately all he wanted to do was get home and drink himself into a fucking frenzy. He needed her to know how much he loved her.

"Look Jen, There's still time to change your mind" he whispered sadly, his face ashen and hurt. Jenna looked up at him open mouthed, shock etched on her pretty mouth as she gazed long and hard into the face of her former lover. He looked like a little boy lost, his eyes were wide and wanting. As though he genuinely was about to burst unless she gave him the answer he needed to hear so desperately. Jenna let out a quick gasping breath as she tried her hardest to maintain her composure. She was stood there in all her wedding finery waiting to marry her best fucking friend and here was Dom trying to pull the theatrics out of the bag not even an hour beforehand. Her head was spinning, she couldn't focus on anything other than the hurt that was furrowed in Dom's brow. He looked defeated and secretly she saw her own hurt mirrored there because she knew that he was her safest bet. He would worship her in ways she never knew possible. But Jenna was a wild spirit and Craig was dangerous, he was everything she wanted and more. She enjoyed being challenged by him and he enjoyed the chase.

"Dom I don't want to argue with you" she whispered as she kissed his brow once more. "I'm sorry but I've made my choice. I hope you understand" she replied, trying her hardest to maintain her happy face.

"but we could have everything" He continued, desperately trying to get her to change her mind, but there was no budging her. She smiled tentatively and turned away. She hugged her son once more and led him back his father.

"I'll see you downstairs, if your not there then I'll understand. I'll always love you Dom. You'll always be special to me. You're the father of my child. Your raising him so so well and I could never thank you enough for everything you've done for me." She stroked his cheek delicately before resuming her position in front of the vanity mirror. She prayed that hormones wouldn't get the better of her today if they did she was worried she'd never bloody stop crying. Dom took Archie by the hand and led him away from the room, his heart was torn in two but he swore he would get through the ceremony as planned. He couldn't wait to see Craig's face as he led her down that fucking aisle and even if it fucking killed him, he would be smiling every fucking step. He was doing this for Jenna, not for Craig's gratification. He plastered the biggest, most fake grin he could manage as he took his position at the foot of the stairs and waited silently, nodding every now and then to the passing guests. Their fake smiles and their prying eyes boring into him as they sauntered past. To them he was just a face.

Craig's nerves were fucking jangling; his nails were in tatters from where he was biting his nails so vigorously. His mind was swimming with every single emotion possible, he was buzzing on his euphoria. He was completely unaware of the faces that were all clapped on him in the open marquee around him. The sun was beaming as he stood at the altar his heart literally pounding his chest. This moment had been building up for so many years that now it was finally here he thought he was going to vomit with excitement. He had been buzzing when Jenna had said yes; it had been the best day of his life so far. He had loved her all the more from that moment onward for her exceptional courage. When they had found out about the baby they had been shocked, overwhelmed even. But they had dealt with it together. As they would deal with all of lives other crazy curve balls. She was his whole entire world and he had put his heart and soul into making today perfect for her. As the sound of UB40's "I Got You babe" played to the congregation began playing in the background Craig burst into a fit of infectious laughter. Jenna had kept the song a secret especially for today and he had almost plagued himself into believing that he would be walking down the aisle to fucking Ke$ha. He turned around for just a second and he was blown away by the most beautiful sight he had ever lay eyes on. His Jenna, she was absolutely stunning, she looked absolutely fucking gorgeous. There were no words left in Craig's mouth, he felt the tears pricking in his eyes as their eyes met as if for the very first time. Piercing green and deep turquoise blue, both smiling mega watt smiles at one another as though time had immediately stood still. Kiki took pride of place as the flower girl, scattering the pretty pink rose petals on the white carpet that adorned the grass beneath their feet. She looked so pretty, Craig's double in every single sense of the word now that she was older, her features were pure Carter. She was a hauntingly beautiful child in looks and demeanour. Craig was incredibly proud of his daughter, she completed him. He smiled as Kiki took her place with the bridesmaids.

As Jenna approached his side, Craig turned and gave her the biggest most boyish grin he could possibly manage.

"You look fucking stunning" he whispered against her veil. Her swollen bump showing each and every single person under the marquee that she was his; He was fucking tempted to rip her dress off her where she stood and fuck her senseless over the buffet table. But he kept his calm as much as he didn't want to. As the pastor took to the congregation there wasn't a dry eye in the house as he relived the story of Craig and Jenna's love story. Claire was a blubbering mess by the time that the vows came. Just as Craig went to mutter the words "I Do" there was a popping noise beside him and within seconds Jenna was on her knees. Her waters had burst and baby Carters imminent arrival was closer than they realised. Dom immediately rushed to Jenna's side, clutching her hand tightly as everyone began reaching panic mode. Someone was screaming about towels and warm water, Jason Harding was gawping open mouthed as Craig was trying to clear out the marquee. A painful contraction stabbed Jenna in back as she squirmed in agony on the floor, clutching her stomach. Her dress drenched from the amniotic fluid that had flooded the floor. Her face crimson with embarrassment and sheer surprise that her child had decided to come and exactly the most inconvenient time ever.

"Craig get a fucking ambulance!" Dom screamed as he noticed the pool of blood that began to seep through Jenna's perfect crisp white dress. Instantly Jenna stared at them both, completely mortified. Fear creeping into each and every face that was still stood in the marquee as Jenna began slipping in and out of consciousness. The voices that hummed around her were nothing more than a strange blur. She could see Craig hovering over her, his face twisted and filled with concern. Completely confused as to what the fuck was going on. But the voice she could hear wasn't Craig's, it was Dom's. Dom and his kind voice telling her everything was going to be okay. That she was going to be fine and that the baby was fine. Jenna slurred some barely audible words before she keeled over into Dom's arms in that moment her world became black and for a moment she wondered..... if she was dead.

Epilogue

The funeral procession gathered outside the church, the pain mirrored in the two men's eyes as they met outside. The funeral had been a spectacular affair in true Craig Carter style. The Cars alone had cost Craig more than his months mortgage payments. But there was no bigger tribute to the first woman to ever steal his heart. She had been a spectacular mother, an amazing friend and the only person who had ever believed in him. He was fucking devastated that she had never got to see the end of the wedding. He was devastated about a lot of things. It had taken every single ounce of strength in his body to get up in the mornings since her death. He wasn't coping well and his panic attacks had come back with a fucking vengeance once again. The only think keeping him sane was waking up each and every day to his baby boy. Sammy Boy Carter or as he was affectionately known to his daddy Sammy B had completely blown Craig away. He was the most amazing baby, so happy and contented it broke Craig's heart. From the minute he had been born by emergency c section on his supposed to be wedding night Craig had been in complete awe of his only son. Sammy Boy had been the missing link, he had eased the hurt that had still remained in Craig's heart from losing Archie.

Every single day he woke up blessed. Kiki doted on him and that was all he could ask for. But in his moment of weakness Craig realised how much of a tower of strength Dom had been for him. He had relied so heavily on Dom and his company ever since her passing. It hurt him of course that he did rely on the man who he had once hated so viciously. But he had become a friend and Craig would always respect him for everything he had ever done for her, especially in her last days on earth.

As they walked away from the floral tributes and messages that adorned the front of the church together, they were no longer enemies. They were brothers. The cremation had been what she had wanted despite Craig's constant fight that she was to be buried. At least she was at peace now and she had told him exactly where she had wanted to be scattered. It seemed appropriate enough that she was back with her family now.

"I can't believe she's gone" Dom snuffled, he had cried his fucking eyes out in the church and Craig was glad that there was no judgement between them. Craig despite how hard he had tried had failed to keep his composure and had cried the whole fucking ceremony. He felt awful. He couldn't face the thought of the wake and so he invited Dom back to his for a drink. There was no better idea now than the two of them sharing a bottle of vodka and getting fucking shitfaced! And Dom agreed surprisingly. Uptight and boring Dom who had always been nothing other than straight toward Craig wanting vodka? The thought amused Craig even under the circumstances. He supposed from that moment on that there was no more poor ground between them. Dom had been amazing for the last few weeks. He had shown Craig just how dedicated he had been to her. When Craig hadn't been able to keep control of his emotions Dom had been there. When Craig had flown off the handle and had started making himself sick in a desperate attempt at emotional attention Dom had been there for him. As much as they had hated one another, and as much as they had despised the fucking thought of one another. Craig would never ever have got through the last few weeks had it not been for Dom. He had been nothing other than a friend. He had moved mountains to make sure Craig's mental state had been fine. He had taken Kiki out for a few days with him and Archie and Craig would be forever in his debt.

"Look Dom I really am sorry for everything" Craig stated, his voice quivering as tears threatened to spill from his eyes. He was finding that even mumbling a sentence together was fucking hard work at the minute so he hated to think how Dom felt.

"Its fine mate" Dom replied and that was that.

As they slipped into the Rolls Royce and Craig indicated for his driver to take them home. They both breathed a sigh of relief. Now that the funeral was over at least they could both try and build upon the shattered ruins that had become their family. At the end of it all they had left was their children and their want for each other to recover. It would take time, it would take strenuous effort but in the end..... It was all they had left.

To Be Continued......

The Joker

Available Winter 2016

Printed in Great Britain
by Amazon

12773749R00118